Praise for

The Last Lie Told

"A complex case fraught with angst and danger ends with surprising revelations."

—*Kirkus Reviews*

"Debra Webb writes the kind of thrillers I love to read. Sure, there is a murder or more. Yes, there's a twisted mystery to be solved. Once again, in *The Last Lie Told*, her characters are fully rendered and reveal themselves authentically as her novel unfolds and careens to its stunning conclusion. *The Last Lie Told* is her best yet. Webb is the queen of smart suspense."

—Gregg Olsen, #1 *New York Times* bestselling author

Can't Go Back

"A complex, exciting mystery."

—*Kirkus Reviews*

"Police procedural fans will be sorry to see the last of Kerri and Luke."
—*Publishers Weekly*

"Threats, violence, and a dramatic climax . . . Good for procedural readers."

—*Library Journal*

Gone Too Far

"An intriguing, fast-paced combination of police procedural and thriller."

—*Kirkus Reviews*

"Those who like a lot of family drama in their police procedurals will be satisfied."

—*Publishers Weekly*

Trust No One

"*Trust No One* is Debra Webb at her finest. Political intrigue and dark family secrets will keep readers feverishly turning pages to uncover all the twists in this stunning thriller."

—Melinda Leigh, #1 *Wall Street Journal* bestselling author of *Cross Her Heart*

"A wild, twisting crime thriller filled with secrets, betrayals, and complex characters that will keep you up until you reach the last darkly satisfying page. A five-star beginning to Debra Webb's explosive series!"

—Allison Brennan, *New York Times* bestselling author

"Debra Webb once again delivers with *Trust No One*, a twisty and gritty page-turning procedural with a cast of complex characters and a compelling cop heroine in Detective Kerri Devlin. I look forward to seeing more of Detectives Devlin and Falco."

—Loreth Anne White, *Washington Post* bestselling author of *In the Deep*

"*Trust No One* is a gritty and exciting ride. Webb skillfully weaves together a mystery filled with twists and turns. I was riveted as each layer of the past peeled away, revealing dark secrets. An intriguing cast of complicated characters, led by the compelling Detective Kerri Devlin, had me holding my breath until the last page."

—Brianna Labuskes, *Washington Post* bestselling author of *Girls of Glass*

"Debra Webb's name says it all."

—Karen Rose, *New York Times* bestselling author

DEEPER
THAN
THE
DEAD

OTHER TITLES BY DEBRA WEBB

Finley O'Sullivan

The Last Lie Told
The Nature of Secrets
All the Little Truths

Devlin & Falco

Trust No One
Gone Too Far
Can't Go Back

DEBRA WEBB

DEEPER THAN THE DEAD

THOMAS & MERCER

Published by Thomas & Mercer, Seattle

www.apub.com

Amazon, the Amazon logo, and Thomas & Mercer are trademarks of Amazon.com, Inc., or its affiliates.

ISBN-13: 9781662516184 (paperback)
ISBN-13: 9781662516177 (digital)

Cover design by Shasti O'Leary Soudant
Cover image: © Connie Miller Photography / Alamy

Printed in the United States of America

This book is dedicated to a lovely lady who has tirelessly supported my books for many, many years now. She's always there to help out, and we love the same college football team (roll tide!). Thank you so much, Teresa Ellett Russ, for all you do and for allowing me to use your name for a character in this story! Cheers!

One picture is worth a thousand words.
—Fred R. Barnard (and many others)

1

Monday, July 22

Memphis Police Department
Public Safety Building
Main Street, Memphis, Tennessee, 9:05 a.m.

It wasn't the end of the world.

Vera Mae Boyett grabbed her coffee mug from her desk and tucked it, coffee stains and all, into the gym bag she'd brought from home. No one paid the slightest bit of attention to gym bags—they were as common as briefcases around here. She could be carrying any manner of nonmetal contraband in this seemingly harmless blue nylon bag, and not a soul would notice or even wonder.

But Vera hadn't gone to the gym this morning. The bag was a just-in-case decision. She had seen the writing on the wall, and if this thing ended up going where she suspected it would, she had no desire to return to the office at a later date for her personal belongings. With that in mind, she'd come prepared to pack up and walk away.

She squared her shoulders and forced back the emotions crowding into her throat. No, this situation was not the end of the world—just the probable end of fifteen years of service to a job she loved.

The stapler she'd bought after the department-issued one broke went into the gym bag next. She wasn't leaving one damned thing that belonged to her. Not for someone to come along one day and pick up, saying, "Oh, this belonged to Deputy Chief Boyett. You remember her, the one who allowed a cutting-edge unit to go to hell in a handbasket?"

She blinked. Lifted her chin in defiance of the damned emotions that now burned behind her eyes. The past couple of days she had told herself repeatedly there was a slim chance this might not be the end. After all, the investigation had barely begun . . .

Who are you kidding, Vee?

It was over, and she knew it.

This was the outcome she had expected from the beginning—no point pretending. The horrific events of last week were bad. The kind of bad where no one involved walked away unscathed—not even those guilty by association only. Public opinion would not see the difference.

Bottom line, the buck stopped with her. *She* was responsible.

Vera closed her eyes and struggled to exile the surge of images that had played over and over on the news and social media cycles for the past seven days.

The whole team was going down. The move would be necessary to mitigate the discontent in the community—particularly among the powers that be. No one understood that reality more than her.

Vera's fingers found their way to the paperweight she'd had since she was a kid. The round, flat rock, polished to a smooth sheen by eons in a river, had been a gift from her mother. She'd painted a *V* surrounded by flowers and given it to Vera for her fifteenth birthday. *A reminder that sometimes things and people need a reason to stay. A little something to hold them in place.* Her mother had said those words to her. She already knew she was dying. Vera and her sister Eve did not learn this sad fact until later. Evelyn Boyett understood that when she was gone, her older daughter would want to run as far away as possible. Vera always had big dreams of going places—anywhere but small-town Tennessee.

Two months after her fifteenth birthday, the last truly happy family event Vera could recall, their father explained that their mother hadn't wanted to ruin Vera's special day. Good mothers wanted to protect their children.

Too bad their father didn't follow through with being good. Fathers were supposed to be good, and dependable, too—even after the worst possible thing that could happen to a family did so.

Vera buried the thought, as she had for more than two decades now, and placed the stone in the bag. Looking back to her childhood, all the way up until just after that birthday, Vera could honestly say hers had been pretty perfect. A mother who'd been fully engaged with raising her children. One who loved life deeply and treasured the smallest of things—like butterflies and flowers and the perfect stone for creating artistic beauty. A father who worked hard and somehow found endless patience no matter how tired he was when he came home from work each evening. A little sister who adored Vera and believed she could do anything.

But within the year that followed that final genuinely happy birthday, their lives fell apart. For Vera, losing her mother felt like the end of everything. If possible, the loss was even more difficult for her little sister—her only sibling at the time. Eve was only eleven.

The untimely loss had been the beginning of the end.

People who talked about their lives falling apart could generally pinpoint the moment the foundation started to crumble. For the Boyett sisters, that moment had started the day after their mother was buried, when they found their father in the barn. Poor Eve thought he was dead, too, but he was only sleeping off the alcohol in which he'd drowned himself the night before. Sadly, the heavy drinking didn't end with that unfortunate episode.

Vernon Ray Boyett had been the perfect husband and an amazing father . . . until he just couldn't be perfect or even good anymore.

Vera closed her eyes and shook her head. Why was she thinking about that now? Her career with the Memphis Police Department had just gone down in flames because of someone else's decision. And there was not one damned thing she could do about it but grieve with the rest of the city.

And go. She had to go. She surveyed the office that had been her home twelve to fourteen hours a day. Rising to the position of deputy chief had been her crowning achievement—the epitome of all she'd worked to accomplish. What would she do now? Where would she go? Staying in Memphis wouldn't be an option.

A hum of vibration snapped her attention to her desk. Wouldn't be hers much longer. She struggled to clear the haze of disbelief from her brain and looked for the source of the sound. Face down on her desk blotter, her cell phone vibrated again. Vera took a deep breath and reached for it. If it was another reporter who had somehow managed to obtain her private number, she was going to be . . .

Luna. A frown tugged Vera's eyebrows together. The possible reasons for a sudden call during work hours from her half sister—not that Vera had ever seen her as anything other than a full sister in every sense of the word—set her nerves on edge. This couldn't be good.

Didn't bad things come in threes?

Her shoulders sagged. Damn. Just what she needed.

Vera braced herself and accepted the call. "Hey, Luna. Everything okay?" That she managed to sound normal under current circumstances startled her. When had she become such a good actress?

More importantly, what did that say about her?

Not going there.

"Vee, you have to come home."

Vera stilled at her sister's words. No, not her words—the sound of her voice. Strained with shock or disbelief. So, this was it. *Deep breath.* She moistened her lips and said the necessary words. "Is it Daddy?"

Their father was only seventy-five, but his health had taken a turn for the worse just over two years ago. The dementia had made it impossible for him to live at home any longer. Not that Vera got home that much anymore. But Luna kept her informed about their father. Even made the occasional video call—which never seemed to come at a good time—from his room at the memory care facility. It wasn't that she didn't love her father—she did. It was just that in light of what happened after her mother's death, Vera had been forced to adjust her thinking toward him. It was the only way to pretend life was even remotely normal.

Right. What was normal?

A fist clenched in Vera's chest. Though she had been expecting this call for a while now, it still felt like the undoing of some invisible tether to which her life had been bound since the beginning. They—she, Eve, and Luna—were officially orphans now. It was the most unexpected, oddest feeling. She should cry, right? Or, at least, feel tears welling in her eyes. She blinked once, twice. Nothing.

Certainly that was not normal.

"No," Luna said, sounding strangely startled. "Daddy's fine."

"Oh. Good. So . . ." Vera started to ask what exactly the trouble was, but her sister began speaking again first.

"I mean . . ." Luna sighed. "You know, he's doing as well as can be expected. But that's not why I'm calling. This is about . . . it's Mama, Vee." Her voice grew shrill with something like excitement. "They found her."

Suddenly thirty-nine-year-old Vera Mae Boyett was seventeen again, soaking wet and cradling her baby sister to her chest. With the burn of fear rushing through her veins and the wail of the nine-month-old echoing in her ears, she had mentally scrambled for how to fix the unfixable.

Vera blinked away the jarring memory. "I don't understand." It was all she could think to say. The fist that had been pressing against the vital organs in her chest now pushed into her throat. Shock, disbelief . . . apprehension rushed through her.

How could this be?

No. No. No. This was not supposed to happen. Two years after her stepmother's disappearance, the consensus among all who knew her had been that Sheree Corbin Boyett either was dead or no longer wanted to be a part of their lives. When her body was never found, they assumed the latter. In spite of the rumors and conclusions, their father never remarried. Vera had wondered if deep down he hoped Sheree would come back one day. Or perhaps he realized that his hasty wedding to another woman after his first wife died had been a mistake that didn't bear repeating.

Please. Like he deserved that much credit.

"They found her," Luna repeated, as if Vera hadn't gotten that part.

Oh, she got it. The ability to breathe had escaped her as that unexpected reality pulsed its way to her brain. Her equilibrium wobbled. Dear God, how had this happened? She squeezed her eyes shut. *No. No. No.*

"She didn't leave us, Vee." Luna's voice broke in, shaking with raw emotion now. "Someone took her from us. Mama's dead. She's been dead all this time."

Luna continued to speak, but two words boomed over and over in Vera's head, drowning out all else. *Mama's dead. Mama's dead.*

Somehow, before the ability to think deserted her completely, Vera managed to promise she would be home as soon as possible. As the call ended, she stared at the screen. Attempted to gather her wits about her, but the sour taste of regret and panic surged into her throat too quickly. Vera dropped her phone onto her desk and rushed from her office.

Forcing herself to move more slowly so as not to draw attention, she concentrated on holding back the bile. Her eyes stung. Her stomach spasmed. She made it through the door of the restroom and as far as the sink before the bitterness spewed forth, leaving a burn from the very bottom of her gut to her nose.

When she stopped gagging, she twisted the faucet's handle and cupped her hand beneath the flow of water to rinse her mouth. She did the same to flush the sink, then braced her hands on the cold porcelain and stared at herself in the mirror.

This couldn't be. Could. Not. Be.

Her career was falling apart . . . spiraling out of control, and now her personal life was tipping over the edge . . . and it was all happening at once.

Breathe. Pull it together.

Barely restraining the surging emotions, she straightened and steadied herself. Ran her fingers through her hair, adjusted her jacket, and then walked out of the restroom. With her gaze locked onto the entrance of her office, she moved in that direction, hoping to God she didn't run into anyone who wanted to offer their regrets regarding her team's crash and burn.

She passed one . . . two colleagues, but both were focused on the files they carried. All she had to do was make it a few more steps, and she would be in the clear.

Deep breath. Keep moving.

As she reached her desk, she sagged with relief. Hand shaking, she picked up her phone and tucked it into her shoulder bag. Another deep breath.

Hold it together a little while longer.

One last survey of her office, and her gaze landed on the framed photo that sat on the corner of her desk, angled so she could see it whenever she looked up from her work. The photograph was of the three of them: her, Eve, and their much younger sister, Luna. They were all smiling. Standing under that big old oak tree in the front yard back home. Seemingly of its own accord, Vera's hand reached for the framed memory and placed it in the gym bag.

Okay. *Breathe.* That was the last of her personal effects. She was done. She could leave now.

Laughter abruptly bubbled into her throat, sputtered past her lips. This was insane.

Two people were dead. The team she had helped create from the ground up would likely be abolished—every single person related to it in any way had been suspended, pending further investigation. The whole thing continued to play out in the media like a bad movie, amplifying the already tragic situation.

Her disillusioned laughter dissolved as the hot sting of tears surged onto her lashes.

Here she'd thought the worst that could happen had done so already . . . then her sister called.

2

Not much had changed.

No surprise there. Vera braked at the traffic light and surveyed the courthouse, which stood proudly in the center of the town's square. The shops that surrounded the Colonial Revival–style structure were mostly the ones she remembered from her childhood. Some had new names and facades. In small towns flexibility was key to survival.

The ice cream shop on the corner had been Vera and Eve's favorite stop whenever they came into town. Strawberry for Eve. Always chocolate for Vera. They'd lick their ice cream cones and spin around on the stools. Tug at each other's long blonde braids.

So many memories. Vera frowned. How long had it been since she last visited?

Years. She hadn't come back in over two years. Luna had insisted that she, Eve, and Vera together—as a family—move their father to the home. Grudgingly, Vera had cooperated. But she'd only stayed the one night. Hurrying back to work had been her excuse.

Can't use that excuse this time, now can you?

Vera blinked away the thought. The swell of dread that had occurred after Luna's call still refused to subside, despite the time required for Vera to go home and pack a bag and then to drive better than halfway across the state. The blare of a car horn behind her made her jump. The light had turned green, and, lost in thought, she hadn't noticed.

Clearing her head, she pressed the accelerator and rolled forward. Pedestrians waited at the ends of blocks to cross the street when the light changed. Her gaze skimmed over faces she didn't recall or maybe didn't want to recall. If she were lucky, no one she encountered would recognize her.

"Oh look, it's Vera Boyett—the woman whose incompetence cost lives."

"Not going there," she muttered as she passed the bank her family had used for as long as she could remember. At the end of the next block was the Presbyterian Church they'd attended before everything changed.

Before their father ruined the remainder of their childhoods.

Looking back on her early life, Vera saw it in two parts—before and after. Before her mother died, when life was good and simple. Then once she was gone, everything changed—the *after*.

Her cell vibrated against the console, and the call flashed on the SUV's dash screen. *Eve.* Vera tapped Ignore Call the same way she had the other half dozen or so times her sister had called. She could not talk to her. Not on a cell phone. Not until they were face to face.

A dozen more knots tightened in her belly. How the hell had this happened?

Luna had probably provided the details of this startling development when she called, but Vera hadn't heard anything after *Mama's dead. She's been dead all this time. She* being Vera and Eve's stepmother, Sheree. Sheree Corbin Boyett—the second wife, the one over twenty years younger than their father. The one who had looked more like a stripper dressed for her next act than a bride about to take on a ready-made family. Air abruptly filled Vera's lungs, reminding her she'd forgotten to breathe.

Don't think. Just drive.

Instinctively, she navigated the road that would take her home. Could have driven it blindfolded.

Home. She blinked repeatedly. This had not been home for a very long time, yet somehow, it always would be. Funny how life was like that. You spent years dreaming of escaping a place, and no matter how far and fast you ran, you could never get completely away. It was part of you. Entrenched on a cellular level. God knew she had rushed to escape with considerably more enthusiasm than most.

The shops and pedestrians faded in the rearview mirror. The landscape shifted to trees and pastures . . . cows, horses, sheep, and the occasional cotton or cornfield. She tapped the dash screen, ushering the air-conditioning fan to a higher level. It was hotter than blazes, and the humidity level felt like 200 percent. By August it would be worse, like trying to breathe underwater. She'd lived in the South her whole life, so one would think she would be used to the heat and the swelter. Who could possibly acclimate to this level of misery?

A left turn onto Good Hollow Road, and she was plunged deeper into the woods. The road narrowed, and the asphalt turned a paler shade of gray as it curled through the trees, the hills rising up on either side. Occasionally a grass-covered hillside dotted with grazing cattle disrupted the thick flow of trees. Then the sudden drop into a hollow between hills would plunge the scenery into denser, darker woods, with the occasional stream snaking a path through the flora just to shake things up.

The farmhouse came into view, and an ache pierced her. The house looked exactly the same. Two tall stories with a broad porch. A redbrick chimney climbed up one side of the white wood-clad exterior, towering above a green metal roof. Wisteria vines streaked up the other end. Even now she could summon the sound of rain on that roof and the cascading purple blooms that appeared on those vines each spring.

A quick glance farther up the road, and Vera spotted a cluster of official vehicles near the narrow dirt road that led to the barn. They had apparently opted to use the road farthest from the house to access the area where the remains had been discovered. That was the most direct route and left the main drive free of parked vehicles. It then cut across the expansive backyard and pasture. The sheriff was likely responsible for the decision. Sheriff Walter Fraley and their father had been friends forever. Fraley's wife, Beatrice, had been a schoolteacher as well as a very close friend of Vera's mother. Vera still considered her the best teacher she'd had during her primary education years.

Hopefully the sheriff's foresight would keep any reporters who showed up focused on the area beyond the house and not on the house itself.

Wishful thinking.

Vera had been in the policing business far too long to believe that sort of luck would hold out, no matter how many guardian angels you had.

She turned onto the gravel drive and made the quarter-mile journey to the parking area near the house. A garage or carport had never been part of the home's amenities. There was just the wide, circular graveled area for keeping vehicles off the grass.

Tall windows banded the front of the house. Her mother had loved the generous amount of light they allowed into the house. She'd made long curtains of gauzy white fabric to decorate each without blocking the sun's radiance. Inside, wood floors and plaster walls with minimal molding filled each room, including the large center entry hall. The house wasn't grand by any means, but it was good sized and warmly decorated. Their stepmother hadn't been around long enough to change the decor. Vera doubted the idea had so much as crossed her mind.

Neutral, Vee. No petty stuff. For Luna's sake, no digging up those old wounds.

Vera parked her Ford SUV next to Luna's little electric Nissan sedan. Next to the Nissan was Eve's ancient Toyota, which had belonged to their mother—the same one their mother had driven for years before her death. The vehicles they drove were as different as she and her sisters were. Luna was young, only twenty-three with brown hair and eyes, like her mother, Sheree. They shared the same exotic olive skin and a vibrant personality. True girlie girls who loved makeup and dressing to the nines. But that was where the similarities between mother and daughter ended. Luna loved books and was the assistant director of the local library. Her little car was silver and sassy and needed no fossil fuels to shuttle her from place to place. But she would not be caught in a bar or under the influence of anything beyond a single glass of wine if her life depended upon it.

Sheree, on the other hand, had loved barhopping. At one point she'd even been a dancer at a club in Huntsville. Sadly, alcohol had not been her only vice. Drugs, two prostitution charges, a DUI, and at least one petty theft charge, but the last had gotten thrown out of court.

Then there was Eve. Vera smiled sadly as she thought of how Eve must be feeling right now. Like Vera, she had the same blonde hair and blue eyes as their mother. They were fair skinned, with all the issues that came with having pale skin in the South. Freckles and sunburns; heightened worries about skin cancer. She and Eve had taken different career paths. Vera had rushed away from Fayetteville as soon as possible after high school graduation. Once safely ensconced in the university life, she waffled a bit about her major but eventually chose criminal justice, later adding a master's degree in psychology.

And what would she do with that now?

Vera kicked the thought aside and rested her gaze on her sister's car. Eve hadn't fared so well. By fifteen she had lost herself in the bottle. Other, more dangerous means of reality avoidance followed. All manner of drugs. She succeeded in graduating high school by the skin of her teeth. After bouncing from one starter job to another and doing a couple of stints in rehab, she crash-landed back home and did nothing for a while. Eventually she worked her way through a mortuary science program and the required apprenticeship to become a mortician.

Basically, they both ended up working in jobs that involved some form of taking care of people, which was an irony of its own.

Don't even go there, Vee.

She opened the door and climbed out of her SUV. The quiet sounds of nature surrounded her, making her more keenly aware of the sweet scents and visceral impressions of home. Their mother had loved most anything that bloomed. The yard was full of blossoming perennials. A couple of old tractor tires overflowed with dahlias and zinnias. Clusters of shrubs obscured the foundation of the house; the lush, vibrant colors anchored the towering walls of white siding. The wisteria had long ago covered the side of the house that faced the pond. Jasmine and honeysuckle grew on trellises and fences. The tweets and chirps of birds crooned in the background. It was all so naturally beautiful and so reminiscent of their mother.

At least that was one thing from Vera's childhood—the *before* years—that Sheree hadn't been able to screw up.

Vera shivered at the memories that attempted to intrude. She reached back into the vehicle and grabbed her shoulder bag and cell phone. Time to face the music and learn just how bad this was going to be. She braced herself and walked the weathered brick path that led to the front porch.

The remembered sound of laughter and the feel of sweating glasses of lemonade whispered across her senses as she climbed the steps. Wicker rockers and vintage chairs that were far older than her thirty-nine years still lined the porch. The floral cushions were faded and tattered in a shabby but elegant way. The urge to have a seat and relax tugged at her. Only this place had ever made her want to unwind. Her life in Memphis had eternally been a roller-coaster ride of adrenaline and urgency. Like a junkie, she had reveled in the highs and ridden out the lows with the knowledge that another high wouldn't be very far away.

Overhead, three ancient ceiling fans in a row turned slowly, churning the thick air just enough to still be considered serviceable. Vera reached to knock on the front door, but it opened before she had a chance.

Wearing her typical black scrubs and her preferred short, spiky hairstyle, Eve stood in the doorway.

The thirty-five-year-old woman in front of Vera suddenly morphed into the twelve-year-old who'd opened this same door twenty-two years ago, her clothes wet, sheer terror in her eyes. Beyond her, somewhere deeper in the house, baby Luna had screamed at the top of her lungs.

"You're here," Eve murmured.

Vera snapped from the disturbing memory and forced a smile that was likely not much of one. "I got here as quickly as I could."

Eve's face creased into a frown as she opened the door wider for Vera to come inside. "What's wrong with your cell phone? I've called you like eight times."

Ten times actually, but who was counting. No matter that a dozen questions nagged at her, Vera responded calmly, "We'll talk later. Where's Luna?"

Eve didn't attempt to conceal her frustration. She cocked her head toward the back of the house. "She's in the kitchen baking." She closed the door behind Vera. "Why can't we talk now?" she whispered, too loudly.

Eve had never mastered the art of patience, much less that of actually whispering. Vera was certain the inability had been inherited from their paternal grandmother. The woman couldn't have lowered her voice to a true whisper if her life had depended upon it.

"Later," Vera warned. "When we can speak privately."

Eve rolled her eyes. "Fine." She executed an about-face and marched to the kitchen, like the little girl she'd once been who had blamed God for their mother dying on them.

A wide center hall led from the front door to the kitchen, which spanned the back of the house. Near the front of the hall was the staircase that climbed to the second floor. Along the way to the kitchen on alternating sides were the main parlor—or "living room," as they'd always called it—a dining room that was only used on holidays and special occasions, their mother's library, and a downstairs powder room. But it was the kitchen where they had spent most of their time.

Debra Webb

The scent of freshly baked cookies filled the room even before Luna drew a baking pan from the oven. She settled it onto the table and then tugged off the oven mitts. Luna was a stress baker. Anytime she was upset or worried, her Betty Crocker side came out—so, so unlike Sheree. Luna's gaze met Vera's, and her lips trembled.

They met in the center of the room and hugged.

Vera drew back and managed a smile. "How are you?"

Luna lifted her shoulders in a shrug. "I waffle between feeling wildly elated and utterly sad." She shrugged again. "I mean, the idea that she might still be alive and residing somewhere was always in the back of my mind. I've lived with the real possibility that she abandoned me my entire life."

"But she didn't," Vera said. "You know that now." This was the upside. No one should spend a lifetime feeling unwanted.

Luna nodded. "But now I can't stop thinking about how she died. Did she suffer? It's a horrible feeling." Her hands went to her flat belly. "Like being torn apart inside."

"Completely understandable," Vera assured her. "Just try to be calm and patient. I'm sure we'll know more soon."

Eve wandered to the big table in the center of the room that had always served as a sort of island and an informal dining spot. She leaned against it, picked up a cookie, and studied it. "Vee's right," she said before taking a bite. When she'd swallowed, she went on. "It won't take long for the cause of death to be determined."

Luna hugged her arms around herself. "The sooner I have all the details, the sooner I can put the not knowing behind me. But all these new questions keep popping into my head now. Like, who did this and why. How could she be dead all this time and the police not have figured it out?"

Vera pasted an understanding smile in place and prayed, for her little sister's sake, the investigation would not drag out. Having been gone for twenty-one years, she had no idea who any of the sheriff's deputies were. Unless things had changed, the remains would be sent to

16

Nashville for official identification and determination of cause of death. A forensic detail for gathering and analyzing evidence would be sent down from Nashville as well, unless Lincoln County had gotten one of its own. Not likely. Eve would surely have mentioned as much. She generally kept Vera up to speed on those sorts of happenings around town.

As if Eve had known Vera was thinking of her, their gazes collided. Ice crusted her insides. This long-buried *thing* between them was no longer just between the two of them. Everyone would know now. Vera's throat struggled with the difficulty of swallowing.

Everyone would have questions. Lots and lots of questions. But for Vera, there was only one that really mattered.

Had she and Eve left behind any incriminating evidence all those years ago?

3

Vera watched as the massive black pickup truck owned by Luna's future husband drove away. Why did anyone need a truck that large? It was a miracle her petite sister could even climb in without assistance. It was an even bigger miracle Luna had fallen for a hard-core country boy. From the time she was in kindergarten, all she'd talked about was being a ballerina in New York City. She had loved ballet. Their father had certainly gone to endless lengths to ensure she'd had all the necessary lessons.

The man had dragged that child all over the Southeast for competitions as she'd gotten older. Thank God Vera had been in Memphis by then, building her career.

The one that fell apart last week . . .

She forced the thought away and focused on the developing situation here. Not that it was a safer place to land, mentally speaking. Maybe not in any respect. But it was somehow easier—at least for now.

"She gone?"

Eve's voice made Vera jump. She turned from the window. Her sister was a few inches shorter than her. Their mother had always said that Vera snagged a little extra height from her father's side of the family.

"She and Jerome are off to the funeral home to pick out a casket," Vera said in answer. There was no way to guess when the remains would be released, but Luna preferred being prepared. Vera desperately hoped she wasn't planning some sort of elaborate funeral.

Eve shrugged. "I'm surprised she didn't insist we help with picking out the casket."

Vera grunted her agreement. It was a miracle—one for which she was immensely grateful.

Eve walked to the window and stared, probably, like Vera, at nothing. Their vehicles were there . . . but not much else beyond the collage of blooms scattered across the landscape. There was the heat that wouldn't abate until well after dark—the signs of it showed in the wilted leaves and drooping blossoms.

No sign of reporters, thankfully.

The extended visual assessment of nothing in particular meant her sister had something to say and was attempting to work up the nerve to get it out. Vera had plenty to say herself, and she wasn't looking forward to a single word of it either. The dialogue opened a door into one of those no-going-back sort of corridors. As silly as it sounded, somehow all this time it had felt like if they didn't say it out loud, it wasn't real.

Oh, but it was. Far too real.

"Why didn't you answer my calls?"

Vera drew in a big breath and crossed her arms over her chest. No more beating around the bush. The worst-case scenario they had long sequestered to the backs of their minds had happened.

"It's better not to talk on cell phones."

Eve grunted. "Right. I get it. It's a cop thing."

Vera forced a patient smile. "Yeah. It's a cop thing. Transcripts of text messages and cell phone conversations can be subpoenaed for use in trials."

Eve's face paled. She crossed her arms, matching Vera's stance. "You think that will happen?"

Vera's jaw gapped. Did Eve not understand just how wrong this could go? Most likely *would* go. Another thought slammed like a punch to the gut. Was Eve drinking again? Taking some drug that made her so laid back?

Just stop. Give her the benefit of the doubt.

"That depends," Vera said more pointedly than she should have—or maybe not, judging by her sister's unrelenting look of confusion—"on whether we left anything incriminating behind."

Surprise widened Eve's eyes. "Wouldn't most things have deteriorated beyond the point of being useful for forensic purposes by now?"

Oh my God. "Please tell me you did not google that." Eve's response sounded exactly like something she'd read on the internet. Vera cringed. "You are aware that a search history can be found even if you delete it?"

"I'm not completely stupid," Eve snapped. She turned her attention back to what lay beyond the window. "I know better than to look up something like that." One shoulder lifted in a shrug. "That's what they preach in the movies and on all those cop shows."

Vera grabbed onto her patience and moved on. The emotional reality of what had occurred had temporarily set aside the other questions she had contemplated over and over on the four-hour drive here. Starting with: "Explain to me how exactly this happened?" She looked to her sister and waited for her to look back. "And when? Luna didn't give me that much information—at least if she did, it didn't sink in."

Eve made a sound that was more a scoff than a laugh. "Two local teenagers, one from town, the other from the Jennings farm next door, evidently had nothing better to do than to go poking around deep in the woods. You know how kids are. When the two grew bored on the Jennings property, they climbed the fence and started exploring on our property. Most people around town know Daddy doesn't live here anymore and Luna and I don't get out in the woods, so there's no fear of getting caught. I've heard hunting dogs, even though we have signs posted all along the property boundary." She shrugged. "Anyway, the kids basically stumbled upon the cave and went inside."

"When did this happen?" It was Monday, but school was out, so the teens could have been there over the weekend or this morning, for that matter.

"After church yesterday afternoon." Eve rolled her eyes as she leaned against the window frame. "I guess they don't teach the 'no trespassing' part anymore. Anyway, the boys ran home and told Mr. Jennings. He followed them back to the cave and then called the police. After that, he came to the house and told Luna what happened."

Yesterday? "Why didn't you or Luna call me last night?"

"I wasn't here," Eve said, her voice reflecting just how weary she was of the conversation. "I had a rare weekend off. Suri and I went to Nashville. Luna didn't call me or you"—Eve shifted to face Vera—"because she figured it was remains from the Civil War or something. It wasn't until this morning when she heard about the purse and the suitcase that Luna realized it could be *her*."

Her. Sheree. The woman who only did one good thing in her whole short, miserable life, and that was to give birth to Luna.

Disgust mingled with regret filtered through Vera. Whatever else she did, it was essential she keep personal feelings out of this. Personal feelings were too easy for experienced interrogators to detect. Personal feelings permitted suspicious comments and actions to seep in during an interview.

Not that she was all that worried about being questioned by Sheriff Fraley. He'd known Vera and Eve their whole lives. He would not view them as suspects under any circumstances . . . unless evidence forced him to do so, and even then he would give them the full benefit of the doubt.

Still, that uneasiness wouldn't relent. What if there was more to how this happened than Eve was telling?

She and Vera had always been extremely close. Closer than most sisters. The thing that happened more than twenty years ago may have even made them closer, in a twisted sort of way. All that said, they had been separated by geography for a very long time. Could her instincts about Eve have been compromised by time and distance? Maybe. Eve was a grown woman now. She was no longer the needy kid sister that Vera had protected and essentially raised.

This next series of questions would not go over well, but they had to be asked. "Have you ever spoken to anyone besides me about what happened?"

"Are you f-ing kidding me?" Eve rolled her eyes and shook her head. "Yeah, I took my whole high school freshman science class on a field trip to that cave to play with the remains. It was the highlight of the year. A girl can't have too many friends, after all."

Vera refused to be shamed into silence. These were necessary questions.

"You started drinking when you were fifteen," Vera reminded her, frustration and no small amount of impatience igniting. "How many times did Daddy have to pick you up from a party where you got shit faced and somebody's parent called him? What about after high school, all the times you were arrested and thrown into jail? Or rehab? The question is a valid one—no matter how badly you want to pretend those things didn't happen."

The glare that arrowed her way was lethal. "I never told anyone," Eve snapped. "As drunk as I have been at times, I have never been *that* drunk."

Still not convinced, Vera forged on. "What about blackouts? I seem to recall you had a few of those."

Eve nodded, her lips pursed tightly. "Yes. Some alcoholics have blackouts when they go on binges. I was one of them."

Defeat twisted inside Vera. "Then you can't say with any real confidence that you never told anyone."

For a time her sister said nothing. Really, what was there to say? They could be in serious trouble here. Vera wondered if Eve had heard about Memphis. Probably. The story had been on the national news for three days now. But then Eve was not like other people. She wasn't big on news. She read the obituaries. When asked about her obsession with reading obits, she insisted it was only to see who had picked the competition over her. According to Eve, funeral homes were very competitive.

Sometimes Vera worried that her sister had a far too unhealthy obsession with death and the dead, period. After what happened, she supposed it wasn't so surprising. Just look at her own decision to go into law enforcement. She'd never once considered that route until her sophomore year at university, then suddenly it was all she could think about. If the full story came out, who wouldn't see that as odd?

Vera let go a heavy breath. There were so many scattered pieces and unexpected turns related to what had once been their lives, she was no longer sure of anything.

"I," Eve said finally, her voice firm, "have been sober for seven years. I would think that if I'd told anyone about what happened, *this* would have happened way before now."

A reasonable expectation. Considering the way Eve used to drink, more often than not with other off-the-rails drunks, if she had told anyone, that person likely hadn't remembered a word of the conversation.

"You're right." Vera turned to her. "I wasn't thinking. And I certainly wasn't trying to make you feel bad by bringing up those unpleasant parts of the past. It had to be done, that's all."

"Even if all is revealed"—Eve met her gaze—"what happened wasn't our fault. We shouldn't take the fall for a murder we didn't commit."

Vera scrubbed at the tension in her forehead. "Let's hope it won't come to that." She recentered her thoughts in an effort to look at the situation objectively. "First thing we need is to know exactly what they've found and deemed as evidence."

Sheree was dead, and her remains had been discovered. Nothing they could do about that now. At this point, it was all about damage control, which required objectivity and emotional distance.

"The three of us own this farm jointly," she went on. "We have a right to know what's happening on the property." Vera set her hands on her hips. "I'll go out there and demand a briefing. I'm sure Sheriff Fraley will oblige."

Property owners had a right to be kept informed unless there was reason to keep certain details from public consumption or if one or all property owners became suspects. Things would change drastically at that point. Luna had obviously given permission for the local cops to search the cave and remove the remains. Vera would have done the same had she been here.

"That brings up something else you should know," Eve said, drawing Vera from the uncomfortable but necessary thoughts.

"What?" What could be worse than their stepmother's remains being found in the cave where they had put her cold, dead body all those years ago?

The memories flooded her before Vera could stop them. Water dripping everywhere. Luna screaming. Eve bellowing. Their father nowhere to be found.

She banished the memories. *No looking back.*

"The sheriff," Eve said. "He's someone you know."

Well, duh. Fayetteville was a small town. Everyone knew everyone else. "How could I not know him? He and Daddy were close friends. Don't you remember? His wife was our favorite teacher." For Christ's sake, Fraley was the one who conducted the investigation into Sheree's disappearance.

Eve moistened her lips, as if what she had to say was going to burn or be too bitter to bear crossing over them without preparation. "There's someone new now. Sheriff Fraley retired two years ago. A few months after Daddy had to be put in Hillside."

"Oh." Well damn. So much for having an in with local law enforcement. "Who replaced him?"

Eve held her gaze a moment before answering. Vera had a bad, bad feeling about what was coming next, if the dread in her sister's expression was any measure.

"It's Bent. Bent took his place."

"What?" Vera felt confident she had heard wrong. The very notion was ridiculous.

"Bent is the sheriff now. He did his time in the military, retired actually, then came home and got elected as sheriff of Lincoln County a few months later."

"Why did Sheriff Fraley suddenly retire? Is he ill?" The man had been sheriff of Lincoln County for nearly forty years. Mostly Vera asked this question because she could not—would not—allow the other information to assimilate completely just yet.

"Multiple sclerosis. Mrs. Fraley had to retire to take care of him. He's like a hermit now. Rarely leaves the house."

Vera flinched. Nodded her understanding. "I'm sorry to hear that." This . . . this Bent thing still didn't make sense. In large part due to the fact that she didn't want to accept the idea. As if that would make it cease to be. "Sheriff Fraley had no deputies interested in the position?"

"There was a big shake-up in the department," Eve explained. "A couple of the senior deputies had gotten involved with some drug dealer out of Nashville. Evidently several others had taken bribes to look the other way. Bent has been working hard to rebuild the force since he took over. He had to do some serious housecleaning. It hasn't been easy for him. He's taken a lot of shit."

"But . . ." Vera hesitated still. The Bent she remembered was a heavy drinker—possibly an alcoholic. At sixteen all she'd cared about was the idea that this gorgeous guy made her feel better. Didn't matter that he was twenty-one and had been seen with most of the women his age or older in town at one point or another. How many husbands had sworn to shoot him on sight for messing around with their wives?

Forever ago. All of it . . . felt like a different life. Yet somehow, that distant past was suddenly bursting its way into her present.

"He's not the same guy you remember," Eve said, while Vera continued to struggle for a reasonable response.

"You mean," she said, unable or unwilling to fully rein in the bitterness, "the womanizing alcoholic?"

Eve made a face. "He still drinks. He's just smarter about it these days. He said the military taught him how to be patient . . . to use restraint in all things. Once in a while he even comes to the AA meetings I lead. He sits in the back and says nothing, but he's there. I asked him one time why he came, and he said just to prove he could."

Didn't sound as if he'd changed much to Vera. "Why wouldn't you tell me this?"

"Why would I?" Eve leveled a pointed gaze on Vera. "You almost never come back home anyway, and the few times you have, you left so fast no one knew you were ever here. Didn't seem relevant. Or maybe I just didn't want to deal with *this*."

Vera supposed she deserved that one. "You're right. Besides, what Bent did or does is completely irrelevant to me, unless it's related to this Sheree situation."

For all she knew he could have a string of former wives and neglected children.

"He never married," Eve said as if Vera had made the statement aloud.

"I'm sure he found the idea of having just one partner too boring." Vera stared out the window once more to prevent her sister from seeing the surprise in her eyes. Not that his marital status affected Vera one way or the other. She could not care less.

"No idea. But he's a damned good sheriff. Everybody likes him now that he's proven himself. Except some of the former deputies. They give him a little trouble now and then. But he handles it well."

Sounded as if her sister was a fan. "You talk to him often?"

"Sure. He asks me about the bodies sometimes."

Vera's instincts stirred. "About the bodies?"

She nodded. "The bodies from crimes—victims. He asks, you know, my thoughts on the matter."

The memory of her sister sitting next to the bathtub after having found their mother plowed into Vera's brain. Vera had been on the phone with one of her friends. The only phone in the house had been in the living room. She glanced around. In this very room. There was an extension in the kitchen now, but that hadn't been added until later.

Her gaze settled on the landline that sat on the end table next to the sofa. She'd been deep in conversation when she heard Eve calling for their mom. By the time Vera realized something was wrong, ended the call, and got up the stairs to the bathroom, her sister was weeping frantically. Her best friend Suri was attempting to comfort her.

Their mother was dead in the bathtub. The doctor had warned days before that it wouldn't be long. That day, they checked on her first thing when they arrived home from school. Then, while Vera was busy on the phone, Eve and Suri helped her into the tub. She wanted a bath, Eve explained later. Evelyn urged her and her friend to go to Eve's room and play. She would let Eve know when she was ready to get out. A little while later, after Evelyn called for Eve, she went to the bathroom and found her unresponsive. Eve had never said, but Vera suspected she hadn't gone immediately when their mother called. It was a question she never intended to ask. Their mother was dying. A minute one way or the other was not the reason she died, and Vera would never say or do anything to make Eve feel in any way responsible or guilty.

But the part that stood out most in Vera's mind was the way Eve had insisted that their mother couldn't be dead because she had told Eve not to cry and that everything was all right *after* Eve found her. No matter how many times Vera asked her, Eve said the same thing. She came into the bathroom, found their mother unresponsive, and started to cry. Only eleven at the time, Eve recognized their mother was dead. Once she'd started crying, Eve claimed their mother opened her eyes, smiled at her, and told her not to cry. Suri didn't come into the room until after that part, so she hadn't been able to say one way or another.

Looking back, Vera understood that her sister had been traumatized and wasn't thinking rationally. But there had been other instances. Folks in small communities tended not to miss paying their respects when a neighbor or friend passed. It just wasn't done. Vera and Eve's parents had taken them to viewings and funerals dozens of times during their childhood. On several occasions Eve whispered to Vera and asked why the person in the coffin was looking at her. Since the corpse's eyes were closed, that was impossible. After the first time, Vera asked her mother about it. She suggested that Eve had a vivid imagination and said not to worry about it.

Vera moistened her lips, giving herself time to carefully choose her words now. "What sort of thoughts does Bent want to know?"

Eve's gaze narrowed. "You know I get these feelings about people who've died. *Instincts*, I suppose you'd call them."

She had stopped mentioning that dead people looked at her or spoke to her after the last time, when their father insisted on taking Eve to see a psychologist. Vera had figured the whole thing was Eve's way of punishing their father for remarrying so quickly after their mother's death. Two months. He'd married only two months after she was buried. And he'd been *dating* Sheree weeks before that obviously, since Luna came only six months into the union. Worse, he'd married a woman who had just turned thirty, and he had been fifty-two. It happened. As an adult Vera thought nothing of those sorts of age differences. But as a fifteen-year-old who'd recently lost her mother, the whole thing had been disgusting.

"I remember," Vera said, careful not to sound judgmental.

Eve stared out the window once more. "Did Daddy ever tell you about what happened to me?"

Vera tensed and felt a frown tugging across her brow. "What're you talking about?"

"He didn't tell me either until I was thirty-two. Just before he started forgetting my name."

Dementia did that. "What did he tell you?"

"When I was five, we were all at old man McCallister's funeral."

Vera smiled. "The drugstore owner. He always gave us cherry colas from the soda fountain."

"That's the one," Eve confirmed. "Anyway, when everyone went home, our parents thought I was going with our grandparents."

They only had one set of grandparents around growing up. Their mother's parents had divorced and moved away.

"Didn't you?" Vera vividly remembered Eve staying with their grandparents often. Vera had preferred being home, but Eve had adored their paternal grandmother. They had a special bond. And the same nose. Vera's lips twitched with the need to smile at the random thought.

"Not that time." Eve shook her head. "That time I had fallen asleep under the chairs. Grandma thought I went home with Mama and Daddy. When I woke up, I was alone in the funeral parlor. The guy on duty was busy in the office with a girlfriend and hadn't put the bodies away for the night. There were three in different parlors. By the time the guy got around to putting them away, he found me asleep—in one of the caskets with the deceased. He freaked out. Mama said when they picked me up, he was the one crying. I just kept saying that the lady in the casket said she was lonely, so I climbed in there with her."

Vera had never heard that story. "Wow. Were you terrified?"

"I don't really remember it, but probably not so much. I like dead people." She breathed a laugh. "At this point, maybe more than the living."

Vera wasn't sure this was a good thing, but her sister had always marched to her own drumbeat. "I feel that way sometimes myself." She exhaled a big breath, mostly at the idea of Gray Benton, a.k.a. Bent, being sheriff. "I should get out there. Find out what I can."

Eve touched her arm. "You think we'll be okay?"

Vera managed a smile. "We will."

Probably a lie, but there was no need to assume the worst at this early stage.

Who knew? Maybe the new sheriff would prove their saving grace.

It was the least he could do after what he'd put Vera through all those years ago.

4

The Cave
Boyett Farm
Good Hollow Road, Fayetteville, 5:50 p.m.

Sweat had beaded on Vera's skin by the time she reached the outer perimeter of the site. Walking had seemed like the best idea. By far the most likely way to arrive at her destination without being spotted by reporters. Having reporters descend upon her would have been far worse than feeling hot and sticky and being under siege from the bees, wasps, and gnats. She'd swatted dozens from her personal space.

Eve had suggested she take the UTV. Their father had bought one of the utility vehicles for riding around the farm before the dementia had taken over. But Vera passed on the suggestion. The place where the remains had been found was maybe a mile and a half from the house. She ran three miles every day. The walk would be a piece of cake.

Yeah, right. The past few years she had spent so much time inside, either behind her desk or in conference rooms, she'd forgotten what it was like to walk through the woods in the heat of a summer afternoon. Even her workouts—including those three-mile runs she was so proud of—were done in a climate-controlled gym. Vera almost laughed at herself. No question about it. There was very little of the country girl left in her now. Give her air-conditioning and bottled vitamin water any time.

Still, this nightmare was happening here, and she had no choice but to take care of it here. Whatever she had to do, whatever she had to endure, she would . . . and then what? Get back to her life?

What life?

She kicked the thought aside and focused on the path that had brought her to the most immediate problem. Even the yellow crime scene tape appeared to droop in the oppressive humidity and ruthless heat. No matter that the sun hovered just above the treetops, it was still as hot as blazes.

As kids, she and Eve had roamed this three-hundred-acre farm from end to end. They had explored every nook and cranny. Their mother would pack them a basket with sandwiches and treats and water and repeat the same instructions every time they left the house.

Don't get separated. Watch for snakes. Drink your water. Get home before dark.

If Vera had ever taken the time to have children, she would never have allowed them to roam the woods this way. But her childhood had been a different time. A more innocent time. Snakes, bobcats, and coyotes had been their only concern. Everyone knew everyone else. There was no fear of being harmed by another human.

Funny how looking back, you realized the danger that was actually there all along.

Focus, Vee. Lurking around in the past would not keep her on her toes in the present.

The trees weren't as thick this far beyond the barn. The soil was rockier. A near impossible place to think of burying anything. But the cave—more of a nook beneath a rock ledge—allowed for stashing things that needed hiding. She and Eve had figured that out even as kids.

Technically a ground cave, their secret place—as she and her sister had referred to it—rose from the hillside like a heavy-lidded gaze. The opening reminded her of one of those eyebrow windows she'd seen on historic homes in Buffalo, New York. For someone who hadn't bothered to buy a home of her own, she was fascinated by historic architecture.

So much so that anytime she traveled, nearly always for work, she took whatever architectural tours were offered. The one in Buffalo remained solidly in her top five. She went there for a joint conference between select law enforcement members and the CIA. No one demonstrated more creativity with interrogation techniques than the CIA. Vera was one of only fifty-nine representatives from departments across the country who were chosen to attend. Not that all the specialized training was going to help her now.

She blinked away the thought. This was not the time for distraction. Or a pity party. Life was complicated sometimes, and she had no right to feel sorry for herself when at least she was alive. Even if her life was burning down and she couldn't seem to find a way to put out the fire, self-pity was for cowards.

The cave opening came into view, and she stalled. Vera had not set foot in this vicinity in more than two decades. And looking at it now, she felt startled by the idea that someone had *accidentally* discovered the place. You basically had to know where it was to see it, the way it was nestled in that copse of cedar trees. Additionally, the opening was almost completely concealed by a pile of boulders that had seemingly erupted from the ground right next to it.

As she studied the landscape, a cop exited the cave opening on his knees. He held a box, which likely contained whatever evidence he'd collected. A tent, maybe eight by eight feet, had been erected a few feet from the opening to create a landing area for the remains and evidence being removed. The remains, as well as any other visible evidence, would be collected, bagged or boxed, and then removed from the site. Soil and other samples from inside would be taken for comparison purposes. Samples of essentially anything inside the cave that may have touched or affected the evidence in some manner would be gathered. A uniformed officer stood guard at the tent to ensure the collections were not compromised in any way.

Another uniform stood at the crime scene perimeter where the yellow tape sagged. He'd already spotted Vera and made a call on his radio.

Probably to Bent. Some part of her braced for the coming reunion. She almost rolled her eyes at the thought. Both she and Bent had gotten out of here twenty-odd years ago. And now here they were, about to come face to face again. Right back where it all started. Fate really had a twisted sense of irony.

But he'd left first, and all these years later she hadn't forgiven him. Or forgotten him. Not that she would *ever* in a million years admit that last part.

So far none of the reporters gathered at the roadside appeared to have dared move closer to the actual scene, which was approximately three quarters of a mile from their location. Or maybe they had, and the observant officer in charge of maintaining the security of the perimeter had sent them packing. That would change in the coming days. Some would no doubt already be talking to friends and neighbors of the Boyett family. A good reporter did what he or she had to do to get the story. When they couldn't get usable or sufficient information elsewhere, they would come back to the source and attempt a connection.

Vera understood. When you needed information, you did whatever necessary to find it. You scratched around, pushed as hard as the law allowed (sometimes harder), and you didn't stop. Ever. Until you had what you needed.

Uneasiness crawled along her spine. She and Eve needed to talk about that aspect of this situation. It wasn't as if they had to figure out what to say in answer to official questions. They had told their stories in April twenty-two years ago when Sheree disappeared. Not in all these years had their stories changed. No reason for modification. No one had ever prompted a review of the case. Sheree hadn't had any close family to nudge law enforcement for closure. When she disappeared, Sheriff Fraley attempted to contact her family, but her parents had passed by then. Not that they would have shown up or cared anyway. Her overly strict parents had insisted their one and only child was dead to them by the time she was fourteen. Apparently, her wild ways had been too horrific for their sensibilities. They'd moved back to Indiana and put

Tennessee behind them for good. Who abandons a child? And Sheree had been a fourteen-year-old child when they cleared out.

In some ways, Vera supposed Sheree hadn't understood how to be a better person. All she'd ever known was taking care of herself and avoiding the disappointment, shame, and abandonment of her heartless parents.

No sympathy, Vee.

Feeling sorry for the woman who had torn their lives apart was not going to help the situation either.

Another figure exited the opening of the cave.

Even without his trademark cowboy hat, Vera recognized him. His hair was long, brushed his shoulders, just as it had back in the day— before he'd run off to join the army. He stood, dusted off his knees, and looked in her direction. Somehow his gaze landing on her—despite the distance—shook her in ways to which she should have grown immune ages ago. Unfortunately, she clearly had not. He began walking toward her, and she braced for whatever would come next.

When she was a teenager, his coming closer would have had her heart pounding and her pulse fluttering. Not unlike now, she realized, frustrated with herself. She dabbed at her forehead with the back of her hand, wishing she'd driven that damned UTV instead of working up a sweat on foot. Her hair was likely a mess. Her Memphis Police Department tee was sticking to her skin. Damn it.

He stopped three feet away, leaving the hanging yellow tape between them. "Vee."

Some part of her had managed to block the memory of how his voice sounded. Deep, the slightest bit gravelly, but the real killer was the soulful aspect to the way he spoke. Slow, focused—as if each word was intended for only you in the most intimate way possible. His voice moved through you, tugged at you . . .

Vera reminded herself to breathe. "Bent." She gave the slightest of nods. "I was surprised to hear you're the sheriff now. When did you get back?"

For the first time, she allowed her gaze to meet his. And he still had that way of looking not just at you but inside you. As if he could see all the way to the thoughts in your head and the hammering in your chest. She steeled herself a little more firmly—for all the good it would do.

"Did my twenty in the army," he said. "Decided to come on home and take my time figuring out what came next. Before I knew what was happening, Sheriff Fraley had talked me into this job." He inclined his head, studied her as if he expected to hear the rest of her story next. "So here I am."

She nodded again—more of a jerk than an actual nod. "I'm glad you found your calling."

Oh hell. Inside she cringed. Could she have said anything more cliché? She blinked. Whatever. She and this man were practically strangers. There was absolutely no reason for her to be concerned as to what he thought of her. At least, not beyond any connection to the human remains found in that damned cave. Whatever brief connection they had shared a lifetime ago had vanished the moment he took off on her.

"Your sisters called you about this"—he hitched his head toward the opening into the hillside—"I'm guessing."

What was that question supposed to mean? "Well, of course they called me. It's my understanding the remains of my stepmother were found."

"We don't have an official ID just yet, but we have reason to believe it's her. Some of her personal belongings were found with the remains, including a driver's license." He studied Vera a moment, as if calculating what he might say next. Every ounce of willpower she possessed was required not to look away.

"As I recall," he finally went on, "you hated Sheree. You can see how I might be surprised that you'd rush back home on her account." He shrugged, that gesture that only men who wanted to prove they gave not one shit could make. "What's it been—two or three years—since you were here?"

Obviously, he was trying to fire her up. "You're right." She squared her shoulders and looked him straight in the eyes. "As a teenager I truly despised Sheree for taking our mama's place too soon. For stealing all our daddy's attention. And I probably wished her dead more than once." She flashed a fake smile. "And I'll be the first one to admit that I was extremely happy when she disappeared. Good riddance. Is that what you wanted to hear?"

He winced, or maybe it was just some sort of tic, then glanced toward the uniform standing guard at the tent a few yards away. "Jesus Christ, Vee, that's something you don't need to repeat to me or to anyone else."

"It's true," she said, not backing down. "But I was a kid, and I was hurt by the loss of my mama. Sometimes you say and do stupid things when you're emotionally ravaged by consecutive life-altering events."

He looked away.

She resisted the temptation to smile. Good. Now he understood how it felt to have the past shoved into his face. "But that's the past. I'm here about what's happening now."

His gaze connected with hers once more. The thumping in her chest hitched. Damn it. After all this time she shouldn't react to the man on such a fundamental level. Ridiculous.

"West Jennings," Bent explained. "Wesley's son. You may or may not know that Wesley took over his family's farm a few years back. His younger son and one of his friends from school, Matt Thompson, were roaming the woods and came upon the cave and what was inside."

"Eve told me," she said, her throat suddenly dry for reasons that had nothing to do with the man watching her entirely too closely.

"You or Eve ever happen upon this?" Again, he hitched his head toward the opening, from which one of his deputies or an evidence tech exited just then. "It's mostly hidden. I can understand if you didn't."

Her first instinct was to say no. But explaining how they'd discovered a good hiding place as kids and then never came back to it after they were older might make more sense. In addition, it would leave room for any potential evidence they may have left behind. Kids loved cool places, particularly those their parents might not know about.

"You two didn't roam around out here the way West and Matt do?" He rephrased the question as if he had decided her lack of an immediate response meant she didn't understand what he'd asked. "Wesley says his son and his friends are in the woods all the time."

"Well, you know how boys are. Always looking for a way to get into trouble. But the answer to your initial question is yes. Eve and I found this place as kids. We used to play here quite often, but eventually we lost interest, so it's been a really long time since we were in there."

His gaze narrowed ever so slightly. The first part of her answer had hit home. Not particularly nice of her to make this uncomfortable for him, but some things just had to be said. The benefit was that if she kept him off his game, he was far less likely to do his best. There were things he could not know.

The simple fact in this whole mess was that there were some things you could never tell anyone. Not for love or money or anything else. You just could never tell.

Vera would not feel guilty about trying to protect her sister and herself from this nightmare. Telling the whole truth wouldn't fix any of this. Sheree was dead. Had she deserved to die? Of course not. Would telling the truth make Luna feel any better? No. There was nothing to do except ride this out and deal with whatever came up as best they could.

No one would be better off with the real story.

Vera refused to analyze the conclusion. It would be like turning over the same rock repeatedly and hoping to find something different beneath it each time. It was what it was.

"You think your father knew about this place?"

"My father?" The question startled her. Otherwise she would have responded with a far more direct and incontestable reply rather than the one her brain spit out without thought. She steadied herself. "Daddy worked hard. He had two kids and a wife who was very ill. The idea that he was roaming around these woods looking for caves is a little silly, if you really think about it."

"Three kids," he countered.

"Obviously if he was busy with Eve and me," she shot back, "he was even busier when Luna came along." Particularly since Sheree hadn't possessed the slightest maternal instinct.

That he flustered her so easily only made her more disconcerted. And angry.

"A man likes to keep an eye on his property," Bent pressed. "You sure he hadn't run upon West messing around out here? Before his illness took over?"

Had West said as much? Vera ignored the thought. "He certainly never mentioned anything about it if he did." She folded her arms over her chest. "What is this? Are you suggesting my daddy had something to do with what happened to Sheree?"

"I'm not suggesting anything," Bent assured her. "I'm only attempting to determine if anyone in the family was aware of the cave."

A thought occurred to Vera. "Maybe Sheree found it. She may have been meeting someone here and things went wrong."

Did Vera feel guilty about throwing her stepmother under the bus? No way. Sheree had done all within her power to make Vera and Eve miserable. To suck everything—his attention, his money—from their father. No way did Vera feel even the slightest guilt for making a negative statement about her.

"Could be," Bent agreed.

"When can I have a look around in there? I'm sure you're aware I'm well qualified to assess a crime scene. More so, I would imagine, not to brag, than anyone in there right now." She was bragging . . . sort of. But it wasn't to show off. It was to accomplish her goal.

His lips—the lips she had loved to kiss as a young, naive girl—quirked with the urge to smile. "Yes, I'm well aware of your qualifications, Vee. But I can't let you in there."

It had been worth a try.

"Because I'm a suspect?" She dared him with her eyes. "Are you actually going there?"

"I didn't say you were a suspect. You know the rules."

Yes, she did, but you never got to bend them unless you tried. "Then I'll expect you to keep me well informed."

With that, she showed him her back and started toward the house. If he refused to permit her to see the crime scene, there was little else she could do here. Other than sweat in this damned humidity and suffer powerful flashbacks of all those times she found herself tangled up with him.

She really had been naive.

Even now she couldn't help wondering if he remembered those days and weeks as graphically as she did. She rolled her eyes. *Idiot.*

More importantly, she loved that she was the one walking away from him right now. She would bet just about anything that he was watching, still wondering what he should have said differently to keep things on a friendlier level.

No matter how badly she wanted to appease the ridiculous curiosity expanding inside her, she did not allow herself to look back. Not when she could feel his gaze burning a hole in her back. Oh, he remembered, she decided. A triumphant smile tugged at the corners of her mouth. In fact, she doubted enough alcohol existed to erase those memories.

The man she had known back then was more mature now, obviously. Less spontaneous, probably. Less self-destructive, maybe. That part was hard to say just yet.

Sadly, if anything, he was far more physically attractive. No doubt wiser.

Bent had always been smart. She had heard her daddy say more than once that he could have done anything he wanted with his life if he hadn't loved the bottle so much. Even back then, Bent had been particularly observant as well . . . but was he perceptive enough to know Vera was lying?

She could only hope that was not the case.

5

The memory care facility had been built on the hillside overlooking the town—thus the name Hillside Manor. A grand old house built in the late eighteen hundreds, the home had represented a status symbol for the wealthy Lott family who'd resided there. The last of the family—a daughter named Sarah—nursed both parents through the horrific stages of dementia. In her will, since she had no children of her own or other family, Sarah left the house and land, as well as the remaining family riches, to the city for the purpose of developing a memory care facility for patients like her parents.

Hillside Manor had been Luna's choice for their father's care. Vera had been okay with that decision. She'd heard mostly good things about the facility. The fees associated with long-term care at Hillside were a bit exuberant, but she, Eve, and Luna all pitched in to supplement their father's savings so it would be enough. As his daughters, they had a duty to ensure he was comfortable for the rest of his days.

Even if he had failed his two older daughters so completely in the *after*.

"You know," Eve said as she and Vera strolled toward the entrance, "they say Sarah Lott's ghost still roams these halls."

"Of all the things—good and bad—said about this place," Vera noted, "only you would latch on to that one."

Eve grinned. "Who's to say ghosts aren't real?"

Vera was not going there. "Be nice. This is important to Luna."

Luna was already at the reception desk when Vera and Eve walked in. Their younger sister hurried over and pressed peel-and-stick visitor badges to their chests.

"Now." She smiled widely, but the expression lacked her usual vivaciousness. "We're ready."

Luna turned and led the way to their father's room. Vera reminded herself that Luna was still very young. Having been spoiled so by all of them, she wasn't quite as mature as she might otherwise be. That said, no one could question her organization skills—or her innate proficiency at being bossy.

Vera had actually hoped after the visit to the funeral home that Luna's fiancé would occupy her for the evening so Vera and Eve could talk further. But that hadn't happened. Vera had barely gotten home from the visit to the crime scene when Luna returned and insisted they go together to see their father and to give him the news about her mother. Like he would grasp the ramifications of what they were saying.

Be nice, Vee.

But it was true. This endeavor was pretty much pointless, since most of the time their father had no idea what planet he was on, much less who his long-missing wife was. But if it made Luna happy, then it had to be—for all their sakes. This was Luna's world, and they were just paying rent. It was the motto Vera and Eve had lived by throughout the *after* period. In truth they still did. Case in point, here they were marching down the corridor like soldiers on a mission—at the behest of their fearless leader.

As they entered the room, Vera drew in a deep breath and pasted on a smile she almost had to choke back. Why was it that no matter how much a place like this cost, it still smelled the same? A combination of medicine, cleaning products, and urine.

"Daddy," Luna said, as if calling him to the stage for an award. "Look who's here!" She turned to Vera and gestured with her hands like Vanna White showing off the next letter in a prize puzzle. "Vera has come all the way from Memphis to see you. Isn't that wonderful?"

Vernon Boyett had already been tucked into bed. He stared at the muted television that was set to a decades-old sitcom. His mouth sagged just enough to leave a crack between his lips. His gray hair was a bit mussed, and his jaw sported a slight evening shadow that was equally gray. As he glanced toward Luna, his gaze remained distant, then swung quickly back to the television.

With a nudge from Luna, Vera moved closer to his bed and increased the wattage of her smile, making her lips feel brittle. "Hey, Daddy. How're you feeling today?"

He looked toward her and blinked but said nothing.

Luna grabbed Eve by the arm and pulled her closer. Eve always lingered in the background, and Luna always tried to integrate her into the forefront of whatever they were doing. It was like family dinners, where everyone talked about their days except Eve. Or gift-giving time at Christmas, when Eve had to be prompted to open her presents when everyone else had already ripped through all theirs.

"Eve's here too."

Another fleeting, blank glance from their father.

"He may be a little tired this evening," Vera offered when his silence continued. Generally, he would say hello or some other greeting in acknowledgment of another human presence, even if he didn't recognize the person.

Vera really would have preferred to just leave. Sensory overload had hours ago exhausted her. She needed to close out all else and let her mind still for a while. This final outing reminded her that it was a full-time job keeping Luna happy. Always had been.

How had she and Eve gotten through as well as they had?

"Daddy," Luna persisted, leaning her folded arms on the bed rail, "we have some important news to share with you."

Whether it was the move closer or her persistence, he regarded his youngest daughter. Even held her gaze until she spoke again.

"They found Mama."

He blinked.

For reasons Vera couldn't fathom, she found herself holding her breath. Would he remember who Sheree was?

He blinked again, then asked, "Where's she been?" His voice sounded eons older. It was rusty and cracked, barely recognizable. His voice used to be so deep . . . so strong. He'd been tall and handsome—was still handsome actually. How sad that this disease had stolen so much of him.

While Luna practically vibrated with joy that he'd spoken, Vera and Eve exchanged a surprised look. It almost seemed that he understood the relevance in Luna's words. It was typically hit or miss as to what he would grasp in a conversation.

"Someone took her from us, Daddy," Luna explained, her voice wobbling. "She's been dead all this time." She reached out and squeezed his hand. "Mama didn't leave us. Someone took her."

Vernon's gaze narrowed as if he was trying to understand the words, or perhaps he did. "Probably not much 'taking' to it," he said finally. "She probably went because she wanted to." He shook his head, the move barely visible. "That one never was happy with what she had."

Luna looked to Vera, her lips trembling, fresh tears perched on her lashes.

Vera put aside her indifference and stepped closer to the bed. "Daddy, what Luna is trying to tell you is that Sheree has been dead all this time. She didn't run off with someone else."

Vernon frowned. "Are you from the police? Where's Fraley? I want to talk to him. He was supposed to take care of all this."

"I am," Vera told him. Technically she was, even if suspended. "Sheriff Fraley has retired, and there's a new sheriff now. You might remember him, Daddy. It's Gray Benton."

He blew out a puff of air. "Is he sober?"

Fair question. Unexpectedly so. "As best as I can tell," Vera said.

"He's a good sheriff, Daddy," Luna said, her voice still sounding shaky. "He thinks someone murdered Mama."

"Did the world a favor," Vernon mumbled.

Luna drew back as if he'd slapped her.

Vera reached for her arm. Gave it a squeeze. "He doesn't know what he's saying," she assured her little sister quietly.

Luna tried to smile but failed miserably.

Vera turned back to the bed. "We'll let you know when we have more news. You rest now, Daddy. I'm sure this has been a shock." Damned sure had been to Vera.

He glared at Vera now. "Where's that Eve? Sheree said she won't listen to a word she says."

"I'm right here, Daddy." Eve sidled in next to Vera. "I'll try to do better."

Vera was grateful Eve hadn't argued with him. Luna didn't need the added stress just now.

"You better," Vernon said. "She's trying her best, and you know it's not easy for her after all she's been through."

"I know, Daddy," Eve said.

Vera reached between them and gave Eve's hand a squeeze to show her appreciation.

"We'll be back to see you soon, Daddy," Luna promised.

Vernon stared at her, his face blank. "Who are you?"

Vera winced. Of all the people he didn't recognize today, Luna shouldn't have been one. She came to see him nearly every day. She had taken care of him the final year he lived at home. Vera was certain it pained Luna, even though she understood that it was the disease talking.

"Why, you know who I am, Daddy. It's Luna."

He stared a moment longer, then nodded. "You don't fool me. I know who you are. I told you I can't marry you. It would hurt my daughters too much. I can't do that to them. They just lost their mama."

Now he obviously thought she was Sheree. If there was even an inkling of truth to what he'd just said, maybe he hadn't so readily blown up their lives only a few weeks after their mother died. Vera wondered if Sheree had purposely gotten pregnant to change his mind.

"I'll see you tomorrow, Daddy." Luna's voice sounded brittle now. Apparently, his words had injured her a second time. Maybe this wasn't the first time he'd spoken to her as if she were Sheree. God only knew what he may have said to her. He and Sheree had navigated some fierce battles in those final weeks before she disappeared.

Luna turned away from the bed. Vera and Eve did the same. The three of them had made it to the door when he called after them. "If Fraley had been any good, he would have found her a long time ago. I kept expecting him to."

The shock his words caused was evident on Luna's and Eve's faces. Vera imagined her expression reflected the same.

Had he known she was dead all this time?

Impossible.

Once they were in the corridor, the expected reaction flew from Luna's mouth. "He couldn't have known . . ."

Vera shook her head. "Of course not. It's the dementia. He didn't know. We watched him grieve. I'm sure he means that her disappearance should have been solved long ago—not that she was dead."

Vera steadied herself. Good God, this was a nightmare.

"He stayed after Fraley all the time," Eve chimed in. "Went to see him every week even years later, wanting an update on what the man was doing to find Sheree."

Luna nodded, seemingly appeased.

As they made their way back to the lobby, every staff member they encountered stopped them to pass along their condolences. Apparently, they had all heard about the find, the probability that it was Sheree, and the fact that she had been murdered.

"Bless your heart," one of the nurses said, "I'm so glad they finally found your sweet mama."

"How terrible," another said. "Sheree was so kind. She certainly didn't deserve such a terrible fate. She was an angel."

It went on and on that way. Vera had no idea who these people were talking about, but it sure as hell wasn't the Sheree she had known. She felt confident they were only being kind.

Luna's fiancé was waiting for her when they reached the house. He said his aunt had called him from Hillside—she was employed there—and told him about seeing Luna in tears. He whisked her away for a quiet dinner.

Vera was grateful. She needed some peace and quiet.

As the truck's taillights disappeared in the distance, Eve asked, "Do you think Daddy knew she was there all this time?"

Vera turned to Eve. "I suppose it's possible, but I really don't think so."

"If he did," Eve went on, "that means he knew what we'd done."

"Maybe," Vera agreed. She weighed the possibility, too damned tired to react on an emotional level. This was strictly her analytical side doing what it was supposed to do: analyze.

But if he had known, why hadn't he said anything? Asked questions?

The chances that they would ever know his reasons or if he even actually knew anything at all were lost to the dementia.

Unless he'd confided in someone.

Vera didn't dare say that part out loud.

If someone else knew . . . they would hear about it soon enough.

6

"We had to come." The older woman, Florence Higdon, thrust the covered casserole dish she held at Vera. "It's the least we can do," she assured her with all the humility a woman who possessed none might fake.

Vera managed a smile. "Thank you. Really, you shouldn't have gone to so much trouble."

"Pop it in the microwave for a minute before serving," Beatrice Fraley chimed in. She stood in the doorway next to Higdon, her life-long friend.

Vera's face hurt from holding the smile in place. "I'll remember that. Thank you as well, Mrs. Fraley."

"You should call me Beatrice, Vee." She smiled, the expression weary, maybe a little sad.

Vera gave her a nod. "Beatrice."

"It's an old family recipe," Florence put in. "Trust me, y'all will love it."

If she had a million dollars, Vera would bet every cent of it that Beatrice—retired fifth-grade teacher and wife of the now-retired sheriff—had prepared the offering. These two and Vera's mother had been friends back in the day, and her mother always said that

Florence loved to gossip and to take credit for what others did, while Beatrice loved to teach and to try new recipes.

"I'm sure we will," Vera agreed.

"We're anxious to see Luna," Florence said. "I hope she's holding up all right."

Now Vera was confused. Florence Higdon, in addition to being the wife of the longtime Lincoln County medical examiner, Dr. Charles Higdon, was the director of the library—Luna's soon-to-retire boss.

"Didn't you see her at the library today?" Vera was under the impression Luna had gone to work this morning.

"Oh no. I had the day off," Florence explained with a shake of her head so adamant that her towering southern-belle hairdo moved, despite the half a bottle of hair spray that had no doubt been showered upon it. "I've been worried sick since Charles told me what they'd found."

"I'm afraid Luna isn't here." Vera mentally crossed her fingers. No need for them to linger in light of that news. "She's out with Jerome and his family tonight. But I'll let her know you came by."

Florence's face lit with renewed enthusiasm. "We won't worry about Luna then. We'll just come in and visit with you and Eve for a spell. Why, I haven't seen you in ages, Vera Mae."

"Where are my manners?" Vera backed up and allowed the ladies inside. She felt ill with the idea of how the next half hour—or God forbid, hour—would go. But then she shouldn't be surprised. Florence would be fishing for juicy tidbits to pass along to her grapevine. The woman hadn't been called "the Radio" her whole adult life for nothing.

"We won't stay long," Beatrice promised, while Florence hurried on down the hall.

"It's always a pleasure to see you," Vera assured her former teacher. Then, to include her friend, she amended, "y'all."

Vera followed the two and wished that Eve hadn't gone to her room for her cell phone charger. If she realized they had company, she would stay hidden until the two were gone.

48

Just Vera's luck.

Oddly, Florence had bypassed the living room and stationed herself in the library. At the door, Vera paused. "I'll just put this in the kitchen."

Florence waved her permission without a glance in Vera's direction. She was too busy surveying the room. Beatrice had perched on the edge of a chair, hands braced on the purse in her lap.

All Vera wanted was for this day to end. She left the casserole on the table and used the phone on the wall to call Eve's cell. Of course it went to voicemail, damn it. "You better get down here and rescue me." Then she hung up, took a breath, and returned to the library.

For the next fifteen minutes Florence effused about poor Luna. Blessed her poor little heart at least a dozen times. She did this even as she slowly perused the shelves around the room. Beatrice nodded her agreement with all that poured out of her friend. The way the two took their cues from each other was like watching a comedy act, only nothing about it was funny.

"But you're here now, Vera," Beatrice threw in. "Luna will be fine. I'm certain you'll take care of everything just as you always have."

"I'll certainly do my best," Vera promised with a glance toward the hall. Still no sign of Eve.

"What do you make of all this?" Florence exclaimed with palpable dismay, finally settling in a chair. "I mean, how could this happen right under our noses and no one figure it out?"

Now Vera felt sorry for Beatrice. Since her husband had been the sheriff at the time of Sheree's disappearance, the jab hit home. Her crestfallen expression said as much.

"We know Sheriff Fraley did everything possible to learn what happened to Sheree," Vera said. "He was the finest sheriff this county ever had."

The former teacher's face showed her appreciation. "He was and still is a good man."

"Well of course," Florence agreed. "No blame lies with Walt. He did all he could."

Somehow the woman's tone transformed the validation into an insult, but Beatrice let it pass.

"Were you girls able to relay this awful news to your father in a way he could understand?" Florence asked, shifting gears again. The woman hopped around from subject to subject like a rabbit on crack.

"We told him, but I'm not sure he understood what we were saying."

"It's such a sad situation when we lose someone to that terrible disease," Beatrice put in.

"It really is," Vera agreed.

"I've always wondered," Florence began, "if he knew more than he was telling." Her eyebrows reared up her forehead. "Not to say he was guilty of any wrongdoing, but it's so strange that he had no idea about what happened to her. She was his wife after all."

Vera tightened her jaw to prevent the sort of response that would only result in gossip fodder.

"Walt always thought that Garth Rimmey character had something to do with her leaving," Beatrice offered. "That man was a pure devil." She turned her full attention to Vera. "We were concerned for your father after he and Sheree married. Walt worried that Rimmey might try and hurt Vernon or one of you girls to get back at him for marrying his longtime girlfriend."

"Then he ended up dead too," Florence said in a suspicious tone. "Just a few days after Sheree disappeared. Someone beat him to death with a baseball bat. Seemed to me that would have been relevant to her disappearance somehow."

"Walt looked into any sort of connection," Beatrice countered. "He found none."

You tell her.

As for Garth Rimmey, Vera hadn't known him, not really. She'd heard the rumors about him, and she'd seen him around. He'd certainly looked mean enough, but that was the extent of her knowledge of the man. Still, the idea that Rimmey had been so close to Sheree . . . that he may have been looking for her after she disappeared unsettled Vera more than a little.

Had he come to their house looking for Sheree? Had he been watching them?

He was dead . . . probably didn't matter.

Unless he'd voiced whatever suspicions he had to a friend. Had he known about the cave?

Vera forced the new worry away.

"I was thinking," Florence went on, "with all your training, Vera, I'm sure you have ideas on what you believe happened."

"I was a kid," Vera countered. "A teenager. I had no clue. I assumed she left." She turned her hands up. "Looking back, based on her reputation, anyone would have thought as much."

"That's right," Florence continued with a slow nod. "You were in high school." A big smile spread across her face. "You and my Preston were in school together. You know he's a judge now. He's been nominated for a position on the Tennessee Supreme Court. We're all so proud of him."

"Congratulations," Vera said, forcing a big smile.

Preston was three or four years older than her, and back in high school, he'd been a bully. Not the type who beat up other kids. His preferred weapons were insulting words and a sharp sense of superiority. Then again, who was surprised, considering his parents had written the book on self-importance.

Florence hummed a note of disappointment. "I would have thought you'd formed some sort of impression."

Obviously the woman couldn't bear not having the skinny on everything, including Vera's thoughts. The truth about what really happened to Sheree was a mystery, and it was killing her. It wasn't doing a lot for Vera's mental health either.

Vera's smile lapsed. She couldn't keep that face on a second longer. "I'm afraid I haven't had much time to consider alternative scenarios regarding this shocking discovery. I arrived home only a few hours ago."

"You're right." Beatrice stood. "We should go. My goodness, you've barely shaken the dust off from your travels." She glanced down at her friend before looking to Vera once more. "We'll pop in again when you've caught your breath."

Vera was on her feet in a heartbeat. She pushed that fake smile back into place and lied, "I look forward to it."

Florence reluctantly rose from the sofa. She studied Vera a moment. "Mercy, you look so much like your mama."

Vera managed a real smile this time. "Thank you. I consider that a great compliment."

"You should," Florence said. "There was no one else like your mama."

With that, she followed the route her friend had taken, all the while babbling on about needing more time to catch up. Vera thanked them again for the casserole. Once they were gone, she closed the door and collapsed against it.

Eve came down the stairs. "They gone?"

Vera glared at her. "Thanks a lot."

Her sister shrugged. "Admit it, you would have done the same thing."

Vera rolled her eyes. "Maybe." She laughed then. "Florence Higdon hasn't changed one little bit. How on earth does that woman keep her hair so high? It's like a cone-shaped tower—like the one at the Twistee Treat shops we stopped at for ice cream when we went to the beach in Florida."

Before.

Eve laughed, and for a moment they were lost to the memories together. The seemingly endless hours in the car to get to Florida and then the ice-cream-swirl-topped buildings where they savored the best cones of the summer.

"Good times," Eve said, her voice distant. "As for the hair," she added, "you know the old saying. The higher the hair, the closer to Jesus."

Vera rolled her eyes. Neither she nor Eve had ever been big-hair types. "Maybe that's where we went wrong. We hardly went to church anymore after Mama died." They were certainly in a mess—one of biblical proportions.

Eve scoffed. "I don't think even Jesus could get us out of this one."

Sadly, Eve was right. They were in trouble here, and all the hard-earned experience and knowledge of fifteen years in the criminal justice system wasn't going to fix it.

Their only hope was plausible deniability.

7

Vera had never liked the silence.

She opened her eyes. Blinked against the darkness. Stared at the ceiling.

Everyone else was likely asleep. Luna had come home just before ten and gone to bed. Her mood hadn't improved much, but at least she was no longer in tears. Eve went to bed before Vera as well. She insisted she needed an early start at the funeral home in the morning.

Since then, Vera had walked the floors. She did some googling, studiously bypassing anything with her name in the lede. She'd avoided the radio and television since leaving Memphis. But past experience with this sort of thing provided plenty of fuel for her imagination.

Oddly enough, the shit show in Memphis now had serious competition for top priority.

Eventually, she forced herself to climb into bed. Then she had tossed and turned.

She threw back the covers and sat up, dropped her feet to the floor. The hardwood felt cool under her bare toes. She pushed her hair back from her face, swiped at her damp forehead with her arm. The damned floor was about the only thing around here that felt cool. Was the air-conditioning broken? She hadn't stopped sweating since she arrived.

She stood. Glanced around the room that had been hers as a kid. The posters of her favorite rock bands and celebrity crushes still lined the walls. The same daisy-covered quilt her grandmother had made when Vera was twelve lay on the bed.

If she looked closely enough, she'd find the scratches in the white paint of the old iron headboard where she'd added her name when she was ten. The books she had loved as a teenager lined the shelves next to the desk her mother had purchased from a tag sale and painted a pale green to match the leaves on the quilt.

Vera dragged her fingers across the top of the desk, memories tugging at her emotions. Life had been good then . . . *before*. Full of hope and possibility. All had gone to hell after her mother died and hadn't been right again until Vera was far away from here and in college. For a long while she'd come back once or twice a year. Then it was just once a year . . . even less, more recently. Work was always her excuse. Of course she and her sisters had spoken by phone regularly. One or the other would usually hand the phone to their father for a quick hello. But coming back just wasn't something Vera had wanted to deal with any more often than absolutely necessary.

She thought of her father now, lying in that bed at Hillside, not even knowing his own name most of the time. Maybe she'd been selfish to avoid him all those years. But he'd had Luna. She'd stayed home even while attending college.

If family commitment determined a person's afterlife reward, Vera was screwed.

She wandered to the window. Coming back forced her to acknowledge what she wanted to pretend away. Loss and pain and terrible secrets.

How did Eve sleep in this damned house?

The memories . . . they haunted Vera even as far away as Memphis. Her intent focus on work had been her only means of escape. Maybe that explained her lack of a personal life.

Enough. Definitely not going there.

The truth was, she hadn't set out to be in law enforcement. Maybe it was some sort of subconscious atonement . . . or just to demonstrate she could. Being a cop proved she was good, didn't it? In some little way maybe it made up for past mistakes.

Hadn't she been doing that—trying to prove something—her whole life? At least in the *after* part. Like when her mother died and then her father up and married a younger woman, Vera had gone out and gotten involved with a bad boy. A bad boy her father had warned her about.

Maybe her choice of law enforcement hadn't been about proving anything or atoning for something. Maybe it had been about this moment. The moment when she would need to protect herself and Eve from a murder charge.

No . . . she refused to chalk years of hard work up to something so self-serving and simple.

Vera evicted the thoughts and stared out the window. As a kid she had loved watching the moonlight trickle through the trees and slink its way over all the blooms of her mother's many shrubs and bushes. Later, in the *after*, she had used that moonlight when it hit the house at just the right angle for her to climb her way down the trellis that her father had installed for more of her mother's vines. The greenery was so thick on it now, finding a foothold on the trellis would be impossible.

It was a miracle she hadn't broken her neck back then.

She leaned her head against the window frame. Eve had never sneaked out of the house. She'd always been the good girl. At least until after Vera was gone. Then the behavioral issues at school started. Eve pushed away all her friends, and then the alcohol and drugs became her go-to buddies.

Vera closed her eyes and thought of her sister in the next room. Life had been so hard for her back then. She'd been a child stuck in that pivotal transition period between kid and teenager.

It was difficult to evaluate just yet how this current situation was affecting her. Vera had watched her during their time at Hillside with their father today. Her facial expressions had remained closed even when she'd spoken to him. Once they were back home, she'd spent most of the time on her phone. Whenever Vera tried to start a conversation to discuss the situation, Eve needed to make another call or to answer another text.

Typical evasion tactics.

Vera got it. Eve didn't want to talk about it. She'd wanted desperately to talk before Vera arrived, but once she was here to take care of things, Eve had withdrawn from the situation.

A degree in psychology wasn't required to understand her strategy. Eve accepted that the situation had happened. Now she was on to the "let's pretend it didn't involve me" level and was focused on moving forward. Put on the blinders and ignore. Let Vera handle the issues.

Not that Vera blamed her sister. It was far easier to not look . . . to pretend. For their entire childhood, Eve had been able to count on Vera to make everything all right. Vera was here now, so to Eve's way of thinking, everything would be fine. Vera would fix it.

Except the chances of her being able to fix this were not good.

Her superpowers had evidently taken leave of late. She couldn't fix any aspect of what was happening in her life. The queasiness she'd been fighting all evening resurrected. She should just go back to bed and fight the covers some more. Sleep would win the battle eventually.

Something out of place snagged her attention as she turned from the window. She leaned closer to the glass and scrutinized the view. Considering the amount of time Vera had spent staring out this window as a teenager, she knew every tree and bush and the way the moonlight hit each one.

Then she spotted the anomaly. A vehicle parked in the driveway, beyond hers, Eve's, and Luna's. A pickup. Dark in color.

If it was a reporter poking around, she was calling the police. Vera grabbed her cell phone and slipped out of her room. She hurried down the stairs as quickly and quietly as possible and opted for the back door rather than the front.

On second thought, she grabbed her daddy's shotgun, which had sat in the corner by the back door for as long as she could remember. If someone was out there snooping around, they were in for a rude awakening.

The click of the back door closing behind her was like a shot fired in the night. Vera held her breath and listened. Silence. She crossed the porch and descended the steps, then disappeared into the thicker part of the trees and bushes on the north end of the house. She could use that cover to reach the end of the parking area. The truck sat just beyond it, in the driveway proper.

The vehicle had no markings. She considered that maybe Bent had a deputy keeping an eye on the place. Maybe it was someone using their own vehicle. As she neared the edge of her cover, she paused and listened.

So damned quiet. Not even a cricket chirping.

This close she could make out a form inside the cab of the truck. Windows were down. She watched for a bit. Listened intently. The occupant made no attempt to get out. Made no sound.

Deep breath. Vera lifted the shotgun and braced it against her shoulder.

She eased to the left, keeping the barrel aimed at the ground—and moved toward the tailgate. Steeling herself, she hunkered down and progressed quickly past the back end of the vehicle and up the side until she was nearly even with the cab. The open windows made the slightest sound dangerous.

Her heart thumping, she straightened. Leveled the weapon on the target. A face turned toward her.

She froze.

Bent.

"I couldn't sleep either," he said, as if his presence should be no surprise.

"What the hell are you doing out here?" Vera lowered the barrel of the shotgun.

Memories of dozens of other times they'd met like this flooded her senses. She would sneak out of the house, rush out here, and climb into his truck. The man always drove a truck. Always an old junker.

She pushed the memories aside, then mentally kicked herself for allowing them to intrude.

"Like I said"—he opened the door, forcing her to take a step back—"I couldn't sleep." He climbed out and closed the door, then leaned against it. His trademark hat low, the brim rendering his face completely unreadable.

How was it that watching him move made her respiration quicken? *Idiot.*

"So you come here like this"—she gestured to his truck—"in the middle of the night? Is that your typical surveillance protocol?"

"Seemed like a reasonable thing to do since I needed to do some thinking. These questions"—he made a circling motion near his head—"keep spinning around in my mind."

"You couldn't call?" This was what normal people did. They called when they had a question. Or knocked on the door. They didn't sit outside in the dark unless they were casing the place or conducting surveillance.

"I didn't figure you'd appreciate a call at eleven o'clock at night."

"You've been sitting out here for better than twenty minutes?"

"Thereabouts."

The shotgun suddenly felt too heavy, and the idea that she wore a nightshirt that had seen better days abruptly occurred to her. The fabric was thin and far too clingy. Worse, she looked a mess from tossing and turning. She would have blushed with embarrassment had she not been so damned annoyed.

"What questions?" she demanded. Might as well get this over with. She knew the routine. Watch a suspect. Make them nervous. Ask odd questions. It was all about getting under the skin. Prodding answers. Forcing reactions.

Yada yada.

After a long pause—also a routine intimidation tactic—he stared directly at her and said, "I'm wondering if you remember anything unusual at all that happened just before Sheree disappeared."

"You mean other than the fact that she made Eve and me utterly miserable?" Then again, she supposed that hadn't really been unusual. Sheree had done that to lots of people. The woman had been a cold-hearted bitch of the highest order. "Or that she ignored her baby?"

"Besides that."

Vera's turn to do the intimidation thing. "I really don't want to be rude, but have you been drinking?" She scrutinized him head to toe and back. "I mean, this is not typically the sort of move a member of law enforcement makes. Showing up in the middle of the night and just sitting outside a house and watching like some psycho stalker. Unless you're conducting surveillance. Is that what you're doing?"

He chuckled, the sound rumbling from his chest. "Yeah. I almost forgot that part. You're a criminal analyst. Should I be calling you Chief Boyett?"

Now he was a comedian. Great.

"Not necessary." She cocked her head and glared at him in the near darkness. "You didn't answer my question."

"You didn't answer mine," he countered.

"Yes I did."

"What you did," he argued, "is throw out a distraction."

Touché. "What I remember," she decided to say, "is that Sheree was complaining about the baby all the time. She was always leaving Luna with me or with Eve and disappearing for several hours. The rumor was that she was cheating on Daddy. Maybe she was, maybe she wasn't. Eve and I both hated her and hoped she would find someone new and disappear."

"And just like that"—he snapped his fingers—"you got your wish."

Vera bit her tongue. She hadn't meant to say *disappear*. "I guess we did. If you're expecting me to say one or both of us felt bad about her going away, don't hold your breath. We were relieved." She considered her answer for a moment. "No, not relieved. We were grateful."

"How about your father? What was his state of mind at the time?"

"He was devastated, of course. Sheriff Fraley questioned him. I remember Daddy crying through the whole interview. Maybe you should check the case file. I'm confident there are notes about the interviews, and I vividly recall that he was questioned more than once."

"But he and Fraley were friends."

Vera laughed. "You really are considering the idea that my daddy did this." She shook her head. "That's impossible. He was madly in love with Sheree." Or maybe it was lust. Either way, he had used very poor judgment.

Her daddy's words about expecting Fraley to have found Sheree sooner echoed in Vera's head. But the statement hadn't meant that he had done something to Sheree. The idea was just not possible. Vera was there . . . she knew what happened.

Had Bent questioned her father?

"Have you been to Hillside and spoken to him?" she asked, the accusation clear in her voice. Her father was mentally incapacitated. Even Bent would know better than to question the man without his legal representative being present.

"Nah," he said. "I just wanted to hear your reaction."

Now she was beyond pissed off. "Good night, Bent."

Before she could walk away, he said, "I know there's something you're not telling me, Vee. I saw it in your eyes when we talked today. I just haven't figured out what it is yet. But I will."

She turned back to him. "Are you trying to intimidate me?"

He pushed off the truck, moved closer. Close enough to have her steeling herself for whatever the hell he intended to say or to do next.

"I wouldn't do that. I might be guilty of many things, but being a bad cop is not one of them."

Evidently he'd heard about Memphis. "Is that another underhanded accusation?"

He studied her a moment. Even in the moonlight his gaze was probing, piercing. And far too paralyzing. "Why would it be?" He gave her a nod. "G'night, Vee. Get some sleep."

He climbed back into his truck. She expected him to start the engine and drive away, but he didn't. He just sat there, waiting for whatever it was he thought he needed to see, hear, or feel.

If he hoped she would join him, he had another thought coming.

She gave him her back. Walked to the house, put the shotgun away, locked the door, and went in search of something to help her sleep.

For a moment she'd considered asking him about Garth Rimmey. Florence Higdon had reminded her that the guy had been involved with Sheree. Vera hadn't found much on the net about him, but what little she did discover, combined with his reputation, fit the profile of the perfect suspect. She would much prefer that Bent focus on him rather than her father or, worse, find the truth.

Rimmey was dead . . . it wasn't like it mattered to him. Being blamed for Sheree's murder wasn't going to make his reputation any worse than it already was.

But digging up the truth could destroy Eve.

Vera could not allow that to happen. Not to mention, it wouldn't do a whole hell of a lot for her.

She located a bottle of Jack Daniel's whiskey in the cupboard above the refrigerator and trudged up the stairs, carrying the bottle by its neck.

Unlike the other men in her life—her father, Bent, and a handful of guys who couldn't possibly have lived up to the memory of her first love—Jack had never let her down.

8

Just like old times.

Eve watched her older sister talking to Bent. The two stood outside his truck. It was the middle of the night, and they were far enough away from the house so as not to be heard if their voices were raised. It could have been twenty-some years ago all over again.

Except nothing was the same.

Vee lived in Memphis. She almost never came home. Their daddy was gone for all intents and purposes. Luna was getting married. Despite how annoying she could be with all her "happy" ideas, Eve had gotten used to her being around. Now she would be moving across town.

Eve would be stuck here all alone with the ghosts of their pasts.

She rolled her eyes. Except for Sheree. She just wouldn't stay in her place. That loathsome bitch had found a way to come back to show her ass one last time.

Anger roiled Eve's gut. The woman had made Eve's life miserable for the sixteen months she had lived in this house. As if that wasn't bad enough, she had stolen their daddy's attention. Not just part of it either—all of it. The woman had single-handedly changed their entire lives.

Bent's truck door abruptly closed. Eve peered harder through the darkness. Was he leaving? Vee must have really pissed him off. Eve scanned the path from the driveway to the house until she spotted Vee just before she disappeared onto the porch. Seconds later Eve heard the door close. A moment more, and she heard the soft footfalls on the stairs, along with the occasional squeak of a tread. Eve turned to the closed door of her bedroom and imagined Vee walking past.

Didn't take any real imagination to figure out Bent had more questions about this "stunning" find—that's what the *Elk Valley Times* had called it. It was possible he'd even been watching the house, concerned that they might be in danger from whoever put Sheree in that cavern in the ground.

As for Vee, she wouldn't trust Bent to get the job done when it came to closing this case. She would believe he was the same old don't-give-a-shit guy he was before. But she'd be wrong. Bent was smart, and he was good at his job. He would figure it out.

That was the part that worried Eve.

Oh well. Nothing she could do to fix it now.

And maybe she didn't care. To Eve's way of thinking, this was far more of a problem for Vee than for her. It was a shame she already had a truckload of problems with her job in Memphis. If she even still had a job. Eve had gone on Google and searched the Memphis headlines. All surviving personnel in that one-of-a-kind team Vee had helped put together had been suspended, pending the outcome of the investigation.

Eve couldn't help feeling bad for her. Vee had been like a second mother to her. Always taking care of her and getting her out of trouble. But then she'd left. For a long time Eve had resented her for leaving, but she eventually understood that Vee hadn't been able to stay. It wasn't her sister's fault that Eve hadn't been able to leave too. Well, she eventually left a couple of times, but she hadn't been able to stay gone. She always failed. Then she would come dragging herself back and drown herself in her drug of choice at the time.

Not Vee's fault.

Eve picked up her phone from the window ledge and stared at the text she had received a few minutes ago.

You still awake?

Eve hadn't answered. Maybe she would now. She suddenly felt rest-less, and being in this house was only making it worse.

She responded. Meet me at our place.

Eve tucked her phone into the hip pocket of her jeans as she eased out of her room, closing the door quietly so Vee wouldn't hear. Her pulse reacted to sneaking out of the house with both her sisters at home. Eve smiled. It had been years since she'd had to do that. And not a soul ever knew it was happening. Not even Vee.

Moving carefully, Eve descended the stairs, avoiding the treads that squeaked. She left via the front door rather than the back. The back door was almost directly beneath the area where the upstairs bedrooms were. Vee and Luna were less likely to hear the front door. An escape technique Eve had honed over the years. She always parked on the far side, closer to the driveway. Another strategic maneuver.

A few seconds later the house was disappearing in her rearview mirror.

She didn't encounter Bent's truck or any official sheriff's department vehicles as she drove along Good Hollow Road. Maybe he'd driven down to the barn to ensure those camped-out reporters were playing nice.

Only ten minutes were required to reach the town limits. The shops around the square were dark, the streets empty. A few blocks from the square she leaned into the curve that cut alongside Rose Hill Cemetery. She took the next right and drove up the hill. At the top, she parked on the side of the street and shut off the engine and lights.

After a moment her vision adjusted to the darkness, then she spotted what she was looking for. *She* was already here. Eve smiled as she climbed out of her car and quietly closed the door. She slipped through the gate and wound her way through the headstones.

The moonlight falling over Suri forced Eve to stall. She lost her breath. Suri was so beautiful and so kind. Eve was immensely grateful for their friendship. There were times when she desperately wished for more, but she wouldn't risk ruining what they shared for those selfish desires.

Suri spotted her and waved.

Eve's heart bumped harder against her chest. She walked faster. Knew the way by heart.

"I know I've told you this dozens of times," Suri said in a whisper, as if she feared disturbing the residents, "but I love your mother's headstone. I swear I want one just like it when I die."

Eve hugged her. She couldn't resist. The feel of her slight body and the silkiness of her long red hair relieved her somehow. Made her feel instantly more relaxed. "If I'm still around, you can be sure that I'll see to it."

Suri sat down on the cool grass, and Eve joined her. The sky was clear. The moon and stars shedding plenty of warm light across the cemetery. This was Eve's favorite place in the world. Anyone else—except Suri—would find it odd. Maybe even a little crazy. But, in truth, Eve felt far more comfortable with the dead than she did with the living. She'd come to understand this fully after her mother's death. That was when she'd started spending time here to be close to her mother.

Being in this spot, on the ground above her remains, was the one place where Eve had been able to find peace after her death. To a large degree this was still true. Few places felt safe to Eve. She was at home in the mortuary when preparing a body. Really any place in the funeral home gave her a feeling of belonging. She wondered now why it had taken her so long to recognize what she needed to do.

Stupidity, immaturity . . . addiction.

One or all of the above.

"You're upset about the remains of your stepmother being found," Suri suggested.

Eve leaned back against the cool black granite of her mother's headstone. "It's unsettling." More than Suri would ever know. They had been friends since first grade, but there were some secrets Eve couldn't share even with Suri.

"Perhaps part of it is Vee's presence."

Eve turned to her dear friend. "Vee is the only person in the world who loves me."

She held her breath, wished with all her heart that Suri would tell her she was wrong and that she loved her too.

"That's so not true." Suri laughed. "Luna adores you. She thinks you're a little strange, but she adores you just the same."

"Maybe." It had taken Eve a very long time to learn to like her little sister. In the beginning she had only tolerated her.

She supposed the softening had come somewhere around the time Eve turned twenty-eight, when Luna had been only sixteen and in the final weeks of her sophomore year in high school. Eve had stumbled and staggered her way into trouble at a motel over in Tullahoma. She'd gotten rip-roaring drunk with friends, and they'd rented a room where they could party. The police were called, but Eve sneaked out the bathroom window before the uniforms barged in. She was so drunk she could hardly walk. Worse, she was barefoot, and it was winter. She had no choice but to call someone for help.

Goody-two-shoes Luna came immediately. She took Eve home, slipped her into the house, and cleaned her up before putting her to bed. Most importantly, she never told their father. Eve had just accepted the position as mortician at Barrett's Funeral Home. That kind of trouble would have cost her the job . . . not to mention it would likely have cost her any future positions in the area.

That was the last time Eve got shit faced. She'd been managing her drinking for a few years prior to that. Limiting those over-the-edge moments. But she knew the morning after that night, when she had so very much to lose, that she couldn't take those sorts of risks ever again. She had to be smart. She loved her work far too much to screw it up. For the first time since her mother died, she was content, and that was saying something. She would not let anything screw it up.

"And you know how much I care about you." Suri leaned against the headstone and propped her head on Eve's shoulder.

The words made Eve feel warm inside. "Ditto."

"Imagine if anyone saw us here." Suri giggled. "Sitting on your mother's grave in the middle of the night like two ghouls."

"This is where we belong," Eve agreed. "Surrounded by the dead. It's so much more peaceful than being crowded by the living."

"Very true," Suri murmured. "I'm glad we get to do what we do."

Suri was the head mortician at Hurst, the largest funeral home in the county. Eve wondered if Suri saw the dead the same way she did. Eve could always tell the good ones from the bad ones. There was something about the bad ones . . . she could sense the evil in their skin . . . in their bodies. No matter. She gave the bad ones the same sort of service she gave the others.

They all deserved a proper preparation for their final presentation to those they'd left behind.

Eve rested her head against Suri's. Right now, her life was pretty perfect—more perfect than she would have believed possible, considering the nightmare it had lapsed into after her mother's death.

Surely fate would not be so cruel as to allow the return of that bitch Sheree to ruin everything all over again.

No. Eve couldn't possibly go to that place again.

No way.

Her heart thundered so hard, she was stunned Suri didn't hear it.

Eve struggled for calm. Told herself it would be okay. Deep breath. Vee was here. She would make everything okay.

She would save Eve . . . just like before.

9

Twenty-Two Years Ago

April

Lincoln County High School
Fayetteville, Tennessee, 11:00 a.m.

Vera hated high school.

It wasn't about the grades. Her GPA was a perfect 4.0. It wasn't even about the annoying people who surrounded her day after day in the classes she would rather do anything than attend.

It was about her life.

For the most part it was over.

Bent had left. Months ago now. The bastard.

Hurt and anger curled in her stomach. She hadn't meant to like him so much. Mostly he had been a distraction. Her mother had died, and then her father had married the crazy Sheree. By the time their love child was born, Vera had been desperate to escape her life. She had another whole year of high school left, and she had zero dollars. The car she drove was a total piece of crap. Her dad should have given her the Toyota, but he refused. Her mama had loved that car so much. It stayed in the shed, and no one was allowed to touch it. Not even Sheree. If he'd given it to Sheree, Vera would have freaked for sure.

In the end, it didn't matter. Vera had nowhere to go.

She glanced around the class. Others were still working on today's test. Another twenty minutes until lunch. Vera supposed she could read until the bell sounded. She reached for the paperback in the front pocket of her backpack, but a rap on the classroom door tugged her and the rest of the class's attention there. If they were lucky, it would be some sort of drill that would take them from class for the next half hour. Wouldn't that be great?

The secretary, Mrs. Parton, stepped into the classroom and walked to the teacher's desk. The two whispered for a moment, then looked straight at Vera.

Vera started. She covertly glanced around to see if maybe there was someone else they were looking at. Another student who had finished his or her test and sat behind her. Before Vera confirmed the target of their collective stare, Mrs. Parton hurried in her direction. Uneasiness slid through her. This couldn't be good.

When the woman stopped at Vera's desk, Vera prayed for the floor to crack open and swallow her. Everyone in the room twisted to look. God, she hated high school.

Mrs. Parton leaned down and whispered, "Vera, you need to go home. There's an emergency."

Fear nudged her. Eve had stayed home sick today. Was she really sick? Vera had figured she was faking it. "What happened?" she demanded several decibels above a whisper.

The older woman frowned at Vera. "I don't know, but your mother called—"

"My mama is dead," Vera pointed out, annoyed that anyone would call Sheree her mother.

Mrs. Parton took a breath. "Your stepmother then, I suppose. Whatever the case, you need to go home."

The secretary scurried away without further explanation or instruction. Vera reached for her backpack. As she stood from her desk, she glanced at the teacher, who nodded in acknowledgment of her need to leave.

Vera hurried from the classroom, sprinted down the hall to the exit. Whatever was going on at home, she couldn't help a sense of elation at being freed from another tedious day of boredom. When the exit doors closed behind her, she drew in a deep breath. As worried as she was that Eve had gotten sicker or that her father was hurt, she was so glad to be out of that classroom.

She climbed into her car and quickly lowered the windows to allow some of the heat to escape, and then she was out of there. If she had a cell phone, she could call and find out what was going on, but her father insisted cell phones were for responsible adults with paying jobs. Not for kids who talked too much anyway instead of helping out around the farm.

Vera rolled her eyes and roared out of the parking lot. If it was an emergency, she had cause to drive fast, right?

Driving too fast made her think of Bent.

She wanted to hate him for leaving . . . but she couldn't bring herself to feel anything except sadness and disappointment. She missed him. Damn it. Why the hell had he joined the army? Without telling her! She could write to him, but then he'd know how pathetic she was. Not happening.

No point dragging it out. They were over.

Hadn't she been through enough the last eighteen months? She'd lost her mom. Her dad had married a joke. And Bent had left.

She poked her head out the car window and screamed.

Vera HATED her life!

As she passed Monroe & Floyd, the distribution center where her father worked, she slowed and scanned the lot for his truck. She spotted it and felt a fraction of relief. He was still at work. That had to be good. If he was sick or hurt, he wouldn't be at work still. She sped up.

"Don't let it be Eve," she murmured. Her little sister was the most important person in her life. She could not lose her too.

Sheree could be dead, and Vera would feel nothing but relief.

Okay, so she didn't wish death on anyone, but for sure her life would be far less miserable without that obnoxious person in it.

She thought of baby Luna. Vera had tried so hard not to like the child. But the baby just wouldn't be ignored. Her smiles and gurgles got to Vera no matter how hard she tried to ignore her.

Just get home. She pressed harder against the accelerator.

The air cooled considerably after she turned onto Good Hollow Road. The trees were turning green again, and their branches and fresh new leaves shaded the road from the sun that was already hot, no matter that it was only April. When she pulled up to the house, Sheree's car sat in the same spot as it had when Vera left for school. Obviously she was home.

Worry gnawed at Vera. Had to be Eve.

Or maybe the baby was sick, and Sheree was passed out drunk or something. It had happened before.

Vera bounced out of her car and hurried across the yard, up the steps, and to the door. If Luna was sick and Sheree was out of it, Vera intended to call her dad. He needed to see how bad she got when he wasn't around.

The door suddenly opened, before Vera could wrap her fingers around the knob.

"Vee."

Eve stood in the doorway. Her clothes were wet. Even her hair was damp, plastered to her head on one side. Somewhere in the house Luna wailed at the top of her lungs.

"What's going on? Where's Sheree?"

Eve moved her head side to side.

Vera noticed for the first time that her sister's face was as white as a sheet. Her eyes as big as saucers. "What happened, Eve?"

"I tried to stop her . . ."

Vera pushed past her sister and rushed up the stairs. She went first to Luna's room. The nine-month-old stood in her crib, naked and screaming. Vera reached for her, pulled her into her arms. The baby was wet too.

A frown pulled at her face. What the hell happened here?

When Vera—Luna in her arms, clinging to her as if her life depended on it—walked out of the room, Eve stood in the hallway that spanned the second floor in either direction from the stairs. She blinked seemingly in slow motion and pointed to the shared hall bathroom.

Vera's heart suddenly started to pound, yet the air wouldn't fill her lungs.

She turned in the direction Eve pointed and walked the dozen or so steps to the bathroom door.

Vera stood in the open doorway for a long moment, her eyes taking in the scene while her brain scrambled to assimilate what she saw.

Sheree on the floor. Eyes open, unblinking.

Water stood in the tub. It had overflowed or sloshed onto the floor.

However many seconds Vera stood there looking, Sheree did not blink, and her chest didn't rise or fall. Oh shit.

Vera turned to Eve, who stood next to her now. "What did you do?"

"Vee, I swear it wasn't my fault."

Luna wailed even louder.

10

Tuesday, July 23

Boyett Farm
Good Hollow Road, Fayetteville, 8:05 a.m.

Vera awoke with a start.

She blinked away the bleariness, then traced a water stain on the whitewashed beadboard ceiling. She blinked again. *Home.*

She groaned and started to flop onto her side, but the brass-and-crystal light fixture her father had hung on her fourteenth birthday drew her into the past. She'd so badly wanted a chandelier. It was nothing elaborate, but it had made her fourteen-year-old self feel special. Eve thought she was crazy for wasting her birthday wish on a dumb light fixture. Didn't matter. Vera had loved it. Her mother smiled and whispered that she wished she'd had one that pretty when she was fourteen.

Before.

Before their mother got cancer. Before she died, leaving Vera and Eve so very sad. Before their father sought out comfort elsewhere, leaving them so utterly and completely alone. And before the rest of the disastrous things that occurred.

Vera was home. She lay in the bed a few more moments, until the more cognitive side of her brain caught up with the emotional part delivering all those tender memories. She was home, and she was in trouble.

Sadly the trouble was coming at her from both aspects of her life.

The other memories, more recent ones, poured into her skull. Years of hard work to bring a cutting-edge investigation team to life. And then the one defining event that destroyed it all.

She squeezed her eyes shut and tried to force the thoughts away, but they refused to go. No more pretending. At some point, her sisters would ask questions about the trouble in Memphis. This other insanity—right here at home—kept her off the hot seat for now, but it wouldn't last.

Nothing ever did.

Vera opened her eyes and allowed the reality to rise inside her, swarm in her brain like bees in the springtime.

No less than a dozen well-trained, focused minds had worked hard to become the very best officers in the elite program. Vera interviewed each one personally and repeatedly. All were the cream of the crop produced by the police academy. Four seasoned veterans had been carefully chosen to lead the unit.

Vera turned on her side and curled into herself.

Still, they had failed. No one had spotted the trouble until it was too late.

Mission after mission went perfectly. The department, the mayor, the governor praised their work. The media turned them all into celebrities. Other police departments were asking for help with creating their own teams that would work 24-7 to stop crime *before* it happened.

The Memphis PD's PAPA (predictive analytics policing action) team was the first truly successful one of its kind. For two years they had ferreted out and stopped perpetrators before they carried out their criminal activities.

And then it all went to shit when a senior detective killed another for reasons that had nothing to do with the work. Vera should have noted the issue and seen the trouble coming, but she missed it completely.

Internally, all were grateful the killing hadn't involved civilians. Still, two fine detectives, a man and a woman, were dead. The woman who had done the killing immediately turned her weapon on herself.

Vera had known this woman. They had been friends, she and Lorna Carver. Lorna's recent divorce set off warning bells for Vera, but Lorna insisted she was glad it was over. She and her ex had no children. The divorce seemed to be amicable. Vera bought her story without question. All was as it should be, and Lorna was ready to move on. End of story.

Except it wasn't.

As it turned out, Lorna had relationship troubles going all the way back to elementary school. Her mother broke down during her very first questioning and admitted that Lorna had hidden it well, but she'd always had issues keeping a relationship together. When her husband moved out, Lorna became involved with a fellow detective—a colleague on the PAPA team. The two were close. Everyone on the team was close. But what no one knew was that he had a history with Lorna's husband. That connection drove him to betray Lorna's trust and ultimately prompted her to unravel.

Even now, Vera tried to find an incident that should have set off new alarm bells, but both detectives had been too careful. For Lorna, her career was all she had left, in her mind, so she worked extra hard to behave as if nothing was amiss. Until she lost control.

No excuses. Vera should have seen it coming.

She reached for her phone and checked the time. *Eight fifteen a.m.* She sighed. Good grief, she should have been up hours ago. Vera tossed her phone onto the bedside table and threw back the covers. As she pushed to her feet, she considered that it was necessary to talk to Bent again about the case here. She needed to know exactly what they had found so far. Ultimately, she was at a standstill as to what to do until she knew what she was up against.

What *they* were up against.

This was bigger than just Vera.

Once she had more information, she needed to have a more in-depth discussion with Eve. She wasn't sure what time Eve and Luna went to work. Before now, apparently. The house was as silent as a tomb, which suggested no one else was here. Vera tidied the covers on her bed out of habit. She dug a pair of jeans and a tee along with underthings from her bag and rushed through a shower. With her hair tucked into a ponytail, she wandered toward the stairs, checking the other bedrooms as she went. Luna's room was exactly what anyone who met her would expect. Pink and flowery. Lots of family photos on the wall. A framed photograph of her fiancé on the bedside table. Everything in its place. Eve's, on the other hand, was cluttered and glum. There was only one family photo, and it was a framed shot from when Vera and Eve were much younger. It sat on the dresser alongside a pile of clothes that needed to be put away. Her bed was unmade, and the window blinds remained closed.

Perfectly Eve. Dark and brooding.

Their father's room smelled musty and unused. Vera doubted anyone went into the room anymore. Unable to help herself, she turned on the light since the shades were drawn and stepped inside. The room looked exactly as it had when he was married to Sheree, which wasn't that different from the way it had been in the *before* part of their lives. Sheree hadn't really changed anything around the house. Doing house stuff, she would say, wasn't her thing. Cleaning of any sort was included in the stuff that wasn't her thing. Eve and Vera had been like little Cinderellas during her tenure as their stepmother.

Sheree hadn't cooked either. Their father would make breakfast before he left for work. Vera and Eve figured out supper so their father wouldn't have to. The summer after he and Sheree married, the two of them had been on their own for lunches as well. Sheree lay around the house watching soap operas all day. This was just before any significant social media launched, so when she wasn't watching television, she stayed on the phone talking to *friends* or she simply disappeared for a few hours. All while Vera and Eve took care of the house, the cooking, and eventually, the new baby.

Early on they stopped complaining to their father. Even then they knew their stepmother was up to no good, but keeping the peace was far easier than dealing with the fallout of tattling. Sheree had been one vindictive bitch.

Vera forced the memories away and drifted down the stairs. It had been so long since she'd spent a night in this house, she'd forgotten about all the wonderful childhood photos her mother had hung on the wall going down the stairs. Thankfully Sheree hadn't touched any of those either. She probably hadn't even paid attention to them. She'd been far too full of herself to notice anyone or anything else.

Downstairs, the vague scent of coffee lingered. A glass dome covered a stack of muffins waiting on the table along with a note from Luna saying she decided it was better to go to work and keep her mind off things. There was no note from Eve, but her favorite mug sat in the sink, with a telltale ring suggesting she had coffee here this morning.

Since the leftover coffee in the pot was cold, Vera grabbed a pod and made a single cup. With her cup brewed, she slid onto a stool and checked her cell. No calls. No emails or text messages. She wished that were a good sign, but it wasn't. What it meant was one of two things—either the powers that be in Memphis had nothing to back up the narrative they wanted to present, or they had something that didn't fit their narrative. In either case, a lid would be kept on things until they figured a way around the issue.

Vera drew in a deep breath and sent a text to Bent to see if there was any news here. She thought of last night and how he sat out there in his truck the way he used to when they were younger . . . and far less intelligent. He left not long after she came back inside, but the impression he'd made stayed with her for hours, because that's how long it took her to finally fall asleep. Damn it.

She had been so enthralled with him back in high school. Her father had warned her about Bent, but there had been a mystique about him she couldn't resist. A dark allure. Neither of which she would have allowed herself to fall into had she not been so desperate to escape what was happening at home. Bent had been this secret, forbidden thing that was hers and hers alone.

Then, six months later he left without saying a word. She had to hear about it from his mean-ass daddy. Since her father hadn't bought her a car yet, she rode her bicycle all the way to Bent's house and beat on the door until someone answered. Howard Benton yanked the door open and staggered onto the porch at four o'clock in the afternoon. He drunkenly told Vera the news and then warned that she'd better "git" before she got more than she came for.

That same night Sheree announced that she and Vernon needed a vacation. The girls could take care of Luna and hold the fort down. The most bizarre part was that their father agreed. When they returned from their long weekend away, he obviously felt bad about the decision, which was likely the only reason he bought that junker of a car for Vera's senior year. Being a teenager, she readily forgave him . . . until the next time.

Surviving that year and escaping to college had been her only hope for relief.

Looking back, she understood that Bent's leaving had been for the best. She had buckled down and refocused on her schoolwork. Went off to college and lived mostly happily ever after—at least until recently.

At first, she'd felt bad for leaving Eve. But that had been the only choice at the time.

Was it her fault that Eve turned to drugs and alcohol?

No. Vera gritted her teeth. She refused to shoulder the full responsibility for what had clearly been her sister's bad decisions and their father's failure. He should have taken care of *all* his children. He stopped being concerned about Vera and Eve as soon as Sheree came into the picture. After Sheree was gone (and once he moved past the self-pity stage), his entire focus had been on Luna.

By the time Vera finished her undergrad work and started on her master's, Eve had left home and started college herself. But time and time again she bombed and returned home to lick her wounds. When it was clear Eve needed rehab, despite their father's denial, Vera took out a loan to ensure that happened. By then she had accepted a position at the Memphis Police Department.

It all seemed a lifetime ago now. Was, actually.

Vera washed out her mug and stared through the window above the sink. Bent had not responded to her text. She really needed to get a handle on what they'd found out there. If he wouldn't share answers with her, then she'd just have to find them herself.

She was going back to that cave.

Mind made up, she grabbed her cell, slipped on her sneakers, and headed out the back door. She'd made it down the steps when a voice stopped her.

"Vera, you are one difficult lady to catch."

Vera stopped in her tracks, swore silently, then forced herself to turn around. Her gaze collided with that of the woman who'd spoken. *Patricia Patton.* Top-of-the-heap reporter from Memphis's ABC bureau. Here she was, standing in the Boyett backyard, in stilettos and a tight skirt and looking all sleek and polished, just like she did on the prime-time news every evening.

For Vera, the big question just this second was *Where had her cameraperson hidden?* He would be here somewhere. Her gaze darted around the yard. No sign of him.

"I spoke to your sisters as they were leaving for work," Patton went on, "but they didn't have much to say. I've been waiting more than an hour for you to make an appearance."

"In our backyard," Vera said, at last finding her voice. "You realize you're trespassing."

It wasn't a question. The ambitious woman knew exactly what she was doing.

Patton smiled. "Well, you know how it is. It's difficult to get ahead and stay there in this business without a little creative step here and there."

Vera pulled off a smile, folded her arms over her chest, and lifted her chin. "Well, I applaud your creativity, Pat"—the woman hated, *hated* being called Pat—"but you'll need to go back to the road like all the others."

No cameraperson popped out from behind a crape myrtle or rosebush. Not yet, anyway.

"How are you handling the situation back in Memphis from here?" Patton asked, ignoring Vera's order and choosing instead to follow her toward the barn.

Vera stopped and faced her. "You can either go now, or I will call a deputy to see that you do."

Rather than depart as directed, Patton looked her up and down. "You have an in with the local cops, don't you? Sheriff Benton. The two of you have a history."

How the hell did she know about that? The thing she'd shared with Bent had not been common knowledge. It had been their secret. Vera decided the woman was bluffing.

"We've known each other most of our lives, if that's what you mean," Vera said. "Now, if you'll get off this property—"

As if he'd received some sort of cue or had been close enough to hear the exchange, a large man, camera on his shoulder, appeared from around the corner of the house.

Vera had known he wouldn't be far away. She was mad enough to spit. Without a word, she turned her back to both. She was not giving this woman a sound bite or a usable image to manipulate or exploit.

"Vera, do you feel singularly responsible for what happened to your team?" Patton shouted to her back.

Vera stalled. She told herself to keep going, but her brain just wouldn't issue the command.

"You and Detective Carver were close. Shouldn't you have seen this coming?"

Vera turned slowly, aware that the camera would be rolling. "Detective Carver was an outstanding member of our team. No one could have foreseen her actions. Whatever caused this tragedy, I refuse to trample her career in light of the years she devoted to the department and the community—for your ratings."

"Perhaps you're more worried about *your* career," Patton argued. "Based on what I'm hearing, you should have spotted the cracks before the breakdown happened."

Vera nodded. The words had hit home. "You're right. It was my job to recognize anyone who was not fit to carry out his or her duties. I did what any other person in my shoes would have done—the best I could. Perhaps it wasn't enough, but I am only human. I cannot read minds or see the future."

"How strange that you would say this when seeing the future is what your glorified PAPA team was all about. Perhaps it was never about anything more than profiling and harassing certain minority groups in poor neighborhoods."

Vera wilted a little despite her best efforts. This was where the tragedy had been headed since the moment Detective Carver pulled the trigger of her weapon in that mission briefing room.

Patricia Patton didn't care about the two detectives who died that day. She only cared about ratings and awards. She cared about promoting unrest and villainizing the department. All for just one thing—staying on top.

"That's a question for the chief of police's office," Vera said before turning her back once more.

"You're no stranger to tragedy, Vera," Patton called after her. "Was the unsolved disappearance of your stepmother the reason you chose a law enforcement career?"

Vera hesitated but kept going. Soon she would hit the tree line, and she doubted the ambitious reporter would have the guts to follow her into the woods, since there would be cops at the crime scene. Not that there was any hope of keeping this thing low profile. The find in the cave was the absolute perfect backstory to the drama unfolding in Memphis, making Vera an ideal target.

"Or maybe," Patton threw out, "your career path was just the safest place to hide from the secrets of your past."

Vera froze.

Was that what she'd been doing all this time . . . hiding?

11

"That's enough."

The fiercely growled statement had Vera pivoting in the direction of the voice. Bent had come out of nowhere and was herding Patton and her cameraman back around the house. Vera followed.

When had he gotten here? She hadn't heard his truck, but then she'd been a little distracted. She'd checked out the window before coming outside and hadn't spotted him or his vehicle, so obviously he'd only just arrived. Since she hadn't seen Patton or a news van either, apparently she and her colleague had walked from wherever they'd parked. Evidently Bent had as well.

Once he had the two herded into the front yard, Bent warned, "If you come on this property uninvited again, I will arrest you."

Patton smiled knowingly. "I'm sure you will, Sheriff."

With that and a final parting glance at Vera, she walked away. The man carrying the camera followed. Sadly this would not be the last time Patton crossed the line. She had a reputation for just this sort of strategy. You didn't rise to the top of the heap in her business by pulling any punches.

Vera should've thanked Bent. Instead, she glared at him. "They were already leaving. It wasn't necessary for you to make a show of force."

He cocked his head and studied her. "You worried she'll think you actually do have an in with the local cops?"

How the hell long had he been listening?

Long enough, obviously. She shouldn't be surprised or worried that he'd heard anything he didn't already know. The whole country knew about Memphis. He couldn't have missed it if he'd wanted to. At least not if he watched the news. Like everyone else, he might not be aware of all the details, but he had the gist of the story.

Vera had made a mistake. A terrible, tragic mistake by not seeing what was right in front of her. Her gut clenched, and the acid from that one hasty cup of coffee she'd downed burned its way up her throat.

"Why are you here, Bent? I was heading to the cave." She wanted to see inside . . . to know what they'd found.

"Can we take a minute? Have a cup of coffee?"

She blinked, dismissed the realization that there was still something about his eyes that drew her in the same way it had all those years ago. How pathetic was that?

Don't even go there, Vee.

His showing up and wanting to have coffee could only mean one of two things. He had news or he had questions. Maybe both.

"Of course." She turned and walked to the porch. "I sent you a text to see if there was news."

"I decided to answer in person."

Great. At the front door the knob turned without resistance, and she realized that she and her sisters were still operating under the assumption that Fayetteville was so safe, no one needed to lock their doors. Fayetteville might well be a very safe place to live still, but with all the reporters around, it was definitely not safe for the Boyett family. Not right now. From this point forward it was essential that the doors to their home be locked. She would talk to Eve and Luna about staying on top of the situation.

"You should keep your doors locked," Bent echoed her thought.

She made a sound of agreement. More a grunt.

Vera led the way to the kitchen and popped another pod into the coffee maker. She placed a mug where the carafe would generally sit and pushed Brew. The smell had her stomach burning again. Not a good sign.

"Cream?" The only thing she'd ever seen him drink was beer or whiskey. She had no idea how he took his coffee.

"No thanks."

Well now she knew. How exciting. He took his coffee the same way he did his whiskey: straight. She silently scolded herself for being so snarky, even if only in her head. Eve seemed to believe Bent was a good sheriff. Vera should be grateful he was in charge, if for no other reason than the fact he might have some amount of guilt related to their past that could potentially work in her and Eve's favor.

A big *if*, but she would take it. At this point, any glimmer of hope was better than none.

Once the coffee maker stopped sputtering, she passed him the mug and slid onto a stool across from him. He'd settled at the table and placed his hat on top. Even all those years ago he'd worn a hat similar to that one. Fancied himself a cowboy, she supposed. Lots of guys around Lincoln County cherished their hats, whether the cowboy style or the baseball type.

"You want to talk about it?"

She stared at him in confusion. "It?" He meant Memphis. She understood this, but she had no intention of showing as much.

"Memphis."

After one, two, three seconds of pretend consideration, she lifted her chin. "No."

"All right then." He picked up his mug and tested the coffee. Winced and placed the mug back onto the table. "Let's talk about the last few months before Sheree disappeared. Go over what you remember from that time."

Vera nodded slowly. "I get it. You have to keep asking that question because you were gone. Poof! Just vanished. So you have no idea what happened those last months I was home."

He flinched.

Okay, that was low, but she hadn't been able to help herself. He'd disappeared on her—ghosted her before ghosting was a trendy thing. If not for her determination to find him and that run-in with his daddy, she wouldn't have had a clue if he was dead or alive. Most days she had hoped for the former. Okay, not true, but it sounded good when she was angry.

"We can talk about that too," he offered, "if it'll make you feel better. Clear the air. Maybe."

Vera waved a hand in a "whatever" gesture. "The air is just fine from where I sit." There was no way she intended to admit how badly he'd hurt her.

He nodded slowly, as she had before. "Tell me the *details* about life in this house those last few months. You can break it down into just before and right after Sheree disappeared if you'd like."

If she'd like? She didn't like any aspect of this, but clearly she had no choice. If she refused to answer his questions, he would eventually compel her to do so.

She forced a smile. "Why don't we just go back to the beginning? We wouldn't want to overlook any aspect of relevancy. If you want *details*, I mean."

He gave a nod. "Even better."

Deep breath. Focus on the facts. Say no more than necessary.

"When Sheree first arrived," Vera began, "Daddy was overjoyed. She pretended to want to fulfill his every wish. She'd take credit for whatever dinner Eve and I had prepared and practically hand-feed him. Then they would disappear into the bedroom and leave us to figure out how to avoid the sounds they made."

The memories sickened her.

For those first two months after her mother died, Vera had been devastated. Lost. But so had Eve and their father. Somehow, the shared suffering made going on easier. They were a team—still a family. Then Sheree became a part of their family, and everything changed. Eve's and Vera's lives became the stuff bad fairy tales were made of. If not for Eve,

Vera would have taken off. But she couldn't leave her sister alone with their wicked stepmother.

And where would she have gone? Vera had never gotten that far in the what-if process because she'd realized it was an impossible idea.

"How long before things changed between Sheree and your father?" Bent tested the coffee again and this time took a long swallow.

"Sheree had Luna six months after they married." Vera rolled her eyes. Which meant their father was sleeping with her at least a whole month before their mother died. Even at sixteen, the reality was a huge letdown. He wasn't the superhero they'd believed. His immature behavior all those months with his new wife stole the remainder of their happy, innocent childhoods . . . prompted feelings that she and Eve had never felt before. Hatred. Disgust.

Their mother would have been disappointed by that most of all.

"Anyway," Vera continued, "after Luna was born, she—Sheree—was suddenly unable to do anything but lay around on the sofa and be waited on hand and foot." Which really wasn't a change other than the fact that she continued this behavior after their father came home each evening. "Daddy treated her like a helpless princess."

"I'm sure it was difficult for you and Eve to watch."

He had no idea. "We survived."

"Did she ever show any real affection for Luna?" he prodded.

"At first," Vera admitted—though she hated giving the woman any sort of credit—"Sheree was sort of captivated with the baby. But the fascination didn't last long. Within a few weeks Eve and I were taking care of the baby, and Sheree was MIA. I can remember coming home from school and finding Luna screaming in her crib. *Alone.* She would be hungry, and it was obvious she'd been wearing the same diaper for hours. Sheree would just leave her. We told Daddy, but Sheree always insisted we were lying, and he took her side."

Bent grimaced. "Not exactly the sort of childhood you were accustomed to."

He knew it wasn't. This was another thing that had drawn Vera to Bent. He had known her mother. She hired him to help with the gardening that final summer of her life. Sometimes he wouldn't show up, and Vera would tell her mother she should hire someone else, because everyone knew Gray Benton was no good. Vera had heard rumors about him. But her mama would always smile and say Bent was a good man, he just needed someone to show him how to be as good as he really was.

The truth was that Vera had been attracted to him on so many levels that it had terrified her. He represented everything she had been taught to avoid. No matter that he was the most handsome guy she had ever seen and that just being in the same room with him made her shiver, she sensed that he was dangerous somehow . . . maybe only to her innocence.

After that summer, Vera hadn't really seen Bent more than twice. Once in town hanging with his buddies, then another time when he'd been standing outside the house, staring up at her mother's bedroom window. Vera had stayed home from school to take care of her. Her mother insisted she would be fine, but Vera knew better. She was really, really sick from the chemo. She asked Vera to push back the curtains and open the window so she could smell the air. Vera did so, and that was when she spotted Bent standing under the big oak her mother loved so much. She told her about him being there, and her mother asked Vera to let him in.

When he came into the bedroom, her mother insisted Vera give them a few minutes alone. Vera was, of course, incensed, but she did as her mother asked. Though she didn't go far. She had stayed right outside the door, and to this day she would swear that she heard Bent sobbing like a child. At first she thought it was her mother, but when she started to come into the room, her mother had asked her to wait outside. Her voice didn't sound like she'd been crying.

She didn't see Bent again after that . . . not until months later. Her mother had been dead and buried, and her father and Sheree were married, and Luna had been born. Everything had so abruptly and so dramatically changed, and Vera wanted to glom on to anything that connected to her mother. She had missed her so much.

The memories flooded her now . . . sending so many emotions whirling through her that it took a moment for her to find her voice again.

"Why did you come to see my mama that last time?"

She'd never asked him about that day. Talking about her mother had been far too difficult for her to bring up the subject. Besides, they didn't spend very much time talking when they were together. This was actually the first time Vera had thought about that day in all this time. How strange for the memory to pop into her head at this precise moment.

"Your mama was nice to me. Mine died when I was just a little boy, and my dad, well you know what a mean bastard he was. Evelyn wanted to help me, I think. She kept telling me what a good person I was. Always had. As far back as I can remember, whenever I would see her, she would smile and tell me how handsome or smart or good I was." He breathed a sound, a sort of gutted laugh. "I just let her say whatever she wanted. I didn't want to hurt her feelings by telling her she was wrong. That my no-good daddy had beat all the good out of me by the time I was old enough to go to school."

The confession startled Vera . . . struck some place deep inside her that still dared to feel compassion for this man. She tried to think of some meaningful response, but nothing came.

He looked away, blinked as if he, too, was overwhelmed by some powerful emotion. And all this time she had been certain he was not capable of such a thing.

"Evelyn was very good to me," he repeated. "She treated me like I mattered, and I appreciated that kindness more than you can imagine."

Vera blocked the second round of emotion that wanted to rise inside her. Damn it, she would not allow herself to be pulled into a compromising position by the past. Not to mention it was too bad his appreciation hadn't filtered down to Vera. He'd sure as hell left her high and dry no matter how good her mother had been to him. She forced the thought away. Refused to acknowledge how he'd devastated her.

"So, yes," she said, going back to his question, which now felt like a much safer place, "everything about our lives changed with Sheree and Luna. Eve and I lost our father, really, but we dealt with it. What else could we do?"

"Did you ever hear your father and Sheree arguing?"

Voices and images filtered through her mind. "Obviously. He eventually saw through her lies and started demanding she stay home and take care of Luna. This resulted in several ugly confrontations."

"Did these confrontations," he asked, choosing his words carefully, "ever become physical?"

Vera recognized where he was going with his questions. "No. Never."

"You're sure," Bent pressed. "Just so you know, I reviewed the case file thoroughly, and there were folks who stated that they saw Sheree with bruises on more than one occasion and with a black eye once."

"What folks?" Vera demanded.

"Folks who knew Sheree back then," he explained. "There were witness statements in her case file. Sheriff Fraley had taken statements from several of her friends after she disappeared."

"What friends? Sheree had no friends, as far as I recall."

"There were a couple of women who frequented the same places she did who claimed to be her friends," Bent explained. "One has since died, and the other moved away."

Vera waved her hands, dismissing the idea entirely. "I'm sure she had so-called friends that she hung with, but not a single one ever came around here. Any bruises or black eyes these friends saw came from whatever Sheree did during all those times she disappeared, leaving me and my little sister to take care of her baby. Daddy would never have hit her."

"You and Eve weren't home all the time," Bent reminded her.

"I am telling you unequivocally that he did not hurt that woman. He would have done anything to keep her happy, but that was an impossible task for any mere mortal." Her frustration and disgust were showing, but she didn't care. This was the truth.

Bent picked up the mug and cradled it in both hands. "Still, I have to talk to him. See what he remembers."

Vera laughed. "Good luck with that. Most days he doesn't even remember his name." Funny how it was so much easier to laugh a little rather than to stop and think about the fact that her father was for all intents and purposes gone. But then, really he'd left a long time ago.

"But, professionally speaking, you understand that I have to try." He knocked back a slug of coffee without ever breaking their mutual gaze. His eyes were the palest blue.

Not what she needed to be thinking about just now.

As for his question, yes, as an investigative analyst, she understood—even if she didn't like it. "I do."

He set his mug aside. "Then you'll consent to the questioning and go with me?"

She turned her hands up. "Sure. I will gladly help you waste your time." She was being overly sarcastic, but it was true. Unless, of course, her father said something odd, the way he had last evening. She supposed it was a necessary risk. Better that he be questioned by the devil she knew. "I'll have to run it by Eve and Luna first."

"What about allowing me to have a look around the house? Maybe a check of his room to see if there's anything that might tell us what the two of them were up to just before she vanished. A note. A receipt. Something."

Vera needed to buy some time on that one too . . . just in case. "Again, I'll have to talk to my sisters first. Make sure the idea is okay with them."

He gave a nod. "I appreciate your help."

Despite her efforts to stay completely calm, her pulse had started to gain momentum. This was really happening. The realization still startled her.

This situation was the last thing she needed at the moment.

And this man . . . her first love . . . was the last person she needed to do this with. Yes, it was possible he could be an asset, but he could also make her vulnerable. She hadn't realized until just this moment how much he still affected her.

"Of course." She straightened. The urge to search her father's bedroom was suddenly pounding in her veins. He wasn't the only one who'd had arguments with Sheree. Vera and Eve had gone head to head with her many times, particularly after the birth of Luna. Vera was fairly positive Sheree wasn't the journaling type, but she wasn't going to assume anything. The absolute wrong thing an investigator could do was to operate on assumptions.

She'd given Bent something he wanted, so maybe now was the perfect time to introduce that other suspect option—the one that wasn't her father.

"Do you remember a man named Garth Rimmey?" he asked before she could.

She barely kept her jaw from falling slack. Apparently they were on the same wavelength. "I remember there was talk that Sheree was involved with him before. He wasn't happy that she'd married Daddy. Otherwise, the only thing I know is that he was a bad guy."

"He *was* a piece of shit," Bent confirmed. "He died not long after Sheree disappeared—four or five days, I think. Fraley was always after him. He was suspected of selling drugs and other things, but he was never caught with the goods."

He scrubbed at his jaw. Vera watched the movement with far too much interest.

"This was all hearsay," he went on. "No one would admit they'd bought anything from him. Too scared to do so, I imagine. The rumors you heard were right, he and Sheree were involved. It was mostly off and on. He would beat the hell out of her, and she'd leave him, then end up going back. This went on from the time she was sixteen until she married your daddy. Some say Rimmey put her up to go after Vernon just to get money, but there was no evidence confirming the stories."

Vera blinked. Gave herself a mental kick for getting distracted by watching his lips move as he spoke. "He was murdered?" The casserole ladies had said as much, and her net search had confirmed this, but more details would be useful. As for the gold digger scenario, Vera had always suspected that to be the case.

"Someone went into his trailer and beat him to death with a baseball bat."

Vera raised her eyebrows in question. "A tough guy like that—who everyone was afraid to rat out—let someone sneak up on him?"

"The medical examiner said judging by his blood alcohol level, he was probably unconscious when the beating started. There was no indication that he fought back. His killer caught him passed out and did the deed. The bat had been wiped clean, and no other evidence was found. Case is still unsolved."

Vera readily saw the potential setup behind that one too. "You think Daddy believed Rimmey had something to do with Sheree's disappearance and killed him to have his revenge?" So not her father's style. He wasn't a bully or a murderer. "You can't be serious."

"It's not impossible," Bent argued.

Speaking in terms of conceivable scenarios, this was true, but she wasn't saying that out loud. "Just highly unlikely, knowing my daddy."

"Rimmey had a strong history of violence, which suggests he could have killed her." Bent studied Vera's face, her eyes closely as he spoke. "Makes sense that he would have placed her body on your father's property to implicate him when or if she was ever found. I can absolutely see him doing something along those lines."

If this theory kept her father off the suspect radar, it worked for Vera.

"A plausible scenario," she agreed. Nothing screamed guilt more than jumping too quickly to place blame elsewhere.

Any good investigator, Bent included, would be looking for exactly that. He watched her too closely for her to believe otherwise. The hint of worry in his expression even suggested that he hated the idea, but she wasn't going there. Whatever guilt or debt he felt toward her was not something she wanted to explore. On the other hand, it was something she fully intended to exploit.

"How thoroughly was he investigated regarding Sheree's disappearance?" She clarified, "I mean, really investigated."

"He was pretty much Fraley's prime suspect, but he never had the evidence or a witness to prove it."

"It's tough to close a case without one or the other," she pointed out.

"No question. Rimmey had a friend," Bent said, "Pete Brooks. I'm working on getting an interview with him. See if he remembers anything else around that time period. According to the statement he made during the investigation, he hadn't seen Rimmey in a couple of weeks. Doesn't seem likely to me, given how close they were."

Pete Brooks. Vera couldn't place the name.

In her hip pocket her cell vibrated. She reached for it, checked the screen.

Eve.

Vera frowned and accepted the call. "Hey."

"Hey, I was coming back home to get a change of clothes and . . ." A sigh echoed across the line.

"What?" Vera's instincts started to hum. Eve's tone sounded off. Worry? Fear? Something in that order.

"Someone ran me off the road."

"Are you all right?" Fear snaked into Vera's chest. "Where are you?"

"I'm okay, yeah. I'm on Molino right after the curve."

She didn't have to say which curve. Vera knew the one. "I'll be right there."

"What's going on?" Bent asked as soon as the call ended.

"It's Eve. Someone ran her off the road."

"My truck's outside," he said, getting to his feet. "I'll take you."

12

Dead Man's Curve
Molino Road, Fayetteville, 10:00 a.m.

The curve didn't officially have a name, but some locals had called it Dead Man's Curve for as long as Vera could recall. For good reason. Several people had lost their lives taking this curve too fast.

She felt sick staring down the steep incline that could have taken her sister to her death. Eve's car sat on the edge of the pavement, one wheel dangling over that precipice. She had frozen at first, she said. Then, terrified and gripping the steering wheel, she realized if she didn't let go, crawl over to the passenger-side door, and get the hell out, she would remain in danger. It was a miracle her movements hadn't shifted the car and caused it to tumble fully over the edge.

Even if she hadn't been killed, she could have been gravely injured.

The possible explanations for how this happened pressed harder and harder against Vera's chest. Had someone rammed into Eve's car with the intention of injuring her? Vera swallowed at the rising emotion. Or worse, killing her? But why? The question twisted inside her. She couldn't see this having anything to do with Sheree's remains being found. But who the hell knew?

"Did you get a glimpse of the license plate number?"

Eve shook her head in response to Bent's question. She had explained that she'd come around the curve and then suddenly a vehicle rammed her from behind. Since it was not safe to take that curve at any rate of speed other than a crawl, the sudden lurch forward caused her to cut the steering wheel sharply to the right to avoid going over the left side of the road. When she cut so sharply, her car skidded, and her rear driver's side tire slipped over the edge of the pavement and into the air. This left the back end of the vehicle perched partially on the rear axle and slanted toward that drop-off.

Her car now sat diagonally blocking the narrow road. Bent had called a wrecker as they left the house, and thankfully, it had arrived. Now that he had assessed the situation from an official perspective, including taking photos with his phone, the wrecker driver was attempting to move Eve's car. The only damage appeared to be at the rear bumper, where she'd been struck by the other vehicle. There could be damage beneath, since the wheel left the road and caused the frame, axle, or whatever to hit the pavement.

The only thing that mattered to Vera at the moment was that her sister was okay. Still, she understood the necessity of determining how this had happened and who was responsible. If it was intentional . . . she didn't even want to go there. Bent, on the other hand, had to go there. He needed every detail Eve could recall.

"Then it was a truck," Bent said, above the grind of the wrecker's progress.

Eve shrugged. "Maybe. Like I said, I really didn't see anything other than the headlight area, and then I was busy trying not to run off the road."

"More details may come to you later," Vera offered in hopes of calming her sister.

"If a vehicle was right on your tail," Bent pressed, "and the headlights were visible in your rear window, then the vehicle sat higher than yours. Had to be an SUV or a truck."

"All I know," Eve insisted, sounding exhausted and exasperated, "is that I felt an impact, and then I was struggling to control my car. When I got out, the other vehicle was gone, and for a moment, I collapsed into a heap on the pavement." She shivered. "I was just glad not to be down there." She nodded toward the rocky drop-off.

Vera's heart lurched all over again. This had been entirely too close.

Bent surveyed the road. "Which tells me," he went on, oblivious to Eve's emotional state, "the driver backed up, turned around, and went in the direction from which he'd come."

Another shrug from Eve. "Guess so."

Vera set her own emotions aside. Bent was right: there was no way the other vehicle could have gotten around Eve's car. Vera scanned the short distance between where Eve's car sat and the curve. The only option would have been to back up beyond the curve and then to turn around on the other side. The move would have been risky considering another vehicle could have happened along.

"There's paint transfer." Bent gestured to the damaged rear end of Eve's car. "A dark green, I think. That could help us identify the vehicle that did this." He surveyed the road once more. "Once you turned onto Molino from Coldwater Creek, you didn't notice anyone in your rearview mirror?"

"I wish I had, but I was thinking about all this other stuff." Eve exhaled a big breath. "I should have paid better attention."

Vera moved closer, draped an arm around her, and gave her a hug. "You're okay. That's what matters."

"You might not want to hug me," Eve said, drawing back. "I had a spill with my pickup. That's why I was coming from Ardmore. We had to borrow one of the chemicals we ran out of. Evidently the lid wasn't closed properly when I picked it up, and I got some on my clothes. I was headed home to change before going back to the funeral home."

The fact that her sister was a mortician made Vera wince and step back. "Good point. We should get you home."

The wrecker driver shouted to Bent that he was ready to go, and Bent waved him on.

The three of them headed for Bent's truck. At the passenger-side door, Eve hesitated. "I doubt Bent wants me in the middle next to him."

Vera didn't see any stains on her sister's clothes, but there was a definite odor about her that she hadn't noticed at first. She'd been too grateful she was uninjured. Rather than argue about who would sit next to Bent, Vera climbed in. Why couldn't he have one of those trucks with a back seat? She supposed she should be glad the truck had a bench seat.

When Eve climbed in next, Vera had no choice but to ease closer to where he would sit. When he slid behind the wheel, he kept his attention straight ahead, which made the situation a bit more tolerable. The drive to Good Hollow Road took only a few minutes. No one spoke during that time. Vera was thankful. She was confident the sound of his voice would have made the ride even more cramped and uncomfortable.

However hard she tried to suppress the images, flashes of her sister going over that precipice kept haunting her.

Thank God she's okay.

Eve had suffered more than anyone with the intrusion of Sheree into their lives. Vera hated, hated that her sister had to go through any of this.

Once Bent had parked in front of their house, Eve clambered out. Vera scooted out behind her. "I can give you a ride back to work when you're ready." She had planned to go to the scene in hopes of getting a look inside the cave. She glanced at Bent. If he was in a charitable mood, he might allow her inside at this point.

"I appreciate the offer," Eve said, "but I have to take a quick shower. I called Suri while I was waiting for you. She'll come pick me up in half an hour. We're having lunch and then we'll both be heading back to work." Eve flashed a smile for the driver. "Thanks, Bent."

"Any time." He returned her smile, but it wasn't one of his killer grins.

Vera regretted immensely that she even noticed the difference. Eve wiggled her fingers at Vera before hurrying into the house. She was glad her sister had a friend like Suri. The two were close. Maybe closer than friends, but Eve hadn't said as much, and Vera wasn't asking. It was none of her business. Eve had always been secretive about her relationships. Some folks just didn't want everyone knowing their business.

Vera turned to Bent. "Like Eve said, thanks. I really appreciate your help."

He studied her for a long, unsettling moment. "Make sure she calls me if she remembers anything else."

"I will." She nodded.

A beat or two of hesitation and then, "You should all be watchful right now . . . just in case."

There was a chance, they both recognized, that Eve's accident was no accident at all.

He glanced toward his truck. "I should get back to that cave."

Anticipation fired in Vera's chest. "Actually," she ventured, "I was hoping to get a closer look. Have your forensic personnel gotten to the point where I could possibly view the scene?"

If the remains had been removed and the area thoroughly searched, with all potential evidence gathered, she didn't see why not. While he considered the request, she didn't dare breathe. Any way she rationalized it, she was asking a lot. Allowing her to be involved in even the smallest way could create problems. She got that. But maybe he would be feeling generous in light of Eve's close call.

"I suppose it couldn't hurt at this point. You and Eve have been in there before."

She nodded. "When we were kids, yes."

He hitched his head. "Let's go then."

They walked to his truck, and when Vera had settled in the seat and fastened her safety belt, he asked, "Did you ever go into that cave with your father?"

"No." She laughed. "Daddy would have locked us in the house and never let us out again if he'd known we dared to venture into places like that." This was mostly true.

Bent backed up, turned around, and headed up the road. "Then you have no idea if he was ever in the cave."

This, she decided, could be a trick question. "Certainly it's possible. This farm has been in his family for three generations. I'm sure Eve and I were not the first kids to explore that cave, but I'm not aware of him ever going in there. He never mentioned a cave on the property. I told you this before."

There was only one reason to ask a question twice—to determine if the person being asked would provide the same answer. Whatever else Bent was thinking, he was suspicious of her and Eve and their father as well. This was to be expected. The remains were those of their father's last wife, and they were found on the family farm. If Bent wasn't at least a little suspicious, his ability to be sheriff would be questionable, to say the least.

He navigated onto the narrow side road that led beyond the barn, bypassing the reporters still loitering in the area and ignoring their shouted questions. "Do you recall the last time you were there? At the cave, I mean."

"Sorry. I don't." She kept her gaze straight ahead. She didn't trust that Bent wouldn't see the lie on her face or in her eyes. There was a time when he'd known her well enough to recognize the slightest nuance of change in how she felt. She doubted he would now, but why take the risk.

"Eve may have gone back there without you." He parked well beyond the barn, on the same patch of pasture grass as the other two official vehicles. "She was only thirteen or fourteen when you left. She may have done some more exploring before she lost interest or just to get away from the house."

To smoke pot, he didn't say. After all, Eve had been stuck . . . a prisoner of the ongoing nightmare. Maybe it actually was Vera's fault her sister had hit rock bottom. What kind of big sister left her little sister behind to deal with all the fallout?

One like me. Evidently.

Did that make her a bad sister? Maybe. But she couldn't go back and do it differently. There were no do-overs. What was done was done.

The only thing she could do at this point was attempt to get the family through this crisis.

She mentally rolled her eyes. Calling this a crisis might be an understatement. It was more like a catastrophe.

"You'd have to ask Eve about that," Vera said, in case he was expecting a response.

"I'll do that." He looked toward the cave then. "I'll check in with Conover, our lead forensic investigator, first. As long as he's okay with you coming in, we're good."

"Thanks." Vera produced a smile and mentally crossed her fingers.

"Sheriff!"

Both Vera and Bent looked toward the voice that had called out. A man, early thirties, dark hair—obviously a member of the forensic investigation team, based on the way he was suited up—was striding their way.

Bent got out; Vera did the same. Until she was told otherwise, she intended to see and hear all possible.

"Conover," Bent said as he closed his door. "What's going on?"

Conover glanced across the hood at Vera. "We have a development." He seemed to have trouble with whatever should come next. Finally, he said, "You need to come into the cave."

Vera's heart started to pound. What now? Her emotions were still frazzled from Eve's accident. Though she didn't know this man, Conover, she recognized his agitation. Whatever had happened, it was big.

"Stay here," Bent ordered. "I'll be right back." He followed Conover to the cave opening.

Vera watched as the two knelt down and crawled on hands and knees through the opening. It wasn't tall enough to walk through, but once you were inside, it opened up considerably. She recalled vividly the first time she and Eve went into the cave. They'd thought for sure there would be pirate booty inside somewhere. But they'd never found anything beyond a few arrowheads and an old spoon.

The space wasn't that big, really.

For the next three or four minutes—which felt like hours—Vera considered what this new development might be. The last time she and Eve were here, there had been nothing—at least, nothing readily visible. Certainly nothing to get excited about. She had never stayed long in the cave. She'd been a bit claustrophobic when it came to areas that tight, especially ones underground. Still was.

She thought again about someone running Eve off the road. Who would do such a thing? With the incident happening at that curve, it was possible the other driver had no idea who Eve was. He or she may have been on his or her cell phone. That sort of thing happened with automobile accidents all the time. The driver may have feared being sued or arrested and took off.

Just because Sheree's remains had been found here was no cause for anyone to suspect Eve or Vera of wrongdoing.

Unless . . . someone *knew* . . .

Ice slid through Vera's body. Even if someone knew or suspected, why go to the trouble of revenge now? After all this time? Sheree had no family left around town. No friends, as far as Vera was aware. Who would care enough to take revenge?

It made no sense.

"Vee."

She jerked. Startled, but grateful to be dragged away from the troubling thought. "What's going on?" His face told her there was something . . . something bad. She braced herself for whatever was coming.

"One of Conover's men is a caver. He did some poking around and found an opening that appeared to lead into a possible second cavern beyond the main space where we've been working." He glanced back to the opening of the cave she and Eve had played in dozens of times as kids. "He assumed it would be a short, narrow dead end, but he was wrong. It led into a slightly larger space." He lifted his hat and ran a hand through his long hair, then fixed his gaze firmly on Vera's. "Vee, they found two more sets of human remains there. From what Conover can determine, they've been there longer than Sheree . . . a few years maybe."

No. That couldn't be right. This place was on *their* farm. No one ever came back here. It was private property.

It was Eve and Vera's secret place.

Except if those kids had found the cave . . . it was possible someone else had as well.

Obviously. It was the only possible explanation for what Bent was saying.

Because there was only supposed to be one set of human remains in that cave. Just one. Vera was absolutely certain about this because she and Eve were the ones who put that body in the cave twenty-two years ago.

Unless someone in her family had . . . killed before.

13

Vera stood on the front porch of her childhood home and watched Bent drive away. It was as hot as blazes, and still she felt chilled to the bone.

Before she could stop it, the memory of tugging with all her might to get Sheree's lifeless body out of that bathroom expanded in her brain like a balloon being blown up, stretching bigger and bigger until it was ready to pop.

Sheree had weighed a lot more than Vera had expected, no matter that she was hip bone–jutting thin. The only things of any size about her had been her breasts and her lips. Both had gotten her enough male attention to go to her head. She'd used those assets to get what she wanted. Never caring one iota about the impact of her behavior and decisions.

Vera shuddered at the memories.

Two more sets of remains.

How could that be?

The memory of Luna wailing made her twitch. The whole time she'd been tugging at Sheree's deadweight, the baby had been strapped on Vera's back in a backpack-style carrier. It wasn't like they could have left her screaming in her play yard or crib. Eve argued the point, but Vera refused to leave Luna alone in the house for the time required to do what they had to do. Taking her with them was the only option, even if it had been horribly gruesome.

As if the memory had summoned her, Luna's little electric car—probably the only one in the whole county—zoomed into the parking area. Vera shook herself. Had to pull it together. She squared her shoulders and cleared her head. Did she tell her sisters about this new find? It wasn't like she could keep it from them, but . . .

This shouldn't be happening.

Vera squeezed her eyes shut a moment in hopes of resetting. Surely there was some mistake.

Pull it together, Vee. There is no mistake.

The solid thump of a car door closing forced Vera's eyes open. She moistened her lips and formed them into a smile. "Hey, you home for lunch? I should have prepared something."

But Vera was just getting back from rescuing Eve . . . from learning that there was something way bigger than their secret in that damned cave. Someone had left two bodies in there—*before* Sheree. In a part of the cave Vera and Eve hadn't known existed.

They had never gone beyond the main cavern. They hadn't realized there was a hidden access to something bigger. Conover said the access was concealed by rocks. No reason they would have seen it.

It was . . . unbelievable.

How the hell had this happened?

There was only one answer: someone else had used that cave as a hiding place.

The possibility that the someone in question may have come back at some point and seen the makeshift burial site that she and Eve had made for Sheree unnerved Vera.

Sent a thread of fear weaving along every nerve ending.

That day . . . twenty-two years ago, Eve had slipped out of the cave while Vera was placing all the rocks she could scrounge up over the body. Her sister returned minutes later with an armload of flowers or blooming weeds (Vera could never tell the difference) she'd picked in the woods and the pasture beyond—anywhere along the path between the house and the barn.

Vera shook off the memories. Anyone going into that cave days or a few weeks later would easily have recognized the emotional connection to the deceased those dead flowers represented.

What a stupid, stupid move. But at the time, barely seventeen-year-old Vera had thought it was a nice gesture.

What idiots they had been.

Just hold up. Vera steadied herself. At this point she had no idea the condition or circumstances of these other remains. Until a forensic pathologist examined them, there was no way to be certain. The estimate Conover had given could be way off. They could actually belong to long-ago residents of the area. Some folks buried family right on their property. The cave could have been used as a tomb. It could be soldiers from the Civil War. Could be injured criminals who had hidden there decades ago and died of natural causes or starvation. There were any number of reasonable explanations that didn't include murder . . . or a member of her family.

Vera wrenched her mind from the worrisome thoughts of the past. Staying grounded and focused, solidly in the present, was far too important right now to be sucked into what-ifs.

Luna climbed the steps to the porch. "It's all right. I'll just have tuna and crackers." She patted her concave belly. "I have to watch my caloric intake if I'm going to get into that wedding dress."

Vera drummed up an effort at a casual laugh. "Women always have to work the hardest for these big events."

Luna rolled her eyes. "I swear, there are just a million things to do." She sighed. "And on top of that, now there's Mama's memorial service." She put a hand on Vera's arm. "I've set it up for Saturday at two. I want everyone to be able to come."

To the best of Vera's memory, Sheree had zero friends and no family in the area. All the other women in town had hated her, because she was always either flirting or sleeping with their men. "That's a good idea," Vera offered, the words tasting sour in her mouth.

"I'll need to go to Huntsville shopping before then," Luna bemoaned. "I'm certain I don't have anything proper to wear. Would you like to go with me, Vee?" Now she wrapped both her arms around Vera's one and held on tight. "That would mean so much to me."

"I'd love to go with you," Vera lied. "Whenever you'd like." Except for now. Vera had to find and talk to Eve. There was no way to put off telling her about the discovery in that damned cave. Word traveled at lighting speed in small towns. A frown furrowed Vera's brow. She should tell Luna about Eve's accident . . .

Not now. There just wasn't time. Maybe later.

"Thank you." Luna gave her arm one last squeeze. "That would be wonderful. I'm planning to bury Mama on the other side of Daddy's plot, if you and Eve have no objections. The plot is available, and that way Daddy has both the women he loved next to him, one on either side. It's perfect, don't you think?"

Vera mustered up another smile. "I'm sure Daddy will love that idea."

Thankfully he wouldn't have a clue what Luna was talking about. Or, if he did, he wouldn't for long. Lucky him.

There were so many things just now that Vera desperately wished she could forget.

Barrett's Funeral Home
Washington Street, Fayetteville, 12:45 p.m.

Vera had seen plenty of dead folks in her time—definitely not as many as her sister, but more than she would have liked. Growing up, the only transgression worse than not putting in an appearance at a viewing or the funeral of a neighbor was taking God's name in vain. Which meant Vera and Eve had loads of experience with funeral homes and the dead.

As an adult, most of the dead that Vera encountered had been homicide victims. Usually victims of violence. She'd sat in on more than her share of autopsies. But she'd only been present at the final preparations for burial once or twice. Both times, like now, with her sister.

When Vera arrived, Eve insisted she put on an apron and gloves, no matter that she had no intention of touching the corpse or any of the equipment in the room. Her sister had begun setting the features of the deceased, an eighty-year-old female heart attack victim named Mary Jo Kaufman. Mrs. Kaufman had played piano at the church they'd attended from the time the elderly woman was fifteen until the Sunday before her death. Like most of the kids who had attended the Presbyterian Church, Vera and Eve had taken lessons from her. Who could forget the ruler Mrs. Kaufman had used to snap their hands when they made mistakes? She wondered if Eve thought about that when she was preparing the body. Vera suspected there were times when the work was particularly satisfying.

Eve had stuffed cotton into the appropriate cavities of Mrs. Kaufman's head. Now she negotiated the suture thread through the lower gum area and up into the palate, passing into the right nostril, through the septum, and into the left nostril before slipping back into the mouth. The two ends of the suture thread were fastened together, and voilà, the jaw was secured shut.

Vera pressed her lips together. She intended to be cremated. If she'd ever had any misgivings, she had none now.

"What happened that made you decide it was necessary to visit me at work?" Eve asked as she massaged Mrs. Kaufman's lips and face. She glanced up. "It couldn't wait until later?"

Eve never liked being interrupted at work. She insisted the preparation process was like art—one needed time and focus to do their best. And it was unquestionably intimate, between her and the deceased.

Vera's stomach twisted at the thought of the less-dignified steps that came next—all for the entertainment of those left behind. Clean it out, stuff it, dress it up for proper presentation, and then stick it in the ground. Inside, she shuddered. "There's been a development at the scene."

Eve glanced up. "In the cave?"

Vera nodded. "They found more remains."

Eve's expectant expression slipped into a frown. "As in human remains?"

Vera made a face. "If they weren't human, it wouldn't be a development and we wouldn't be having this conversation."

Eve stared down at the gray-skinned woman on the table. "Ignore her tone, Mrs. Kaufman. Vee has always been snippy, as you well know."

Frustration lit inside Vera. "This is a serious matter."

Eve met her pointed look with an indifferent one of her own. "I'm not stupid, Vee. I totally get it. This complicates matters."

That was one way to put it.

"How could someone else bring a body," Vera challenged, "not once, but twice—into that cave without our knowledge? How did they even know about the cave?" She shook her head. "And if they ever came back and saw her . . ."

Eve made a "whatever" face. "They probably didn't. But even if they did, what were they going to say? Hey, I hid a body or two in your cave. Did you put one there too?"

Vera bit her lips together to hold back an equally smart-ass response. "I mean, why wouldn't they try and use the information for personal gain?"

Eve glanced down at Mrs. Kaufman, then hummed. "Who knows? Could be people who lived on the farm generations ago."

Vera reminded herself that patience was essential. "I understand that might be the case. But it's the possibility that someone involved with those remains returned *after* Sheree that we have to be prepared to deal with. Think, Eve. In all this time," Vera demanded, "have you been aware of anyone exploring the farm? Maybe someone who asked to hunt on the property?" Preparation was key. They had to be in a position to provide some sort of reasonable explanation for any surprises.

"Daddy never allowed anyone to hunt the land." Eve looked down at the deceased woman again, inclined her head, and frowned, as if noting some issue.

"What are you looking at?" Vera studied the dead woman's face. She saw nothing that should be distracting Eve from the conversation. This was an *important* conversation.

Eve's frown deepened, as if Vera had spoken in a foreign language. "I'm not looking *at* anything."

"You keep looking down at Mrs. Kaufman as if there's a problem."

Eve scrutinized Mrs. Kaufman again, then shifted her consideration back to Vera. "Well, she's right there. It's not like I can ignore her. You did interrupt my work."

Mrs. Kaufman's once brown eyes were gray and opaque with death. Admittedly, having the deceased lying on the table, eyes open, was hard to ignore. But the real trouble was that Eve just kept glancing down at her while she and Vera were having this very important conversation. It was unsettling.

"Why haven't you set her eyes?" Vera turned back to her sister. "Having this discussion with her lying there that way is a little distracting."

"I do the eyes last." Eve shrugged. "I wouldn't want my eyes closed while I was still being worked on."

Dear God, her sister had the strangest ideas about dead people. Always had.

"And no," Eve continued, "I do not know of anyone ever hunting on or exploring our farm. I can't say for an absolute certainty that it hasn't happened, because I've heard hunting dogs a time or two, but they may have been on the Jennings farm. Sound carries at night, you know."

A reasonable explanation.

"Did you," Vera continued, "ever go back into the cave after that day?"

This was the biggest question, looming like a black cloud. Bent hadn't mentioned discovering any trace evidence, but she couldn't be sure that he would share his findings at this point. Just because they had once been lovers didn't mean he felt he owed her anything. Least of all information related to an ongoing investigation.

Eve made a face. "Why would I go back to the cave?"

"I don't know, maybe because," Vera glanced down at Mrs. Kaufman, "you have a morbid fascination with death."

Eve had always, always liked watching things die and hanging out with the dead. Not that she'd gone around injuring animals or birds or even insects, but whenever they had come upon something fatally injured, she had insisted on watching until it was over. Then there would be the burial. Vera had never understood that creepy need.

For a moment Eve said nothing. Finally, she looked to her sister and responded. "I always hated the thought of anything dying alone. It's too sad."

"I'm sorry," Vera offered. "I never considered that you might feel compelled in that way." Maybe she was the creepy one for not being more sympathetic. "But I need to know if you ever went back. If you saw anything that looked out of place from when we were there last."

Eve stared at her a moment. "Yes. I did. Twice, just to see how she was doing, and then I left."

Vera groaned. She knew it! Damn it. "How she was doing? For God's sake! She was decomposing. What'd you think? That she'd gotten up and left? Gotten a new hairdo?"

"I'll pretend you didn't say any of that. But, for your information, my visits were a really long time ago," Eve argued. "Like only a few months after. I never went back to see her after that."

Vera gave herself a mental scolding. So much for calm and understanding. "Thank you for telling me."

"By the way, I'll probably stay with Suri until my car is repaired," Eve said, dragging Vera to a different topic. "It's just easier for getting to work."

"Sure," Vera agreed. She opted not to mention that this would leave her at home alone with Luna. She'd already been more than a little insensitive to Eve's feelings during this conversation. The idea that she could have been killed in that accident still twisted Vera's stomach into knots.

But what if it wasn't an accident? Could someone know what they had done and have been waiting all this time to take action? The possibility didn't make sense. Why not come after one or both of them twenty-two years ago? Fifteen or even ten years ago?

"Do we know who these people are?" Eve asked.

Vera shook off the other thoughts and frowned. "People?"

"The remains," Eve explained. "Have they ID'd them yet?"

"If they have, Bent didn't tell me." She and Eve had put Sheree's handbag and a suitcase with some of her things inside in the cave with her. At the time it had felt like the right thing to do. The missing items went along with the scenario that she'd run off.

Vera tried to remember what on earth had given her such an idea. Had she seen it on television, or had sheer desperation prompted a plan that had been completely her own? Poor Eve had been far too distraught.

"I guess we'll just have to wait and see what they learn," Eve noted. She returned her focus to Mrs. Kaufman.

"I suppose so," Vera agreed. "I should go. I'll touch base with Bent and see if he knows anything more."

Eve was smiling down at Mrs. Kaufman now. She'd done the necessary massaging to loosen the muscles of her face and lips. A quick application of glue, and then the final step of adjusting the lips into a smile. A far more pleasant expression than the woman had ever worn when she was alive.

"Do you still talk to them?" Vera ventured. Their parents had caught Eve more than once talking to the deceased at a viewing when no one else was looking. She had insisted that she wanted to be nice, since they were so lonely and no one else would talk to them.

Eve scoffed. "Of course not. That was just a phase when I was a kid." She shook her head. "This is my job, Vee. I like giving it my best. Believe it or not, being attentive and considerate makes my job easier. Makes all this"—she waved her hands around to indicate the room at large—"easier."

Vera believed her. The clients who passed through this funeral home were lucky to have Eve. "I'm sure the family is grateful for all you do."

"Let me know what you find out from Bent," Eve said almost absently as she readied to set Mrs. Kaufman's eyes.

Vera winced as she lined first one and then the other eyelid with glue. Sometimes, Eve had told her, the eyes didn't want to stay shut. One method to facilitate closure of stubborn lids was the glue she'd just used. If that didn't work or didn't provide the look she was going for, she used eye caps.

Vera blinked at the thought, hated when anything touched her eyes. "Sure, I'll let you know what he says. Talk to you later." Vera hesitated. "Be careful. If someone does know something and what happened to you today is an indication of that, he or she may try something again."

Eve nodded. "I'm working hard not to think about it at the moment, but you're right."

"Just stay watchful," Vera suggested.

"Promise." Eve used her forefingers to push the woman's nose more to the center.

Vera hesitated again. Thought of all the times her sister had made her promises. Sometimes her follow-through left something to be desired. Vera could only hope this wouldn't be one of those times. She made her way to the door, discarded her gloves and apron into the hamper there. Once she stepped outside the room, she didn't allow the door to close completely so she could covertly watch her sister for a moment.

It wasn't that she didn't trust Eve to tell her the truth. It was just that she might be trying to protect Vera from worrying. As the oldest, Vera had always been the worrier.

"Now," Eve said, peering down at Mrs. Kaufman, "where were we? A little birdie told me your older son was thinking of retiring. He's the one who found a wife online, isn't he?"

Vera's hopes that everything was as it should be deflated a little as she eased the door shut and walked away.

All these years she had, deep down, known that something was a little different with Eve. Well, that wasn't fair. What Vera had just witnessed could be chalked up to eccentricity. Whatever the case, she just hoped it hadn't amplified or evolved over time.

Vera needed Eve to be okay.

She loved her sister, and she would do anything to protect her.

14

Vera stood on the sidewalk outside the funeral home.

Thankfully the parking lot was empty. Since the board showed two viewings scheduled for this evening, the lot wouldn't be empty for long. God, she hated funeral homes. How could Eve work with the dead after what they'd been through?

And talk to them, for God's sake. How in the world could that be normal?

But then Vera supposed the same could be said about her own work.

Vera thought of going back home, but the idea held no appeal whatsoever. What she wanted was to have a look inside that cave or, more importantly, at what they had found in that cave.

Her cell vibrated, and she dug it from her shoulder bag.

Bent.

Seeing his name on the screen of her cell phone still rattled her. She'd added him as a contact last night. Obviously this situation wasn't going to resolve anytime soon. The two of them would be in contact for a while. Better to recognize his number when he called.

The fact that he was calling so soon had her wondering if there was more news already. Or had she been on his mind? Vera rolled her eyes. She was likely the last person on his mind, ever.

Bracing herself, she accepted the call. "Hey. You have news?"

"I think we need to talk. Just the two of us."

Oh hell. "All right. You want to come to the house?" She preferred to maintain the home field advantage.

"With the reporters watching your house, I was thinking maybe you could come to mine. I'll pick up lunch on the way."

Her stomach reminded her she needed food. She hadn't bothered with breakfast, and it was lunchtime already. "Sure." She took a breath. "Where do you live now?"

Before, he'd still lived in his father's house. At least that had been his official address. Truth was, he was rarely there, and knowing his father, she could understand why.

"I'm over on Old Molino." He provided the number that went with the road.

"I'll head that way." Vera knew the address. She'd never been to the home there, but one of the girls in her AP English class sophomore year had gotten off the school bus at that location.

"Good. See you in a few."

Benton Ranch
Old Molino Road, Fayetteville, 1:30 p.m.

The driveway was at least half a mile long. It wound through the trees, finally coming to an end at the house, which overlooked a pasture that was more like a meadow and absolutely stunning. Two horses grazed in the distance where the pasture spread toward the woods.

This was not what she had expected at all.

Vera turned back to the house. More a cottage. Not too small, but certainly not large. Stone and timber. It could have been lifted from a scene in the Cotswolds of England and placed on this hillside. Blooming vines grew over the stone portion of the wall in front. A small porch was tucked neatly on the other side. A gray metal roof highlighted the gray in the stone.

The extensive landscaping had to have been here already. Her mind simply refused to see Bent clipping hedges and fertilizing blooming shrubs. She climbed out of her SUV and closed the door. The sun bore down on her, amplifying the muggy heat and prompting her toward the shady porch. The house was surrounded by massive trees. Their broad reach provided generous protection from the sun. The soft fragrances of the variety of shrubs and perennial flowers drifted in the air and reminded her of her mother's gardens.

On the porch was a bench. A pair of mucking boots sat next to it. Men's. Vera turned and peered toward the horses. In the tree line, almost completely camouflaged, was a barn. She surveyed the yard for a UTV. Had to be one in the detached garage, which looked more like an old-fashioned carriage house. If not, that was one heck of a long walk to the barn every morning and every evening. Then again, Bent looked quite fit. Maybe he liked the walk. Or maybe he jogged to the barn and back twice a day. The notion reminded her that the only working out she'd done since her arrival was the emotional kind.

Vera shook her head and lowered onto the bench. This whole situation felt surreal.

She was back home in small-town Tennessee—after her career crashed and burned—to try to head off any trouble related to the body she and her sister had hidden twenty-two years ago. And the man who had been her first lover was in charge of the investigation.

How was that for one hell of a twist of fate?

The crackling sound of gravel beneath tires drew her attention to the long driveway, as Bent's truck rolled into sight. Vera drank in the view: the horses meandering through lush grass, the trees standing sentinel, the sweeping drive. It was really the quintessential country setting.

How had Bent ended up here?

This setting simply didn't fit with the man she knew.

But the fact was, she didn't really know him. Not anymore. She hadn't known him since she was a kid, and he'd barely been more than one himself. They were different people now. She surveyed the yard. This was his grown-up life.

She thought of her Central Gardens town house in Memphis. She had all the amenities and convenience that city living could provide. But she would never have this kind of view. Would never smell the sweet, clean scent of this air in the city.

She exiled the thoughts. She didn't want this. The city was her home.

Her career with MPD might be over, but her life was still in Memphis or someplace like it.

She thought of Eve and Luna and her daddy. The past was here . . . the people she loved were here. But there was no coming back to stay. That possibility just wasn't an option. The mere thought made her restless.

As if fate had wanted to prove her wrong, Bent emerged from his truck, and her heart skipped at least one beat.

Vera almost laughed out loud. Oh. Dear. God. She was not in love or anything else with Bent. Maybe she once was—as a kid. More likely what they'd shared was mutual need . . . equal measures desperation and lust.

A huge difference.

And she wasn't a teenager anymore.

He climbed the three steps and gave her a nod. "Thanks for coming."

She glanced at the bag in his hand. The logo from the town's most popular slaw-burger café had her stomach sending stronger hunger messages.

"Nice place." She stood, swept her gaze across the landscape once more. "I wouldn't have guessed you for a farm sort of guy."

"It's a ranch," he tossed back as he unlocked the door.

She glanced at the horses. "Ranch," she amended. He had always worn that cowboy vibe with pride.

He opened the door and waited for her to go in first. "Make yourself at home," he offered.

Inside was a little more western, a little more masculine. The stone and wood theme carried through in the structure. A huge fireplace spanned a good portion of one wall. The ceilings were vaulted with wood beams. The sofa was leather, with the two accompanying side chairs upholstered in a Southwest style. The only thing in the room that gave a nod to the cottage style was the vintage wood rocking chair.

"My mom's," he said, noting her attention on the rocker. "It's the one thing of hers my old man didn't throw away or destroy during one of his drunken binges."

Vera spotted the oval brass-framed photo on the table next to the rocker. She crossed the room and picked it up. The woman in the photograph was his mother. She didn't have to ask. His mother had the same dark-blonde hair and stunning blue eyes.

"She was beautiful."

"She was," he agreed.

Vera placed the photograph back on the table and turned to her host. "What made you buy this place?"

The living space was one big room, with the kitchen on the far side and a big old round table standing in the middle. The cabinets were painted a white that had dulled in brightness over time and sported a few dings but somehow looked exactly the way they were supposed to. Homey and well loved. Bent stood at the rustic table, unbagging their food.

"Just before my mother died, we came here together once." He chuckled softly as if the memory gave him pleasure. "The couple who owned the place had hired her as a housekeeper. She cleaned houses to make ends meet. God knows my old man drank up most of the money he earned. Anyway, we were here, and I was wishing I was in the woods somewhere."

Vera couldn't help smiling. She remembered Bent saying he was far more at home in the woods than anywhere else. He'd never been a hunter. His love of the woods had been about feeling close to nature. The man was a walking cluster of contradictions. As soon as you thought you had him figured out, and that he didn't care about anything, you realized you knew nothing at all and that he cared deeply about many things.

"As bored as I was that day, I remember her saying how she loved this place. When we were driving away in that old junker my dad somehow managed to keep running, she said this was her dream home. Imagine that." He laughed softly, glanced around. "When I moved back to town, I heard it had been sitting empty for years, and I bought it. Did a little TLC, and here I am."

Vera couldn't think what to say for a moment. It was such a moving explanation, and she did not want to be moved by it . . . or by him.

"Keep in mind, you asked," he pointed out, noting her inability to decide what to say next.

She walked toward the table and him. "I'm impressed that you would want to do something in her memory." She looked around, taking in more fully the comfortable, relaxed setting. "It's a really nice place, and I'm certain your mother would be so proud of you for remembering . . ." She took a breath. "For everything you've accomplished."

There, she'd said it. Given him a compliment. A well-deserved one, she confessed to herself. It was more than he would be able to do for her. Her life was in tatters, and she was confident even more trouble was coming.

"Thank you." He gestured to the table. "Have a seat. You want water? Beer? Sweet tea or coffee?"

"Water is fine." Vera settled into one of the chairs. "What made you decide to come back? You could have landed anywhere after your time in the military."

He filled first one, then another glass from a pitcher he'd taken from the refrigerator. "I did my twenty and decided I was done." He put the pitcher back in the fridge, grabbed the glasses, and headed to the table. "I still had the homeplace here, and I figured I'd land there for a while until I decided what came next." He sat a glass in front of her, took his seat, and drew a long drink from the other glass.

"Did you sell the house where you grew up?" She unwrapped her burger and took a bite. It would be a lie if she pretended she didn't love a good cheeseburger loaded with slaw. She'd gotten hooked on the combination as a kid. This one made her want to moan with satisfaction.

"I did not." He unwrapped his own burger. "I donated it to the church for temporary housing for those in need. Victims who lose everything in a house fire or a wife and kids who need to escape an abusive situation."

Stunned all over again, Vera finished chewing and swallowed. The man was just full of surprises. "That was very generous of you."

He lifted one shoulder. "Not really. I didn't need it. Clint—you remember Clint Grider, the pastor at the Baptist Church over on Elk Avenue?—he was always good to my mother and me."

Vera sipped her water, then nodded. "I see. You came back to prove something."

"You think I'm proving something?" The ghost of a grin twitched his lips.

"You're making a safe place," she suggested, "from the home where you and your mother were abused. You're the sheriff, keeping the community where you grew up as an outcast safe from threat."

"I'm honored you think I'm that deep. Anyway, Fraley asked me to run for sheriff. He was desperate for someone with the right background. He served during Vietnam, so he saw my military service as the right background. It was a job. I figured why not—for a while anyway." He looked her straight in the eyes then. "And maybe giving the house to the church was an up-yours to the old man. He would have hated that."

Vera bit her lip, but she couldn't stop the smile. "That would have been my alternate scenario."

They ate in silence for a bit, but eventually the subject she'd hoped wouldn't come up did. Of course.

"What happened in Memphis?"

As much as she'd enjoyed his story about buying this place, she had no desire to talk to anyone here or anywhere else about what happened in Memphis. The news media was doing a bang-up job of that for her. She couldn't wait to see what they made of today's development.

"You don't watch the news?" she tossed back, rather than give any sort of response.

"What gets reported isn't always what really happened." His gaze rested on hers. "I want to know what really happened. From you."

She supposed if she expected him to keep sharing with her, she needed to do the same. But not about this. "It's a difficult situation, and at this point, my attorney has advised me not to talk about it to anyone."

When had she become such a consummate liar? She hadn't spoken to an attorney yet. No matter that her police union rep had urged her to do exactly that, she simply hadn't been able to go there. The truth was, maybe she didn't deserve an easy way out of this.

If Bent had said something—"okay" or "I see"—she might have been able to move on and change the subject. But he didn't. Instead, he watched her . . . just watched her and waited for a real answer.

Vera took a breath, let it go. "I made a mistake."

The statement hung in the tension that swirled inside her, around her, despite her best efforts to tamp it down. Again he said nothing, just waited for her to go on.

"I should have noticed the trouble with a member of the team, but I didn't. I mean, I did, but I thought she was okay. I should have recognized she wasn't. Two people are dead, and it wouldn't have happened if I hadn't allowed my friendship with a team member to override my judgment."

"One thing I've learned"—he crumpled his burger wrapper and tossed it back into the bag—"is sometimes we can't see what's right in front of us." He inclined his head and studied her. "It isn't always about being blind or distracted. It's about not wanting to believe what we see."

Valid point. "Unfortunately, dead is dead, and no amount of rationalizing will bring those people back." She couldn't finish her burger, pushed it aside. "And someone has to answer for that. It was my job to see, and I didn't." She wadded the remainder of the burger in the paper and placed it into the bag. To prevent herself from fidgeting, she placed her clasped hands in her lap and held on tight for whatever was coming next.

"I'm sorry. I know this is difficult."

She drummed up a grateful expression. "Thanks." Subject change. "What's the situation at the cave now? Two more sets of remains were found. Is there anything else you can tell me?"

"You want some coffee?" He pushed back his chair and stood, clearly wanting coffee himself.

"Sure." Why not feed more caffeine to her jangling nerves?

He placed the grounds in the filter, poured water into the reservoir, and started the process. Then leaned against the counter next to the coffee maker and settled his gaze on hers. "There are similarities between the sets of remains."

"Between the two found in the other cavern?" That had to be what he meant. Those two could not be related in any way to Sheree.

"Between all three."

Vera's heart nearly stopped. "What sort of similarities?"

"All the victims are female, and all were posed similarly. Rocks were placed on the bodies in an effort, I imagine, to prevent them being bothered or dragged off by animals."

The memory of piling rocks on Sheree's body flashed in her head. "Okay."

"Their arms were folded over their abdomens before the rocks were piled on, but more telling were the things left with the remains."

His words had her heart lunging into a gallop. "What sort of things?" She thought of Sheree's handbag and her suitcase. Tendrils of tension riddled with trepidation stretched through her.

"Crosses on chains." He touched his throat. "Necklaces. They each had one, and they were all exactly the same. Silver plated, thin chains, all a bit rusty now."

Vera felt hot and then icy cold. She could see Eve leaving a cross necklace on Sheree's remains . . . but she couldn't have on the others. It wasn't possible. "How long"—she paused, steadied her voice—"have the two in the second cavern been there? Any ideas on the timeline?"

"One, we believe, has been there twenty-five years, maybe less. She was wearing two rings. One was a silver band—the real thing—and there was a date inscribed inside. August first, twenty-five years ago. The other was silver also, but it was one of the best friends rings teenagers buy each other."

She nodded, the movement jerky. "I know the kind you mean."

"This is the part that you're going to find interesting." He said this with a knowing look. "The other vic was wearing the matching ring."

"Which suggests they knew each other," Vera proposed. "Is the estimate on her time of death the same?"

"Now that's the strange part, when you consider the matching rings. The first victim was put there months, maybe a year before the second one, Conover estimates." He lifted one shoulder in a vague shrug. "It's difficult to be certain at this point, but that's the best estimate he can give me. We'll see what the lab says."

Holy shit. Her head was still reeling. Who the hell could have put them there? And why? *Okay, Vee, think like an analyst, not a perpetrator.*

"What's your conclusion then?" God, she hated that her voice sounded a little pitchy.

"I believe it's possible the same perp left all three victims in the cave. I don't know why the older remains were hidden more carefully than Sheree's. Maybe the killer didn't have as much time to hide the body of his last kill. Or maybe some physical limitation prevented him from doing the same as he had the two times before."

Vera cleared her throat. His assessment was a reasonable one. "What about cause of death? Any similarities there?"

"Again, I can't say for sure, but there's indication of head trauma on all three victims."

Jesus Christ. She understood now. He was leaning toward the idea that this was the work of a serial killer. She managed a shaky breath. Of course he was. Three murders with numerous similarities. Bodies dumped in the same place. Made sense.

Her gut clenched at the little voice whispering things she did not want to hear. She hushed it. Would not go there. No way.

"I've asked for support from the TBI. One of their agents, as well as a member of their forensic group, is coming tomorrow to have a look."

Vera reminded herself to breathe. "Good move." Not that he needed her to tell him that calling in the Tennessee Bureau of Investigation was smart, but it was better than saying nothing. "As I've said before, I would be happy to help if you need me."

Her lips felt numb, her tongue awkward. She struggled to slow her pounding heart. She had to keep her wits about her. Had to maintain analyst mode. So far nothing to worry about. Nothing she and Eve couldn't deal with. It was all okay . . . *so far*.

"I appreciate the offer." He smiled, then turned to the coffee maker and proceeded to fill two mugs with the freshly brewed coffee.

She ordered her fingers to unlock so that she could accept the mug he passed to her. "Thanks."

He settled back into his chair and placed his mug on the table. "I'll bring you in as soon as I can. For now, I have to keep the scene pristine. You understand."

"I do, yes." She did. Really. She wasn't part of official law enforcement around here, and as someone with access to the crime scene prior to the discovery, she was a person of interest. The additional remains had taken this thing to the next level for those investigating. Bent's people, however well trained and experienced, simply didn't have all that was needed for a case like this one. There was a level of expertise and experience required that typically wasn't found in small-town police departments.

"When Sheree's remains were discovered," he began, "my primary persons of interest were your father, obviously, and Garth Rimmey. Both had motive and opportunity."

Obviously. Her father was the husband. Of course he was a suspect. "But we know my father wouldn't have hurt Sheree or anyone else."

This was true, even if it would have been far easier to let him take the fall. He wouldn't know or understand what was happening, and Eve would be in the clear.

Didn't matter now. This was bigger than just Sheree.

How the hell had two other bodies gotten into that cave?

The glimmer of a scenario she did not want to expand upon nudged her again. *Couldn't be. Couldn't be.* There had to be another explanation. Her father wouldn't kill anyone . . . the idea that he'd killed multiple victims was ludicrous.

Wasn't it?

All the times he'd gotten angry after their mother died . . . all the drinking . . . but the timeline didn't fit.

Not going there . . . not yet.

"As for Rimmey," Bent went on, "the other two victims don't really fit a scenario that involves him. What would be his motive for disposing of his victims on your property prior to Sheree's marriage to your father? I can't see a connection there."

Vera managed a sip of her coffee. "Agreed. So . . . how long before you plan to make this new information public?"

Not something she was looking forward to. The nightmare would expand exponentially for the Boyett family, and the story would gain momentum in the media. Mass shooters and serial killers were viewer magnets. The coverage would be nonstop from now until the case was solved.

"I'll see what the agent from the TBI has to say about releasing information and go from there. For now, considering there are no recent victims, we have no reason to believe the killer is an imminent threat. For all we know, he could be dead or in prison."

"True." Her right knee began to bounce. She cradled her coffee mug in hopes that he wouldn't see the way her hands had started to shake as well.

She had to get out of here. He wasn't going to allow her into the scene today. Which was just as well. She needed to think, and then she needed to talk to Eve again. Alone. Some place where there was zero chance of being overheard or distracted.

"I should let you get back to work," she suggested. "Thank you for lunch."

"I'm glad you agreed to come. It means a lot to me that we can talk like this."

Why was she having such difficulty reading him? Did he or did he not suspect her and/or Eve of being involved with this somehow? Or their father? There were moments when she was certain he had suspicions related to one or all three of them, and then he would do something like this lunch, and she would be convinced he did not.

But then again, this could just be his way of regaining her trust.

On the porch, he hesitated and reached for his cell. "Benton," he said in greeting to the caller.

Vera wandered down the steps and surveyed the landscaping around the house that really was so un-Bent-like. She took a long, lingering look at the meadow, where the horses grazed. It was a peaceful place.

The call ended, and she waited for him to join her, then they walked to her SUV together. Vera settled into the driver's seat.

Bent paused a moment before closing her door. "Just remember," he said, searching her eyes, "anything you can remember from when Sheree disappeared that you may not have mentioned before could make all the difference in figuring out this mess."

"I assure you," she promised, "I've told you everything I can remember."

Still, he hesitated, held her gaze. "I'm counting on that, Vee, because this situation just got a little worse."

The call. "What now?"

"We have a fourth set of remains."

15

Bent scrubbed a hand over his jaw as he considered the new aspect of this expanding hornet's nest. Each layer seemed to reveal another.

"What can you tell me so far?" he asked, not entirely sure he wanted to hear the answer.

Will Conover nodded. "One more set—four total. Three female, one male. As we've already discussed, the female vics were arranged in place, arms folded, rocks on top of the bodies. Sheree was the only one with an assortment of personal possessions—a handbag, wallet, and suitcase. The jewelry worn by the other two females is the only personal items left with those remains." He shrugged. "The male vic is newer—I'm guessing he died three or four years ago, maybe a little less. Still got meat on the bones. Judging by the condition of the back of his skull, he died of head trauma, like the others. No wallet or anything like money or nail clippers, et cetera in his pockets. No cross necklace. But there is a school ring. University of Alabama in Huntsville."

Hope sparked in Bent's chest. "Tell me there's a name inscribed."

"Not his name, but there is what I'm thinking is a nickname. Either that or the guy was überreligious. The inscription reads *God*."

Bent nodded slowly. "*God?* That's it?"

Conover nodded. "Yep. I'm thinking I can track down the owner of the ring through the manufacturer. They generally keep records. We have the school, the inscription, and a year—which should be the year of graduation."

"Give it a shot." Bent surveyed the craggy walls, which right now felt as if they were closing in. "Thanks, Conover."

"No problem," he said. "I'm curious as hell about the inscription."

Conover made his way out of the cavern, but Bent stuck around. The folks from TBI wouldn't arrive until tomorrow. Just as well. He needed some time to think. He surveyed the mounds of rocks that had been removed from the two sets of female remains. The misplaced piles made the space a little crowded. Maybe eight feet by ten feet, it was not such a large area. The female victims had been placed on a slightly elevated ledge that time or water or whatever had carved out of the rock wall along one side. They had been easy to see upon entering the hidden cavern. The other victim—the male—had been placed in a corner at the back of the space, with fewer rocks hiding him. He'd been tucked into a wide crevice at the base of the cave wall, where it met the floor, making his remains almost unnoticeable.

Each victim was against the rock walls of the area, none in the center of the space. The loose stones that had been placed over the bodies seemed a fairly large number. Bent suspected some had been brought from outside the cave. He had no idea how many—if any—had been inside.

The process of removing all the remains would wait until after the TBI folks had a look. Bent had assigned two deputies to keep the cave secure tonight. Two more tomorrow. He didn't want anything walking out of here.

It wasn't like Lincoln County was crime-free, and it hadn't been that long ago that six people were murdered in a drug retaliation hit. But this was different. These were four sets of remains from two different time periods. Conover estimated that the three females had died within a few years of each other. It was the last find that changed everything.

Not only because the victim was male but also because the murder had occurred no more than three to four years ago. Since he had been shoved into a crevice, there was no posing. No cross and chain. The difference, he suspected, meant something about why he was murdered and maybe by whom. Possibly the male vic had learned something about the killer . . . or someone close to the killer, and that knowledge had gotten him murdered. Or maybe he was the one who'd killed the three females and someone close to one or all three had levied revenge.

Bent shook his head. Could be a serial killer—the TBI would no doubt see it that way. Either that or there were different perpetrators involved who just happened to use the same dump site.

"Not very fucking likely," he muttered. There would be a connection of some sort.

Bent walked back to the access point that separated this space from the primary one the cave's exterior opening entered into. Since the opening was only about two feet tall and three feet wide, he had to low crawl through to the other side. The way the access was hidden behind a boulder, it wasn't readily noticeable when first entering the cave. You had to be looking for it. The big question in Bent's mind was *Why not drag Sheree through that small access and hide her with the other two?* Her remains were the only ones in this front area of the cave.

Maybe the killer had a specific reason for keeping Sheree separate from the others. Or he just hadn't taken or had the time.

The bigger worry here was the more recent murder. There was a greater likelihood that the killer could still be in the area and active. Someone Bent knew. A neighbor. Even one of his deputies.

Not to mention the equally troubling bad feeling growing in his gut. Vee was not being completely up front with him. He couldn't say for sure that she was lying, but she wasn't telling him everything she believed or knew. Though it had been a long time since the two of them had been involved, and they'd been damned young for sure, he knew her eyes . . . knew her voice.

Not to mention he'd searched for her on the internet many times over the years. He'd watched countless interviews. Kind of dumb, but he hadn't been able to ignore the need. No matter that it had been more than twenty years since they were close, he had watched her and listened to her enough to know something was not quite right.

She was hiding something.

Maybe nothing earth shattering . . . but something relevant.

He made his way through the cave's exterior entrance, which actually wasn't that much larger than the one going into the secondary cavern. Conover and his team were outside in the tent-style temporary processing area they'd set up for preparing the remains for movement.

One thing was damned clear, they were going to need a bigger tent.

16

Vera paced the length of the room once more. Bent had called with an update on the latest find. In her opinion, the news changed everything.

What the hell was taking Eve so long? She was supposed to be here twenty minutes ago. They only had so much time before Luna would be home. Luna wanted Vera to go shopping in Huntsville with her. She'd promised she would, so there was no backing out.

But first, Eve and Vera needed to talk.

Her cell vibrated, and she tugged it from her back pocket. If her sister was sending some lame excuse about not being able to come . . .

I know what you did.

A chill washed straight to her bones.

Vera stared at the screen. Opened the text message fully. The sender was not in her contacts.

She felt sick. Blinked. What the hell?

This couldn't be right. Vera shook her head. Tried to slow the racing in her chest.

A glimpse of movement beyond the window jerked her attention there. She eased in that direction. A small black car—a Mini

Cooper—had pulled in next to Vera's SUV. She held her breath as the driver's side door opened. Eve emerged.

"Thank God," she muttered, relief roaring through her veins.

Vera rushed to the front door, unlocked and opened it, then waited for Eve to reach the porch.

"I had to borrow Suri's car."

As soon as Eve was across the threshold far enough, Vera closed the door. She couldn't hold this in any longer. "They found another set of remains."

Eve made a face. "What?"

"As if that's not bad enough, then there's this." Vera held her cell phone in front of her sister's face. The message she had received mere moments ago on the screen.

I know what you did.

Eve stared at the screen, then blinked. "Yeah. I got one of those too."

Vera's jaw dropped. "And you didn't tell me?"

Eve shrugged. "I just told you. And you just told me about yours."

True. But Vera had only just gotten hers like five minutes ago. "When did you get yours?"

Eve checked her cell. Showed Vera the screen. Four seventeen. Only two minutes after Vera received hers.

God, she wanted a drink. Something to steady herself, but she couldn't go there. It wouldn't be fair to her sister. Who the hell would be sending messages like this? No one knew . . . at least not if Eve was to be believed. Was it someone toying with them? Someone who hoped to prompt a response of some sort?

Eve searched her face. "They found another set of remains. Really?"

This was her reaction? *Really?*

Vera reached deep for calm. "Really. The latest victim was male and appears to have been put in the cave three or four years ago."

"Shit." Eve's eyes widened with something like surprise.

Vera studied her pupils. Had she been smoking pot? She was way too calm. The truth was, Vera could only control so much, and there was even less she could do. Particularly if Eve wasn't being completely forthcoming.

Just keep going. "The females were all posed exactly like Sheree. But not the male. Apparently he was shoved into a crevice." Vera closed her eyes a moment. Dear God, she couldn't get the image of Eve posing Sheree out of her head. Just a kid trying to make this dead woman look like the people in the coffins at all those damned viewings they'd attended. Vera had rounded up and placed the rocks. Eve had run back outside to gather wildflowers to put on the rocks.

All the while the bodies of two other women had been only a dozen or so feet away.

Who the hell had been using their cave? Even before they did?

Vera's heart pummeled her sternum.

This was insane. She had to sit down. She shuffled into the living room and collapsedm into the nearest chair. "I don't understand." She watched as Eve came into the room and settled onto the sofa. "How the hell could this happen? How could we not know about the others?"

This part—this unbelievable escalating development—was far more troubling than some jerk sending the two of them messages. The messages could be some fool playing games.

"No clue," Eve said, her voice sounding weary of the subject, her face equally so. "But whoever did this seems to know we were the ones who put Sheree there." She shook her head. "I mean, the text messages sort of suggest that's the case. What else could they mean?"

Eve had a valid point. Vera scrubbed at her forehead. "Who could possibly know what we did?"

More importantly, who could have been killing people and leaving their bodies in that damned cave on *their* damned farm?

Take a breath. This was not the time to lose it.

"I've racked my brain, and nothing comes to mind." Eve stared at her cell. "This is really crazy. Who would hate us this much? Enough to try and run me off the road and to send these messages?"

Oh Jesus. Vera had put the event at the curve completely out of her mind after learning about the other remains. Maybe the driver actually had been nothing more than an idiot who'd been preoccupied with his phone and ran to avoid the insurance and legal issues of an accident. Then again, what if the driver was the person who killed those other victims? Had he watched their inept efforts with Sheree? Had he gotten a good laugh? Or was he pissed that their carelessness—compared to his disposal of victims—had caused his work to be discovered?

"If they're connected," Vera ventured, "the accident and the text messages, then we're in over our heads and we're going to need help."

"You want to tell Bent what we did?"

That was the last thing she wanted to do. "I honestly have no idea what to do."

"Well," Eve offered, "considering you're a cop yourself with fifteen years' experience, if you don't know what to do, I sure as hell don't know what to do."

Vera rolled her eyes. "On an ethical and cognitive level, I know what to do, Eve. I just don't know what to do on an emotional level. This was always about protecting you. Now it's grown into something far larger."

"Now it's about protecting you too," Eve suggested.

"Clearly." Vera hated that she sounded sarcastic, but it wasn't necessary for her sister to point out the obvious. Eve was likely thinking the same way. They couldn't go down that path. Playing the blame game wouldn't help. "What happened was an accident," Vera went on. "If I'd been the one at home that day, it would have probably turned out the same way."

"I know," Eve agreed, sounding bored of the subject.

"This thing that's happening now," Vera said, looking Eve straight in the eyes to ensure she was paying attention, "is different. Someone killed three people and hid their bodies in our cave. Killing three people at three different times is *not* an accident. The problem for us is that the killer ignored or reveled in finding Sheree's remains and probably decided we were responsible or maybe watched us do it. Or thought our father did. We can't be certain of anything. Except—the person who put those other remains in the cave is a murderer. If he's still out there, then we have reason to be concerned for our safety."

Vera took a deep breath. "His work has been discovered, and he likely blames us—hence, the text messages, and maybe what happened on that curve as well. If we hadn't put Sheree where we did, the others might never have been found."

"Yeah, I get it." Eve shifted her attention to her phone rather than maintain eye contact. "I guess that was my fault."

A too-familiar sick feeling attacked Vera again. What was Eve hiding from her? There was something. Vera could not shake the feeling or ignore her sister's obvious detachment. "What do you mean?"

"I'm the one who suggested the cave." She glanced up. "That makes it my fault."

Vera tried to recall the frantic conversation all those years ago. She was certain the decision had been a mutual one. "We did this together," she reminded her sister.

Eve nodded but kept her attention on her phone or her hands.

"You're certain there's nothing else you need to tell me," Vera nudged. Despite her need to trust Eve completely, she found herself holding her breath.

"I don't believe this." Eve stared heavenward and heaved a big breath. "What happened with Sheree"—she glared at Vera—"was an accident. You know that. You just said it. I damned sure haven't killed three other people. How could you think that?"

Sadly that was the part that bothered Vera the most. Bent mentioned it just a little while ago. Rarely did a person see what was right in front of them when it involved a close family member or a close friend. She'd experienced a devastating reminder just last week.

"I know you didn't kill those two women. You were only eight or nine when they were murdered. I just need to know that everything is on the table—you're not holding back even to protect someone else."

"We've talked about this," Eve argued. "The fact is, it seems like there's a lot we both need to know. Like who the heck sent those text messages. My first thought was Luna."

Eve's suggestion annoyed Vera. But more importantly Vera recognized it for what it was—an attempt to shift the focus. Her sister was definitely hiding something. But Eve had never responded well to being pushed. The issue would have to wait a little longer.

"I think it's safe to say," Vera countered, "that Luna is not involved with this. She has no idea we are."

"I don't know why you think she's so innocent. What if Daddy figured out what we'd done and told her at some point after his dementia got so bad? It's not impossible."

Vera supposed that scenario was conceivable. But she couldn't see her father knowing and never saying anything to her or to Eve. Still, it wasn't out of the question.

Vera shook her head. "If Luna had learned the truth, we would have known it long ago. She would not have pretended otherwise."

"Then who can it be?" Eve demanded.

There was the rub. If Eve hadn't told anyone, and Vera certainly had not, that left only their father. But if he'd discovered their secret, why would he not have demanded answers from one or both of them? Had he somehow discovered Sheree's remains after his dementia but before they were aware of the problem? Could he have decided she and Eve were responsible and had intended to confront them and then forgot? Or could he have, in the throes of his illness, believed he did it? Then again, maybe he killed the other two women and later, when he discovered Sheree, decided he couldn't confront his daughters for fear of them finding his secret?

Who the hell knew? What a freaking mess!

"Bent has Daddy at the top of his suspect list," Vera admitted, in case Eve wasn't aware. Garth Rimmey had been there, too, but the older remains had dropped him lower on the list.

"Makes sense. He was Sheree's husband. And maybe it was him. We can't be sure."

Vera's face pinched. "You think Daddy could have killed those other two women? Then all these years later a man? Why?" She made a "what the hell" face. "I mean, at least with Sheree we can point to a potential motive, except it's irrelevant since we know what happened to her. The others . . ." This was crazy. There was just no way their father was a killer. "It can't be him. It just can't."

"You're positive you didn't tell Bent what we did?" Eve said quietly.

Vera drew back at the question. "Of course I didn't tell Bent. He was gone before *that* happened. Remember? I had no way of contacting him. Until yesterday, he and I had not spoken in all this time."

"Then how do we figure out who it is?" Eve held up the phone, indicating the text message she had received.

"I have a friend in Memphis who can run a check on the number the messages came from. Chances are it's a burner phone, and we won't be able to locate the owner. But we can try. Bent will do all he can to determine who ran you off the road, but frankly, that won't be easy, either, since we have basically no details about the other vehicle."

"So what do we do in the meantime?"

"We stay alert. Make sure we're watchful and don't end up in a ditch somewhere. We keep each other informed of every little thing."

"And keep pretending like we don't know anything?"

Vera drew in a big breath. "We don't know anything. What happened to Sheree has nothing to do with the other victims."

Eve's expression clouded. "What if we're wrong and Daddy is a serial killer? Maybe he had it under control for all those years and then the dementia set him off, so he killed the last victim? He didn't argue when we decided to put him in Hillside. It was like he was glad to go."

The worst thing about her sister's suggestion was that it could be true.

17

Wednesday, July 24

Methodist Church
Elk Avenue, Fayetteville, 7:30 a.m.

Eve sometimes wondered why she bothered with this.

The meetings were more for Suri and Vee than for Eve. She had stopped needing Alcoholics Anonymous ages ago. If she said this to Suri or to Vee, they would think she was crazy. Maybe she was. But she had found the way to assuage her needs, and alcohol was not the answer any more than the other drugs she had tried.

She surveyed the gathered group that sat before her. Most of them were people she had known her whole life. Some were from outside the county. Those were the ones who didn't want their neighbors or friends and family to be aware of their AA attendance. In her opinion, those were also the ones who would more likely fail. Based on Eve's experience, people who felt the need to hide their problems were the ones who never stayed sober.

But who was she to judge?

Seated in the back, away from the others, was Bent.

He only came occasionally. Since he'd come last week, she figured he had some other reason for coming today. It wasn't like he couldn't have come on another day of the week. Wednesdays were her day to lead. He knew she would be here, and he probably had questions, which meant she'd have to figure out how to answer them. The knack to providing satisfactory answers—even when not being completely truthful—was in the ability to respond without hesitation. So, while the attendees in the circle talked about their battles, she mulled over how to answer what Bent would most likely ask.

She liked Bent. He was kind of like the brother she never had. After her mom died, he'd made it a point to be extra nice to Eve. In part maybe because he had been screwing her sister. But Eve hadn't cared. She'd needed someone to show some level of attention to her, especially since her daddy had been reliving his youth with Sheree and Vee had been busy proving she could feel something.

They'd all had their issues.

When Bent left town, and with Sheree and baby Luna the only things their father cared about, Eve started sneaking around to get high. Even Vee didn't know. Eve stayed over with friends whose parents kept liquor in the house. She did a lot of things to get her hands on alcohol. Her sister didn't lose her virginity until she was sixteen, nearly seventeen. Eve, on the other hand, did before she was fourteen. She had no other tradeable assets, and she needed alcohol or whatever—something to ease the pain.

Trevor Redmond stopped talking, and Eve forced an affirming nod. "Thank you for sharing, Trevor." It wasn't necessary to hear his story. It was the same every time. His latest girlfriend had dumped him, and no one—relative or friend—would let him stay over anymore. He'd passed out and pissed on their sofas too many times. Now he slept in his truck in front of their houses.

It was sad. But at least he was coming here and saying the words. That was something.

Eve forced herself to pay some measure of attention as one after the other had a turn at spilling whatever was on his or her mind. She didn't wait for Bent to speak up. He never did. Just showed up once in a while and listened. Maybe it was his way of reminding himself that his life didn't suck as much as he thought. Maybe to prove he was a sheriff for all in the community.

Or maybe just because he had nothing better to do.

When the meeting was over and the dozen gathered had wandered out, Eve started the cleanup. Whoever was in charge made sure that was done before leaving. Most of the attendees tossed their coffee cups in the trash and put away their chairs, but some didn't. Bent took care of the remaining chairs while Eve removed the trash bag from the can. Whenever Bent showed up, he always helped. Eve had figured out that part of the reason he did was so he could ask questions about Vee. He didn't ask about her every time he came, but nearly every time.

"Did you get your car back?" he asked as he put away the last chair.

"Friday," she said, grateful for an easy question. "Luckily Mr. Garner was able to find used parts, so the cost wasn't as bad as it could have been."

Bent picked up his hat from the table where the stack of flyers about the AA program sat. "Mr. Garner was close friends with your daddy back before your mother passed."

"He was."

Vee had let Eve know that Bent was asking questions about their father. No big surprise. There had been plenty of that back when Sheree first disappeared. But Sheriff Fraley had known Vernon Boyett since they were schoolboys, and nothing would have made him believe his old friend would ever hurt another human. Except he had. He'd hurt Eve and Vee. But he hadn't really meant to. He'd just been easing his grief the only way he thought would work. They'd all done that in one way or another.

"The Garners helped out for a while after she was gone," Eve went on, hoping to direct the conversation rather than allow Bent to go where he would. "His wife cooked for us for weeks."

"Until," Bent said, "Garner and your daddy had a falling out."

Eve cringed inwardly. Damn it. She'd forgotten about that stupid incident. Mrs. Garner had come around so much her husband had gotten jealous. He and his lifelong friend—Eve and Vera's daddy—had a very public argument about how much of Mrs. Garner's attention he was getting. They worked it out soon after, but no one forgot the incident. Folks would be talking and trying to remember every little thing from that time frame. As Vee would say, it was human nature.

"You remember they worked it all out," she said, putting the flyers away in the drawer designated for AA's stuff.

"You're right, but I also remember there was an issue at one time between your mom and dad about the hospice nurse who saw her in those final weeks."

Okay so he just wanted to talk about the past. She could handle that with no sweat. "Taylor Williams. He was a good nurse. Vee and I took care of her bathing needs. There was no reason for Daddy to be upset about a male nurse. Mama liked him."

"But your daddy thought he was coming around a little too much that last week or two."

"Daddy was just mad because he couldn't take off work enough to see after Mama himself." This was true. He'd blamed himself for not being there the way he thought he should have been. Eve remembered the way he cried when he thought no one was looking. She also knew for a fact that his boss would have allowed him to take an extended leave. She heard the man say as much to her daddy on one of his visits. The truth was, Eve suspected, her daddy wanted to stay, to do all possible for his wife, but he couldn't bear it, so he didn't. As strong as he had been, he just hadn't been strong enough.

"Taylor had a bad accident one night after leaving your farm."

There was that. She opted not to comment since it wasn't a question.

"I seem to recall," Bent said as they walked toward the stairs, "there was an issue with the brake line or something like that."

Eve paused at the bottom step. "Sheriff Fraley said the brake line broke. It was just one of those bizarre things that happen sometimes with older cars." She frowned. "Are you accusing Daddy of something, Bent?"

He settled his hat into place. "Just confirming a few things I read in the case file."

Eve pushed through the lower-level street entrance. Bent followed. The morning sun was already oppressive. "Daddy wouldn't have hurt anyone," Eve pointed out. "You're wasting your time digging up those old rumors."

He glanced at the line of cars parked along the street before settling his attention back on her. "This is just between you and me, Eve. I won't be stirring this pot publicly. But you need to be prepared, because others likely will."

She'd figured it was just a matter of time before the gossipmongers got started. "If what you want to know is if I recall anything unusual related to Daddy's activities after Sheree's disappearance, there's just one thing."

Vee had told her how Bent was pressing the idea. Eve was prepared. "What's that?"

"He was devastated. The same way he was when Mama died. Personally, I thought it was damned shitty of him for being so torn up over that woman after the way she treated us and disappeared on him and Luna."

"Could've been guilt," Bent suggested.

Eve shrugged. "Maybe. He was pretty upset with her for cheating on him, but he would have done anything to keep her, so I'm fairly certain killing her wouldn't have been on his mind. I mean, I suppose it could have been some sort of freak accident. But if he had been involved with whatever happened, he would have called an ambulance or taken her to the hospital himself. He wouldn't have left her to just die."

Bent considered what she said for a moment. "Whoever did this to Sheree, I have my doubts as to whether it was an accident. There were multiple fractures to her skull. Her head was hit with something hard or banged against something hard more than once."

Eve stilled. Inside, the beating of her heart, the rush of her blood all seemed to quiet. "Unless she was arguing with someone and accidentally fell down the stairs." Her voice sounded strained, distant even to her own ears. "Our stairs are steep—not like the stairs in new houses."

"Do you think she was arguing with someone?" he asked. "Wouldn't you have heard their voices? You were home that day, right?"

One, two, three . . . Eve held her tongue. Ordered her heart to slow its racing. Calmed her thinking. Sounding calm was far more important than not hesitating. "I don't know." She swallowed to wet her throat. "But, yeah, I was home. I didn't hear any arguing . . . just the baby crying. Like I said back then."

Bent inclined his head as if weighing the possibility. "A fall down the stairs could cause multiple head injuries. The lab in Nashville will tell us more. All we have right now is the preliminary report."

Had he told Vee about this? Eve's heart abruptly started to pound and all that sound—the thundering beneath her sternum and the roar in her veins—nearly deafened her.

She forced her lips apart and her tongue to work. "What did Vee say about the skull fractures?"

"I haven't talked to her yet about those specifics. I'm meeting with her later today. The TBI folks are on the way, so I have to rendezvous at the scene with them in half an hour."

Eve forced her head up and down. "But you believe," she dared to venture, "it was not an accident."

An icy chill flowed through her during the long seconds that elapsed before he responded.

This was the worst possible news. How would they ever get Bent or anyone else to believe the truth . . . if doing so became necessary?

He bracketed his hands on his hips. "I really can't say. On first look, the accident scenario seems unlikely, but as you suggested, she could potentially have hit her head multiple times falling down the staircase. Whoever was with her may have gotten scared and buried her. Tried to make it look as if she'd run off. The state lab has people who specialize in determining how these things happen. They measure all the different aspects of injuries. Determine the types of fractures, depressed or ring or whatever. Hopefully they'll give us something soon, and then we'll know with some measure of certainty."

"So they won't be releasing her remains as quickly as we first thought?" Luna would not be happy. She already had a memorial planned. She dragged Vera to the mall in Huntsville last night for dress shopping.

"It might be a little while, yes."

Eve nodded. "I'll let Luna know. She's anxious to have a memorial service."

"She can have a memorial service anytime she likes," Bent said. "Just no burial."

"I'll be sure to explain the situation to her."

Bent started to go. Eve's knees almost gave way with relief. But then he paused and turned to her once more.

"Think about that time frame, Eve," he said. "If you recall anything that might be relevant to what happened to Sheree, let me know. I don't want folks speculating too much. Better to figure this out and wrap the case up before the rumors and the speculation get out of hand."

"Sure." She nodded. "I'll do all I can. Vee and I will put our heads together. See what we can recall. Maybe one of us will remember something useful."

"That would be really helpful. Thanks, Eve."

She watched him go. The only thing Eve could think was that she really, really needed to call Vee.

18

Vera stood in the middle of her father's bedroom. She wasn't looking forward to this. But it had to be done before any sort of official search—which was no doubt coming.

As soon as Luna had left for work that morning, Vera had started going through the house. With last night's shopping foray, there had been no time until now. But she'd made great headway this morning. She'd started in the living room and then moved on to the kitchen. Then the dining room and the library. Even the laundry room and powder room. The downstairs hadn't been so difficult.

On the other hand, upstairs hadn't been nearly as simple. Vera had gone through Luna's room first. She came home for lunch often, and the last thing Vera wanted was to be caught rifling through her things. Luna had kept a number of items that belonged to her mother. Mostly little things, like jewelry and trinkets. Like a child in a woman's body, Sheree had been a fan of shiny things. Vera scolded herself for being so unkind, but the woman had made their lives miserable.

Thankfully it hadn't lasted long.

No one should ever be grateful about another person's death . . . except she and Eve couldn't help being thankful for the reprieve. Being responsible for Sheree's death had never been their intent . . . the same way killing the Wicked Witch of the West hadn't been Dorothy's.

Vera shook off the weird metaphor.

The new dress Luna had chosen last evening for the upcoming memorial still hung in the plastic the store clerk had pulled over the hanger. It was a conservative black dress that fit Luna beautifully. She insisted that Vera choose something as well. Since Vera hadn't come prepared to attend a memorial service, she grabbed a black sheath and a pair of matching heels. She felt bad that Eve wasn't with them, so she bought her a little black dress as well.

She doubted Eve would appreciate the effort, but it made Vera feel better. Sometimes you did things for others just to boost your own self-esteem.

Speaking of Eve, her room had been relatively easy. She wasn't a clotheshorse or a collector of things. Her room was sparsely furnished. Oddly so. And dark. Vera couldn't remember her sister being brooding when they were kids. But then, people changed. Especially after major trauma.

She thought of Bent and decided that maybe she hadn't handled things quite so well after all. But she had survived with somewhat fewer scars than Eve.

The longer she stood here in her father's room and put off what she needed to do, the longer it would take. She surveyed the space. Might as well get this over with.

Vera started with the bedside tables. Luna had ensured that everything—except those items she had taken to Hillside for him—had stayed just as it was. Luna or Eve had placed the framed photo of Vera's and Eve's mother next to the one of Sheree on the table on their father's side of the bed. Or maybe he'd put it there himself at some point. Honestly, Vera couldn't recall him speaking of her mother those last two years she was at home before she went off to college. The first year because he'd been totally enthralled with Sheree and the second because he'd been far too devastated about her behavior and then her disappearance. After that, Sheree and Luna were all he had talked about.

Vera shook her head at the letters in the drawer of her father's bedside table. He'd written letters to Sheree after she was gone. Eve read them back then, which only made her feel worse. Vera tossed the faded envelopes aside. The whole thing had disgusted her. Maybe she'd never been so madly in love with someone to understand how emotion would run a person into the ground. Her father had lost his ability to reason . . . to function. Not so great for his children.

Eve was likely the only reason Luna had turned out okay.

Vera hadn't been around. But she had helped from afar.

She thought of the times Luna had come to spend a couple of weeks with her during the summer. She'd been so in awe of Vera's life and work.

"Nothing to be inspired by now," she muttered as she moved on to the bedside table her mother had used before Sheree.

Everything inside was Sheree's. Glittering barrettes for her hair. Three kinds of lip gloss. An eye mask for sleeping undisturbed by light. A perfume bottle. Vera frowned. She'd always hated the stout smell of Sheree's perfume.

She moved on to the dresser. Nothing but the usual in those drawers. Underthings and socks. Scarves. Gloves. Belts. The closet offered nothing exciting either. Some of their father's clothes. Some of Sheree's. Way in the back, beyond their father's stuff, were some of Evelyn's things. Vera smiled as she dragged her fingers over the one elegant dress her mother had owned. It was silk. A rose color that had looked so beautiful with her blonde hair and blue eyes. Vera had only ever seen her wear it once. To a friend's wedding. Vera remembered she and Eve had worn floral print dresses with a hint of that same rose scattered through the pattern. Numerous people had mentioned how beautiful they looked.

Vera shook off the bittersweet memories and continued her search of the room. So far there was nothing of interest. Just to be sure, she checked under the bed and the dresser. Beneath the side tables and under the mattress. If there had been anything here related to Sheree and whatever she was doing just before she vanished, Vera couldn't find it. Nothing about the other victims in the cave. Not that she really thought there would be.

The three- or four-year-old set of remains had kept Vera awake most of the night.

Who was he, and how the hell had he ended up in their cave? It made no sense at all. But the truth was that her father had been fully capable of being out and about until just over two years ago. Was it possible he'd had an encounter with this person and the incident ended in murder? Possibly.

But why? Vera just couldn't get right with any sort of motive.

She dismissed the idea and moved on in her search. Nothing relevant in the upstairs bathroom. Finally she did a walk-through of her own room. She hadn't left much when she headed off to college. Clothes from her high school years and a journal from when she was twelve. Her cell vibrated in her hip pocket. She checked the screen. *Eve.* Vera braced for more trouble.

Vera accepted the call. "Hey."

"We need to talk. Now. In person."

Definitely bad news.

"Where are you?" Vera walked out of her room and headed for the stairs.

"Rose Hill. Meet me at Mama's grave. We'll have privacy there."

"Coming now," Vera promised.

Rose Hill Cemetery
Washington Street, Fayetteville, 11:40 a.m.

Eve had said to come right away . . . that she would be waiting. Twelve minutes after Vera arrived, her sister still wasn't there. Damn it. The funeral home wasn't that far away. She glanced across the headstones toward Morgan Avenue and then College Street. She and her sister always parked on the Washington side of the cemetery.

Finally Vera spotted her sister walking down the hill. Vera sat down on the bench she'd added—thankfully next to her mother's grave, since Luna had decided Sheree would be interred on the other side of their father.

"I thought you were coming right over," Vera said when Eve was in earshot.

She shook her head. "I forgot I didn't have a car. I had to find someone who could bring me."

Vera made a face. "When are you getting your car back? We could order you a rental." No one hated waiting more than Vera. It was a serious pet peeve.

Eve sat down beside her. "I'll have it on Friday. No big deal."

"So what's happened now?" Vera wasn't looking forward to the news. Wouldn't be good. Eve's voice had told her that when she called.

"Bent was at the AA meeting this morning."

"You said he comes sometimes." Vera didn't see the reason for this impromptu meeting in that statement. Sadly, she suspected the shoe just hadn't dropped yet.

"Yeah, but today he wanted to talk about back when Sheree disappeared and how Daddy acted. He wanted to know what happened with Mr. Garner and with Taylor, the nurse. It's like he's pushing the idea of pinning this on Daddy."

"The spouses are always considered first," Vera explained. "His scrutiny of Daddy is not unusual. Didn't we talk about this already? He asked me basically the same questions."

"Yeah, yeah." Eve waved off the reminder. "It's the other part that worries me."

Dread settled in Vera's gut. "What other part? If you're referring to the three sets of remains besides Sheree's, I've been thinking that those might actually help our situation." She could hope. Jesus, what was she saying? Three other people had been murdered and placed in that cave. Being grateful for the news was . . . not right somehow.

Eve hesitated a moment before launching into her explanation. "He said the preliminary examination showed multiple fractures to Sheree's skull."

Why hadn't he told Vera this? Worry tightened its way through her chest. "Based on what happened, I don't see how that's possible. I mean, obviously she died of head trauma, which would likely result in a skull fracture. You said her head hit the sink, but how would that have created multiple fractures?"

Eve shrugged. "How do I know? Luna was screaming. Sheree was trying to shove her head under the bathwater. I just understood in that moment that I had to stop her. So yeah, her head hit the sink." Her face twisted in confusion. "But then we did drop her a couple of times going down the stairs. And we tossed her into that trailer pretty hard. Wouldn't that do it?"

Vera chewed her lip. Her sister had a point. "I suppose it's possible."

She tried to recall more precisely the details of those moments when they were grunting and hefting Sheree's lifeless body. She'd felt like a ton of bricks. They had dropped her at least once. Vera shook off the memory of how they'd swung her back and forth for a moment, then pitched her into the trailer. It was the only way they could get her in there. At least in their adolescent minds.

Still, the news was troubling. Sweat beaded on Vera's skin as her gut turned and twisted with the need to vomit. It was conceivable that Sheree's head had hit the stair tread or the metal rails on the trailer hard enough to cause a fracture. They hadn't exactly been thinking about protecting her from further injury. She was dead, for God's sake.

"So we don't worry about this," Eve said, her expression hopeful.

"Right. We just stay calm and wait for the final autopsy report," Vera agreed. "We'll know more about the type and pattern of fractures then. There is nothing to be gained by borrowing trouble at this point."

Frankly, Sheree's injuries might end up being the least of their worries.

"Okay," Eve said, sounding only marginally relieved. "I'll try not to worry about it."

"There's something else I learned late yesterday, but since I didn't see you last night, I wasn't able to share the details."

Eve made a face. "Why? All you had to do was call."

"I wanted to do it in person. Remember what I said about phone calls."

Eve made a frustrated sound. "Yeah. Yeah. I meant you could have called for a meeting."

"I was just too exhausted after going to the mall with Luna." Vera had needed to be more rested and alert for this—to analyze her sister's reaction to the latest news.

Guilt heaped onto her shoulders for allowing the notion of distrust to linger.

"The other remains—except for the male vic—were posed the same as Sheree. But the really bizarre part is that all three had a silver cross necklace—the exact same type. If there was one with the male victim, they haven't found it."

Eve blinked, once, twice. "Are you serious?"

"As a heart attack."

Her sister made one of those groans of disbelief. "How did that happen?"

"I don't know." The resigned admission sent more of that ice forming in Vera's veins.

"Then somebody does know what we did," Eve suggested, obviously referring to the text messages they had received. "They know, and maybe they think we copied what they did. Now that the police are involved, they're trying to scare us or maybe pin their shit on us."

Vera looked away. Felt sick with the notion that her sister could possibly be correct in her assumption. "The question is *Who knew about the cave?*"

"I did not tell anyone," Eve snapped, "and even if I had when I was on a binge, that would have been years ago. Besides two of the victims were there before we . . ."

Her words trailed off. Obviously, she'd just had the same thought as Vera. No matter how they looked at it, this appeared more and more like their father was involved . . . or, at the very least, someone he knew.

Jesus Christ.

"Okay"—Vera drew in a big breath—"no matter what we think we know, we need to confirm the details we're certain about. For that matter, the victims who were killed before Sheree may not have been put in the cave until after we put her there." The idea gained momentum as Vera talked. "We won't know for sure on that until the remains and everything around them have been analyzed. The approximate time of death doesn't necessarily mean the cave was their first resting place. Considering the extended time involved, the results could be inconclusive, and we might never know when or how they ended up in the cave."

Eve shook her head. "I'm confused. What do you mean we have to confirm the details we're certain about?"

"We need to recall every single thing we saw that day. Only what we saw with our own eyes is certain." Vera allowed the memories to flash through her brain. "Maybe we saw something in that cave the day we put Sheree there that might make a difference in regard to the other victims."

Eve nodded slowly. "When you really think about it, this could be good, right? The extra victims, I mean. Bent could determine that the same person killed them all. If that person is no longer alive or around . . . then we wouldn't have to worry anymore."

Vera couldn't deny having had the same thought. "Maybe. At this point, I'm not sure of anything. And there is the man who was murdered more recently." She stood. "Come on, I should let you get back to the funeral home." She cast a final look at their mother's grave. Their lives would have been so different if she hadn't died.

Vera almost laughed at herself for indulging in that fantasy. Her grandmother always said that if a frog had wings, it wouldn't bump its butt when it hopped.

She and Eve didn't talk as they wove their way through the cemetery. What was there to say? There was a big chance they were in serious trouble here, but it wasn't as bad as it could be. Based on Vera's experience, it would be difficult to pin Sheree's death on them—on anyone for that matter. Even if some evidence was found on or near her remains that implicated Eve or Vera, they had lived in the same house with the woman. Most things could be explained away.

The thing that worried Vera was the other victims. How had those happened? Who in this little town had killed three people without anyone noticing their disappearances? The only reasonable explanation was that the victims were not from the area. The biggest mystery was the identity of the person who knew about the cave. The answer to that one was what they needed.

"Has anyone around the county gone missing and the case remains unsolved?" she asked, more a thought spoken. Bent was likely looking into this already.

Eve slowed to a stop next to a tall headstone, seemed to consider the question. "People have gone missing for sure, but I can't recall anyone specifically who was never found like Sheree. Not around here anyway. It would have been on the news and in the papers."

They moved toward the street once more. If Vera had been at the top of her game, she and Bent would have talked about this already. Damn it.

Eve suddenly stopped again.

Vera almost bumped into her. She started to ask what was wrong, but then she saw the trouble. Someone had written words on the driver's side window of her SUV.

I know what you did.

Before Vera could move closer and touch the letters, her cell vibrated. She ignored it and continued toward her car. The vibrating stopped but then immediately started again. This time she dragged out her phone and checked the screen. Could be Bent with more news.

Luna.

Vera accepted the call. "Hey, Lu. What's up?"

Eve turned and stared at her, waiting for whatever was coming next. At this point they were both gun shy. Every call was like a warning blast.

"You need to find Eve," Luna said sounding frantic, "and come home. Right now."

Vera looked to Eve. "We'll be right there."

19

The message at the house was not at all like the one on Vera's car. That one had been very specific—very pointed—yet made no actual threat.

But this one was different. This one was a direct threat.

I should have killed you all when I had the chance.

On the porch, Vera, Eve, and Luna stood shoulder to shoulder, staring at the words spray-painted across the front door in four lines.

This message was a scare tactic. For Luna, it had done its job extremely well.

"Who would do such a thing?" Luna wailed. She'd settled down after Vera and Eve arrived, but now her emotions were getting the better of her again.

"Someone who's playing a game," Vera suggested. "Who wants to take advantage of the situation."

"It could be the person who hurt Sheree," Eve said, her gaze glued to the words.

Vera wanted to shake her. What was the point of scaring Luna further with that suggestion? Damn it. "The person who hurt Sheree," Vera challenged, "could be dead himself by now. Or too old to get around. We can't know for sure that this is related to who hurt Sheree.

It could be someone who wants to make us miserable. To capitalize on the situation. Grab a minute of fame."

"Just saying," Eve argued. "My explanation makes a lot more sense."

Vera glared at her, but it did no good since Eve wouldn't meet her gaze. Did she really think her suggestion was going to help?

Moments after Vera and Eve had arrived, a news van from Memphis stopped at the road in front of the house. Patricia Patton and her cameraman stood next to it, staying well away from the property line. Vera had wanted to walk out there and demand that they leave, but they were in the road, so she couldn't. What she and her sisters could do was keep their backs to the camera, which she had warned them to do. Although the house sat back from the road a good distance, a zoom lens could zero right in on the situation.

Bent pulled up, and Vera, keeping her back to Patton, waited for him at the bottom of the steps. She and Eve had decided weren't going to tell him about the other messages. Those would only lead to questions neither of them wanted to answer. Fortunately, the message on her SUV had been written using one of those glass markers designed to put for-sale information on cars. The wet wipes she carried in her car contained alcohol, which made removing the words easy enough.

Besides, Vera had someone working on the text messages. Bent couldn't do any more than what she had already set in motion.

"Someone left an ugly message on the front door," she said, rather than hello. "Luna's very upset." She turned to her sisters, who huddled near the door, staring at the assault on their home as well as their senses. "Eve's taking it fairly well, but it takes a lot to faze her."

"Yeah," Bent agreed, "she's pretty unflappable." He studied Vera as they made their way up the porch steps. "You okay?"

"I'm fine." She saw far worse than this all the time in Memphis.

"I'm sure you've seen way worse," he said, reading her mind, "but this is personal."

Maybe he was right. She should be more affected. But it was difficult, knowing what she knew. "I'm trying to keep my reactions in neutral territory until we know more. And for them." She nodded to her sisters. "As well as the vultures on the road."

Vera didn't dislike reporters in general. Just this one. Many reporters were helpful during investigations. Not Patricia Patton.

"That's smart—if you can manage it," Bent commented.

She scoffed. "Believe me, I'm an expert."

As soon as the words were out of her mouth, she regretted having said them. Statements like that could come back to haunt a person. Thankfully this investigation had not pointed to Vera and Eve just yet, but it very well could eventually.

It was all these extra little surprises—like three additional sets of remains—creating havoc deep inside Vera.

Her instinct was to start questioning people who had known and been friends of the family during that time period. Find out if anyone worked on the farm for her father. Cut hay or trimmed trees. There was a time when they had horses and a few head of cattle. It was possible someone had helped with the animals. Vera had no memory of a handyman or a helper of any sort.

As she and Bent neared, Luna and Eve stepped apart, clearing the path for him to see the message left on their front door.

"Afternoon, ladies," he said, his gaze fixed on the words spelled out in red paint across the yellow front door.

The house was white, and the door had once been a pale green—their mother had loved green. Sheree, wanting to put her stamp on at least a few things, insisted it be painted her favorite color—yellow. After Sheree was gone, Vera and Eve painted it green again. Looking back, it seemed a bit childish, but it had made them feel better. Later, when Luna was twelve, she noticed a photo of her mother standing on the front porch and saw that the door was yellow. Their father had told her how Sheree loved the color. Luna begged him to repaint it that bright daffodil.

Vera had been immensely grateful she was long gone by then. Eve had been furious about the change.

Since neither of them would hurt Luna by commenting negatively, the door remained yellow evermore. Besides, after Sheree disappeared, Luna had become Daddy's little girl, while Vera and Eve had become irrelevant. She supposed it was understandable to some degree, since Luna had been a baby. Within a year Vera was off to college and Eve was in trouble all the time. Luna was by far the easiest to love, and it didn't hurt that she had adored their father. Vera and Eve hadn't done that in a very long time. Not since he brought home a woman to take their dead mother's place.

"Do we have a time frame when someone may have done this?"

"It had to be between eleven thirtyish," Vera said, "and whatever time Luna arrived, because I was here until then."

"I got home about ten after twelve," Luna said. "I come home for lunch a couple of times each week."

"We can assume then that it was someone who knows your routine," Bent suggested. "Otherwise, they were taking a big risk on being caught."

Vera agreed with this to a point. "Whoever vandalized the door had to be watching the house, because my being here is not part of the routine."

Bent nodded. His gaze meeting hers. "Good point." He shifted his attention to Eve and Luna. "I'll have someone drop by and check for prints in case the perp touched the doorknob or some part of the door. I'm doubtful we'll find anything, but we'll try."

Luna shook her head. "Can we just cover it up?" She glanced farther down the road, beyond the trees that provided some amount of cover for them. "I don't want more of those reporters rushing over here."

"We can," Bent said. "If that's what you prefer."

"Luna's right," Vera agreed. "Since it's unlikely you'll find anything useful, the harm those reporters could do represents the bigger threat."

"All right then." Bent looked from one to the other. "Any yellow paint around here?"

"I'll get it," Luna offered. "But if it's all right, I'll go back to the library and have lunch there. I can't be here right now."

"I should get back to work too," Eve said. She turned to Vera then. "If that's okay."

Vera waved her hand in dismissal. "Sure. I can handle this."

"We," Bent corrected. "I'm pretty good with a paintbrush."

The surprises just kept coming—from this man . . . and whoever else was intent on making their lives miserable.

Luna rounded up the can of yellow paint she used to refresh the door from time to time and a couple of brushes, along with a stir stick. By the time the paint was blended sufficiently and Bent and Vera were applying it to the door, Eve and Luna were long gone. And, thankfully, so were Patricia Patton and her sidekick.

For a while Vera and Bent didn't talk. She had a feeling he had something to say, but it required some fortification.

Finally Bent said, "I need to try and question your dad, Vee. I can't put it off any longer."

She'd expected that would be coming.

"Like I told you already," Vera reminded him, "I don't believe it'll do you any good, but if you feel it's necessary, then we're okay with that."

Although she hadn't mentioned it to her sisters, it was unnecessary. That excuse had been for buying time, nothing more. At this point, she recognized there was no avoiding the step.

Long ago she had learned that when trouble started, it was best to choose her battles. She had a very bad feeling that the real war was yet to come.

Hillside Manor
Molino Road, Fayetteville, 2:55 p.m.

When they found her father, he sat in a chair in the garden beneath the shade of trees. Nearby, a bubbling fountain in a small pond appeared to have his interest. The residents loved the pond. It was full of koi, and whenever they were outside, one of the attendants manned the perimeter of the shallow water to ensure no one decided to take a dip or tried to catch a fish.

"Hi, Daddy." Vera sat down next to him.

"Vee," he said, smiling, "what're you doing here? Did you finally decide you could leave the big city long enough for a visit?"

She smiled, grateful he seemed lucid for the moment. She'd seen him when she first arrived, but obviously he'd forgotten. He'd probably forgotten that Sheree's remains had been found, as well.

"It was time for a visit, Daddy."

Bent sat down on a matching bench that stood at an angle to the one where Vera and her father sat, giving all seated nice views of the pond.

"Daddy, you remember Bent, don't you?"

"Course I do," he said, his smile gone now. "Evelyn was always trying to help him." He shook his head. "But I had him figured for a lost cause." His gaze narrowed in on Bent. "Guess I was wrong."

Maybe they really had caught him on a rare good day.

"I'll take that as a compliment, Mr. Boyett," Bent said. "I came by today to ask if you recalled anything from when Sheree went missing that might help us find out who took her away."

Vera's father shook his head. "I tried to do right by that girl. Tried to give her a nice home and everything she needed, but there was no making her happy. She just kept cheating and whoring around."

Vera cringed. "Daddy, I need you to think carefully before you speak. You loved Sheree."

He nodded. "I did, but I also knew what she was. I finally had enough, and I told her to leave."

His words stunned Vera. "When did you do that?"

"Right after I found out she was back with that no-good bastard again. I told her to leave and never come back. If she did, I intended to make her regret it. I meant every word of it too."

Oh hell. "Daddy," Vera warned, "I'm sure you had no intention of hurting Sheree."

"I thought about it," he said, eyeing Vera now as if he suspected she was some stranger, "but lucky for her, she took off before I had no other choice. At least she left Luna with me. That was likely the best thing she did in her whole rotten life. I couldn't bear the thought of her dragging that baby off to her disgusting rendezvous."

"Can you tell me who she was involved with at the time she disappeared?" Bent asked.

The question had been asked and answered twenty-two years ago, and Vera saw no reason for him to dig up that business now. Her father had suffered enough. She started to say as much, but her father spoke first.

"Who wasn't she involved with?" he snapped. "I'm surprised some of the wives hadn't gotten together and skinned her alive. She screwed around with husbands and single men alike. Whore." He mumbled the last.

Vera was so grateful Luna wasn't here. She'd never heard her father speak like this about Sheree. Right now was not a good time for him to start.

"But at the time of her disappearance," he went on, "I had reason to believe she'd gone back to Garth Rimmey. But really, who knows? I told all this to Walt."

"Any husbands in particular that you recall?" Bent asked.

Vera closed her eyes at the reality that Bent was digging for suspects to go after. The investigative analyst in her wanted to tell him not to waste his time.

But the sister in her wouldn't allow her to do so. She had to protect Eve.

"Burt Roberson over at the market," he said. "Clive Todd at the bank." He made a disgusted sound. "Take your pick. If they had money or any sort of authority around town, they were her targets. Course, it

163

didn't seem to matter when it came to that damned Rimmey. He was a nobody who had nothing. She never could fully break ties with him."

"Daddy," Vera countered, "I've never heard you say things like this about Sheree before. Are you sure this is all true?" It was. She knew it was. But casting doubt in Bent's mind was important.

"Believe me, Vee. I know the things she did. If I hadn't been a fool, I would have killed her myself well before someone else did. But I had you girls to think about."

Vera shrank into herself. Maybe it was better if she said nothing.

"Did you and Sheree argue frequently?" Bent asked.

"After Luna was born, that's all we did was argue."

Vera desperately wished her father would go back to that place where he couldn't remember. At least for the next few minutes.

"Did the two of you ever go to that cave about a mile behind the barn? The one that you have to get down on all fours to go into?"

Vera froze. She had no idea what her father would say in answer to that one. How many times had he raised hell with her and Eve about playing in that cave?

Rather than answer Bent, he turned to Vera. "I told you and your sister not to be going in that cave. It's no place to play."

Vera opened her mouth to assure him that she and Eve only went a few times, but Bent spoke first.

"The girls played there a lot?" He didn't look at Vera as he asked this question.

"All the time." Her daddy shook his head. "I warned them that they could get hurt in there, but it didn't do one bit of good. Both are as hardheaded as a rock."

"Do you recall the last time you caught them there?"

Vera's mouth gaped. She stared at Bent, but he wouldn't look at her.

"Not long before Sheree disappeared," her father said. "I think they were trying to get away from her and the baby. Sheree put poor Luna off on them every chance she got. They were just kids themselves, you know."

No matter that she was as mad as hell at Bent, Vera felt stunned that her father had been so aware of all that was going on. He'd seemed removed most of the time. Uncaring, even.

"You're sure about the timing?" Bent asked, daring to look at her then.

Vera glared right back at him. What the hell was he up to?

"Of course I am." Vernon tapped the side of his head. "Memory like a steel trap."

If only, Vera mused.

"But after Sheree disappeared," her father went on without provocation, "they knew better than to go back in there."

"Why is that?" Bent pressed.

Vera stood. "Well, Daddy, it was good to see you, but Bent and I need to be on our way." She glowered at him. "We have things to do."

"One last question, Mr. Boyett," Bent said, ignoring her edict.

So much for hoping she could count on him for leeway in all this. Her father raised his chin. "I'm listening."

"Were you aware there were more remains—of other people— tucked away in that cave?"

"Daddy—" Vera started, but he cut her off.

"I told them," he said. "I told them to stay away from that cave. But they didn't listen."

Vera leaned down and kissed his cheek. "We have to go, Daddy. You enjoy the rest of your day."

Before she could move away, he grabbed her arm with surprising strength. "Don't go in that cave, Vee. There are things in there no one needs to see."

Bent was suddenly right beside her. "What kind of—"

Vera got between her father and Bent, cutting him off. "This ends now."

Bent nodded his understanding, but it was impossible to read his reaction. "Good day, Mr. Boyett."

It wasn't until they were outside the facility and headed to Bent's truck that Vera turned on him.

"What the hell was that about? Were you trying to make my father incriminate himself when most of the time he can't even remember the names of his own daughters? We cannot be sure a single word of what he said is accurate."

"I did what I had to do." Bent paused at the passenger-side door of his truck. "You know the drill. You would have done the same thing if this was your case."

He had her there, but that wasn't the point.

"First, anything he says will be thrown out by a judge, and you know it." She would see to it.

Bent inclined his head and considered her as if he didn't understand why she was so angry. "But he told me the names of other people who may have wanted Sheree to disappear. Isn't that our goal? To find out who killed her and to see that justice is done?"

Bent had no idea that in this situation there was no justice any way one looked at closing the case. But how did she make that clear without giving away the one part she couldn't share with anyone?

Before she could figure out a response to his question, her cell vibrated. She yanked it from her pocket, grateful for the distraction. William Talbert's name and face flashed on the screen.

The chief of special operations in Memphis . . . *her boss.*

"I have to take this." Vera walked several yards away and accepted the call.

At this point she wasn't sure which was worse, going down this path with Bent or hearing from her boss about the investigation of her team.

One was about as appealing as the other.

20

"Chief Talbert, I'm glad you called." Vera swallowed against the burn of that whopping lie. "I've just been on pins and needles waiting to hear something." That part was mostly true.

"I wish I could say I had good news, Vera." He exhaled a big breath.

Vera held hers. He'd braced her for the worst. The idea that she was just a little surprised was ridiculous. She had known this was coming. There were no other conclusions or decisions to be reached. Someone had to pay for what happened. End of story. Made complete sense that the one to pay would be the one who made the mistake. God knows the other two involved had already paid the ultimate price.

"I understand," she said, bracing her free hand on her hip to stem its shaking. She refused to sound weak or cowardly about this. "Just tell me how this is going to happen, and be done with it."

"The investigation has concluded that Detective Bedwell was not without fault in all this," Talbert explained. "There were things said and actions taken that may have led Detective Carver to believe he was interested in a relationship."

When that news had come out, Vera had been blindsided. She was completely unaware of any inappropriate behavior on Detective Bedwell's part, much less his connection to Detective Carver's husband, Lee. Just another of Vera's epic failures. She felt compelled to repeat her previous statement on the matter. "Neither Detective Bedwell nor

Detective Carver showed any inappropriate behavior in the workplace. Not once."

"Every member of the team has confirmed as much," he agreed. "Apparently it was all an act—on Bedwell's part—kept carefully away from everyone, save Detective Carver. Detective Carver was suing her soon-to-be ex-husband for half of certain assets, and he needed to prove she had cheated on him to get her off his back."

The words stung like a slap. Vera started to pace. Couldn't help herself. Lorna had insisted she hadn't needed any extra time off to sort out her personal issues. How could she have fooled Vera so completely?

"Detective Carver had no idea what was happening between her husband and Detective Bedwell until the day of the event. We've learned the two went to college together—I believe you've been made aware they had a history."

"Yes." Vera's throat constricted with the idea that this went far deeper than just old acquaintances.

"They were buddies. They'd lost touch years ago, until Bedwell joined PAPA. To get to the point, Bedwell agreed to help Lee Carver prove his wife was unfaithful, since apparently, the man had done him a similar favor some years back. We have no idea what that favor was, since the husband has lawyered up and isn't talking."

Oh dear God. This was even more twisted than she had known. "He set Lorna up."

What the hell was wrong with people? Vera had not recognized what was happening, because there was no way to see it if Lorna truly believed all was well. As for Bedwell, he was only returning a favor . . . he wasn't worried or upset in any way. It was just a ruse. A game.

One that ultimately got him and Lorna killed.

"He did. It was all supposed to be quick and painless, except Lorna found out and, well, you know what happened then. Either way, she snapped, went over the edge, taking Bedwell with her. The DA is working on the charges that will be brought against Lee Carver for his part in this. It's a real nightmare here, Vee."

The silence that followed was more telling than anything Talbert could have said.

"Just say the rest," she told him. Why put it off?

"The recommendation is that you be relieved from duty and reassigned. I'm sorry, Vera. No matter that we can see this couldn't possibly have been your fault, the powers that be need a scapegoat. I'm working on the reassignment part. But don't worry, I'll find the right place for you."

Vera forced herself to take a breath. "No," she said tightly. "That's not necessary, Chief. Although I appreciate the offer, I'll tender my resignation, and this will be done."

"No. The MPD needs you, Vera." The urgency in his voice underscored his words.

"I appreciate your saying so, but we both know what needs to happen." She battled back the sting of emotion. "The MPD needs to evict me from its ranks and move on from this. Let's not pretend it will fade away, Will." She rarely called her boss by his first name, no matter that they had been friends for a very long time. "I'll be fine. Really. You don't need to worry about me."

"Vera," he argued, "you are far too valuable a resource for us to lose. We need you."

Her lips trembled into a smile. "I appreciate your saying so, but let's not beat around the bush here. This is the best for all involved." Her gaze locked on Bent. "I have to go, Will. Take care of yourself and the team. Maybe we'll talk again sometime." She ended the call before he could argue.

Their team. PAPA had been their brainchild, his and hers. Now it was his. At this point, she had no problem with that. She had bigger troubles right here in her hometown. She'd just have to figure out where her life went once this was done.

Assuming the answer wasn't prison.

She groaned, slid her phone back into her pocket, and strode toward the other man who held the rest of her life in his hands.

And all this time she'd thought she was in charge of her own destiny. Turns out she had control over nothing at all.

"You okay?"

"Are you seriously looking at my father as a suspect in the murder of my stepmother?" she demanded. She could not talk about Memphis right now. Instead, she made a face and snapped, "Why wouldn't I be okay?"

He held his hands up. "Dumb question."

When she stood directly in front of him, she said, "You didn't answer my question."

"Your father was closest to Sheree, but I personally have no reason to believe he did this. Officially, since Sheree was his wife, he has to be ruled out—the same way Fraley ruled him out last time. You know the way this works."

She did. Her point was to see if there was more than relationship dynamics at play. The discovery of those additional remains changed everything. "All right." She gestured to the facility they'd just exited. "Clearly ruling him out won't be easy, considering his condition and the new development in the cave, so what now?"

"We need to talk about what we know so far."

Vera thought that was what they were doing, but maybe there was more he had been holding back. He surely was aware Eve had passed along his thoughts from this morning. "Where would you like to do this?"

"There's something I'd like to show you back at my place."

She raised her eyebrows at him. That sounded exactly like something the old Bent would have said.

"About the case," he added. He held up three fingers with his thumb holding his pinkie finger down. "Scout's honor."

Vera rolled her eyes. "Yeah, right." Like he'd ever been a Boy Scout.

They climbed into his truck, and on the drive back to his place, she concentrated on trying to put Memphis out of her mind. She supposed she should be grateful that for her it was over, but somehow she couldn't summon any gratitude.

No matter how many cases she had helped to close or how much hard work she had put in toward that effort, this single event would haunt her name forevermore in that department. Going back wasn't an option. That life was over . . . all because of a cheating, scumbag husband.

Since she'd cleared out her office when she left, no worries about that. The only detail hanging over her head in Memphis was her town house. The best option would be to pay out the lease and walk away. A moving company could pack up her things and ship them . . . where?

Where the hell would she go?

Will—Chief Talbert—would give her a good recommendation, but that wouldn't be worth all that much, with the situation in Memphis still dominating the news cycles. It would take time for the smoke to clear and for people to stop remembering her in association with a preventable tragedy.

As they turned onto Bent's driveway, the landscape drew her from the painful thoughts. Vera leaned forward, not wanting to miss a single nuance of the picturesque view . . . the way the trees stood against the sky. A bird dipping down to land on a limb. The horses galloping along the fence line, keeping pace with Bent's truck. It was like a painting come to life.

"Even after two years, I ask myself every day, What the hell did I do to deserve this."

She studied his profile a moment. When had he turned into such a sentimental guy? After he grew up, maybe, she realized. They had been just stupid kids two-plus decades ago. Kids with unhappy home lives who needed something or someone to grab onto. The truth was, she didn't know Bent the man.

She looked away from him. The dead-last thing she needed to do was to get caught up in learning him.

"I'm glad you're happy, Bent, but why are we here?"

He parked in front of the cottage. "Come on. I'll show you." He reached for his door and climbed out.

Vera did the same, just a little slower. The weight pressing down on her shoulders suddenly became all the clearer, all the heavier. She couldn't salvage her career. Her family was all she had left just now, and protecting them was paramount.

Whatever she had to do . . . whatever the cost.

Bent walked past the cottage, and she followed. That leisurely swagger somehow managed to draw her attention, despite current circumstances. She shook her head. She really was losing it.

His destination appeared to be a smaller structure. Sort of looked like a potting shed. What on earth would he be doing in a potting shed?

He unlocked the padlock on the door and reached in to turn on a light. Then he gestured for her to go in ahead of him.

She did. Even though she couldn't deny that the ridiculous idea he planned to lock her in here for some reason kept playing in her head. Maybe to interrogate her. After all, he'd spent twenty years in the military. She was familiar with their interrogation techniques through her training with the CIA. Cold rushed over her skin despite the heat clinging to her clothing as she stepped inside.

Don't be ridiculous, Vee. You are not afraid of this man.

She was only afraid of what he might discover during the course of his investigation.

As if the thought had guided her, her gaze landed on a large whiteboard on the far side of the room. Photos of the remains and the crime scene populated the board.

This was his home office.

A smile tugged at her lips as she relaxed a little. "Wow."

She walked deeper into the climate-controlled space. There were two such boards. Both standing on wheeled legs. In addition to the photos, the first board was also covered with notes about the case. The final image on the second row of photos showed the most recent set of remains, with some amount of dark fleshy material that was a nasty combo of what had once been skin, organs, and other tissue. It was no doubt hard and crusty now, still working with the environment to disappear from the bones. If left on its own, it would likely be gone completely in a couple more years.

This was the victim from about three years ago. The proverbial wrench in the works.

The second whiteboard had a canvas tarp or drop cloth thrown over whatever was on it. "Very thorough work, Sheriff."

"A little something I learned during my last five years in the army, working with CID."

She turned to him. He'd removed his hat and tossed it onto a table she hadn't even noticed standing in the middle of the room. A desk of sorts, she decided. There were bookcases too. File cabinets. Everything one needed to stay organized.

His statement filtered through the surprise still swaddling her brain. "You spent five years in the Criminal Investigation Division of the military?"

He nodded. "A lieutenant from CID had been assigned with our unit during a mission, and he was impressed with my work. He didn't shut up until I agreed to a transfer. It came with an instant promotion. Why wouldn't I be game once he told me that part?"

Which likely meant the promotion offer had come from above in order to achieve their goal. The government was like that. When they wanted something, they didn't stop until they got it. This would suggest that Bent had done quite well with his military career.

The man was one surprise after another.

Vera turned around slowly and took in the other details of the space once more. The bookcases that lined the walls were actually filled with books. Were those law books? She wandered over to check, and sure enough, they were. The file cabinets sat next to those. The table, desk, whatever in the center of the space was like a big conference table made from two-by-fours and plywood—all obviously salvaged from somewhere on the property, since the patina screamed vintage. Two stools stood beneath the table.

"This is your private war room." She turned to him then. "Do you bring your deputies here to work out cases with you?"

He shook his head. "This is just for me." His forehead furrowed in thought. "And now you."

She wanted to be flattered, but she decided not just yet. No letting this become personal. "Why is the other whiteboard covered?"

He waited a moment, and in those few seconds she understood there was something more he needed to tell her about the case. A detail or details that would change everything.

Oh hell.

He took the few steps required to reach the other whiteboard and methodically folded and removed the covering so as not to disturb what was underneath. She studied the items and words there. Bent had made a list of potential suspects and motives. Her throat went bone dry as she read her name, Eve's name. Their father's. Garth Rimmey and his friend Pete Brooks. Howard Benton—his own father. Along with various other prominent men of Fayetteville. An arrow from each name pointed to a motive. Yet another pointed to opportunity, and yet another to means.

Somehow she managed to draw in a breath. Instinctively her arms folded over her chest. Vera turned to her host. All the heat in her body felt as if it had rushed out through her feet, leaving an icy cold behind. "I see you made your suspect list a family affair. Is this seriously all you've been able to come up with? Surely there was more than this in the old case file on Sheree's disappearance."

He continued to stare at her, and her knees knocked together a little, and she struggled to steady herself. Bent moved in next to her— right next to her—which only unnerved her further. He surveyed the list and then turned to her once more, searched her face, then her eyes. That definitely didn't help either. She dropped her shoulder bag to the floor and braced her hands on her hips.

Keep it together. No losing it in front of this man. Look at this like work—just another case being investigated by your team.

Except she didn't have a team anymore. She didn't have a job anymore.

The bottom dropped from her stomach.

"You have a name or two you want to add?"

"You didn't answer my question," she said, attempting to sound unaffected.

"Rimmey and your father were the only suspects when Sheree disappeared," he said. His deep voice was calm, and despite the subject matter, it still got to her somehow.

Vera worked to compose herself against the feelings he prompted. "Your killer has to be someone strong enough to hoist the bodies through those tight passages. Someone who knew enough about my family and our farm to feel no concern going to the cave to carry out this task."

He nodded. "You're right. Which to me suggests the killer is male."

Vera turned her back on the boards and walked a few steps away. She knew what he was thinking. Her father was the one. Damn it! But the newly discovered remains indicated the person they were looking for had killed *before* Sheree and *after*. Could Eve's off-the-cuff theory be right? Their father had done these things but stopped, and then the dementia prompted his old ways . . . his old needs.

No. Her father was not a killer. Certainly not a serial killer. This didn't make sense. She abandoned that line of thinking and opted to center on taking herself and her family out of this equation. The good news, it seemed, was that Bent was actively looking for other suspects.

"I believe our initial assessment that this might be a serial killer is a logical one." The need to breathe had her inhaling deeply. "Either that, or we have more than one killer."

From the moment she learned about the additional remains, she knew this was no coincidence. That cave had been used as a dumping ground. There was no other explanation. Absolutely there was more than one killer. She knew this with complete certainty. The problem was, she couldn't press her certainty about that without giving a reason.

Sheree was that reason.

Vera could not go there. But she could suggest options.

"The TBI agrees with the serial killer scenario," Bent admitted. "They want to call in the FBI."

Of course they did. No unit or agency wanted to deal with a situation like this one unless they had no choice. The investigation could go on for years. Resources would be sucked dry. But there was something else, she realized. Bent hadn't said he believed this was the work of a serial killer. Very likely this was a fishing expedition. He hadn't brought her here just to show off his cool home office. This was about getting her take on the case.

She moistened her lips and asked the next logical question. "Do you have any evidence pointing to a suspect?" Surely in all this—Vera turned back to the photos—they had found some little thing. Any damned thing. No one deposited multiple victims without screwing up somehow. Well, almost no one.

He shook his head. "Nothing so far. No shoe prints anywhere. Not one thing was left behind. The killer or killers were very careful with cleanup. There aren't even any indications of drag marks, and we both know those bodies had to be dragged through those damned tunnellike holes. I can only assume he or she or they covered any and all tracks each time." He shrugged. "Then again, time and visiting animals could have done the same."

The words echoed in her brain. The accompanying images clicked past, one after the other. She and Eve hadn't covered their tracks like that . . . it hadn't occurred to them. "Then our killer is smart. Methodical. Neat. Obsessively so." Vera did an about-face and walked back to the first whiteboard. She surveyed the images and notes there. "Are any of the victims besides Sheree from the area?"

"Don't know yet."

Vera felt sick. "What do you make of Sheree being apart from all the others?" She faced him then. Needed to hear his voice and see his face in hopes of assessing the thoughts beneath the words he spoke. Turnabout was fair play, wasn't it?

Was he thinking the same thing she was? How could he be? He didn't know the things she knew.

His hesitation put her further on edge. Had her holding her breath again.

"When our killer was in the market for a hiding place," Bent began, "the cave on your property fit the bill, which tells me he's a local. He used the secondary cavern so his victims wouldn't be found by just anyone."

"But why would he leave Sheree away from the others?" It was the question he would expect her to ask.

Another pause had her nerves jangling.

"Because I don't think he killed Sheree."

The impact of the statement blasted against her chest. So he wasn't convinced this was a serial killer. He was leaning toward the multiple-killers theory.

"Wait." Vera reached down deep for the mettle she needed. "There are many similarities between the female victims. Even the timeline fits. How did you come to that conclusion?" She wasn't cutting him any slack. He wouldn't expect her to.

"Maybe," he argued, "whoever killed Sheree posed her the way the other victims in the cave had been posed so that whoever found her would believe she was a victim of the same killer. She's the only one who had a suitcase with her. Sheree's killer definitely knew her. He knew her well, and he was aware of her marital issues. He used that knowledge to make it look as if she'd run out on her husband and kid."

Vera remained steady, despite the fact that the damned floor had just shifted under her feet. Not because she was surprised he'd concluded Sheree wasn't a part of the other killings . . . but because he'd nailed several details and the associated motive so damned close. Eve had said Bent was a good sheriff. Clearly she was right.

"Maybe she had her things with her because she was running away," Vera suggested. "She crossed paths with the killer, and that's why the MO was a little different."

What she wouldn't give for a glass of water. Her throat felt so dry she couldn't swallow if her life depended upon it.

"I don't know," Bent countered. "If someone stumbled upon the cave and the victims that were already there—it was the perfect setup to add Sheree to the lineup. The authorities would tie all the murders together. The same way we've talked about." He gave a dry laugh. "I can just imagine the original killer's surprise if he returned for a visit and found Sheree there looking like one of his victims."

He was confident—too confident—in this scenario. That was his only mistake. Once an investigator locked onto a scenario, he put on blinders. Seeing anything else after that was nearly impossible. Did this work in their favor? Vera couldn't say yet.

"Then you're convinced that we have two killers," she tossed out.

"Two killers, for sure. Maybe three, considering how the male vic was disposed of. The TBI still wants to toy with the idea of a serial killer, but like I said, I'm not really buying it."

Breathe. She moved to the nearest stool and slid onto it rather than risk her knees buckling beneath her. No matter that she'd investigated and analyzed evidence from hundreds of cases . . . as he'd said before, this was personal.

She moistened her lips again and asked the question that had to be raised. "What does the TBI think of your theory?"

"I haven't told them."

"Why?" She couldn't wait to hear his answer. Call her a glutton for punishment. Actually, call her desperate.

"I want to find out who killed Sheree before I put that scenario out there."

"Why?" she repeated, every part of her anticipating his next words—the ones that could change everything . . . that could end everything.

"Because I want to be sure I know all there is to know first. Chances are, the others will come up with the same conclusion, but until then, I'm dragging it out for the extra time."

"All you need to know?" she echoed as she pretended to study the case boards. "What does that mean?" Could he possibly be afraid it was Eve or her who'd done this? Was this his way of giving them an out or a heads-up? It sure sounded that way.

Or a clever way of getting her to confess? A distraction to confuse her or make her overconfident.

Impossible to know just yet.

"It means preparation is the key," he said. His lips tilted upward slightly at her startled expression. "I watched an interview where you said that. I want to be prepared before I go tossing out scenarios to another agency."

She couldn't argue the point. "It's a good strategy." *Deep breath.* "There's always the possibility that the male victim killed the three females. Then, years later, someone close to one or all three learned his identity and had his or her revenge." She watched for his reaction. It was as reasonable a theory as any other.

"Maybe. There's still a lot to learn about the other victims," he admitted. "We believe the two female victims found together were possibly best friends. We believe the male vic may have attended the University of Alabama—based on the ring he wore."

She moved closer to the board, studied the photos of the crime scene. "Where are the photos of the rings and the necklaces you mentioned before?"

He withdrew his cell. "I didn't stop by the office and pick them up, but I have them here." He passed her the phone.

Vera studied each of the photographs. The cross necklaces . . . the rings the women wore . . . and lastly the college ring that belonged to the male. "Is that *God* in the inscription?"

Bent chuckled. "Yeah, Conover and I have a bet as to whether it was a nickname for how he viewed himself or an indication of his faith."

Vera noted the manufacturer and the year. "It's not much." She handed the phone back to him. "But it's something. I'm just not clear on how this will help you with finding out who killed Sheree—unless it's the same killer?"

"Maybe it will help," he said. "Maybe it won't. I just need more time."

How could she tell him that no amount of time would change the facts surrounding what happened to Sheree?

She couldn't . . . not for any reason.

21

Luna was waiting just inside the front door when Bent dropped Vera off at the house.

"It's all over the news," she said, her hands wrung together in front of her as if she were praying fervently. "Please tell me this awful, awful story about more remains being found isn't true."

Beyond Luna, Eve lingered, watching. When she saw that Vera was watching her, she shrugged and gestured to their younger sister.

"Let's go in the kitchen and sit down to talk about this." Vera couldn't remember the last time she had felt so utterly exhausted. She had to find a way to remedy this situation that would allow what was left of her family to remain intact.

Was that even possible at this point?

Luna searched Vera's face, as if she expected some answer to be spelled out there. Finally, she nodded and turned away. She wrapped her arms around herself and headed in that direction.

"She's not taking this very well," Eve said, with a lingering look after her.

Vera paused next to Eve. "We have to talk." Eve looked at her. "Privately." Vera gestured to the kitchen. "As soon as we get Luna calmed down."

Eve nodded. "'Kay."

The two of them walked side by side to the kitchen. Luna had settled onto a stool, still hugging herself.

Where was her fiancé? Jerome should be here, reassuring her.

Vera took the stool on the opposite side of the table from Luna. Eve slid onto a seat at the end to Vera's left. Vera looked from one to the other and decided that putting off what had to be said wouldn't help.

"A reporter, a guy Luna knew in high school," Eve said, before Vera could start, "from the *Elk Valley Times* came to the funeral home."

Vera's stomach twisted into knots. "Did you talk to him?"

Eve shook her head. "I did not. But then he went to the library and upset Luna."

Vera looked to their younger sister. "Did you speak with him, Lu?"

She wagged her head slowly side to side as if it took every ounce of strength she had to respond. "Mrs. Higdon ordered him out of the library." She rolled her eyes. "The idea that he and I graduated together should have made him nicer to me, under the circumstances. Instead, he treated me like a criminal, demanding answers and making accusations."

Vera didn't need to ask what sort of accusations. She could imagine. "Folks will be saying a lot of things about Daddy and your mom," she said. "About the farm and that cave. About us, too, probably. We have to keep in mind that people talk when something like this happens. It's not personal. They're just doing what they do. As for the reporter, there will be more. They will push hard and play all manner of dirty tricks in an effort to get the story. And when they can't get something to use, sometimes they make it up. So don't be surprised at what you hear and see—even from people you thought you knew. Just remember that it will go away eventually. Something else will happen to distract them. We just have to be strong enough to ride it out."

Luna drew in a big breath and nodded. "Okay. But I would stay away from the library if I was that sort of reporter." She gave Vera a knowing look. "Mrs. Higdon carries a tiny little pistol in her purse, and she insists she knows how to use it."

Vera made a face. "Really? Well, I suppose—given the circumstances—that's . . . handy." She couldn't think of anything else to say, and the goal here was to calm Luna down, not tell her that her boss might be a little off her rocker.

"Lots of folks carry weapons," Eve reminded her sisters. "This isn't the big city."

Vera had nothing against weapons or those who owned them, as long as they were mentally balanced, properly trained, and smart about the handling and storage. It was the mentally balanced part that worried Vera where Mrs. Higdon was concerned. She was just as likely to go off half-cocked—no pun intended—as not.

"I'm aware," she said to Eve, before going on. "We should warn Hillside not to allow anyone at all to talk to Daddy unless one of us is there. We've already seen there's no telling what he might say." He'd proved that again when Bent questioned him.

"I called them," Luna said. "Right after Nolan—the reporter, Nolan Baker—left the library. I was terrified he'd go there next."

Vera's mouth gaped. "Carl Baker's boy Nolan?"

Luna nodded.

"I can tell you," Vera warned, "he inherited that mean streak from his mother. She was awful back in high school." She turned to Eve. "You remember her? Elizabeth Bogus—Baker now. She was two years ahead of me, I think. When Mama died, she made fun of the dress I wore to the funeral. She always thought she was better than everyone else. Always winning beauty pageants. She thought she owned the world."

"I remember her, and she was mean as a snake," Eve agreed, then she grinned. "Her nickname was Boggie."

Vera almost snorted. That was the thing about small towns. Everyone knew everyone else. The good, the bad, and the ugly.

"What did Bent tell you? Is there anything new?" Luna asked, drawing her back to the more pressing conversation.

Vera studied her sister for a moment. She could lie and say there was no news. It would be a little bit before an update was issued in the media. But what was the point? It was coming. She'd already told Eve. Luna might as well brace herself as well.

"There are a total of four sets of remains."

"Oh my God," Luna wailed. "How is that even possible? You said the cave was really small. How could they not have seen the other sets of remains right at the beginning? Oh my God. I have to call Jerome."

Before Vera could explain, Luna rushed from the room in a fit of tears. Maybe ripping off the bandage so quickly hadn't been the best idea.

"Jerome's parents are Baptist," Eve explained. "This is not going to go over well with them. They already think Luna is not the perfect girl for their son because she might have inherited some of her mama's tendencies."

"Well they're idiots," Vera grumbled. Then she listened for a few seconds to ensure their younger sister had gone upstairs. Once she heard Luna's bedroom door slam, she turned to Eve. "I want you to think long and hard before you answer my next questions, Eve. I need the whole truth."

Eve's eyebrows reared up. "What does that even mean? Why would I lie to you? Haven't we had this same conversation like three times already?"

Vera struggled to tamp down the frustration and half a dozen other emotions welling inside her. She glanced in the direction Luna had disappeared and lowered her voice to a stage whisper. "Bent thinks there are two killers. Sheree's and whoever killed the other three. The TBI is still tossing around the serial killer theory, but Bent isn't buying it."

Eve nodded slowly. "I told you he's a good sheriff. Even though right now I sort of wish he wasn't."

Vera hesitated but then decided there could be no secrets between her and Eve. "I'm pretty sure he thinks it was Daddy who killed Sheree."

"Maybe that's a good thing," Eve suggested. "It's not like they would put him in jail."

Vera couldn't deny having had similar thoughts, but it was just wrong. Before she could say as much, Eve started talking again.

"Has he figured out how someone who isn't part of our family would know about the cave? West isn't the only teenager who has lived close by during the time frame we're looking at. He has a thirty-year-old brother. You remember Wyman? He was a real shithead. Those two may have taken plenty of friends into that cave."

Vera struggled to draw to mind what would have been an eight- or nine-year-old kid when she left for college. "Eve, that makes no sense. Wyman would have been a little kid when the first two victims were put there."

"Oh." Eve frowned. "Right. Then what about his daddy? He could have told someone," she insisted, her chin lifted defiantly. "We should face the fact that no matter what we did, someone was doing it before us."

There was one question related to this new development Vera had to ask. "Did you"—her throat felt bone dry—"decide to pose Sheree the way you did because you had seen the other bodies?"

Eve stared blankly at her for a few seconds, then she burst out laughing. "Did Bent put you up to this?"

Vera clutched her hands together to keep them still. She had started down this path. Couldn't stop now. "It can't be coincidence that the other female victims were posed exactly that way. Those crosses can't be coincidence. I know how you feel about the dead. It makes me wonder if you knew they were there."

Eve blinked. "You're serious."

"Sadly, I am."

Eve stared at her. Silent. Unflinching. Unblinking.

Vera ordered herself to inhale to feed her starved lungs, but her brain wouldn't obey.

Eve suddenly made a face that was somewhere between disappointed and irritated. "I thought you were a big-time, famous crime solver. Is this how you got your reputation? Picking the easiest solution?"

Anger fired in Vera, but surprisingly, she restrained it. "All right then, tell me why you chose that pose."

Eve's gaze narrowed. "I thought it was innocent until proven guilty, not the other way around."

Vera wanted to believe her. She really did. But the problem was, if not Eve, then who? Their father? Who the hell had put that cross necklace with Sheree?

Maybe it was their father, but that still didn't explain how Eve had chosen that exact pose. Unless their father had taken her into the cave with him when he left the bodies or visited them. Eve could be protecting him.

Oh hell. Vera exiled the thought. Their father was not a serial killer! Eve might want to protect him if that were the case, but it could not be. Could. Not. Be.

"I just need to hear you say the words," Vera urged. "Tell me you didn't know about the other bodies. Tell me," she pressed, "that this fascination you have with the dead isn't a symptom of a deeper issue and that whoever is leaving these messages for us doesn't know something you're not sharing with me—like maybe that Daddy or someone else we know did this."

"I don't know any murderers." Eve scrubbed her hands over her makeup-free face.

She'd never been one to wear makeup. Vera had always thought of her that way. Young. Innocent. Unpretentious. Was that why, until this investigation, she'd missed the possibility that she was hiding something? Some secret she'd kept all these years. Because she hadn't wanted to see?

Or was Vera just overreacting to what *she* had missed in Memphis?

"How could you even think such a thing?" Eve demanded, when Vera said nothing. "What the hell?" She turned away, shook her head. "I can't believe this."

Vera nodded. "Okay. Then tell me how you decided on the pose."

"I just posed her the way most dead people are posed. With her arms crossed in front." Eve exhaled a big breath. "How could you think I would keep something like that from you?"

All the times she had noticed her sister doing odd things flashed like a bad movie reel in her brain. "I don't know. With the way this investigation is building, I just have to be sure I am aware of everything, Eve."

God, now she sounded like Bent.

Eve blew out a big breath. "I don't think about killing people, Vee. I think about the dead and how I can help them."

The difference was significant. Vera hated that she'd even brought it up, but she'd had to be certain—if that was even possible. She settled her gaze on Eve's. Did this mean there were no secrets between them? Maybe. Maybe not. But at least she had opened that dialogue.

"I understand. I wasn't suggesting you killed anyone." Vera braced her elbows on the table and rested her head in her hands. "Just please know that anything you need to talk about, I am here. You don't have to think twice about telling me anything at all. Complete transparency is the only way I can protect us."

Eve smiled sadly. "I wish you still lived here."

Maybe this news would lighten the mood. "If it's any consolation, I won't be going back to Memphis."

"Really?" Hope flared in her sister's eyes. "You're staying here?"

Vera shrugged. "At least for the foreseeable future."

"I'm sorry if that means things went even further south in Memphis."

Vera worked up a smile. "Thanks. Life sucks sometimes."

Eve laughed. "I knew if things didn't work out, you'd decide to stay here. You want another chance with Bent, don't you?"

Before Vera could explain that her decision had nothing to do with Bent, the house phone started to ring.

Eve slid off her stool. "I'll get it."

She crossed to the extension that hung on the wall near the back door. Vera closed her eyes and rubbed at her forehead. Maybe if she'd been here more, she would have picked up on anything that was happening with their father. Or with Eve.

And what would you have done, Vee?

God, she didn't know. She just did not know.

"Hello." Eve's face paled. "I don't know who you are, but you'd better not call here again." She slammed down the receiver.

Vera shot to her feet. "What was that about?"

"Our friendly 'I know what you did' fan." Eve's arms went around her middle. "What if he's the person who did all this?"

"It was a he?" Vera's instincts stirred.

Eve nodded. "I'll bet the person who ran me off the road is the same one sending us these messages."

This thing—this person taunting them—was the unknown that worried Vera the most. "We may need that protection detail after all."

"Maybe so." Eve searched her face for a long moment. "Seriously, Vee, I hope Bent is really on top of this. As easy as it would be to lay it all on Daddy, we know he isn't sending us these messages."

Vera considered the work Bent had done on the case. "He's on it. No question."

Would he find more than she wanted him to find? Maybe. But not if she could find the missing pieces first.

11:00 p.m.

Vera lay in bed and stared at the ceiling. Her mind refused to shut down. Was it actually possible that someone in her family was a murderer? The idea was ludicrous. Wasn't it? What happened to Sheree was an accident. Clearly they had made a mistake by not calling their father and letting the whole thing play out the way it should have. But it was easy to see that now—as adults. As kids, living in the hell Sheree's entrance into their lives had launched, they had been afraid to do anything except exactly what they did.

Then there were the other victims. The women, posed exactly like Sheree and all with cross necklaces. Those details could not be coincidence, and that was a big problem. The male victim was the odd one out. Completely different MO. Unless, of course, he was the killer—which left the identity of the revenge killer.

Damn . . . this was a mess.

Vera had called her friend again. Asked for one more favor. *Friend.* Eric Jones was that for sure, but—at one time—the two of them had been more. They had dated for five or six months. He'd wanted to move to the next level, and Vera had not. In the end, thankfully, they had been able to retain their friendship. Considering recent events and the fact that she was no longer a part of the department, she was immensely grateful he was still willing to help.

He had assured her he could track down who had ordered the University of Alabama ring with its *God* inscription. Not that it was such a difficult task. Call the manufacturer, provide the details, and bam—there was the name. A member of law enforcement could get the information with little effort. But Vera wasn't part of that club anymore. She was a civilian . . . one who was a suspect in the ongoing case, whether Bent wanted to admit it or not.

Eric had promised to get back to her as quickly as possible. All things, no matter how seemingly simple, took time.

Her cell vibrated, and she flopped onto her side and reached for it. *Bent.*

"Hey." She braced for more trouble. Christ, would this never end?

"Hey. Come to the window."

She threw the covers back and crossed to the window that overlooked the front yard and driveway. He was there. She waved to him. He leaned against the driver's side door of his truck. Judging by how he'd pulled over into the parking area, he'd been to the cave. It didn't take much imagination to envision all the auxiliary lights inside and uniformed personnel milling about in the area. The crime scene tape and guards in place to hold back the curious and the reporters—some of whom would camp out in the area to ensure they missed nothing.

"Any news?"

"Nah. I was just checking to see that security was in place for the night."

Which meant he had been to the cave.

"Did you call the FBI?" She eased down onto the window ledge. She'd forgotten how deep the window ledges were in this old house. She had loved sitting in this window reading as a kid. Later she'd watched for Bent from here. Hoping and praying he would show up and she could sneak out to be with him.

"I did. They'll have someone here tomorrow."

"I guess that's a good thing." She sighed. "Reporters are giving Eve and Luna a hard time."

"If they'll let me know the names, I'll take care of it."

"I'm sure they'll appreciate it. One is Nolan Baker."

"I will talk to Baker."

"Thanks."

Seconds ticked off in silence, with him looking up at the window and her staring down at his truck—at him, really. They used to do this . . . back when this thing between them first started. At first she was too afraid of sneaking out of the house. She got over that pretty quickly, but until she did, they did this—stared at each other across the darkness. Her in the window, him braced against that old truck he drove back then. There had been cell phones at the time, but Bent couldn't have afforded one, and her daddy would never have allowed her to have one.

"I'm worried about this, Vee."

The deep, smooth sound of his voice made her shiver. She rolled her eyes. She was thirty-nine years old. Her high school crush should not have the power to make her shiver, particularly under the circumstances.

"Yeah, me too." As desperately as she wanted to believe this couldn't be their father, she still had reservations . . . doubts. About him . . . about something Eve might know.

And, God, she hated herself for the doubts.

"I say," he offered, "we conduct our own parallel investigation. Off the record, of course. We know this place and the people better than the outsiders. If there's something to find, we can find it."

The idea was certainly feasible. He already had a case board—two case boards—set up in his home office. He could keep her up to date on whatever the official investigation found. She could provide input. Anticipation welled inside her. It was a good idea. A win-win situation for his case and for her protecting her family.

They could do this . . . teamwork.

Except she couldn't be a totally dedicated team player. For instance, she saw no reason to mention her calls to Eric. At least not until he got back to her.

Ignoring the tiny ping of guilt, she said, "I think that's a great idea. Can we use your home office?"

"We can meet for breakfast in the morning," he offered. "I'll pick up something from the diner and see you at, say, eight?"

"Sure," she agreed. "See you then. Night."

"Night."

The call ended. Vera watched as he climbed back into his truck and drove away. Finding the truth and closing the case would be quicker and easier with them sharing the details they discovered.

Except for the ones she had to do all in her power to ensure he never knew. Like who really put Sheree in that cave.

22

Twenty-Two Years Ago

April

Boyett Farm
Good Hollow Road, Fayetteville, 11:38 a.m.

Paralyzed, Vera stood in the doorway, staring at Sheree, who was obviously dead. She hugged the baby tighter to her chest.

What the hell happened here?

"It wasn't my fault, Vee," Eve urged. "You have to believe me. I was in bed, sick."

Vera turned her head to look at her sister. She was still wearing her pajamas. She was soaked to the bone.

"Why is Luna naked?" she demanded. The baby's little body shook with sobs but at least the wailing had stopped.

Of all the things that came to mind to ask, that seemed the least important, yet it was easier than asking how the hell their stepmother had ended up on the floor . . . *dead*.

Eve took a long, deep breath as if needing to steady herself. "I was asleep. Luna screaming woke me up." She gestured to her bedroom door. "I got up and came out here to see what was going on." Her face turned an even whiter shade. "Sheree was . . . giving the baby a bath. I . . . I thought, but as I watched, I realized she was trying . . . to drown her."

"What?" The idea took horrifying shape in Vera's head. "Are you sure?"

Eve's head popped up and down so fast it was a miracle it didn't break her neck.

"What did you do?" Vera's stomach tied into knots. Luna wailed again. Vera bounced her up and down and made shushing sounds in her ear. Her heart thundered in time with the baby's. This couldn't be real. *Please let it be a dream.*

Her gaze landed on Sheree again. But it was real. The wicked witch was dead . . . but how did they explain this to Daddy? She glared at Eve. "Tell me what you did," she growled as quietly as her temper would allow.

"I ran to the bathtub and started trying to take Luna away from her. We struggled, and she fell backward and . . ." Her voice trailed off, and her gaze settled on the scene in the bathroom. "She hit her head. Real hard. I tried to pull her up, but she just lay there. She blinked a few times and then . . . she just stopped."

"Okay." Vera nodded. Took a breath. "We . . . we should call Daddy."

"No!" Eve rushed to her side. Luna whimpered. "You know he'll blame me. Sheree has him believing I'm always doing things to make her unhappy. Everything that happens around here is my fault."

Studiously bouncing the baby and smoothing a hand up and down her back, Vera tried to think. Her sister was right. They would be blamed for this—no matter that Vera hadn't even been home. Her heart twisted. Eve was the only family she had left. Their daddy had a new family since Mama died. He would probably be happy if they were sent away to reform school or some sort of prison.

"Okay," Vera said, then she took a deep breath. "We have to make it look like this didn't happen."

Hope welled in her sister's eyes. "You'll help me?"

"Of course, dummy. I'm your sister." She held Luna tighter. She was baby Luna's too. "First, we have to . . ." Her gaze drifted back to the floor, where water had sloshed from the tub . . . and where Sheree's body lay motionless, her eyes open. "We have to get rid of . . . her."

Eve nodded, her head doing that wild up and down motion again. "But where will we put her?"

Had to be someplace no one would find her. Vera's mind raced over the possibilities.

"The cave," they said in unison.

Vera's gaze locked with Eve's. "We're getting too old to play there anyway."

Eve nodded. "Daddy will never think to look there, because we're not supposed to be in there."

"No one will look there," Vera agreed. "No one even knows about it."

"Mama knew."

Her sister's voice sounded so small and pitiful, it made tears well in Vera's eyes. "Mama would think it's the best plan too."

Eve looked at Sheree. "How do we do this?"

"We'll need the baby carrier so I can strap Luna to my back."

"We're taking the baby with us?" Eve made a face. "That's crazy."

Vera sent a look that warned her sister that she better shut up. "I'm not leaving her here alone."

Eve shrugged. "Whatever."

Better than half an hour was lost to strapping the baby onto Vera's back and dragging Sheree into the hall and onto a bed sheet. As they rolled her up, Vera was surprised her body didn't feel stiff like she'd expected. Maybe that happened later. Then it took even more time to clean up the bathroom just in case their daddy came home before they got back.

"Okay." Vera picked up the end of the sheet at Sheree's feet. "Grab that end," she said to Eve, "and lift."

Eve knotted both hands in the other end of the sheet and pulled. "Oh my God, she weighs a ton."

They lowered her back to the floor.

Vera had not expected her to be so heavy. "I guess we'll just . . . have to drag her."

The plan worked pretty well until they reached the stairs. The first time her head bumped against a tread, Vera flinched.

"Jesus! This might not work either," Eve fretted.

"Let's just get this done," Vera urged. The tremor in her voice gave away her own uncertainty. "It's not like she feels it."

"Oh yeah." Eve pulled on the sheet again, dragging her down a couple more steps.

Sheree's head bumped along with a hollow *thump-thump* like a watermelon rolling down an uneven path.

Vera gritted her teeth against the panic that threatened and grabbed the sheet once more. Together she and Eve pulled the body down the stairs and along the hall to the kitchen. Now all they had to do was get her outside. Vera would get the four-wheeler with the utility trailer. They could drive to the cave. The real trouble would be in getting Sheree through that little opening.

Gotta do it.

By the time they reached the cave, Vera was sweating. Luna had fallen asleep in the carrier draped on her back. Vera was thankful. Though she doubted Luna would remember any of this, still it felt wrong for her to see it.

Eve climbed off the four-wheeler, where she'd sat nestled against Luna and Vera. "What now?"

Vera climbed off next. "We get her in there somehow."

Eve nodded. "Okay."

The fact that her little sister didn't argue was proof of how exhausted they both were. The movies made carrying a body look so easy, but it was not.

Dragging Sheree across the ground ripped the sheet in a couple of places, but there was nothing they could do about that. Getting her into the cave was like trying to push and then pull a ball of wax through a keyhole. Once inside, they collapsed on the rocky ground. When they caught their breath, Eve went back to the four-wheeler for the flashlight Vera had remembered to bring. It was dark as pitch in that cave, even in the middle of the day.

"We'll put her on that." Eve roved the beam of light over the rock ledge on the far wall. "Cover her up with rocks."

Worked for Vera.

They lifted Sheree onto the ledge. Eve posed her arms the way the folks they'd seen in caskets were done. Then they covered her with rocks. Eve gathered flowers to put on top. Vera decided to go back to the house and get Sheree's purse and a suitcase with some of her stuff packed in it. Once those things were in place, they were done.

"We should pray or something, right?" Eve asked, her gaze glued to the mound of rocks. Even with nothing more than the beam of the flashlight, she looked pitiful in her dirty pajamas and with her frazzled hair.

Vera started to say no, but if it made Eve feel better . . . "Sure."

"Dear Lord," Eve said, head bowed, eyes closed.

Vera closed her eyes as well.

"Please take this woman into your loving arms." Eve paused. "I don't know what to say next," she whispered in that voice that was never a real whisper.

Vera rolled her eyes. "Yes, Lord, take this woman in your loving arms and . . . and send her straight to hell where she belongs."

Eve looked at her for a moment. Vera worried that she'd upset her, but then her sister said, "Amen."

As they scrambled out of the cave, Vera told her sister, "We'll have to burn this sheet and wash our clothes."

Eve said nothing as they got to their feet and started forward. Then she stalled and stared back at the cave.

"Eve," Vera urged. "We have to go."

Reluctantly she turned to look at Vera, then nodded. "'Kay."

Even as they walked away, Eve kept looking back.

"What're you looking at?" Vera demanded. She felt ready to drop . . . like an elephant had been strapped to her back and she'd run ten miles.

"Nothing." Eve hurried forward, as if she'd snapped out of whatever trance she'd fallen into.

Climbing onto the four-wheeler, Vera hoped her sister wasn't suffering some crazy trauma like PTSD. Eve settled behind her, careful not to crowd Luna. Now, Vera was the one staring at the cave . . . hesitating.

What had they done?

Her heart started to thunder again.

"Vee?"

Vera kicked aside the worry. Didn't matter. All that mattered right now was not letting their daddy find out what happened.

It had to be their secret . . . forever.

23

Thursday, July 25

Boyett Farm
Good Hollow Road, Fayetteville, 6:58 a.m.

Vera should have packed more clothes.

As she towel dried her hair, she stared at the last pair of clean jeans and the plain white tee that remained in her bag. Nothing she could do about it now. The worry was irrelevant, really. She wasn't here to impress anyone with her wardrobe. Comfort was far more important, considering she intended to get into that cave today. Once the FBI was on site, it would be far more difficult.

She needed to see with her own eyes what had happened in that cave since the last time she had been in there. And before . . . she realized . . . before they had put Sheree in there.

She gathered the clothes she'd already worn to go in the wash.

Downstairs the scent of coffee filled the air. And something sweet. Vera followed the smell to the kitchen. Fresh cinnamon rolls sat on the table.

Eve looked up from her coffee. She had decided to stay with the family last night after all that had happened. "Luna was up baking at five thirty this morning."

"She left already?"

"Jerome picked her up for breakfast with his family." Eve lifted an eyebrow. "We'll see how that goes. If you think life is miserable now, just let them hurt Luna's feelings about all this. We may never have peace again."

Vera gave a short laugh. "They should keep in mind that Luna will be the mother of their grandchildren. Making her miserable would not be a smart move."

Eve nibbled at her cinnamon roll. "Good point. Oh yeah, and Luna postponed the memorial service. She felt it would be better to wait until this all settles down."

Vera opted to not respond. Waiting for all this to settle might take far longer than her little sister realized. "I need to pop this into the laundry." Vera showed Eve the bundle she carried, then headed across the room.

When she returned to the table, Eve passed a cup of steaming coffee to her. "You sleep okay?"

Vera grabbed the cup in both hands and enjoyed a long swallow. She moaned. "Thank you." She studied her sister. "I did. How about you?"

"I don't know." Eve made a face. "I kept obsessing over what we talked about and how this could have happened."

"Yeah. It was rambling around the edges of my thoughts every time I woke up." The scent of Luna's stress-relieving strategy tugged at her. "I need a cinnamon roll."

For a time they picked at the pan of cinnamon rolls without talking.

Eventually Vera prompted, "What were you thinking? Last night, I mean."

Eve wiped her sticky fingers on a napkin. "I don't know. Maybe that during my alcohol binging blackouts, maybe I killed people and put them in that cave."

Vera made a face. "What the hell, Eve? Don't say things like that. Don't even think along those lines." Jesus! Had she lost her mind? "Besides, the women were put there when we were just little kids."

Eve shrugged. "So maybe I did the guy. I could be a blackout killer."

Vera so regretted opening that Pandora's box. "Okay. To put your mind at ease, let's talk about that possibility then." She reached for her coffee. "Have you ever woken up with scratches or bruises you couldn't remember getting? Maybe with your clothes or shoes soiled or your car left someplace you don't remember going?"

Eve considered her questions, then laughed: a dry sound. "Actually, yes to all of the above."

A groan welled in Vera's throat. "Was this something that happened often?"

Eve made a face as she considered the question. "Remember, when I drink, I don't have just a couple of beers or cocktails. I go all out. I drink myself to the verge of alcohol poisoning. I rarely remember anything."

Vera decided she'd lost her appetite. Somehow knowing this was a possibility and hearing Eve say it out loud were different. "All right then. How about anyone who saw you out, and you didn't remember seeing them? Have you ever had anyone insist they saw you somewhere you don't recall going?"

"Only like a gazillion times." Eve finished off her cinnamon roll. "I never had anyone tell me I got into a fight or left with some stranger. Maybe that's a plus."

Definitely a plus. "Have you ever found any items in your car or in your room that didn't belong to you, and you didn't recall how you came to be in possession of them?"

She moved her head side to side. "Not that I can remember."

"Has Suri ever mentioned you saying things in your sleep or any other odd behavior?"

Another shake of her head. "Never. She says I sleep like a rock."

Vera slid off her stool and walked around to her sister. She put her arm around her shoulders and hugged her. "I'm sorry I made you feel you had to question yourself this way."

"No biggie." Eve searched her face. "Will the FBI be wanting to talk to us?"

Deeper Than the Dead

Her sister looked worried now. Vera wished she could make her understand this was just a step in the process. "They will. But you don't talk to anyone without me present. Understood?"

Eve nodded.

"I'll make sure Luna knows to do the same." Vera was well aware how conversations could be manipulated in an effort to prompt the desired response. She was an expert at exactly that sort of interrogation. Funny how different it looked when you were on the receiving side of the manipulation.

Her cell vibrated, and she tugged it from her jeans. Text message. *Eric.* She smiled. The content of the message pulled her smile into a frown. "The cell phone that sent us the text messages," she said to Eve, "was a burner."

"Like in the TV cop shows? Untraceable?"

"Pretty much." A second text told her he'd be in touch about her other request soon. She sent a thank-you with multiple exclamation points, then slid her cell back into her pocket. "There's no way to determine if our messenger is a legitimate threat or just some asshole playing games. Our best course of action is to play it safe—assume he's a real threat. Which means"—she looked directly into Eve's eyes as she spoke—"we should be careful and always watchful."

Eve grinned. "I love you so much. I've always wanted to be you."

Vera laughed. "Don't be ridiculous. Then who would be the amazing Eve?"

Vera's cell vibrated again, with an incoming call this time. She dug it out once more. "Bent." She looked to Eve. "If he tells me we have another set of remains, I might just scream."

"How the hell many more could be in there? It's not that big."

The fact that Eve didn't mention the deeper cavern provided Vera with a measure of relief. She should never have allowed her imagination to run away with her. Her sister couldn't have known the others were there.

"Hey, Bent. What's up? I was just about to head to your place."

201

Eve shot her a look that said "told you so." Vera rolled her eyes.

"Meet me downtown, Vee. We have a problem."

Vera swallowed to dampen her suddenly dry throat. "I'm coming now."

Lincoln County Sheriff's Department
Thornton Taylor Parkway, Fayetteville, 8:30 a.m.

"You remember Dr. Higdon," Bent said, gesturing to the man seated in the chair in front of his desk.

Vera paused only for a second as she crossed the room. Bent's assistant had sent her into his office. Vera hadn't known there was someone already there. "Of course I do." She walked straight over and extended her hand toward the man who had served as Lincoln County's medical examiner for nearly forty years. "Dr. Higdon, it's good to see you again. I hope you'll tell Mrs. Higdon how much we appreciated that casserole she and Mrs. Fraley dropped by." To Vera's knowledge it was still in the fridge, but a little buttering up of local officials never hurt.

Higdon stood, accepted her hand, and gave it a shake. "It's been a good long time. I wish it were under more pleasant circumstances."

Vera forced her smile to stay in place. "It's a strange time, for sure." She turned to Bent, who stood behind his desk. "So what's going on?" Though she imagined Higdon had already gotten a preliminary look at all the remains, chances were, the FBI would want their own people to do an assessment, which invited the question, Why was she here?

Higdon lowered back into his chair, and Bent gestured for her to have a seat as well. Vera complied. Evidently he wasn't going to proceed until everyone was seated. Lastly, Bent settled into his chair.

"Dr. Higdon, why don't you explain the problem to Vera?"

Vera looked from Bent to the older man. It would certainly be nice if someone would. Her instincts were suddenly humming a tune she knew far too well—something was up. Bent had said there was a problem. Evidently it involved the ME.

"I was the person, you may recall," Higdon said, his focus on Vera, "who pronounced your mother after her death."

"I do. Yes." Vera blocked images from that horrible day. It was the worst day of her life.

"We didn't do an autopsy because of the cancer diagnosis," he explained, "but I did conduct a quick examination as per standard procedure."

Vera nodded. *Where was this going?*

Higdon leaned forward—not an easy feat, considering his size. The man wasn't that tall, but he made up for it in girth. With his Sunday-go-to-meeting jacket and his perfectly starched bow tie, he'd always reminded Vera of Porky Pig. She blinked to banish the image. Bit her lips together to prevent a smile.

"I suppose I should have asked about this back then, but you girls were crying something pitiful. Poor Vernon was beside himself. I just couldn't bring myself to do it."

Vera looked from Higdon to Bent and back once more. "Ask what, Dr. Higdon? I'm not following."

"There's really no way to do this but just to say it." He cleared his throat. "While examining your mother, I noted a number of bruises to the throat and shoulder area." He gestured to his own nearly non-existent throat. "At the time I considered that the discoloration might perhaps be related to the cancer treatments. But now, thinking back, the positioning of the bruises . . . well it just feels wrong."

Vera tilted her head, studying the man as she locked down the emotions welling inside her. Now this—this place where Higdon had just gone—was territory where no one wanted to go after the loss of a loved one. The trouble in this instance was that the loved one in question had been dead for more than two decades. And she was Vera's mother.

"What exactly are you implying, Dr. Higdon?"

A covert glance at Bent showed his full attention resting on the medical examiner. Evidently he wasn't giving her a damned thing.

"I know your father well," Higdon said. "I've always considered him a good friend, and I was so sad for him when Evelyn died. For you girls as well. Perhaps my personal feelings prevented me from looking as closely as I should have. From doing my job to the best of my ability."

Fury roared through her like a freight train. He was seriously going there. "I would advise you to tread carefully, sir. This sort of thing can be quite libelous."

Higdon turned to Bent then. "I am only telling you what I saw. And now, in light of what we know happened to Sheree and the other remains—those deaths may not have been the first murder perpetrated by Vernon Boyett." He swung his gaze back to Vera. "You can call it whatever you like, young lady, but I can't in good conscience cover for your father any longer."

Vera stood so fast her chair almost tipped over. "I will not listen to these ridiculous and unfounded accusations. I'm stunned that you would even go down this path." She swung her attention to the sheriff. "I can't believe you would go along with this, Bent."

"We should exhume Evelyn's body," Higdon insisted to Bent, totally ignoring Vera.

"I will not agree to that," Vera stated without reservation. Was the man insane? "And if this leaks to the media, I will sue."

Higdon glared up at her. "If you're so certain your father never harmed your mother, why not allow me to rule out the possibility once and for all?"

Oh, she had used that same line so many times in the course of investigations. "First," she said, "whatever bruising may or may not have been present on my mother's body would not be there now—not in any identifiable manner, at least. As you well know. Therefore what you're suggesting is nothing more than a dog and pony show to buy you some relevance in the media with this current case. We all know how rarely a case like this comes along in a small town, and when it does, everyone wants to be the star of the show."

The man's face bloomed a bright red. "I didn't look for fractures or other indications of previous abuse. I had too much respect for your father. But a man who would kill his wife would think nothing of abusing her in other ways."

Another blast of outrage reverberated through Vera. "You would have been wasting your time. My mother was not abused. My father took very good care of her and all of us. I was there." Her body shook with outrage.

"I would agree," the old bastard said. "Except everything changed when Sheree came into your lives," he pointed out almost giddily. "Considering how quickly she and your father married and Luna came along, it would be foolish not to recognize they were involved before your mother's death."

"Well"—Vera gave a slow, thoughtful nod—"if you did notice something at the time of my mother's death and failed to investigate, then you were negligent in the carrying out of the duties of your office." When he attempted to argue, she held up her hand. "In which case, every death you've investigated since that time will and should come under scrutiny." She aimed a knowing smile at him. "I'm not sure you understand the ramifications of opening that can of worms, Dr. Higdon, but I will be more than happy to show you what they are."

"Vee"—Bent stood—"Higdon has already gone to the FBI with this."

Higdon's eyes fairly glittered with excitement as he watched her stunned and somewhat deflated reaction to the news.

There were many things Vera wanted to say, but words eluded her in that moment. Finally, she summoned her wherewithal and warned, "Exhume my mother, and I will make sure every news outlet in this part of the country knows about your admitted negligence."

"Vee," Bent said, his voice low and urgent, "whatever else Higdon does, the FBI will not let this go now that it's on the table."

She ignored the point he made . . . didn't want to hear it.

"I'm sure the funeral home has photos from when my mother was prepared for burial. You have my permission to use those to review the case," she said to Higdon. "That should be sufficient."

Higdon smiled, as if that had been his intent all along. "Very well. As you say, I'm sure that will suffice."

Bastard.

"Now"—Vera drew in a deep breath—"if you'll excuse me. I have to speak with my sisters and warn them about this latest travesty."

She turned her back and walked out.

"Vee." Bent was right on her heels.

"Not now," she warned with a lethal glance in his direction.

He backed off.

It took every ounce of strength she possessed to get out of the building and into her SUV before the damned tears started. It was one thing to go after her father, but it was entirely another to use her mother's death in such a way.

This was wrong. And she intended to prove it, with or without Bent's support.

24

Bent didn't try to stop her. He just stood there and watched her walk away.

Vera was too angry. She wouldn't have listened to him anyway.

Higdon pushed out of his chair. "Well, I'll get right on requesting those photos." He looked to Bent. "You did the right thing, son. The only thing you could do. Those sisters will just have to get right with what their daddy likely did."

Bent forced his jaw to relax, unclamped his gritted teeth. "First of all, Vera's right—this is wrong. Second, I am not your son."

Higdon only glared at him, then strutted out of the office, shoulders back and chest puffed out like a gobbler during mating season.

Fury twisted in Bent's gut. It wouldn't be so bad if the old bastard's point was finding the truth, but it wasn't. It was just like Vee said. He wanted to make himself a significant part of this investigation now that it had moved to the next level. He wanted his face on the news.

If the truth had been so damned important, he would have demanded it from Vernon Boyett twenty-some years ago when, in his capacity as medical examiner, he claimed to have noticed the bruises on Vernon's dead wife.

Bent set his hands on his hips. Since he couldn't exactly punch an old man, he felt like he needed to do something. Try to talk to Vera. Some damned thing. And he got how this accusation made her feel. He'd been damned angry himself when Higdon brought this to him. Worse, when he admitted that he'd spoken to the FBI about it, Bent had barely restrained himself from going off on him.

Not exactly the kind of thing to do if he wanted to maintain the people's trust.

Damn it, Bent had known Evelyn Boyett, and he'd thought the world of her. He hadn't been that close to Vernon, but he hadn't heard anything bad about him. Well, beyond the idea that he was a fool for having married Sheree Corbin. But most men had their weaknesses. For some those showed up early, making them rowdy and irresponsible in their youth. Like him, he was sad to say. He had no proper raising, which left him to fend for himself. He learned early on that his looks and the right words could get him all sorts of things—none of which he'd needed.

He regretted so much of what he'd done before joining the army. Most of all, he regretted having hurt Vee. She'd reminded him so much of her mother. That was the draw at first. But then he got to know Vera, and he couldn't let go. She made him feel things and want things he knew he would never have.

Vera was the reason he left so suddenly.

He recognized that he was no good for her. Being involved with him could have ruined her life. It was a flat-out miracle she hadn't ended up pregnant. He hadn't taken any precautions with her . . . he'd been too crazy about her. Crazy, period.

One Friday morning he walked into the army recruiter's office, and a few days later he was gone.

Leaving was the one good, selfless thing he did in those days. Leaving gave Vera the opportunity to achieve all the things she had spoken about so enthusiastically. She had big dreams, and he hadn't wanted to stand in her way.

She still held leaving against him, but he could live with that.

Just like he'd known she would, she had done great things. The trouble in Memphis wouldn't stop her from continuing to do great things. As soon as this mess was behind her, she would move on to something even bigger. Some people were just meant to change the world, and Vera was one of them.

This time he would be the one left behind.

He dropped into his chair. The selfish part of him wished she would stay. But he'd never say that out loud. Vera didn't belong in this little town, and she sure as hell didn't belong to him.

But he would damned well feel a lot better if she would trust him enough to tell him what she was hiding. He figured it was something related to what happened to Sheree, but he couldn't be sure. He didn't want to believe Vernon had killed Sheree, but a man could do some dumb shit when he was angry—especially when it came to the woman in his life.

Even knowing what he did, Bent still couldn't get right with the idea that Vernon had cheated on Evelyn. She had been an amazing woman. A beautiful woman. A good and kind woman. But if she were alive today, she would be the first to look back and say her husband had made a mistake. She would forgive him and show nothing but complete understanding. She'd been ill, after all. Dying. He'd needed something she couldn't give him.

Vera was a lot like her. Except for the forgiveness part.

Bent wanted desperately to protect her. Eve too. He owed it to Evelyn to do all in his power to see that her daughters came through this unscathed.

The problem was, he might not be able to get the job done if they didn't trust him enough to tell him the parts of the story they were leaving out. Whenever he brought up the idea, Vera bit his head off.

Eve was a little more subtle about it, but the result was the same.

A soft rap on his door sounded just before it opened, and Myra, his assistant, poked her head in. "Sheriff, Willard Carmichael is on the phone for you."

He gave her a nod. "Thanks."

Myra Jordan was one of the few good people he inherited from Fraley's last years in office. She told him the way it really was. If he wanted to know if a deputy was on the up-and-up, all he had to do was ask Myra. Fraley had assured him he could trust her when he couldn't trust anyone else. All through those first few months, she stood up for Bent, and she stood behind his decisions.

He appreciated her support more than she would ever know.

Pulling his head back into the present, he took a breath, picked up the handset from the phone on his desk, and pressed the blinking light for line one. Willard Carmichael was a deacon at the Church of Christ. There was likely a church fundraiser coming up that required assistance from the sheriff's department. The upside was that these days he had plenty of fine deputies who were happy to volunteer their time off for a good cause.

"Mr. Carmichael, what can I do for you?"

"Sheriff, I need you to come over to the church. Somebody's vandalized my truck."

"How do you mean, sir?" Bent wasn't sure the elderly man should even be driving anymore, but he wasn't going to be the one to tell him he should give up his driver's license. Bent wasn't afraid of much, but he never liked pissing off a man of the cloth.

He already had plenty of reason to suspect he was going to hell when this life was over. Why push his luck?

"Well, I can't really explain it. You know my eyes aren't what they used to be. You should come see for yourself. I'm just trying to figure out how in the world it happened. Quite frankly, it's a complete mystery."

"I'll be right over."

"I'll be waiting," Carmichael said before hanging up.

Bent dropped the handset into the cradle and stood. Just what he needed. Another mystery.

25

Eve was already waiting when Vera arrived.

During the nearly two years Vera had been home after their mother died, she and Eve had met at her grave many times. It was the best place to get away from the house and have some privacy. Sometimes to cry. Sometimes just to talk. Now was one of those times.

As Vera neared the bench where Eve sat, her sister said, "I'm not sure I want to know what's happened now."

"Believe me, you don't." Vera sat down beside her on the granite bench. "Dr. Higdon has decided that maybe the cancer didn't kill Mama."

Eve made a "what the hell" face. "You're kidding, right?"

"He claims he saw bruises on her throat and shoulders when he pronounced her. He thinks Daddy hastened her death to get her out of the way."

Eve blinked, looked away for a moment before turning back to Vera. "Doesn't he know I was the one to find her?" She scoffed. "Daddy wasn't even home. He was at work. Suri was there with me, you remember."

Vera nodded. How could she forget?

"Are we supposed to believe Daddy sneaked into the house, pushed Mama under the water and held her there while we weren't looking, and then sneaked out again?"

The realization shook Vera just a little. She should have thought of exactly that, but Higdon's ridiculous revelation had caught her completely off guard. If she hadn't been so angry, she would have logically explained to Higdon that his suggestion about her mother's death was impossible . . . except it had been too late. As Bent said, the ME had put the idea on the table, and there was no pulling it back. No amount of logic was going to stop some sort of look into the accusation.

"You're right. Daddy wasn't home." Proving it after such an extended period might be problematic. Vera tried to recall where exactly she was when her sister had started yelling for her. The remembered sound of her voice—frantic and brimming with pain—echoed in her brain. "I was in the living room on the phone with Cindy Reynolds."

"I screamed for you, and you came running up the stairs." Eve shook her head. "Higdon is an idiot. I swear that man needs to retire and let someone younger take on the position. He must be what, seventy-five or -six?"

"Maybe he has Mama confused with someone else who died from cancer back then." Vera chewed her lip, tried to think of a preemptive move. "I need to see those photos from the funeral home."

"I can get them." Eve sat up straighter.

Hope swelled in Vera's chest. "You can? We don't have much time," she reminded Eve. "Higdon is probably drafting the request as we speak. The funeral home would want his request in writing for their records. Unfortunately, if he decides to go for an exhumation, he has a judge in his pocket—his son."

"Screw him and his full-of-himself son." Eve pulled her cell from her back pocket. "I have my own secret weapon. Give me a minute."

Vera listened as Eve called Suri and asked her to pull their mother's file. While Suri searched, Eve explained the reason for the odd and abrupt request. Like Vera and Eve, Suri was horrified to hear that Higdon would suggest such a thing.

This whole situation had turned into a total nightmare. Every last detail of their lives was going to shit in a far too public way. Vera was weary of it, and the show was far from over.

Eve made a face and thanked her friend before hanging up.

"Did she find the photos?" Vera needed a copy, optimally before Higdon got his hands on them.

"There are no photos in the file."

Vera drew back. "What? Hurst always took photos. Daddy said so when Mama died." She exhaled a frustrated breath. Where the hell were those photos? "The funeral director asked if Daddy wanted a copy, and he said he didn't even want to see them. It was too painful."

"Well," Eve countered, "they're missing now."

"Could Higdon have gotten over there already?"

"Suri said she was the only one there."

"Maybe they're just misfiled," Vera suggested.

"It's possible," Eve agreed.

Damn it. Vera forced away the frustration and surveyed the cemetery. She needed to clear her head and think for a moment.

Their mother had loved this cemetery. She always participated whenever there was a cleanup or other activity. She insisted that Vera and Eve come along and help out. Now that Vera thought about it, maybe that was where Eve had gotten her fondness for the dead.

"Daddy could have asked for the photos at some point after the funeral," Eve offered, drawing Vera back to the problem at hand.

"I suppose so," Vera agreed. "I just can't imagine why. Either way, if Higdon can't find the photos," she went on, her mind circling the possibilities, "he will want to exhume her. Not that it will do one damned bit of good."

Not unless there were fractures. Vera searched her memory for any time her mother had ever been injured. Nothing came to mind.

"This is ridiculous and utterly insane," she muttered.

"Try not to worry," Eve urged. "Suri will look through all the files. If the photos are in the building, she will find them."

"I hope so." Vera couldn't bear the idea of her mother being disturbed and their father's and family's reputation being trashed in the headlines and on the gossip grapevine for no reason.

Vernon Boyett was not an abuser or a murderer.

Vera's stomach tied itself into knots. *Was he?*

For a time, she and Eve only sat there, the worries crowding in around Vera. How could this be happening? There had been a hell of a lot of misery in the *after* part of their lives, but did fate have to try to damage the good from the *before* part too?

"Do you remember how she looked? In the bathtub, I mean." The words were out before Vera could stop them, and she wanted to kick herself for asking. It had been a really tough time for both of them, but especially for Eve, since she had found her.

"She was wearing that pink scarf," Eve said, her voice sounding a thousand miles away. "She'd even picked pink panties and bra to match. Remember toward the end she wore her undies even in the bath or shower."

"You're right." Vera smiled sadly. "I'd forgotten about that."

Since her death was imminent, their mother had worried about suddenly dropping dead. She didn't want to risk the EMTs coming in to find her naked. Vera thought it was the silliest thing she'd ever heard at the time, but later she understood.

"The pink ones were her favorite. It was like she knew that was the day," Eve went on. "I'm still mad at her a little, you know."

Vera frowned, searched her sister's face. "Why? Because she died and left us? It's not like she wanted to."

Eve shook her head. "I know that. I mean because she didn't tell me the truth."

Vera's frown deepened. She had no idea what Eve meant. "About what?"

"She said it would be better after she was gone. That she wouldn't be suffering anymore, and we would be able to get on with our lives. She said over and over that I would feel better. But I didn't. It was a lie. I shouldn't have believed her."

Vera put an arm around her sister and hugged her, despite the way she stiffened at the gesture. "Her suffering did end," she offered. "And I think she thought we would feel better knowing that."

"I was eleven years old," Eve reminded her. "There was absolutely no scenario where having my mother die was going to make me feel better. I shouldn't have believed her."

"I never knew you felt this way." Vera couldn't recall Eve ever talking about that particular aspect before.

A flash of memory cut through her brain. Sitting on the bathroom floor with Eve. The two of them holding tightly to each other. Their mother lying on the wet tile where they had pulled her from the tub. Suri leaning against the wall, watching in a sort of shock.

"*I shouldn't have believed her,*" Eve had cried. "*It doesn't feel better. It doesn't feel better at all.*"

Vera remembered holding her sister, rocking her until the ambulance arrived. Then their father appeared, and the rest was an emotional roller-coaster ride barreling toward the end of the track. Their father had cried harder than anyone.

"Maybe I made the bruises trying to get her up out of the water," Eve said. "Until you got in there to help me, I kept grabbing at her and trying to heave her up. Suri had panicked and was just sitting there in shock."

"He's suggesting these were bruises showing her body had been held down in the water," Vera explained. "I'm sure you didn't hold her down."

Eve made a face. "I don't think so."

"I don't want you worrying about this," Vera urged. "You didn't do anything wrong any more than I did. She was weak from the chemo. It was the last round because her oncologist didn't believe she could tolerate any more. It wasn't really helping anyway. That final cycle was just a last-ditch effort to buy a little more time."

"Everyone always wants more time," Eve noted. "The concept is overrated when you're that deep into such a wicked disease."

Vera wasn't sure it was possible to overrate more time when it came to life. Most people would gladly give just about anything for even a minute more.

They sat for a while, silent, remembering. A rare late-July breeze provided some relief from the heat, stirring the leaves and reminding Vera of waking up on summer mornings to hear the soft wind chimes through her bedroom windows. Their mother had loved wind chimes. They were hanging everywhere around the house. Sheree hadn't liked them very much. She claimed they kept her awake, and she intended to take them down. Eve came up with the idea to tell her that they warded off evil spirits. Sheree didn't dare take one down after that.

The woman really had been naive in some ways.

Vera closed her eyes against the memories that flashed from that final day with Sheree. They had so much trouble getting her body to the cave and then inside. How the hell had someone put three others in there? Even deeper inside, at that?

"I have to get back to work." Eve stood.

Vera exiled the memories and pushed herself to her feet. "Let me know if Suri has any luck finding those photographs."

"Will do. Thanks for the update." She scoffed. "Not really. I hate all this."

Vera could not agree more. "Me too. But don't worry. As long as we stick to our stories, we'll get through this."

"Famous last words," Eve suggested. She waved as she walked away.

Unfortunately, her sister might be right about that one.

Fraley Farm
Jenkins Road, Fayetteville, 10:20 a.m.

Vera parked and sat for a moment. A truck was in the driveway. She hoped that was an indication the Fraleys were home.

She really hoped this was not a bad move, but since leaving the cemetery, she couldn't stop thinking about her mother. She had been a very smart woman. A bright and perceptive woman. Vera just couldn't see her being married to a man who secretly committed murder without suspecting something. The two had been so close. So happy . . . until the cancer. Call it wishful thinking, but she couldn't get past it . . . not just yet anyway.

The more-probable scenario was that Vernon Boyett had allowed a friend to use the cave. Vera chewed her lip. But would he have done such a thing twice? The third time, the male victim, might have been a situation he knew nothing about. Just because her father had helped a friend once didn't mean he had known about one or both of the other murders. The friend could have taken advantage of the situation. It was difficult to analyze without an iota of information about the victims.

Whatever the case, Vera simply could not see her father doing this and keeping it secret from her mother. Would he have risked allowing the situation to come back to haunt his wife and daughters? To destroy their lives?

Vera needed to speak with someone who had known her parents well enough to have some idea who such a friend might have been back in those days.

A friend who was also a murderer.

Someone . . . anyone but her father. Possibly the unidentified male victim found in that crevice.

Mind made up, Vera opened her door and got out. By the time she reached the steps, the front door had opened, and Beatrice pushed open the screen door and walked out onto the porch.

"Vera, what a nice surprise."

"I hope you don't mind me dropping by unannounced." Vera smiled, fingers mentally crossed.

"Don't be silly." The older woman waved off the notion. "Walt's having a nap. Last night was a rough one. Shall we sit on the porch and chat?"

"Perfect. I could use some fresh air."

Beatrice settled into a rocking chair that looked much like the ones on the porch at home. Vera lowered into the second of the two, appreciated the ceiling fans that stirred the air, however slowly. The floral cushions and hanging ferns all reminded Vera of her mother's decorating style. She and Beatrice had been good friends, after all. They likely shared ideas and inspiration.

"Tell me how I can help, Vee." Beatrice set the rocker into a slow, easy motion.

She seemed so much more relaxed when she wasn't with Florence Higdon. Who wouldn't be?

"I don't have to tell you," Vera began, "how difficult the investigation related to Sheree and the other remains has been for my family."

"I can only imagine," Beatrice agreed. "It's a terrible situation."

Vera hesitated only a moment, then went for it. "One of the scenarios on the table, so to speak, is that my father allowed a friend to use the cave."

The older woman nodded knowingly. "I can see something like that happening. Your father was always kind to everyone. Generous too."

"We're thinking," Vera pressed on, "this friend may have taken advantage of the situation and continued to use the cave for his own personal dumping ground."

"For his victims, you mean."

"Sorry, yes." Vera forged on. "We can't, of course, be certain if my father knew what the friend was doing—assuming the theory pans out. Obviously, he can't tell us now, considering his dementia." Vera looked to the former schoolteacher. "Long story short, I need your help putting together a list of people who were close to my father."

Beatrice stared at her for a long moment.

Vera felt the urge to shrink into herself. The woman clearly thought she was mad.

"Of course." Beatrice nodded. "In fact, when Walt wakes up, I'll have him help me. He might actually know better than me when it comes to your father's friends."

Relief rushed through Vera. "That would be so helpful. Really, when you cut through all the rumors and the innuendos, don't you think this perpetrator had to be someone my parents knew? You and the sheriff and my parents were friends for so long, you know what I mean. Who could possibly believe that either of them was capable of murder?"

Beatrice reached over, placed a hand on Vera's. "You don't have to convince me. Your parents would never have harmed anyone."

The relief at hearing that confirmation made her want to hug the woman.

Before she could ask about any unsolved disappearances from the time frame the victims were put in the cave, Vera's cell vibrated against her hip. She'd forgotten it was in her pocket.

"Excuse me." She fished it out and checked the screen. A text from Bent.

Meet me at the Church of Christ on Washington Street. Important.

Seemed an odd place to meet, but maybe going to his place today wasn't feasible, and the FBI was likely hanging out at his office or the cave by now.

She sent him a thumbs-up and turned back to Beatrice. "Thank you so much for understanding and agreeing to help. I really appreciate it. I have a meeting with Bent, so I have to go." She stood.

Beatrice pushed to her feet a little slower. "You go on and don't worry. Walt and I will do all we can to help."

Thank God for friends like the Fraleys.

Church of Christ
Washington Street, Fayetteville, 11:30 a.m.

Bent waited for Vera in the parking lot behind the church. There was another truck parked next to his. Dark in color. Black or dark blue. Not one she recognized.

Vera parked nose to nose with Bent's truck and climbed out. "What's going on?"

She imagined Higdon had already called to complain that he hadn't been able to get his hands on the photographs. Mentally, she was working at getting prepared for what came next. Her conversation with Eve had reminded her of all the reasons Higdon's suggestion about their father harming their mother was impossible. She would fight him over the exhumation.

"There's something I need to show you."

She walked closer to where he waited between his truck and the other one. As she neared, she noted damage on the front end of the other truck. Not blue, she decided. Black, maybe.

"I think I've found the truck involved in the incident with your sister's car." He gestured to the damage on the front end.

Now that she was closer, it was obvious the blackish color was actually a really dark green. Vera looked from the truck to the church. "Did a member of the church leave it here?" That was one way to avoid having the damage spotted. She doubted the police perused church parking lots in search of hit-and-run vehicles. Except, here they were.

"It belongs to Willard Carmichael. You might remember him. He's a deacon here."

Vera made a face. If this was the Willard Carmichael she remembered, he was old. Like ninety. "Does he still drive? Maybe he allowed someone to borrow it."

Bent shook his head in answer to her suggestion. "He said it's been sitting here for nearly two weeks. There's a mechanical issue, and the man who's making the repairs is waiting on parts."

How was that possible, considering the truck ran into Eve's car just the day before yesterday? She said as much to Bent.

"It won't start," Bent explained. "Carmichael gave me the keys, and I tried myself. It's been sitting right here all this time." He pointed to the pavement directly in front of the truck. "If you'll notice there's a bit of a skid mark. Like another vehicle made a sudden stop right *there*."

"Okay." Wait. Vera held up her hands. "What're you suggesting?"

"I'm saying that the paint on this truck matches what rubbed off on your sister's car, which pretty much confirms that this is the truck that collided with her car."

"But you just said this truck doesn't—"

"Eve came to this parking lot, Vee, and she backed into the truck. That's what I'm telling you."

Ice frosted in her veins. "You're suggesting she made up the whole story."

He nodded. "I don't know why, but I'm as confident as I can be without an eyewitness and without testing the paint transfer."

Vera surveyed the other buildings in the area. "No security cameras around here?"

He shook his head. "Not the first one."

Why in the world would Eve do this?

"Can you think of any reason Eve would try and toss out a distraction related to this investigation?"

Slashes of memory—the two of them hefting Sheree's cold, wet body into that utility trailer—cut through her brain. Still, she shook her head. "None at all."

"I'll have to talk to her about this," Bent said. "Not only did she damage this vehicle, but she falsified an accident report. Whatever is going on with Eve, we need to get it under control before it becomes a real issue."

In Vera's opinion this alone made it a very real issue. What the hell had Eve been thinking?

"Let me talk to her," Vera urged. As if she hadn't just done so a few minutes ago. "I'll get to the bottom of this. But I want you to keep something in mind related to our earlier meeting with Higdon." She explained the impossibility of what the ME was suggesting about their father in relationship to the time of their mother's death. "Daddy couldn't have done what Higdon is suggesting."

Bent nodded. "You're right. And I will talk to him."

"Thanks." Vera pressed her lips together, told herself to let it go. Bent had only been doing his job.

He stared at the ground a moment. "I feel really bad about that business, Vee." He lifted his gaze to hers. "I wanted to shut him down, but he already thinks I lack objectivity on this case. That's why he went to the FBI."

"I get it. You did the right thing." As difficult as that meeting had been, he'd handled it exactly as he should have. "And thank you for telling me about this"—she gestured to the truck—"so I can figure it out. I'll call you after I speak with Eve."

His lips lifted in a smile. "I'm sure she'll have a good explanation."

Vera laughed a pathetic sound. "No doubt."

"I'll call you when we can get together at my home office."

She gave him a nod and headed back to her SUV. She wanted to be relieved that maybe they were off the hook with this exhumation business, but what Bent was suggesting about Eve was equally troubling. She sent her sister a text to meet her at the house ASAP.

What on earth had Eve been trying to do?

26

Why the hell would Eve lie to her?

By the time Vera reached the house, she was thoroughly pissed.

She climbed out of her SUV and shoved the door shut. Lying to Bent was one thing. Even lying to Luna was acceptable, if it was for the right reason. They'd been lying to their little sister and basically everyone else for years. But having Eve lie to her? After what they had been through together—that was just over the top. Unacceptable.

She shoved the key into the door and gave it a twist. If Eve was hiding something awful, and Vera feared she was, she had better get ready to come clean. Vera could not help her if she wasn't honest.

Wasn't that the way of it? Damn it.

The ones who did bad things never understood why friends and family didn't help them more often. It was difficult—no, impossible—to help a person who hid things from you and/or lied to you.

Her omissions with Bent were different. *Yeah right.*

She slammed the front door. What the hell was she even doing here? She should have just told Bent the truth from the beginning and accepted whatever charges the man saw fit to try to drum up. There really wasn't much of anything. Sheree wasn't murdered. It was an accident.

Wasn't it?

There were multiple skull fractures suggested in the preliminary examination.

She stalled, struggled to draw in a breath. Maybe Eve hadn't been completely honest about what happened.

Vera tossed her bag onto the bench by the door. "Damn it!"

But Eve had been a kid. Why would she lie?

The memory of dragging Sheree's lifeless body down those stairs bloomed in her mind. Her head bumping down one step after the other. Vera's shoulders sagged. There was that . . .

Whatever happened, Sheree had been dead when Vera arrived at the house. She had helped her sister haul the body and then tuck it into that damned cave. Sure, she had tampered with evidence. Probably abused a corpse—sort of. But both of those things were no longer even relevant where the law was concerned. The statute of limitations had long ago run out.

Murder was the only crime from that day that could survive twenty-two years.

But no one had committed murder . . . *had they*?

A clunk on the wood floor over her head jerked Vera's attention upward.

She froze.

Footsteps.

Someone was up there.

"Eve?" Her sister hadn't gotten her car back yet. Maybe Suri had dropped her off.

If it was Eve, no problem. If it was a reporter, by God, Vera intended to kick his or her ass. She hit the stairs at a run.

She bounded up the final step, rounded the railing, and immediately rammed into a solid body in the shadows of the upstairs hall. She stumbled back. Tried to see, but there was something in the way.

Mask.

Son of a bitch.

Anger and frustration coalesced inside her. No visible weapon . . . dark clothes . . . dark mask. She charged toward the intruder.

Strong gloved hands pushed her away. Vera hit the wall on the opposite side of the hall.

The dark figure bolted down the stairs.

Vera regained her balance and rushed after him. No way was she letting this bastard get away.

Halfway down the stairs, she grabbed at the back of his shirt, and an elbow jammed her in the chest, knocked her onto her butt.

He kept going, heading toward the kitchen.

Vera attempted to right herself and capture her balance, but she failed. She tumbled the rest of the way down the stairs, hit the floor. Hard.

She grimaced at the pain, scrambled up, and hobbled toward the kitchen.

Too late. He was already out the back door, leaving it standing wide open. She stood on the porch and stared into the woods that surrounded the backyard. He was gone.

"What's going on?"

The demand came from Eve, who now stood in the kitchen with her hands on her hips, glaring at Vera as if she'd put her out by insisting she come home straightaway.

A fresh wave of fury whipped through Vera. "Someone was in the house. He knocked me down the stairs getting away." She gestured to the door. "Then disappeared."

"Are you okay?" Eve surveyed her, from mussed blonde hair to worn sneakers, her frustration turning to concern.

Vera moved her shoulders and then flexed her feet, one at a time. "I'll live. I don't think he took anything—I didn't see a bag or anything in his hands. But we need to be sure."

Eve closed and locked the door, then the two of them walked back to the front hall and climbed the stairs, a hell of a lot more slowly this time. Vera noted an ache in her right hip and her chest. She was going to be sore. Damn it.

Vera's and Eve's rooms were undisturbed. Nothing appeared to be moved or missing in Luna's either.

Their father's room was a different story. The dresser drawers had been opened and items were slung onto the floor. The closet door stood open, and items that had been folded and stored on shelves now lay on the floor.

"What would anyone be looking for in here?" Eve asked, surveying the mess. "Daddy has been in Hillside for two years."

"Who the hell knows?" Vera collapsed onto the bed. "We should call Bent."

Eve sat down beside her. "Maybe he can find some prints."

"The bastard had on gloves."

"Oh."

Vera hated to go down this path with Eve, but she had no choice. "Before we call . . . Bent knows you backed into that deacon's truck, and he knows you made up the story about being run off the road. I'm hoping there's a reasonable explanation for why in the world you decided to fake the event."

God, she was tired and frustrated and flat-out pissed off.

Eve huffed out a put-upon breath. "I never was very good at being sneaky."

Vera's whole body sagged with the new weight of her sister's admission. She bit back the first thing that came to mind. "Why did you do it, Eve? Damn, don't we have enough trouble without adding some stupid thing like this to the mix?"

"I thought I could make Bent believe someone was after us." She shook her head. "That maybe it was the person who killed Sheree. If I was successful, maybe he wouldn't be looking only at our family." She stared at the floor. "I wanted you to believe too. I mean, that there was someone else."

More of that load settled on Vera's shoulders. This was exactly the reason people who might never have been caught after committing a crime often were for the most seemingly insignificant reasons. "I have told you a dozen times. All we have to do is stick with our story. This thing you did"—she shook her head at Eve—"is not going to help. And you should know me better than this. I would never *not* look at all the possibilities."

"I'm sorry, Vee. I should have trusted you. Bent too. I'll pay for the damages. Maybe Bent can arrange it where I can do it anonymously."

Vera sighed. "So what're you going to tell him to explain why you did this?"

"The truth, I guess." Eve scrunched her face. "That I was worried they were going to try and blame Daddy and I wanted them to look further."

Vera couldn't argue her good intentions. "I suppose that's as good an excuse as any." She stretched her back and groaned, then another thought suddenly occurred to her. "Please tell me you didn't put that message on the front door." The mere thought irritated her. "And on my car at the cemetery."

Eve leaned away. "I should take the Fifth."

Vera's jaw dropped. "And the text messages?"

Eve winced as if Vera had landed a blow. "Like I said, I had to be sure you were taking the possibility of other suspects seriously."

Vera rubbed at her forehead. "No more. Got it? No more!"

Eve held up her hands in surrender. "I promise."

Vera narrowed her gaze, anger stirring. "You didn't have anything to do with this intruder, did you?"

"No! Oh my God, do you think I'm crazy?"

Vera sent her a pointed look that said she didn't want to hear the answer to that one. "I have to call Bent about this break-in."

As she opened her contacts, she started a mental inventory of what she remembered about the intruder. Taller than her. Heavier, muscular. Smelled . . . like an aftershave she'd encountered before. Something unique. She couldn't call the one to mind just now, but she would in time.

She made the call, and while they waited for Bent to arrive, they looked for the point of entry. The front door had been locked when Vera arrived.

"He could have unlocked the back door," Eve said. "It's an old lock."

"True," Vera agreed. She checked both the locks, front and back, spotted no indications of forced entry. "Unless I left it unlocked this morning, which is entirely possible. If not, the intruder either came in through a window or he had a key."

"I haven't given anyone a key," Eve said, as if the statement was an accusation. "I know I've done some stupid stuff in my time, but I've never given away a house key."

Vera opted not to go there just now.

Her concern was the motive for the break-in. "Why would anyone think there was something in Daddy's room?" Vera didn't get it. Although their family was reasonably financially secure, they weren't rich. There were no family jewels or precious metals hidden in the house.

"Maybe it was a reporter," Eve suggested. "You said that was your first thought. Maybe he hoped to find a journal or something."

Vera laughed, a not-so-kind sound. "Can you see Sheree having a journal?"

Eve smirked. "That's a hard no. And we both know Daddy wouldn't have been journaling."

"But," Vera supposed, "if it was a reporter, he wouldn't have any way of knowing this."

"You're pretty sure it was a he," Eve said.

"I am. And I think I recognized his aftershave."

A rap at the front door announced Bent's arrival.

Just to be certain, Vera checked out the window first, then opened the door. It would be just like Patricia Patton to show up unannounced again. The memory of her tall, broad-shouldered cameraman had Vera trying to recall if she'd gotten close enough to smell his aftershave. She didn't think so.

Bent walked in, closed the door, and looked from Vera to Eve and back. "What happened?"

"Come with me." Vera grabbed him by the arm and started for the stairs. Her hip complained, but she ignored it as she focused on repeating the details of her encounter with the intruder.

Eve followed, but stalled at the door as they walked into the ransacked bedroom.

"You said he was wearing gloves."

Vera nodded. "Looking for prints or anything else is likely a waste of time. I'm thinking I must have interrupted him before he found whatever he was looking for, because his hands were empty. There was no bag or backpack."

"Okay then." Bent surveyed her. "You're sure you're okay?"

"I'll be sore, but nothing is broken." She hugged her arms around herself, feeling vulnerable. Maybe it was Bent's slow perusal, or maybe the confrontation with the intruder was catching up with her. Charging him the way she had wasn't exactly smart, no matter that she hadn't spotted a weapon.

Bent removed his hat and ran his fingers through his hair, his gaze roving the room now. "Any ideas as to what he may have been looking for?"

"Vera thinks he was looking for a journal," Eve said, stepping into the room. "He may have thought Sheree left one."

Bent eyed her for a moment. "I'm thinking he was more interested in a journal one of you—or maybe Luna—might have."

Eve and Vera shared a look. "Did you ever do any journaling?" Vera asked.

Eve moved her head side to side. "No. You didn't, either, did you?"

"Not since I was like twelve. What about Luna?" Vera had been gone for most of Luna's posttoddler life. She really had no concrete idea what the girl had done during her adolescent years.

Eve shrugged. "Maybe. She was always very private about her thoughts, so if she did, I didn't know anything about it."

"I'm posting a security detail," Bent said. "I should have already."

That was his guilt talking. Besides, Vera didn't want an extra pair of ears around listening unless there was no other choice. She suggested, "I really don't want to be diverting resources. Maybe we should just get a security system."

Eve nodded. "That would probably be better."

"As long as you get it today—tomorrow at the latest," Bent said, "I'm good with that."

"I'll call someone," Eve said. She stared at the floor a moment, then reluctantly met Bent's gaze. "I'm sorry about what I did." She glanced at Vera before turning back to him. "I was afraid y'all were just going to try and blame this on Daddy and wouldn't look for anyone else."

"You should know me better than that, Eve," Bent said. "I've known your family for a very long time. I would never take the easy way out or try and blame your father for something he didn't do."

"I know. I'm sorry. I'll pay for the damages, and I'll even apologize to Mr. Carmichael." Eve shrugged. "I was going to ask if I could do it anonymously, but I should just bite the bullet and make it right."

Bent smiled. "I'm glad to hear it." To Vera, he said, "When we're finished up here, we'll go to the cave. You've been asking for access. I can give you that now. Conover and his guys are done. The Feds will be on site later today or early tomorrow. It's now or . . . way later."

"Great." Vera needed to see the scene firsthand. Pictures were better than nothing but never as good as the real thing. No matter that she'd been in that cave as a kid, memories sometimes took on a life of their own. Changed, expanded. She wasn't sure what she hoped to learn, but she had to try.

The front door opened, and Vera jumped.

Luna stood in the doorway, looking from one to the next. "What's going on?"

Vera ushered her inside and explained about the intruder.

"Do you know if he took anything?"

"We can't be sure."

"Oh my God. I need to check everything." Luna rushed up the stairs.

Eve sighed. "I'll see if she needs any help."

When the two had disappeared down the upstairs hall, Bent turned to Vera. "So you're good with Eve's explanation?"

"I can see her trying to protect Daddy. She was so young when Mama died. She wouldn't have wanted to lose him under any circumstances." She laughed, a dry, humorless attempt. "I, on the other hand, might have been more than happy to send him up the river."

"We do that when we're teenagers," he reminded her. "Draw away. It's part of the process of becoming independent."

"Yeah, well anyway, I find it a reasonable—however not very well-thought-out—explanation." Vera shook her head. "I really worry about her. Between all that happened when Mama died and later, the drugs and drinking, it's possible she's a little behind the curve with emotional development. It's not unusual to find some level of immaturity in those circumstances."

He glanced toward the stairs, and Vera had the sudden impression there was something more he wanted to say.

"Is there news from the scene or the lab?" she asked.

By now the remains were likely all at the crime lab in Nashville, though she felt confident there had not been enough time for autopsies.

"Nothing they're sharing. You know the TBI, they're like the Feds, they don't like to share on anyone else's timeline."

Vera shook her head. "I've always found that so strange. After all, they are here to assist the local police, and somehow they always wind up taking over and setting the locals aside."

"The intruder didn't take anything from my room," Luna announced as she and Eve descended the stairs. "He wouldn't have figured out where I kept my journal in a million years."

231

"That's for sure," Eve commented.

Vera didn't ask. "I'm glad your things were secure."

As Luna came down the final step, her jaw dropped. "Oh my gosh, I almost forgot to tell you." She looked from Vera to Eve and then to Bent. "A woman who lives in Huntsville called me."

Huntsville was just across the state line in Alabama. Vera hoped it wasn't another reporter.

"She claims she was a friend of my mother," Luna went on. "She wants to meet with us. She says she has information that might help with the case."

Now there was the kind of news Vera liked to hear. Sheree never really appeared to have any female friends—at least not locally. Maybe all her friends had been in Huntsville, where the bigger nightclubs were.

"I can follow up," Bent offered. "Make sure she's legit before we invite her for a meeting."

"I think that's a very good idea," Vera agreed.

"For sure," Eve seconded. "Because . . ."

The way her eyes rounded told Vera that she realized what she was about to say would be hurtful to Luna.

"Well," Eve said, "a lot of women were jealous of Sheree—she was so beautiful and everything. I wouldn't want some stranger to say something hurtful just because they were jealous."

Luna made a sad face. "Oh, Eve." She hugged her sister, who looked pained, as usual, at the gesture. "You are so thoughtful. Thank you. I never even thought of that." She drew back and turned to Bent. "Her name is Teresa Russ. I'll send you her cell phone number. I would really appreciate you checking up on who she is."

"Be glad to," Bent confirmed.

Teresa Russ. The name didn't ring a bell for Vera, but if she was a friend of Sheree's, there was one thing Vera knew for sure. She was trouble.

27

Bent went first. Vera insisted. She really didn't want to get down on all fours and stick her butt in the air while he watched.

When he was through the opening, Vera crouched down but hesitated before going inside. The path they'd taken from the house ensured the reporters hadn't seen their arrival. There was just the uniform guarding the cave entrance nearby. The evidence collected had already been transferred to the lab. The tent was gone. Vera glanced at the deputy. She didn't know him. He only knew her by name, she suspected. She'd been gone so long, she doubted anyone under the age of thirty-five remembered her.

Hesitating was ridiculous. It wasn't like she hadn't been in there before. But it had been a long time. The possibility that Bent had finally agreed to allow her on the scene only because he wanted to show her something that would prove she was keeping secrets had crossed her mind. Now she was just being paranoid.

"Get over it," she muttered. Big breath, and she went for it. Crawled through the opening and braced for whatever would come next. Bent waited for her on the other side. He offered his hand, and she accepted the assist.

Dusting off her knees, she glanced around. The place was lit by auxiliary lights, so it didn't look the same as the last time she was here. Back then, there had been no lights except their pathetic flashlight.

Funny how light made such a difference.

It looked like a cave. With its rock ledges and worn-smooth-by-time walls and rocky, sandy floor. When they were kids and it had been mostly dark, it had felt like a scary, evil place where all manner of unknown creatures might be lurking or hidden.

The ceiling was lower than she'd realized. Funny how it all seemed so big back then.

"Sheree was here." He gestured to the ledge wall that ran a short distance on that side of the cave.

Vera stared at the ledge, flashes of memory slashing across her brain. Lifting Sheree's lifeless body. Mindlessly placing rock after rock over her. Eve rushing out of the cave to find flowers. Luna feeling so heavy on Vera's back.

She blinked the memories away. "What about the others?"

"The others were in the next cavern. The opening is over here." He hitched his head toward the other side of the space. "This way."

In the opposite corner, once you got down on your hands and knees, you could see another narrow tunnel passage.

He asked, "You want to have a look there too?"

Vera wasn't looking forward to it, but it was necessary. "Might as well."

Again, Bent led the way.

"I think," Bent said, once they were on the other side and back on their feet, "whoever put the bodies in here hoped they would never be found. Whoever left Sheree didn't seem to be so concerned about discovery."

Vera couldn't tell him that Sheree was where she was because they had been kids. Just damned kids who had been desperate and had no idea what they were doing. It hadn't seemed real . . .

"Any headway on ID'ing any of the other remains?"

"Nothing yet."

She looked around the smaller space. All those times as kids when she and Eve had played here, they had never come into this part of the cave. Vera hadn't even known it existed. There was no reason to believe Eve had either.

Standing here like this . . . with all that was happening, she felt the walls closing in on her. She felt trapped and out of options. Her career was over . . . her personal life was unraveling.

Maybe her and Eve's secret wasn't the only one in the family.

Was it actually possible her father did have something to do with this?

No. She refused to believe such a thing.

A hunter or caver—maybe the dead guy who'd been tucked in here or someone he'd known. Someone who'd found it obviously by accident and used it for his own private dumping ground. Unless there was a friend of her father's who'd taken advantage of their family.

Had her mother ever been in here?

The possibility that Eve knew things that she was keeping from Vera still terrified her. She walked closer to the ledge where the two women's remains had lain. She surveyed the area slowly, carefully, and still she almost missed it.

Her attention jerked back a few feet to the small, scattered stones . . . white stones about the size of a dollar coin. Their mother, Vera, and Eve had spent hours searching for stones like that . . . just the right size and color for artwork.

Cold flashed through her. Didn't mean anything. Those stones could have been in here already. The cave could be full of them for all she knew—she glanced around, scanned the ground—except it wasn't.

"The FBI wants to interview your father."

Vera jerked back to the present, and her gaze collided with his. "You know what they'll do. Twist his words and make him out to be the killer behind all this."

"I've told them you and your sisters will have an answer for them tomorrow." He looked around, as if needing a place for his attention to land. "If you get the doctor to go to a judge and attest that nothing your father says can reasonably be considered true or accurate, we can likely either stop the interview or have it ruled as inadmissible in court."

Vera struggled to push the stones out of her head. *Focus on his words.* It was important for her to know every step Bent and the FBI took. As for the medical opinion, she was well aware of this, but she appreciated his bringing up the possibility.

"As much as I would hate to appear like an impediment to justice," she said, "it's the only way to protect him. At this stage in his illness, we really can't know for sure that anything he says is accurate. He could confess to kidnapping the Lindbergh baby in his current state."

"You're right." Bent set his hands on his hips. "The trouble is, they won't stop until there's a break."

No good cop would. "I get it. They want to solve this thing."

"Don't we all," he said, more to himself than to Vera. Then he set his gaze solidly on her. "I'm worried about Eve. I still think she's holding back."

Okay, so this was about more than showing her the crime scene. "I'm not going down that road, Bent." She held up her hands. "We've talked about this more than once. You think I'm hiding something. You think Eve is."

Forcing her gaze straight ahead and away from where the stones lay scattered, she headed for the narrow opening that would get her the hell out of here.

"Don't do that, Vee," he said, coming up behind her, daring to put a hand on her arm. "I'm not trying to pin anything on you or Eve or your father."

She shook off his touch and rounded on him. "What happened to the two of us conducting our own parallel investigation?"

He scrubbed a hand over his jaw. "Higdon usurped our morning. You were there. As for the other, whether you want to see it or not, Eve is hiding something."

Vera damned well knew they were both hiding one big-ass secret, but there was no way in the world she could tell this man. She couldn't even tell him about those little pale stones until she knew what they meant.

So she lied. What else was there to do? "I have no idea what you're talking about."

He chuckled. "Really? I've kept up with you, too, Vee. I know just how good you are at what you do. In my humble opinion, there's no way you've missed the signs."

Humble? Ha! The man didn't have a humble bone in his body.

"You're right." She summoned all the anger simmering inside her. "I wouldn't miss the signs. So maybe you're just seeing what you need to see to close your case. I'm fairly certain all eyes are on you right now. 'Will he be able to see the truth when it comes to his former lover? Will he see that justice is served? Can he really fill Walt Fraley's shoes?'"

He bowed his head in acknowledgment. "Now those were some seriously low blows."

"Our father did not murder anyone," Vera snapped, tired of this back and forth. "Eve and Luna didn't murder anyone."

He looked at her then. No, not looked at . . . looked *inside* her. "Whatever you think you know, understand this: They're going to dissect the lives of everyone around these remains," he insisted, as if she didn't know how these things were done. "They're going to question every single person who knew Sheree and the other vics, as soon as they've been identified. And then they'll go after anyone close to them. Because they will conclude exactly what I have: whoever did this did not do it alone, and they were familiar with this cave."

"I am well versed in how the FBI works, so my advice," she offered, "is to do your best to find what you need to find. The problem is, you're not going to find it where you're looking."

She had nothing else to say. Not to him or to anyone else.

For Vera the real trouble in this tangled mess was the extra sets of remains. There was no way a killer brought remains all the way out here without some idea of where he intended to plant them.

An organized killer didn't work that way, and this killer had definitely been organized.

Whoever took the lives of these victims knew about the cave . . . obviously knew her parents and the farm.

That meant only one thing to Vera: it had to be someone close to them.

28

Bent braked to a stop and turned to Vera. "You sure you want to do this?"

Vera got it that he really didn't want to. He'd thrown out that question already when she first mentioned the idea. They walked away from the cave, and she asked—no, demanded—to see former Sheriff Fraley. Maybe the request came at that moment only to get under Bent's skin after the way he'd grilled her, or maybe all his queries had been a reminder of things she didn't want to examine too closely. Either way, this was something she needed to do.

And if he was intent on clearing her family as he said, he needed this as much as she did.

"Why wouldn't I?" She angled her head and pointed a questioning glare at him. "Is there some reason I shouldn't?"

She had spoken to Beatrice earlier today. She'd seemed eager to help. The former sheriff had been resting. Hopefully, he was up by now and Beatrice had discussed Vera's request with him.

Bent shoved the gear shift into Park. "I guess not."

He was frustrated, maybe even a little angry. *Join the club.*

She opened her door and got out. Without waiting for him, she strode toward the house. Walter "Walt" and Beatrice Fraley owned a sizable property with a couple of barns, a big old farmhouse, and a half dozen or so cows grazing in a distant pasture. Massive trees shaded the house. Flowers bloomed all around the porch. Beatrice's doing, probably. The woman had always kept a vase of flowers on her desk every day at school. She and Vera's mother had that in common. The truck that had been in the drive earlier was gone now. Vera hoped that was no indication the Fraleys weren't home. She needed that list. Hopefully, there had been time for Beatrice to speak with her husband about Vera's request.

Today's visit with Beatrice had been relaxed and friendly, the way Vera remembered her former teacher. When she and Florence had delivered that casserole, however, Vera had sensed something troubling Beatrice. She'd obviously been uncomfortable with the way her friend had conducted herself. Vera's gut clenched when she thought of Florence Higdon. Like her husband and son, the judge, the woman was utterly full of herself. But she was Luna's boss—one who would be retiring soon. Luna loved her work at the library. She would be stepping into that position. Vera did not want to do anything to screw that up for her.

Vera waited at the front door until Bent caught up with her. When he did, she gestured to the door for him to knock. Since she had told him about the earlier visit, she didn't understand why he was so hesitant about this one.

His gaze sticking to hers, he opened the screen door and knocked on the wood one behind it. He kept that steady watch on her until a voice on the other side of the door shouted, "It's unlocked. Come on in."

Maybe Bent worried his presence would make the visit feel like an interrogation.

Whatever his hesitation, he opened the door and waited for her to step inside first. She walked past him and into the long narrow hall.

"In here," the feeble voice called.

Vera was startled at how weak the man's voice sounded. She entered the room on the left, where he waited in a wheelchair. Like her father,

Walter Fraley had aged far beyond his years. But then, ill health did that. Multiple sclerosis was a hideous disease. The frail man before her was proof.

"Sheriff Fraley." She smiled. "You remember me? Vera Boyett."

"How could I forget you?" He chuckled, then coughed. "You'll have to excuse me for not standing." He gestured to the chair.

"I understand, sir."

"Bent." Fraley gave him a nod of acknowledgment. "Y'all have a seat."

"Thanks for seeing us without notice, Walt." Bent waited for Vera to sit first.

Fraley chuckled. "It's not like my calendar is full."

Vera perched on the edge of the sofa nearer to Fraley. His wheelchair was parked next to a side table only a few feet away.

Bent settled at the other end, giving her much-appreciated space.

"I was sorry to hear," Fraley began, "about Sheree. Course this is the outcome I expected when she first went missing."

"You never considered the possibility that she ran off with another man?" Vera was interested in the former sheriff's reasons for the conclusion.

Fraley contemplated her for a moment. "I did, of course, but deep down it didn't feel right. Mostly because she had it made with your daddy. He gave her anything she wanted and seemed oblivious to her running around."

This was accurate, for the most part. Toward the end there had been some arguing between the two, generally instigated by Sheree.

"Did Beatrice mention that she and I talked this morning while you were resting?"

He frowned. "She didn't, but then at our age things slip our minds more easily than they once did."

Regret and frustration nudged Vera, but she let it slide. No need to press the issue.

"Can you walk me through your investigation?" Vera asked. Bent shifted his position, and she glanced at him. "Bent has gone over some of it with me, but not the finer details."

He didn't look at her, kept his attention on Fraley. Just as well, he wouldn't have liked the look she fired back.

"When Sheree didn't come home that first night," Fraley said, "Vernon came to see me. I told him we needed to give her another day to see if she showed up before we panicked."

Her father had panicked anyway. He'd searched all night. She and Eve were scared to death. They both had to miss school the next day to take care of Luna. Then they had the weekend to figure something out for the baby. Their father was in no condition to do anything for his daughters, not even baby Luna. Beatrice arranged a rotating lineup of sitters among her ladies group from church. Vera appreciated the help, but the sympathetic and sometimes judgmental looks from the volunteers were not what they needed. The unpleasant attitudes hadn't bothered Vera as much as they had Eve. She'd been devastated by all of it.

Understandable, given what had happened in that bathroom.

"Vernon and I," Fraley went on, "discussed anyone who might be considered close to Sheree or a friend, but to tell the truth, she didn't really have any friends. Most of the women in town didn't like her for reasons I'm sure you're aware of."

As Fraley spoke, Bent checked the screen on his cell phone, then stood and walked out of the room.

Vera's gut knotted. Probably something else about the case.

Strong-arming her attention back to the former sheriff, she asked, "What about this Garth Rimmey?" Vera vaguely recalled him coming to the house once and arguing with Sheree. Her father wasn't home, but Vera called him. Afterward, she wished she hadn't. The two, her father and Rimmey, argued fiercely. They didn't come to blows, but Vera and Eve were terrified. Evidently their father had called Sheriff Fraley en route, and he showed up just in time.

"I grilled that man," Fraley said with a shaky nod. "I even kept him in holding for nearly seventy-two hours. Nowadays you couldn't get away with that without an arrest, but things were a little different back then. He got himself a lawyer and complained that we'd tried to beat a confession out of him, but the truth is, he was all beat up when we picked him up."

The memory of a hushed conversation between her father and the sheriff whispered through her mind. The sheriff demanding to know if her father was sure and him insisting that if Rimmey had known anything, he would have talked.

"Don't you just hate the ones who do that sort of thing." Vera smiled, no matter that the remark was a bit on the sarcastic side. Fraley or one of his deputies had likely beat the hell out of Rimmey. Then again, she supposed it could have been her father. He had been out searching for Sheree that whole night after she disappeared.

Not that Vera had any sympathy for the scumbag either way, but there were laws protecting those suspected of crimes. No matter how undeserving.

You mean like you, a little voice said. Vera dismissed it. She hadn't committed a serious crime . . . she'd only cleaned up after what might have been one. No. It was an accident.

"You're satisfied," Vera asked, moving on, "with the people you interviewed and the extent to which you went to determine what happened to Sheree?"

"I am. We interviewed all your neighbors. All the shopkeepers and folks around town who might have had reason to run into Sheree. A few husbands and boyfriends who preferred to stay anonymous to prevent their wives and girlfriends from learning about their bad behavior—Bent won't have found statements in the file from those. As long as they had an alibi I could confirm, I respected their requests for privacy." He gave a solemn nod. "Your daddy even offered a reward to anyone who could provide information leading to an arrest. A few came forward with stories, but none that survived close scrutiny."

Vera had forgotten about the reward. Ten thousand dollars. A lot of money in those days. Not exactly a pittance now.

"What about my father?" Vera ventured. "Did you have any reason whatsoever to believe he might be involved in her disappearance?"

Fraley shook his head. "None at all. I've never seen a man more devastated over the loss of his wife. Still, I didn't let him off so easy. I've seen a few who can fake devastation. Not on that level, still I did my due diligence. I checked with his coworkers. He was at work the day Sheree disappeared. Went in at eight that morning and didn't leave until just past five."

He'd come home at 5:30 p.m. Eve had been terrified that he would recognize they were lying about not having seen Sheree that afternoon. Turned out, they were convincing enough. He'd never appeared to doubt their story.

"A month later we'd all concluded that—as long as she was still breathing—she'd left and didn't want to be found."

"But now," Vera said, "you know that wasn't the case."

"I'm sorry to say that's right."

"Looking back," Vera said, "would you have done anything differently?"

Fraley's wrinkled brow furrowed deeper in concentration as his gaze turned distant. After at least thirty endless seconds pounded out in her veins, he blinked, set his gaze back on hers. "Not one thing."

In Vera's opinion, that was saying something. Apparently she and Eve had been better at covering up what really happened than she'd realized.

"What about the other remains found in the cave?" she ventured. "Was there anyone who went missing in the two or three years before Sheree? Or in the past five years? Another case that was never solved?"

Fraley gave a wobbly shake of his head. "I can confidently say that Sheree was the only unsolved missing persons case we had in this county during my tenure as sheriff."

"A fine record," Vera said. He'd been a good sheriff. Her parents had always spoken highly of him.

"Just doing my job."

"When I spoke to Beatrice," Vera went on, "I asked her to put together a list of my parents' friends. I'm hoping to talk to anyone close enough to have known about the cave. She was going to speak with you to get your input."

"I'm sure she will. She had to run out this afternoon. As you can imagine, she has to work around my needs for most everything."

Vera understood. It was a difficult situation. "Do you recall anyone who might have been that close to my parents?"

He pondered her question for a good long while. Maybe a whole minute. Felt like ten. "Well," he began, "to the best of my knowledge, your mama and daddy had two sets of close friends. Me and Beatrice and Charles and Florence. No one else that I know of were so close. But the two had many friends, to be sure. I'm just not sure any of those folks were close enough to have had your daddy or your mama covering for murder, if that's what you're looking for."

Not exactly the answer Vera had hoped for. "What about helpers? Maybe someone who did work around the house or the farm? Cut the hay? Someone like that may have known about the cave."

Walt bent forward, rubbed at his forehead. He'd obviously lost the ability to reach upward. When he raised up again, he said, "No one who comes to mind right off. Your daddy had horses at one time, which prevented the need to cut the pastures for hay. He never allowed any hunting, so I'm guessing the answer is no. He and your mother took care of the maintenance around the house. Does that mean there wasn't somebody who snooped around and found the cave? Course not. Folks do things they aren't supposed to do all the time."

Vera exhaled a breath of disappointed exhaustion. "Thank you, Sheriff Fraley. I suppose I'm grasping at straws."

"You should call me Walt, Vee. I've known you since before you were born."

"Walt," she repeated, somehow managing a smile. "I appreciate your time."

"Talk to Bea again and to Florence," he suggested. "They knew all the gossip on everyone—still do." He laughed, then coughed long and hard for the effort. "If someone was close enough to one of your parents to know about the cave, those two could tell you. They know everything that happens around here. They were my go-to informants for local gossip." He frowned then. "When Sheree went missing was the one and only time those two seemed to fall down on the job." He smiled sadly. "I suppose everyone gets it wrong sometimes. In fact, they were so wrong I warned them that I'd better never hear any such rumor floating around town."

Vera hesitated. Part of her didn't want to ask . . . but she had to know. "The ladies had a scenario about who was responsible for Sheree's disappearance that they shared with you?"

"Oh yeah." He nodded. "But I don't think you're going to like it."

"I need to know," she assured him.

He gave a wobbly nod. "They were both convinced it was you girls."

29

As Bent parked in the drive next to her SUV, Vera realized she hadn't spoken since they left Fraley's home. Each time she'd considered asking a question or making a comment based on that unexpected disclosure from Walt, she just couldn't bring herself to open that door.

They were both convinced it was you girls.

Beatrice and Florence had suspected she and Eve were responsible for Sheree's disappearance. They'd believed this so strongly they had gone to Walt about it.

How in the world had they come to that conclusion? And why the hell had she asked? It was the sort of information you couldn't unhear . . . and it was too damned close to the truth.

"While you were interrogating Fraley, I received a call from Conover."

Bent's voice startled her. Vera shook off the disturbing thoughts. *Conover.* His lead forensic guy. She steeled herself for even worse news. He hadn't told her what the call was about. By the time he'd come back inside, she had heard Walt's damning statement and wanted to leave before the man could repeat it for Bent. Then she'd been lost in thought on the drive here.

Why hadn't Beatrice said anything to her today? This was not the sort of thing she should have kept to herself. It just didn't make sense.

Vera steadied herself and cleared her throat. "Judging by how long you were outside, there must be an important development." She didn't even want to hazard a guess. The shit just kept getting deeper.

"The school ring the male vic was wearing belonged to a Norton Gates of Huntsville. Fifty-four at the time of his disappearance. Divorced. A teacher at Huntsville High School, as well as a professor at Calhoun College. Gates was reported missing in May three years ago by his girlfriend."

Vera had never heard the name. Huntsville was the largest city in Alabama and only thirty miles south of Fayetteville. Known as the Rocket City because of its ties to NASA, it was also a university town and had garnered the nickname the MIT of the South. A good many of Lincoln County's residents worked in Huntsville. Plenty of others attended university there.

Vera struggled to focus on the appropriate response. "Is there anyone, a family, the girl who reported him missing, you can talk to about who he might have known in this area?" Sounded plausible to her. They could be looking for one of his students, a coworker . . . a friend who killed him and tucked him into that cave. Someone with ties in Fayetteville obviously. Eric would likely be calling with the same information. Vera was going to need another favor from him. Maybe two.

But that wasn't her biggest worry at the moment.

"I'm working on that," Bent told her.

The tone of his voice drew her eyes to him. She stared at his profile. Followed his gaze forward. There was nothing to look at other than the trees and scattered blooms in the landscape. Whatever was on his mind, he didn't want to look at her when he spit it out.

Good God, what else? Maybe he'd already known what Walt told her.

When the silence lingered, she demanded, "What?"

He turned, his eyes searching hers. "You know the likelihood that this doesn't involve your family or someone close to your family is practically nil at this point."

How well she knew, and still cold enveloped her at hearing the words from him.

"When you find evidence to prove your theory, let me know." She reached for the door handle.

He put his hand on her arm but didn't speak again until she met his gaze. "We can't stop this thing. I'm not sure we can even slow it down. You need to be prepared for the worst."

"What the hell does that mean?" If he had something to say, he should just say it.

"I think you know what I mean."

"You now have another potential suspect," she snapped. "Maybe this Gates was a serial killer, and the women in that cave were his victims. Maybe someone figured it out and had their revenge and tucked him into that cave?" It wasn't impossible. Damn it.

"Based on what we know about Gates so far, I'd say that's a long shot. Particularly in Sheree's case. The personal items found with her remains don't exactly fit."

He was right, damn it. But rather than respond, Vera opened the door and climbed out. She walked, ignoring the pain in her hip, straight to her front door without looking back. His eyes on her had her skin feeling as if it would catch fire. Thankfully the door was unlocked, preventing her from having to dig for a key. She escaped inside and closed and locked the door.

Who the hell was Norton Gates?

A clatter from the direction of the kitchen snapped her to attention.

Was someone here? Luna's car wasn't outside. Eve's was still in the shop. She'd mentioned staying with Suri.

But the door had been unlocked . . .

If there was another intruder.

A figure appeared in the doorway. Vera's breath stuck deep in her lungs.

Eve.

Peanut butter sandwich in one hand, a Coke in the other, Eve stared at her. "You okay?"

Vera's muscles went so lax she almost wilted to the floor. "Damn it, Eve. You're supposed to keep the door locked."

"Sorry." She tore off a bite of her sandwich and started to chew.

It wasn't until that moment that Vera realized she was starving. "I need one of those."

Eve swallowed with effort. "Come on. I'll make you one."

Vera followed her sister to the kitchen. She quickly prepared a sandwich, placed it on a paper towel, and then rounded up a cold can of cola.

Once Vera had settled at the table and the meal was in front of her, she announced the latest news. "They've ID'd the male victim."

She took a bite of her sandwich and instantly felt her body relaxing. Peanut butter sandwiches weren't at the top of her favorite foods list, but it was food, and she was starving.

"Do we know him?" Eve sipped her cola.

Vera shook her head. "Never heard of him. Norton Gates from Huntsville. Teacher."

Eve blinked. "How'd he die?"

Vera took another bite and chewed for a bit before answering. "Same as the others, head trauma. At least that's the preliminary finding."

"But you said he wasn't like the others. Not posed or whatever."

"He was more or less stuffed into a crevice. The way the killer disposed of the body spoke volumes about the emotional tie. He was angry with him. Disgusted." Maybe because whoever killed him knew him to be a murderer. She needed Bent to seriously consider that possibility. And he would. She knew this.

Eve's eyebrows reared up. "You got all that from the way he was buried?"

Vera shrugged. "Every action tells a story. You just have to take the time to read it closely enough." She frowned. "Didn't you say you were staying with Suri until your car was fixed?"

"I changed my mind." She downed the last of her soft drink. "Things are getting too interesting around here. It's like a streaming family drama. I can't wait for the next episode."

Vera studied her sandwich, felt abruptly overfull. Her sister was right in that this thing kept stacking up the episodes. Each time a phone rang, she tensed. Would this be another set of remains discovered on their property? Or some other element that made her family look guilty?

"Bent thinks the FBI will go for pinning Sheree's death on someone in the family. I'm guessing Daddy." The bread and peanut butter turned into a hard lump in Vera's belly.

"If you set aside the fact that he's our father," Eve said, "and you put your analyst hat on, what do you think?"

Vera sipped her drink, hoped the sugar would brace her. "If I didn't know what I know about Sheree, I would tend to agree—simply based on the facts we have so far. This is his property. The cave is not a place easily found. Sheree was his wife. She cheated."

Eve finished off her sandwich. "Or maybe Daddy allowed someone else to put his kills there. To protect that person. You know, a favor for a friend."

This was not a far-fetched scenario for sure. They had talked about how someone outside the family could have used the cave as a dumping place. What they hadn't discussed, though Vera had considered it, was the possibility that their father or mother had been protecting that someone.

"But Walt Fraley says the only really close friends of Mama and Daddy were him and his wife and the Higdons. He said there were never any farmhands, no handymen. No one. And, honestly, I think he would know."

"Maybe it was Sheree," Eve offered. "Maybe she killed the competition."

Vera made a face. "Can you see Sheree dragging a body into that cave?"

Eve poked her thumb into her chest, then pointed a finger at Vera. "We did."

"Anyway," Vera countered, opting not to respond to the comment, "the timeline is wrong for that to be a legitimate scenario. Sheree and her boyfriend Rimmey had no reason to know anything about this family until she set her sights on our daddy, and that was years later."

"So, we're screwed." Eve propped her elbows on the table and plunked her head into her hands.

"Maybe more than we know." Vera had at first thought she might not mention this to Eve, but it was best if they stayed completely open with each other. "Sheriff Fraley—Walt—said that the wives, Beatrice and Florence, always knew everything. They were his go-to informants for the gossip in Fayetteville."

Eve harrumphed. "They don't call Mrs. Higdon 'the Radio' for nothing."

There was that. "Anyway, he insisted they were never wrong. Whatever info or theory they passed along always panned out . . . except once. When Sheree died."

A frown furrowed across Eve's brow. "I'm assuming they had a theory."

Vera nodded. "They were convinced it was us—you and me."

Her sister's eyes rounded. "Are you fucking serious?"

"I am really fucking serious."

"What did Bent say?"

"Thank God he was outside taking a call at the time." The thought stopped Vera. "But, I'm guessing Walt has told him this already. Which would explain why he's always asking if we're hiding something." Or maybe he hadn't and only told Vera because Bent was not around.

"So what do we do?"

"We both know what happened to Sheree," Vera said. "We stick with our story. It's the others that we need to figure out. I swear, my gut—my instincts—are telling me that one, probably our father, or both of our parents may have helped out a friend. It's making more and more sense."

Eve eyed her for a moment. "You really think that's a possibility?"

"It's the only one that makes sense—beyond the idea that some random person just happened to find the cave and start using it as his dump site. Maybe this Norton Gates."

"I guess you're right." Her sister picked up her cell and started to scroll.

Vera hated this feeling that there was a wall or a door between them at pivotal moments like this . . . that there was more Eve needed to say but wouldn't for whatever reason. When she started scrolling on her phone, she was done.

"I really need you to tell me," Vera urged, "if you recall anything I should know. Any little thing. It could be important, and you just don't realize it. Something you saw one of them do or overheard one of them say. We need to be ahead of anything that might be found by the FBI."

"I get it," Eve snapped. Then she took a breath. "Look, we've been over this. I've told you all I know." She frowned at her phone. "Shoot. Gotta go. Suri needs my help with a late arrival. She's waiting for me outside." She tucked her phone away. "We do that sometimes. Help each other out when a late one comes in and the family needs them ready to go ASAP."

"You're coming back tonight, right?" Vera certainly hoped she was. This thing had just escalated to critical. "I was thinking we might look through photo albums and see if anything sparks a memory."

"Can we do that tomorrow night?" Eve was backing out of the kitchen. "If I make it back tonight it'll be late."

"Okay. Tomorrow then."

"For sure."

Eve pivoted but then faced Vera once more. "The security people can't come until next week. Bent won't like it."

Vera waved her off. "I'll tell him." *Eventually.*

"Thanks." Eve hurried away.

"Lock the door," Vera called after her.

She sat for a moment. Listened to the sound of emptiness in the house. Tried to ignore the numerous voices urging her to see what she did not want to see. Then she straightened.

She had research to do. Who was Norton Gates? Who was Teresa Russ? How did they play into all this?

Who could her parents have been helping? And why the hell hadn't Beatrice warned her about how she and Florence Higdon had felt when Sheree disappeared?

Vera found her courage and took the fastest, most reliable route for part of what she needed. She put through another call to Eric.

"Vera," he said in greeting. "I was just about to call you about *God*."

She laughed. "I just found out he's Norton Gates."

"Your locals work fast."

She smiled. "They had a head start. Look"—she moved around the table and gathered their dinner remains as she talked—"I know I said I needed just one more favor, but I actually need another."

He laughed. "Any time, any place, lady. I am always available."

A flutter in her chest made her just a little sad. He was such a nice guy. Maybe she'd made a mistake not going to that next level with him. Bent immediately appeared in her head, and she dismissed his image, as well as the entire notion.

"I need everything you can find on our Norton Gates and also on a Teresa Russ, both of Huntsville, Alabama. And, Eric, I need it yesterday."

"You got it."

Vera needed answers . . . it was the only way to protect her family.

30

Friday, July 26

Boyett Farm
Good Hollow Road, Fayetteville, 5:50 a.m.

A sound hummed in Vera's head. She told herself to open her eyes, but her body wasn't cooperating. She needed to sleep . . . to stay in this warm place . . .

The buzzing sounded again.

Her eyes fluttered open.

The vibration against wood had her gaze moving toward the bed-side table. The screen of her cell phone was lit up.

Someone was calling.

Pushing further out of sleep's hold, she reached toward the nuisance. She hadn't slept well last night—all week for that matter. She was fairly certain it had no longer been last night when she finally drifted off. More like some point this morning.

Phone in hand, she studied the screen. Bent's name and face stared back at her.

She accepted the call and pressed the phone to her ear. "Hey." What time was it?

Several cold hard facts battered their way into her consciousness at once. Human remains. The cave. Lies. Secrets.

Her career was over.

She flopped onto her back, snatched the hair out of her eyes.

What the hell now?

"I'm sorry to have to wake you," Bent said.

"No." She cleared her throat. "I was awake. Just lying here." What a lie. Her own voice gave away that one. "What's going on?"

"I'm at the cemetery." A breath hissed across the connection. "Your mama, Vee. A court order prevented me from stopping the exhumation."

Vera bolted to a sitting position. A sharp twinge in her hip reminded her of the intruder, but there was no time to worry about that now. "I'll be right there."

She ended the call and grabbed her clothes from where they'd landed on the floor last night. She dragged on the jeans and slid her feet into her shoes. She frowned at the wrinkled tee. Maybe there was something she could wear in her closet.

Her head ached. Her chest and hip were sore. She needed coffee. No time. She opened the door to her closet and snatched the tee on the first hanger, tugged it on, and rounded up her bag. A quick pee, then she ran the brush through her hair and headed out.

It wasn't until she was downstairs that she realized she should tell her sisters she was leaving. No time.

Vera had to get to that damned cemetery. Her sisters and coffee would have to wait.

Rose Hill Cemetery
Washington Street, Fayetteville, 6:15 a.m.

She was too late.

The lift was already drawing the coffin from the vault.

Vera slammed her SUV door and stormed in that direction. The numerous vehicles lining the narrow street had forced her to park a block up and walk back.

Reporters shouted questions at her as she marched toward the gate. *Vera, why are they exhuming your mother? Vera, do they consider your father a suspect? Vera, did you know your father killed your stepmother? Did he kill your mother too? What's happening with the investigation in Memphis?*

She ignored them all, no matter that they made her blood boil even hotter. She was very good at ignoring the questions that couldn't be answered at a given time.

Not to mention that if she opened her mouth to say something to one of them, there was no telling what sort of fury would lash out. Anytime your emotions were out of control, it was better to say nothing at all. A single misspoken or slipped word could cause irreparable damage.

A police officer, Fayetteville City judging by his uniform, stepped in front of her at the gate. "I'm sorry, ma'am, but you can't come into the cemetery right now."

Vera didn't need a mirror to know her face had contorted with the rage now bubbling over. She opened her mouth to launch a tirade, but thankfully Bent appeared.

"Let her through," he said to the officer.

"Sorry, ma'am." The officer stepped aside.

Now that she'd had to stop, Vera couldn't seem to set herself back into motion. Her gaze was glued to the movements at her mother's grave . . . her mind was a hurricane of thoughts and emotions. No. No. No.

They can't do this . . . the little girl in her cried.

Except they could . . . the woman trained in law enforcement understood. Higdon wanted it, and no doubt, his son who just happened to be a judge had given him the permission he needed or had a colleague attend to it.

Bent's fingers wrapped around her upper arm and gently ushered her along. She stumbled but somehow managed to follow his lead. This should not be happening. Her mother was innocent in all this. It was wrong to disturb her.

The thoughts were emotional, childish . . . but Vera felt like that little girl right now. *Oh, Mama, I'm so sorry about all this.*

The logical, trained part of her recognized that putting Higdon's foolish accusations to rest was a step forward. As difficult as this was, it was best to get it over with and move on. But she didn't have to make it easy or like it.

Bent pulled her to the far side of the official activity, away from the prying eyes of the reporters. A final glimpse of the line of people along the cemetery fence warned that many of those gathered were lookie-loos. People who perhaps knew one of her sisters or her father. People who would never forget—no matter the outcome of this investigation—the threads of criminal accusation that went with this official act.

Luna would be mortified.

Not that Vera wasn't, but she and Eve weren't totally innocent in all this and had no right to feel personally affronted by the ramifications of their own actions. Luna was completely innocent. Their mother was innocent.

That was a definite oversimplification, but Vera wasn't thinking straight. She needed coffee. Another life.

"I know you're upset, Vee," Bent was saying.

She shifted her focus to him, and he made a surprised face. "Maybe *upset* isn't the right word," he amended.

Vera pulled free of his hold on her arm. "Where the hell is Higdon?" He was the one she wanted to yell at. This wasn't Bent's doing.

"Vee, he's not here." He nodded toward the two suits standing next to Fayetteville Police Chief Ray Teller. "Those are FBI agents."

Like she didn't recognize an FBI agent when she saw one, but she kept the comment to herself.

"This is bigger than us now."

As if someone had pulled the plug in the bathtub, all the anger and ferocity suddenly drained out of Vera. She wilted. The urge to cry was a palpable force. But she refused to give anyone in or around this damned cemetery snippets for their wagging tongues or their bylines. Damn it all to hell.

She took one last look at her mother's coffin, and her heart lurched. "I need to get out of here."

Without question, Bent escorted her from the cemetery. The reporters shouted the same questions, which they both ignored.

Once she was in her SUV, he hesitated before closing her door. He glanced at her chest. "Nice T-shirt."

She stared down at the tee. Her gaze zeroed in on the logo. Bon Jovi. The lyrics of the song "It's My Life" echoed in her brain. Bent had given her this tee. He didn't even like Bon Jovi, but he knew she did, and he bought the tee from a guy who had gone to a concert in Atlanta. He even claimed that Bon Jovi had autographed it. The evidence was faded, and who knew if it was real or a forgery, but back then Vera had been thrilled at the notion that the shirt had hung in the same air (meaning in the Philips Arena) that Jon Bon Jovi had breathed.

She stared straight ahead, drew in a breath. "Keep me posted about this, will you?" Her attention shifted to him. He looked worried. Tired, like her. Stressed. And too damned handsome for his or her own good. Extreme stress prompted thoughtless actions. Nothing good could come of her behaving without thought with this man. No matter how easy it would be at this pain-filled moment.

He gave her a nod. "I will."

He closed her door and she drove away. In her rearview mirror, she watched as Bent plowed back through the crowd without stopping.

She appreciated that he wasn't giving them anything.

The urge to cry was back, but what she really wanted to do was scream.

31

Vera adjusted the strap on her shoulder bag, mostly to buy time. She stood outside the door of her father's room. Visiting hours weren't until 9:00 a.m., but she'd talked her way beyond the lobby. She had considered calling Eve to see if she could come with her, but ultimately she'd made the decision to come alone.

There really was no firm reason she could pinpoint, just a feeling that she needed to speak with him alone. Needed to explain to him what was happening.

Possibly because she was terrified of what he might say, given the right prompts by anyone else.

Vera took a breath and reached for the knob. *No time like the present.*

She gave a short knock, opened the door, and stepped inside. With a big smile, she said, "Good morning, Daddy."

Vernon Boyett sat in a chair, staring at the television. The sound was so low it was nearly muted. His hands were folded in his lap. The tan-colored sweatpants and matching tee made his skin look even paler. His hair had long ago grayed, and there was far less of it than in his younger days.

A smile tugged at Vera's lips. As a little girl she could remember thinking she had the handsomest daddy in all of Lincoln County. Her mother had been beautiful as well. They'd made a gorgeous couple. How many times had Vera heard people say to her parents, "My, what a beautiful family you have."

How had everything gone so wrong? The cancer. Damn it. It had taken their mother, and their father had fallen apart. The sisters had clung together like two desperate souls lost at sea.

"I'm ready for breakfast," her father announced, his attention settling on Vera.

"It's me, Daddy. Vee," she said, walking closer. "I thought I'd drop by and see you this morning. You feeling okay?" She sat down in the chair that stood to his left and shared the same side table.

He stared at her, studied her face closely for a while, then his lips spread into a smile. His face lit as if Jesus himself had taken a seat next to him. "Evelyn, I'm so glad you came. I sure have missed you."

"Oh no, Da—" Vera stopped herself. "It's good to see you too." She held her breath, prayed her voice didn't give her away.

His expression turned anxious. "I've been so worried about what you told me." He shook his head. "What if someone finds out? I don't know what I'd do if there was trouble and you had to go away. What would the girls do?"

Fear spread through Vera's chest. What did he mean? What had her mother done? She moistened her lips and considered how to respond. "No need to worry. It's all going to be okay."

Please keep talking, Daddy.

All she needed was some idea of what the hell he was talking about. The image of those other two women's remains kept flashing in her mind like a fluorescent light going bad.

He shook his head again, tears shining in his eyes now.

Vera felt sick that she was in some way the cause of his pain.

"I can see how you thought you were doing the right thing . . ." He stared at his hands.

Vera held her breath. So often when he paused, he lost whatever he was saying or his grasp on where he was at the time.

His gaze lifted to hers once more. "I should have taken care of it."

A new tension slid through her. She clamped her teeth together to prevent herself from saying a word. To interrupt him now would be a mistake.

"I should have protected you. It was my place."

She leaned forward in anticipation of what he would say next.

He blinked. "Forgive me."

What had he done? Vera silently screamed for him to go on. When he didn't, she offered, "I forgave you a long time ago."

He smiled, the saddest expression Vera had ever seen. Her heart fractured just a little, looking at it. *Oh Daddy, what did one or both of you do?*

"Be careful," he warned, glancing around as if he feared someone might be listening. "A secret isn't a secret if anyone else knows."

Vera waited. Afraid to move . . . to breathe. Tension vibrated in the air while the seconds ticked off, and still he said nothing more. Eventually he shifted his gaze back to the television screen and that empty expression overtook his face once more.

Vera reached out, placed her hand over his. "I love you, Daddy."

His attention shifted to her, but there was no recognition there. "Yes, I'm ready for breakfast."

A few minutes were required to gather herself together and prepare to leave. When she stood to go, he didn't look up, so she left him without saying more.

Her heart ached. She hated the disease. Hated the one that had taken her mother.

She dropped by the desk and told them he wanted his breakfast, and then she hurried from the facility, the disinfectant smell suddenly overwhelming. Outside, she sat in her SUV and cried. She hadn't meant to, but she couldn't stop the flow. Damn it.

After a minute or so, Vera pulled herself together and called Eve. They had to figure out what secret their parents had been keeping.

It couldn't possibly be as bad as the one she and her sister had kept for two-plus decades. Their mother had been far too kind and good to hurt anyone. Ever.

The call went to voicemail. Which meant her sister was in the process of preparing someone. Vera left a message for Eve to call as soon as she could.

Her sister needed to know about the exhumation and . . . whatever the hell their father had been talking about.

She started the engine. Thought about going to Bent and telling him what her father said, but she couldn't. Not yet. Not until she knew more.

But she had to do something.

She had gone through the house and found nothing.

There were the barn, the chicken house, and the well house. Oh, and her mother's potting shed.

Feeling a purpose now, Vera headed for the farm.

With the discoveries in the cave, it was a miracle there hadn't already been a request to search the remainder of their property, including the house. No doubt because Bent was in charge. But the FBI was involved now. They were likely planning the search at this very moment.

Vera pressed harder on the accelerator.

Boyett Farm
Good Hollow Road, Fayetteville, 10:00 a.m.

She started with the barn.

Because it was closer to the cave, she wanted to get it done first. She found nothing but old farm tools and implements. A tractor, the lawn mower, and a whole host of yard gadgets. There were still a few old bales of hay in the loft. She checked around and under those. Heavy suckers.

She poked her head into the old shed that stood closer to the house and found nothing but her father's truck. Thankfully it was unlocked, so she had a look inside. Gas receipts, tag receipts, and little else. Then she checked the well house and the chicken house. After their mother died, the chickens had all eventually disappeared. Whether they'd been nabbed by predators or had just wandered away to another farm, Vera had no idea. At some point her father had cleaned out the chicken mansion, as her mother had called it, so going through it was easy enough.

The chicken house had actually been an old smokehouse her father had turned into a glorious home for chickens just to make her mother happy. The old coop had been a shabby little thing, not much bigger than a doghouse. The new one had been for Evelyn's thirty-fifth birthday. Vera had only been seven, but she remembered how happy her mother had been. They had danced around the yard. Eve had only been two, but she'd tried to join in and kept falling on her backside.

Her heart aching with the memories, Vera opened the door to her mother's potting shed. She probably should have looked here first, but she had recognized the task would not be an easy one. Her mother had spent so much time in this shed. She had loved it . . . touched every single thing inside.

The heat was slightly lower in the shady interior, but it was still sweltering. It smelled earthy, with an underlying hint of various fertilizers—organic ones, of course. Her mother had been very conscious of those things. She doubted her father had come back in here after her death. Vera and Eve only had once. They had sat in the middle of the floor and cried.

Evelyn's gardening tools hung on the hooks she had organized over her potting table. Every single thing, from pots to seedling trays, was in its place. Containers that held soil and other items required for gardening lined one wall. There were lots of windows. Vera touched her mother's gloves. Smiled as she traced the handle of her favorite garden trowel.

When she was able to move on, she searched the antique apothecary cabinet her mother had used for seed packets and other small items. Drawer after drawer, she picked through the contents.

When she had exhausted all possibilities, she collapsed onto the wooden stool next to the potting table. There was nothing here except the usual gardening stuff.

She reminded herself that this was the way of investigations: finding evidence was never as easy as you hoped it would be, even when all appearances suggested it should be. There were moments in every investigation when the "aha" finds came unexpectedly quickly, but there were far more moments when they came slowly and miles apart.

Vera stepped outside. The bright sun blinded her for a moment. She closed the door and used her forearm to swipe the sweat from her forehead. Surely her mother had used a fan or something when working out here. More likely she came out early, before breakfast, and did her work.

The twinge in her hip wasn't so pronounced as she walked back toward the house. She suddenly stalled. Beneath her feet, the stepping stones her mother had made by hand captured her attention. Small white stones embedded in concrete. Vera's heart stumbled. Each around the size of a dollar coin. *River rocks.* Her mother would use the white or light-colored ones around a darker one, aligning them in the pattern of a daisy. Eve and Vera had loved helping with the simple design. Evelyn had likely chosen it for that reason.

There had been several of those same stones in the cave at each place where remains had been discovered. Could have been there already, Vera argued with herself. The stones didn't mean her mother or Eve had put them there. But there hadn't been others readily visible in the cave.

Vera wilted, her gut seizing with the need to empty its contents . . . to purge from her body the very thought swimming through her brain.

She thought of the cross necklaces, the poses, and now the stones. This was simply one too many coincidences.

Vera didn't believe in coincidences. Her father's fears confirmed what Vera did not want to see.

The other remains . . . the two women . . . somehow her mother was involved. It was the only explanation. But why? Because of her father?

Had he been having an affair then too? Was Sheree not his first betrayal? Could her mother have known Norton Gates?

Jesus Christ. Her heart felt on the verge of rupturing. All of this seemed to point at her parents.

But what about the cross necklace and the stones with Sheree's remains? Her mother had already been dead when Sheree ended up in that cave.

Their father? Not likely. He'd gone to church to make Evelyn happy. Buying a cross on a chain to leave with Sheree—particularly if he'd murdered her—wasn't logical. The stones were something she and Eve had done with their mother. Vera sure as hell hadn't put them in that cave.

Eve.

Had to be. Vera had known she was hiding something.

Forcing herself to move, she headed into the house. Right now, her goal was to stay calm. In the kitchen she washed her hands and forearms, then her face. She needed a band to put her hair up, and then she needed to think this through.

Her phone pinged with an incoming text. It was about time Eve got back to her.

Not Eve. *Eric.*

Check your email. ☺

Vera opened her email app. She quickly scanned the information, her heart thudding faster and faster. Everything from Norton Gates's shoe size to his University of Alabama GPA was included. Eric had even spoken with someone at Calhoun College, and the class rosters for the fifteen years he had taught there before disappearing were waiting for pickup at the administration office.

Vera grinned. "The man is a magician."

The same detailed report about Teresa Russ filled another page. She operated a private investigation agency in Huntsville. Interesting. The possibilities as to who had hired Russ to look into Sheree's case prompted an uneasy feeling. Was Russ actually an old friend that no one had known about . . . or had someone who expected the findings to lead back to the Boyett family hired her, and the friend thing was just a cover?

Only one way to find out.

Vera sent Eric a thank-you and grabbed her bag. It was time for a road trip. She wasn't waiting for Bent to give her whatever details he chose to share. Or for him to decide they could do the parallel investigation thing.

And she wasn't waiting for Eve . . . her sister had kept a huge truth from her, and Vera would learn the reason why. But not right now.

This road trip wouldn't wait. She needed these answers before anyone else.

32

"Chief Boyett?"

Vera relaxed and managed a smile. "That's me."

It was just like Eric to use her former official title. She appreciated the acknowledgment, but more importantly the assist with research.

The woman behind the counter, young enough to be a college student herself, smiled at Vera. "I love Bon Jovi."

Thank God Vera had left a suit jacket in her SUV. Carrying one for those unexpected moments had become a habit over the years. Nothing she could have done about the worn jeans and the tee.

Vera placed a hand on her chest. "Atlanta—probably before you were born."

Telly, according to her nameplate, smiled. "If you need anything else"—she tapped the folder—"give me a call. I put my card inside. Eric said this was a very important case."

Eric. He was a charmer.

"Thank you. This will help a lot."

Telly glanced around, as if needing to ensure they were still alone. "I knew Professor Gates."

Anticipation zipped through Vera. "Really? It's a shame he went missing the way he did."

"Yeah, it was." She bit her lip. "Your colleague told me his remains may have been found."

Eric shared the details necessary for getting what he wanted. Vera knew the routine too well. "We believe so," she agreed.

"To tell you the truth, I'm not surprised. He had that god-complex thing," she said quietly, so quietly Vera barely heard her.

"How so?" Vera nudged. "Was he some sort of genius? Or saw himself as one?"

She shook her head. "He thought he was a god—sexually, I mean. Like he thought all women wanted him and should submit to him. It was totally bizarre."

Vera's instincts went on point. "Were there complaints from students or staff?"

"Nothing official. Just rumors. Gossip, you know."

"I appreciate the information, and I'll pass that along to the investigators."

"Don't use my name, okay? I don't want to get into trouble."

"Don't worry," Vera assured her. "I won't." She gave Telly a business card. "Call me, please, if you think of anything else we need to know."

Telly looked from the card to Vera. "I will."

Vera thanked her again and exited the office before anyone could stop her and ask for credentials. *Thank you, Eric.* And Telly.

Once she was in her SUV, she started the engine and cranked up the air-conditioning. And she locked her doors. She surveyed the parking lot. Deep breath. She opened the folder and removed the printed lists.

According to the email from Eric, Gates had spent most of his career teaching at Huntsville High School. He'd also taught a microbiology class at the college. Vera felt confident what she was looking for would more likely be here at the college than at the high school. If someone lived in the Fayetteville area—someone who had access to the Boyett farm—he or she more likely met Gates at the college versus the high school.

If this was even the connection. Could be a dozen other things, but this was the simplest, most logical place to start.

There were sixty rosters. Two classes per semester, two semesters for each of the fifteen years on staff. Thankfully the rosters were only one page each. The classes averaged around twenty students, sometimes fewer.

Vera took a deep breath and began the tedious task of scanning the names. Her gaze snagged on a name from thirteen years ago. That same name appeared in two consecutive semesters.

Microbiology I and II. *Suri Khatri.*

Vera sank back into her seat. Defeat sucked at her.

Too soon to overreact, she told herself. Suri was a mortician . . . of course she'd taken microbiology.

Vera blinked. This didn't mean anything. There were surely other Lincoln County residents in this list of more than a thousand names.

But this one was connected to the Boyett family . . . this one was Eve's best friend. Heart pounding, Vera ran through every single page—thank God the names were in alphabetical order—and checked for Eve. She wasn't there. Relief rushed through her. So maybe Eve hadn't lied about not knowing Gates.

Except Suri was her best friend . . .

Vera's pulse reacted to a new thought. Eve would help her friend, no question.

But which of them committed the murder? And why?

Russ Agency
9th Avenue SW, Huntsville, Alabama, 1:30 p.m.

The office space where Teresa Russ ran her PI agency was nicer than Vera expected. A neat brick building that was once an elementary school in a gentrified part of town.

Rather than show up cold as she'd originally planned, Vera had called and made an appointment for 1:30 p.m. Russ had been happy to rearrange her calendar to make room for Vera. In fact, she had sounded ecstatic.

The door opened to a small lobby, which led into a series of office spaces, some still vacant but all newly updated. Russ had sent a text message with her photo enclosed. Vera had done the same. She'd also reread the research material Eric had provided. Russ was sixty. She had been a licensed private investigator for close to thirty years. She'd started right out of high school as the secretary for a low-rent PI in the West Huntsville area. When he passed away seventeen years later, she'd taken over his shop and earned a damned good reputation in the business, if the reviews on Google were any indication. No issues had been filed with the Better Business Bureau. No reason not to expect the woman to be on the up-and-up.

If Vera were lucky, this could be a good lead. Though she still wasn't convinced Sheree had any real friends, particularly ones who remembered her twenty-odd years later. But if someone had hired Russ . . . that name could be very relevant.

A woman stepped from what Vera presumed was an office and smiled. Blonde. Trim. Attractive. Russ.

"Ms. Russ." Vera offered her hand. "Thank you for making time to speak with me."

Russ grasped her hand, gave it a shake. "Of course. I appreciate you coming. I hoped Luna would pass my message along to you."

"She actually passed it along to Sheriff Benton, but I'm assuming the two of you haven't connected." Bent hadn't mentioned it anyway.

Russ took an audible breath. "Let me say one thing up front: your sheriff did call me, but I chose not to speak with him." She put up her hands in a stop sign fashion. "No offense to local law enforcement, but let's just say I have my reasons."

"I see." Vera could live with that . . . maybe. Technically she was not in law enforcement. "My sister tells me you knew her mother, Sheree."

"Let's go into my office. I have my files there for you to see."

"All right." Vera followed her into the office. Right off the bat Russ had evaded a question. Not a good sign.

Russ closed the door and gestured to a round conference table on the far side of the room. Vera took a seat, and the PI did the same. Hope had started to sing in her blood. She really needed this lead to be useful. The ability to protect her family was swiftly diminishing.

Russ placed her hands atop a file folder and looked directly at Vera. "The truth is, I didn't know Sheree."

Oh hell. Vera put up a hand. "Let me stop you right there. We are not—"

"Please," Russ interrupted, "let me explain. I did not contact your family on anyone else's behalf. No one hired me to look into her case. I'm not working with a reporter. My goal is to help you and *me*."

Vera had no patience for this sort of setup. "You have two minutes, and then I'm walking out." She so disliked having her time wasted. Mostly she felt sick at the letdown.

Russ nodded. "I'll get right to it then. Twenty-five years ago, right after I took over the agency from my boss, I accepted a client whose daughter had gone missing. Mrs. Sutton didn't have much for me to go on, but what little she did know was that her daughter had gone to Fayetteville, Tennessee, and then simply disappeared."

Twenty-five years ago . . . the unidentified female remains instantly zoomed into Vera's mind.

"Trina, her daughter," Russ went on, "had recently been released from jail. She'd done a year for a stack of petty charges that involved prostitution and drugs. It was a shit sentencing, but that's the way things were back then."

"You're saying," Vera reiterated, "she was released from jail, went to Fayetteville, and never came back."

"Yes."

"Why?" Vera held her arms out. "Did she know someone in Fayetteville?"

"Her reason for going to Fayetteville," Russ explained, "was because just before she was arrested and ended up in jail, her best friend, Latesha Johnson, went missing—also while visiting your little town."

Two more sets of female remains. Bent's voice echoed in Vera's brain, and she felt suddenly ill.

"Latesha," Russ went on, "had told Trina about a rich boyfriend and how he was going to take care of her until they could be married. She wouldn't say his name. She insisted it was a big secret and that she would tell Trina when she could. One Friday, just over twenty-six years ago, she packed up and headed to Fayetteville, and Trina never heard from her again. Before she could look for her friend, Trina was arrested."

"This Trina," Vera ventured, "was sure her friend came to Fayetteville that weekend."

"Oh yes, her *sugar daddy*"—Russ made air quotes—"was moving her into an apartment that weekend. His family was out of town, so he was available to get her set up." Russ shook her head. "Bastard. You have no idea, as a PI, how often I see this sort of thing."

Vera could imagine. She wrestled with the need to stand up and pace. "Trina gets out of jail a year later," she repeated to be sure she had this right, "and hires you to look for her friend."

"No." Russ shook her head again. "She went looking for her friend and never came home again."

About a ton of worry settled on Vera's shoulders, flattening her rising hopes.

"Two months later," Russ went on, "her mother came to me. She hadn't heard from Trina in all that time. She was the one who hired me."

"But," Vera challenged, forcing logic to rise to the top of the thoughts whirling in her head, "if Trina was involved in drugs and prostitution, she may have met the wrong connection or just disappeared for whatever reason. It happens far too often."

"I agree, but that's not what happened," Russ argued emphatically. "Trina's mother was very well aware of her daughter's issues. But when she came home after doing her time, she was different. She'd gotten cleaned up, and her first order of business was to find her friend . . . or find out what happened to her."

"Any ideas on who this sugar daddy was?" Vera chewed the inside of her jaw to prevent herself from spewing a dozen other questions. This was a solid lead for sure, but she needed more. She needed a firm connection to someone—any damned one.

Russ shook her head. "Mrs. Sutton only knew that he was supposed to be important and wealthy. And, obviously, married—thus all the secrecy."

"If Latesha Johnson frequented Fayetteville," Vera suggested, "she may have known or hung out with Sheree." Wishful thinking maybe, but it wasn't impossible.

"Perhaps. I've found no proof of that. You see when Sheree disappeared," Russ explained, "I went back to Fayetteville and talked to dozens of people. I hoped that maybe—since the circumstances were similar—someone might be able to help me in my search. That maybe Sheree had fallen victim to whoever caused Latesha and Trina to disappear. But I found not a single witness who had seen Sheree with Latesha or Trina. Is it possible they met at some point? Maybe. But I suspect Sheree was busy with trapping and keeping her own sugar daddy at the time Latesha and Trina disappeared."

Made sense in terms of the timeline.

"What I did find," Russ added, "was that Sheree's case was just as perplexing as the others. Whoever made her disappear did a damned good job."

Vera held her breath for a beat before forging on. "Why come to my family now?"

The remains, of course, but Vera wanted to confirm that she was indeed fishing for information in order to close her old case—not for a spot in this investigation to garner attention for her business.

"Two other sets of remains—female—besides your stepmother," Russ said without hesitation, "were found in that cave on your property. The estimated age of those remains fits the timeline in my case."

At Vera's look of surprise, since few facts about the discoveries had been released, Russ shrugged. "I made a friend in the Lincoln County courthouse all those years ago, she called me."

"They haven't been identified," Vera said. A voice in the back of her mind was now shouting that this couldn't be right, when in truth, it made so much sense it was impossible for her to get a deep breath.

Russ picked up the file that lay on the table in front of her. "I can share this information with you," she said. "Who knows if those remains belong to the women I'm looking for. If not, this could potentially rule them out. That would be tremendously helpful for me and for you."

Vera sat up straighter, leaned forward a bit in anticipation of whatever she was about to see. Her heart had started to race at the possibility, no matter that her brain wasn't ready to accept the idea. Putting a face and a name to human remains was always a great relief, as well as a huge responsibility.

It was the possible identity of the "sugar daddy" that had her logic debating itself.

"These are copies, of course." Russ opened the file, and right there on top was a dental record. "These are Trina's. There were none as far as I could find for Latesha. She had no family here, and I wasn't able to locate anyone who knew their names or where they might be."

Struggling to keep her respiration steady, Vera watched as she moved that page aside and uncovered a copy of an eight-by-ten photo.

"These aren't the actual rings," Russ explained as she turned the photo around for Vera to see better, "but Trina and Latesha had been best friends since first grade. When they were in high school, they got these rings, and both were still wearing them when they were last seen."

The rings were the sort that when put together formed the words "Best Friends." Apprehension and more of that anxiety rushed into Vera's throat and stuck there, stealing her ability to comment.

Russ moved to the next page, a single sheet of typed notes. "I don't know very much about Latesha, and Trina's mother wasn't sure about any potential distinguishing marks, but Latesha had a broken arm her junior year of high school. Her right arm, Mrs. Sutton recalled. Also, Trina wore a silver band with her prison release date engraved inside. I don't have a photo of it, but her mother bought it for her. She said this was to remind her daughter that her new life had started on August first that year."

Vera's pulse shot into hyperspeed.

Then Russ revealed the final item. Another eight-by-ten photo. This one of two young women. Twenty, maybe twenty-one years old. Vera's chest tightened to the point of crushing her ribs.

"This is Latesha." Russ tapped the image of a striking blonde. "This one"—she pointed to the girl next to Latesha, a brunette, and gorgeous as well—"is Trina. Both had just turned twenty-one that year. They had their whole lives ahead of them."

Vera stared at the items Russ had removed from the manilla folder. She'd seen all but the dental records and the photo of the women before . . . in Bent's home office. Deep inside she knew without additional proof that these were the two women who had been murdered and hidden in that damned cave. The truth of it pounded in her veins. Would this "sugar daddy" story further implicate her father?

Could it have been him? Had her mother been protecting him?

Or the other way around?

Regret pierced her, denial right on its heels. Didn't matter. She knew what she had to do. To pretend otherwise would be preposterous at this point. Vera found her voice. "May I keep these?"

"Yes, I made these copies for you." Russ placed the pages back in the folder and passed it to Vera.

"All right." Deep breath. "I'll see that the proper authorities receive them."

Considering what she had here, Vera didn't really get why Russ hadn't gone straight to the sheriff's office. Bent's image had been all over the news. He'd asked for information in his press briefings. Not trusting the police didn't actually make sense in view of this kind of evidence.

"Thank you." Russ smiled sadly. "You may not understand this, and I apologize in advance if you don't. Making it in this business—as a woman—wasn't easy. My experience with the male-dominated world of criminal investigation—both private and civil—has been somewhat less than pleasant. Don't get me wrong, I have the utmost respect for law enforcement, but I have rarely found the kind of support I needed there." She laughed dryly. "It's a little better now but, as they say, nothing to brag about."

Vera struggled to keep her breathing level, waited for her to go on.

"Anyway, when I learned about the remains being found on your family farm, I did some digging. I read about you, Vera. What happened in Memphis is a tragedy, but your reputation in law enforcement is nothing short of incredible. I don't know the sheriff there, and I damned sure don't know the FBI agents, but I feel like I know you from all I've read. Help me give this mother some peace."

And there it was . . . the eight-hundred-pound gorilla had just been placed on Vera's back. No matter that this information might very well implicate her father in other affairs and possibly in murder—and maybe her mother in the cover-up—it was Vera's responsibility to do the right thing. Suddenly she wished she hadn't come . . . that she didn't know. But she did know, and there was no way to keep this a secret.

With the folder gripped in one hand, she reached for her bag. "I'll be in touch."

Russ stood. "I recognize this is a huge favor I'm asking of you."

The woman had no idea.

"But I genuinely appreciate your help."

Vera nodded, unable to trust her voice at this point. She walked out without looking back. Then she climbed into her SUV and got the hell out of there as quickly as she could. Once she was blocks away, she pulled over.

Hands shaking, she called Bent. He answered the same way he always did: "Hey."

Vera took a deep breath. "Have you changed your mind about working together?" Their first official meeting had been delayed by the exhumation, and he hadn't attempted to reschedule. Admittedly, he had been a little busy.

"No way. I'm ready when you are, Vee."

"Good. We need to talk in person. I can be at your place in an hour."

33

Vera stood next to her SUV and waited for Bent to arrive.

The manilla folder in her hand felt as hot as the sun beating down on her. This late into July was like hell on earth in the South. Didn't help that her life suddenly felt exactly like it had gone straight to hell. Part of her wanted to burn this file and pretend she'd never heard of Teresa Russ. It would be so easy to take the stand that none of what was in that cave was in any way relevant to her family.

But it was . . . Sheree had been married to their father. Mother to their youngest sister. Killed—possibly murdered—in their home. And the whole thing covered up by the dead woman's two stepdaughters.

All this time Vera had been so certain that what happened that day was just as Eve told her. An accident. Eve had been trying to protect Luna. But what if the whole thing had been staged—a lie. What if their father had killed Sheree because she had started cheating again and refused to leave? He'd admitted right in front of Bent that he had said those things to Sheree!

Vera groaned. That just couldn't be true. But it wasn't impossible. She knew that Eve had been hiding something from her. The discovery at Calhoun College had at first convinced her that the connection between Suri and Gates was Eve's secret.

But then, after hearing Russ's story, Vera had spent the past hour on the road obsessing on the possibility that there had been other women in her father's life before Sheree. Had Vernon Boyett murdered Latesha when she grew too demanding? And then her friend when she'd come poking around? It was an easy leap from there to the idea that he had come home that day and murdered Sheree. Eve would have protected him. No question.

Just as their mother may have protected him.

Memories of her childhood rushed through Vera's mind like old eight-millimeter film on an out-of-control reel. They had been so happy *before*. Until the death of their mother, she and Eve had enjoyed the picture-perfect childhood. Vera would have been thirteen when the first woman went missing and fourteen when her friend disappeared. Surely she would have recognized if something was wrong between her parents.

How could she not have seen this level of evil in her father?

And how the hell did Gates fit into it? Certainly, he was no "sugar daddy" from Fayetteville. Bearing in mind what she had learned from Russ, he likely had nothing to do with the other female victims.

Bent's truck rounded the curve in his long driveway, roaring past the meadow where the horses grazed. Vera wanted to feel relieved that he was finally here, but that only meant one thing—she had to tell him what she'd learned from Russ.

Bent had been right about this coming down to her family. The most credible scenario in this whole mess was narrowing in on her family. And the FBI would recognize it soon, if they hadn't already. She had to trust Bent . . . there was no one else who could help.

Bent parked, climbed out of his truck, and walked toward her.

Vera's heart reacted to the sight of him . . . to the way he walked . . . to that damned hat he wore that made her want to rip it off his head and . . .

She was losing her grip . . . clearly.

"I don't have any updates," he said as he closed in on her.

His voice . . . she had always been affected by his voice. The deep, steady sound of it. It made her feel safe and warm and made her want to . . .

Stop! Damn it.

"I have one." Her own voice sounded hollow and fearful. What the hell? She'd been back here only a few days, and already she'd regressed decades. Where was the fearless analyst who'd solved so many cases? Didn't matter. She waved the folder.

"You want to go inside and talk about it?" His eyes searched hers. She nodded. "Yes."

"Okay."

He waited, let her lead the way to where she wanted to go. What she wanted was to go into his house and into his bed and lose herself for a few hours. But that would be a monumental mistake, and it wouldn't fix the problem.

Instead, she walked around the house to his home office. He followed closely enough for her to feel his presence, but he didn't crowd her or rush her.

When they reached the former potting shed, she stepped aside while he unlocked the door and pushed it inward. Inside was cool. Vera was grateful for the reprieve. Bent turned on the overhead light, chasing away the shadows lurking in the corners of the space.

With a deep breath, Vera squared her shoulders. "I tracked down Teresa Russ."

He removed his hat, ran his fingers through his hair. "I've been trying to reach her, but no luck. Keep getting her voicemail." He placed his hat on a table and studied her. "You want something to drink?"

She shook her head. Her throat was far too constricted to swallow. Before she could stop it, her gaze settled on the case board, where the images of the stones and the remains taunted her.

"Have a seat," he urged.

She moved to the nearest stool at his worktable and lowered onto it. He took a seat across from her.

"Before I called Russ, I called a friend of mine in Memphis to do some digging for me." She cleared her throat. Decided she couldn't tell him about finding Suri's name on that student roster. Not yet. It was only fair that she talk to Eve first. Blindsiding her sister like that . . . Vera couldn't do it.

"My friend," she went on, "discovered that Russ was legit. Good reputation." She handed him the folder, and while he studied the items inside, she explained about Latesha Johnson and Trina Sutton. Then she pressed her lips together and wished she had asked for water, since her mouth felt dry enough for the tissue to crack. Her pulse raced as if she'd run a marathon.

Bent placed the items back in the folder and left it on the table. His gaze settled on hers. "You're worried your father did this."

It wasn't a question. He read her that easily . . . still, and the evidence was right there as plain as day. She wondered if he could see the crack widening in her heart. This might very well destroy her family. "I've considered that it looks that way, yes."

She would die before she implicated her mother.

He braced both hands on the table. "It's feasible. The remains were on his property. Sheree, his second wife, is one of the victims. Based on her reputation for cheating, he had motive." Bent shook his head. "But I know your father, and he's not a killer. He wouldn't have cheated on your mother before the cancer . . . he loved her too much. He just wasn't that kind of man."

Emotion crowded into Vera's eyes, and she wanted to kick herself for daring to tear up in front of this man. "But—in Sheree's case"—she had to get this all out—"it is the most likely scenario."

Bent watched her for a moment before responding. "You're right." He gave an affirming nod. "But we also know that he adored Sheree, and you said yourself how devastated he was when she disappeared."

The determination and strength that had so abruptly and thoroughly deserted her suddenly returned. Her sense of loyalty and obligation to her family resurrected in full force. She wasn't doing this. No way. She would not allow this investigation to destroy everything. Bent was right. Her father wasn't that kind of man. Her mother not that sort of woman. They were good people—whatever their faults.

There had to be another explanation.

"You're right, of course. The evidence felt so overwhelming as I listened to Russ's story that I got caught up for a moment. Perhaps I overreacted."

"It's tough to stay objective when it's personal," he reminded her.

She stood. "In any event, maybe there's something in that"—she gestured to the folder—"that will help ID the other remains. You should notify Russ if Sutton and Johnson are the victims. She knows the family."

As desperately as she had needed to turn this over to Bent, she suddenly needed to be away from him. To get out of here. Finding Eve and updating her were essential. They needed to talk about how this would potentially impact their family. Equally important, Vera needed to understand if the connection between Suri and Gates was something to worry about.

As she turned away, she hesitated. At this point she felt like a fool for having rushed here with accusations about her father. "To be clear," she said, "I love my father. No matter how all this looks, Sheree and that damned cave are the only two elements that connect him to any of this. There's no evidence and certainly no witnesses. You, the FBI, and everyone involved need to remember that."

"I'm with you one hundred percent," Bent confirmed.

She appreciated this more than he could know. "This situation has been difficult for us all. Remember that as well, particularly when factoring in some of Eve's actions."

"That's why she faked the accident," Bent pointed out. "To distract the investigation from her father."

Vera nodded. "She also left that warning." Might as well get it all out there. "On the door." He didn't know about the others, and she intended to keep it that way.

"I can see her doing that." He hesitated a second, then asked, "You don't think she hired the intruder, do you?"

"No. She did not. We talked about that. She would never go that far and risk hurting anyone." She thought of Suri and the man, Norton Gates. Vera certainly hoped she was right about that part.

"All right then," Bent said. "Thank you for getting Russ to talk and for bringing me the folder." He smiled, a weary one. "You do good work."

"Thanks. I'm counting on you to see that this is done right."

He gave her a nod. "No question. I'll give this information to Conover, and we'll go from there."

Vera hesitated again. "What about my mother's remains?" Just thinking about what Higdon had done made her sick all over again.

"On the way to the lab in Nashville." He shook his head. "I really am sorry about that, Vee. I wish I could have stopped it."

"Some things just can't be stopped."

Like this momentum toward a crash and burn the Boyett sisters seemed headed for.

"Unfortunately, you're right about that." He exhaled a big breath. "The FBI has requested a meeting at five thirty in my office. Can you be there? I can put them off maybe another day."

She should just get it over with. It wasn't like she didn't know how to handle the feds. "No, don't put them off. I'll be there."

"See you then."

"Yeah."

She could just imagine the fun they were going to have.

As she drove away from Bent's place, she called Eve and got her voicemail. Vera ended the call. "Damn it, Eve."

She set a course for Barrett's. As she drove, she replayed all that had happened since her return. So much about their family history was suddenly upside down or in question. What happened to that happy family they once were? How could this thing have turned all her good memories into questions or potential cover-ups?

Looking back, she wondered when it had all started to fall apart.

Her mother's smiling face slipped into the midst of the other jumbled images. She'd been such a joyful and upbeat person. Always found the bright side.

There was no one like her.

Florence Higdon's words echoed in Vera's brain. She'd said something very close to that when she and Beatrice Fraley delivered the food. Another memory punched through the thought. Vera's mother and two other women laughing and drinking lemonade in the backyard. But that had been before her mother died.

Vera mulled over the memory. Talking to Eve would have to wait . . . there was something Vera had to do first.

Her foot bearing down harder on the accelerator, Vera drove straight to the farm. Why hadn't Beatrice or Florence called to convey their sympathy that her mother had been exhumed? She and Beatrice had just chatted on her front porch, and she hadn't said a word. Florence had come by that once with the casserole, and then radio silence. Such good friends should have been horrified by the news.

Or maybe, Vera decided, they were afraid of being presumed guilty by association.

She thought of this morning's conversation with her father, when he was so worried about something her mother had done . . . something no one could know . . . that could take her away from the girls. He even mentioned understanding that she thought she was doing the right thing.

Vera parked in front of the house. Obviously her mother had done something wrong, maybe illegal. Her father had been afraid for her. Vera got out of her SUV and hurried to the front door. Her fingers fumbled as she unlocked it. The house was quiet, so no one else was home yet.

Vaguely she considered that there had been an intruder, and they still didn't have a security system. The thought prompted an ache in her hip. She should not just rush into the house without thought.

Forget that. This could not wait. She kicked the door shut and went straight to the library room. She grabbed as many photo albums as her arms would hold and carried them to the table in the center of the room. One by one she flipped through the pages. She alternately smiled and cried. Right there was proof of all those happy memories. They really had been happy. Smiles like the ones in the photographs couldn't be faked. The love so obvious between her parents could not have been an act.

Vera's lips drifted down into a frown. What happened to change everything?

Her father had said it was his place—he should have done the protecting. What could he have meant? Vera replayed the conversation yet again. He was worried that Evelyn had done something wrong. Vera refused to believe her mother had harmed anyone, much less murdered two women. She had to have been protecting Vera's father. And someone else knew . . . maybe that someone was threatening her. Or was involved somehow.

Who better to know a secret than one's best friends?

There were literally dozens of photos of her mother with her two best friends. Florence Higdon and Beatrice Fraley. Best friends who had, obviously, spent a great deal of time with her. All the way up to the year before she died, there was evidence of the three's closeness.

Vera frowned. Why had those two abandoned her mother during her most profound time of need? She had suffered with that damned cancer for just over a year, yet there was not one photo of her friends gathered around her. Now that she considered it, Vera could not call to mind a single instance of the two dropping by or bringing food.

What had happened to destroy their friendship?

A secret . . . one that could destroy one or all of them.

Maybe her mother hadn't been protecting her father.

Bent and even Walt Fraley insisted that whoever put those bodies in the cave was someone her father knew well. Teresa Russ said Latesha Johnson's sugar daddy was someone important . . . someone wealthy.

Vernon Boyett wasn't particularly wealthy or a prominent member of the community.

Dr. Charles Higdon, the medical examiner, certainly fit the bill far better, and he seemed all too determined to find a way to cast suspicion on her father.

Then there was Walt Fraley, friend to her father and sheriff during the time the victims went missing. He swore to Vera there were no unsolved missing persons cases during his time as sheriff. Yet there were Latesha and Trina. Teresa Russ had come to Fayetteville often enough to have developed a contact in the courthouse.

Why had Fraley lied about that? Had he simply forgotten? Or was he protecting someone? Himself? Higdon?

Why had all those best friends suddenly become frenemies?

Vera needed to catch Beatrice alone again and play interrogator. She was the weak link among the four. The most likely to break.

The upcoming meeting with the FBI had pushed Vera into a corner. She no longer had time to let this play out and see what happened.

She had to find answers.

34

Eve added a little blush to Mrs. Carter's face. "There. That's much better." She smiled. Mrs. Carter was never one to wear makeup, but there were times when a touch was simply necessary. "You'll thank me when you hear the comments from your viewers."

Her work done, Eve navigated Mrs. Carter from the room. Typically, cosmetics wouldn't be applied until the visitor was dressed and placed in her coffin, but it had seemed like the right thing to do at this point. The elderly woman had run the ice cream shop on the square for fifty years. Whenever their mother took Vera and Eve for ice cream, Mrs. Carter's cheeks were always rosy and her smile wide and beaming.

Eve tried to remember the little things like that for those she prepared. The viewings and the funeral were their final social engagements. Few would want to be remembered as looking "dead" or "not like themselves."

The route to refrigeration required her to pass the office, where Mr. Barrett's attention was glued to the small television perched on one corner of his desk. It was probably the oldest working portable television in all of Fayetteville. Today, rather than his favorite soaps, the news blared from the small screen.

"No identification has been released on the new remains found in the cave on the Boyett farm," the reporter exclaimed, with all the drama of someone who'd just spotted flames in his kitchen. "Special agents from the FBI have now joined Lincoln County Sheriff Benton in the search for answers . . ."

Eve opened the wide door to refrigeration and parked Mrs. Carter on the right of Chester Hawkins. His viewing was this evening. He'd been a nice man. The best barber in town, her father had insisted. Eve had liked him. He'd always sent lollipops home for her and Vera. She doubted barbers did those sorts of things anymore.

When she turned for the door, Eve hesitated. She turned back to Mrs. Carter. Had she said something?

Eve blinked. For just a moment she wondered if she might be schizophrenic. The idea always crossed her mind when this happened. But then the moment would pass, and the possibility never seemed to materialize . . . or maybe she just didn't know it yet. It had been this way since she was a child.

Like just now. She had the most overpowering sensation that Mrs. Carter wanted to warn her that Vera might be in trouble.

"Good night," Eve announced. She stepped out and closed the door, ensured it was locked.

She actually was worried about Vee. Her sister had called and left a message. Judging by the sound of her voice, something big had happened.

This whole thing just kept getting worse.

Eve hurried past Barrett's office. The last thing she wanted was to fend off more of his questions about the investigation.

Eve returned to her space and inhaled the familiar scent of chemicals used to clean and prepare the dead. Some staff members hated the smell, but it was comforting to Eve. Something she trusted to do what it was supposed to do.

Not like people—at least those still alive, anyway.

In her entire life she had met few who did what they said they would do or kept their word in any way. Really, Vee was the only person in Eve's universe who had kept her word without fail. Telling her sister the whole truth was something Eve had dreaded for decades.

No one was ever supposed to know about the bodies in the cave.

They were Eve's secret. Hers and her mother's.

She peeled off her gloves and threw them into the red trash can.

Vee had enjoyed four years with their mother before Eve came along. Her sister was the one who looked most like their mother . . . even talked like her. Eve had her hair and eye color, too, but her facial features were different. Not as pretty. Her voice was kind of weird. Too deep or something. And not nearly compelling enough. Not lyrical and strong like Vee's and their mother's.

Looking back, Eve understood that her mother hadn't set out to make her a part of *it*, but Eve had never been very good at doing as she was told. She leaned against the embalming table. She remembered that day, as the saying went, like it was yesterday.

Her mother and her two best friends had been in a tizzy—one of her mother's favorite words. Something bad had happened. That part was unclear in Eve's memory. What was perfectly clear was her mother insisting Eve was not to leave the house under any circumstances.

Not such a hard request to follow . . . until she saw her mother and her friends hurrying across the backyard. Eve had gone to the window and watched as the three struggled with her daddy's big old wheelbarrow. There was something in it . . . all wrapped in a quilt or bedspread with flowers on it. Turned out to be a tablecloth.

Eve had to know what they were doing. She had been certain it was the staging of a new mystery night. Once a month or so, her mother would stage a mystery for Vee and Eve to solve. It had always been marvelous fun.

She wondered if Vee remembered those times. Eve hoped so. They were the best memories. For Vee's twelfth birthday their mother had created a big special mystery for the party. The other kids had loved it. Eve had never been so proud of her amazing mama. There wasn't another one like her.

It had been an easy leap from what Eve was seeing on that day to what she decided was an upcoming mystery night.

She had to know what they were doing. She rarely beat Vee at finding clues. Maybe this time she could secretly get a head start. All she had to do was make sure her mother didn't see her.

Eve had sneaked out of the house and followed the three. They went past the barn and deep into the woods. When they reached the cave and stopped there, Eve gasped. She slammed her hand over her mouth. The others hadn't heard, but her mother had looked around. She rarely missed anything.

Heart pounding, Eve watched as they struggled to pick up the bulky thing in the wheelbarrow. When the ladies went down on their knees and dragged it into the cave, Eve was ecstatic. Mystery night would be at the cave!

She decided it would be best if she went back to the house now, and later when her mama was busy making supper, Eve could come back and see what they'd hidden.

Her father was at work, and even though it was a day off from school—a teacher's in-service day—Vee wasn't home. She'd gone to Lake Winnie with a friend and her family. Eve had been jealous at first. She'd wanted to go to the amusement park, too, but she wasn't invited.

Her mama had promised that the whole family would go soon, and for today she insisted that she and Eve would have a special day all to themselves.

A long time later, after the ladies left, her mama came up to Eve's room and sat down on her bed. Eve pretended not to notice and just kept playing with her Barbies. Finally, her mother spoke.

"Eve, there's something I need to show you."

First she and her mother picked flowers from her garden, then they went to the cave. Mama showed her what they had hidden there. A lady . . . only this one was dead—like the ones at the funeral home when they visited. Her mother and her friends had tucked her into a part of the cave Eve hadn't known existed and covered her with rocks. Eve and her mother placed the flowers on the rocks and said a little prayer. She promised Eve that this would be their special secret and that she could never tell anyone, not even Vera.

Afterward, they went back to the house and baked her favorite chocolate-chip-peanut-butter bars. Eve helped her mama prepare supper, and when Vee finally got home with her exciting stories about Lake Winnie, Eve was giddy with happiness that she knew something her sister didn't.

It was barely a year later when it happened again. This time Eve hadn't been home, so she couldn't be sure what day, but she caught her Mama sneaking off to the cave one Saturday morning while everyone was still in bed. She took flowers and left them on a second pile of rocks in that hidden place in the cave. Eve had no idea if the other two ladies had helped bring this one there.

This time Eve's mama was crying. When she spotted Eve watching, she explained that sometimes accidents happened, but there was never an acceptable excuse for purposely taking a life. Eve hadn't understood what she meant at the time. Maybe her mama was so sad because someone had died or because her friends never visited again, or maybe she'd already found out about the cancer.

Fifteen months later her mother died. But shortly before she died, she and Eve went to the cave and placed cross necklaces on the stones. She said it was the right thing to do, and she reminded Eve that she was never ever to tell a soul. Eve promised she wouldn't.

Then her mother stared at the stones and whispered something Eve almost missed. *The cancer is my punishment.*

Several times before she died, her mother told Eve how sorry she was about the burden she had left on her. But Eve hadn't minded. In fact, she had gone back many times over the years and taken flowers. She'd arranged the little stones into daisies the way her mother had shown her. And after Sheree was put in the cave, Eve had taken flowers and a cross necklace to her.

Eve's biggest regret was that she hadn't been able to keep the one other promise she'd made to her mother.

But she could still keep her promise to Vera. Her mama wouldn't mind now that the bodies had all been found.

It was only right that Eve tell her sister the truth now.

But she wasn't sure anything—not even the truth—would save them at this point.

35

Vera hadn't found Beatrice Fraley. She hadn't been at home. If her husband was there, he hadn't answered the door. Maybe she'd taken the man to an appointment. Vera's calls went unanswered, her voicemails unreturned.

Next she'd gone in search of Eve. Not at Barrett's. Not at the farm. No one had been at home at Suri's, and Suri wasn't at work either. Maybe Suri had taken Eve to pick up her car. The repairs were supposed to be finished today.

Then Vera had run out of time, and *this* had been necessary.

Bent was stationed at the head of the conference table. Vera was seated to his right, and the two FBI agents sat like stone statues on his left. Bent had made the introductions. Special Agent Wayne Gallagher was the senior agent, at least in age. Gray hair and eyes set in a face worn and furrowed by time and the work. The typical "I've been at this too long" face. Special Agent Arnold Trotter was on the other side of the spectrum. Young, maybe thirty, fresh faced, with military-short black hair and brown eyes. His cocky posture told Vera he wanted to be the boss, but that wasn't happening as long as Gallagher was breathing.

The TBI agent, whom she'd never met, was not in the meeting. It was possible he'd stepped aside since the FBI had basically taken over the case. Or he was playing out his part by coordinating between the investigation here and the lab in Nashville.

Vera had psyched herself up for this meeting—assumed the critical analyst persona that had made her a star at Memphis PD.

Except she wasn't a star. A star would have spotted the trouble before it happened.

She banished the thought. There could be no distractions during this crucial meeting.

"Should I address you by your rank, Chief Boyett?" Gallagher asked.

So he already knew she'd tendered her resignation. Of course he did. The FBI was very good at fact gathering. It was the actual solving of crime where they failed more regularly of late.

"Not necessary. As I'm sure you're aware, I recently resigned from the MPD."

Bent's expression showed his surprise. She should have told him, but there hadn't been a time when it felt relevant amid this building mess.

Gallagher nodded. "Very well, Ms. Boyett. We appreciate your cooperation."

Vera said nothing.

"Let's go back," the senior agent suggested, "to April, twenty-two years ago. On the seventeenth of that month you were in school, but your sister, Eve, had stayed home since she wasn't feeling well. Is that correct?"

"That's correct." Vera answered the question without the addition of extraneous information. *Never give them more than they ask for.*

"According to yours and your sister's statements when the missing persons report was filed, Eve was awakened by the baby—Luna—crying. That was when she realized your stepmother was missing."

Vera saw no need to respond since he didn't ask a question.

"Why did Eve call you at school?" Trotter tossed out. "Was she afraid to be at home alone with an infant?"

"Eve wasn't feeling well," Vera explained. "She needed me to come home and see after Luna until Sheree returned."

"But she didn't return," Trotter pointed out.

Effort was required not to roll her eyes. No doubt her silence conveyed the feeling.

Gallagher waved his hands. "We could go over all the details of your statement, but I'm sure you recall what you said."

Another nonquestion, so she waited for wherever he intended to go next.

"You were at school," he went on. "Eve was at home, and your father was at work."

When he appeared determined to wait for a response, she said, "Is there a question related to that statement?"

"Were you aware," Gallagher said, "that your father left work at nine forty-five that morning? He returned at eleven fifteen."

If he had wanted to surprise Vera, he'd done so. But she'd learned the art of keeping her feelings to herself.

"No." She felt Bent's gaze on her, but she didn't glance in his direction. It would be seen as a sign of weakness or uncertainty.

"Your father," Trotter said, "was the manager of the accounting division at Monroe & Floyd. As such he didn't need an excuse for leaving the office in the middle of the morning."

Vera waited for a query relevant to his statement. To her knowledge, no one had come forward to say he'd left work that day.

"But," Gallagher picked up from there, "one of his staff members who wasn't interviewed twenty-two years ago has told us that your father borrowed his car to run home for a few minutes. This staff member recalled that he seemed a bit frazzled when he returned."

Again, there was nothing she could or would say to his statement.

"Let's be candid here, Ms. Boyett," Gallagher suggested, when she remained silent. "I don't fully understand why this particular person at your father's place of employment was not interviewed at the time of your stepmother's disappearance, but obviously he should have been.

As you know, your father had motive and, we now understand, opportunity to murder her."

"Do you have a question for me?" He wanted to rattle her, and to some degree, he had succeeded, but she would not allow him to see any measure of success. "Otherwise I would refer you to former Sheriff Walter Fraley, since he was the sheriff who conducted the investigation."

"Less than a week after she disappeared," Trotter said, "the man she was rumored to be cheating on your father with was murdered. Beaten to death with a baseball bat."

This was growing tedious.

"We've spoken with your father's physician," Gallagher said. "He has agreed that an interview won't be detrimental to his condition."

Vera laughed. "Nor will it be useful to your investigation. As you well know, anything he says isn't going to make it to a courtroom. He is mentally incompetent."

"We don't need his testimony for a courtroom," Trotter said, angling his head to study her. "We're hoping for a detail that will help us determine who else had a motive to want Sheree out of the way. You have any ideas about that?" His gaze narrowed. "Seems as if you and your sister didn't really like her."

"Well." Vera pushed back her chair and stood. "This has been . . . interesting, if not enlightening. You know where to reach me if you have other questions."

Bent was on his feet but made no attempt to slow or to stop her departure. She would thank him later.

The agents said nothing.

She closed the door behind her and walked down the long corridor that led past the sheriff's office, as well as the offices of others in the department, until she reached the lobby. Once she was out of the building, she strode straight to her SUV, climbed in, and drove away.

It wasn't until she was on the Thornton Taylor Parkway that she let out all the emotions that had built inside her. She screamed.

Then she took a breath and drove straight to Sweet Things Ice Cream Shoppe. She went inside, ordered a vanilla ice cream cone, and asked to borrow the phone. She called Barrett's Funeral Home and asked for Eve—rather than calling her cell.

While Vera's phone was silenced during the meeting with the FBI, Eve had tried to call her back. That was just like her sister to return a call at the most inopportune time.

As soon as Eve said hello, Vera instructed her to go to the park where they played as kids. They had to talk.

If Eve was protecting their father . . . or their mother, Vera needed to know why and to what extent.

36

Vera parked in the lot and walked down to the spot by the water she and Eve had loved most. The park wasn't so large, but it was interesting. With a trail that meandered along the water and a gazebo hidden in the trees. Ducks waddled along, heading for the water. It was peaceful and somewhat secluded, no matter that it was actually in the middle of their little town.

Within two or three minutes of Vera's arrival, Eve showed up. Vera had already taken a seat on her favorite boulder. More of the big rocks were scattered about in the park and along the river. Eve settled on the one she had favored as a child. Funny how some things you just never forgot.

"This must be bad," Eve suggested.

"Depends on how you define *bad*. If being questioned by the FBI fits your definition for *bad*, then, yeah, it's bad."

Eve's eyes widened a little. Her body eased back a fraction, as if drawing away from the danger. "How did it go?" She shook her head. "I mean, have they figured anything out?"

For a few seconds Vera thought about how to answer that question. "Too early to tell." As much as she wanted to, Vera couldn't put off the other. "I need some answers from you, Eve. I need the whole truth about everything, and I need it now."

"I know." Eve bowed her head for a moment, toed the grass. "Fire away."

Fire away? Vera made a face. What the hell? Where was the insistence that she'd told Vera everything already? The roll of her eyes and remark about having been over this territory before? Since her sister stared expectantly at her, Vera opted to let it go and press on.

"Let's start with the easiest question first," she suggested. "Was the dead guy in our cave Suri's microbiology instructor?"

Eve sighed. "I was hoping they wouldn't figure out that part."

"*They* didn't," Vera said. "I did."

Eve stiffened visibly. "Did you tell Bent?"

Of all the things she could have asked. "No, not yet."

She relaxed. "Good."

Good? Vera wanted to shake her. But she needed her to keep talking. "Next question: Did you not notice the two other sets of remains in there when you helped your friend dispose of her dead teacher?" Vera took a second, steadied the emotions raging inside her. "And why in the world did Suri kill him?"

"She didn't." Eve bit her lower lip.

Vera froze. Oh hell. "You killed him?"

"He was a really bad guy, Vee. I wouldn't have—"

"Holy shit! What're you now? Dexter?"

Jesus Christ. Just when she thought things couldn't get worse. Her sister had killed a man and hid him in the cave on their property! Almost worse, rather than explain how such a tragic event had been some sort of accident, she offered why he deserved to die.

"How the hell did this happen?" Vera demanded.

"When Suri was his student, he raped her."

Some of Vera's anger bled away. "I'm really sorry to hear that, Eve, but still. Did you have to kill him?" Her voice rose with each word.

"I know." Eve looked away. "We were in Huntsville at the mall. We ran into him, and he was oh so talky, talky. Telling Suri how proud he was that she'd done so well for herself. He said he'd kept up with her all these years. Suri said almost nothing, and when he finally moved on, she rushed to the bathroom and vomited. It took me awhile, but I dragged the story out of her."

"Why didn't she go to the police when the rape happened?"

"Because he warned that if she told anyone, she would fail his class, and he'd turn it around as if she pursued him. She was young and afraid," Eve explained, her face urging her sister to understand.

Apparently the young woman at the college had been right about the professor having a god complex.

Too many women had been scared away from going to the police with tactics like the one Eve's friend had experienced. "I'm with you so far, but how did running into him again lead to murder?"

"He started coming around. She would go to dinner here in town and see him there. At the Walmart . . . at the grocery store. Suddenly he was here all the time like he was stalking her."

Vera didn't want to doubt the story, but that would have meant the guy was pretty stupid. Or a serial rapist with obsession issues . . . as well as a god complex. Damn.

"While all this was going on," Eve said, "I did a little research on the guy. I found out there were rumors he'd had relationships with other students. I tracked down one woman, and she had basically the same experience as Suri. He raped her. But she wouldn't go to the police then, and she wouldn't when I begged her to. She was too afraid of the arrogant prick."

Vera hated men like the bastard Eve was describing. "You know you could have called me."

"I was going to call you," Eve agreed. "But then he showed up at Suri's place."

"Where she lives now?"

Eve nodded. "It's on the edge of town, that little house she inherited from her grandmother. You remember, the school bus used to stop there for her brother."

Vera did remember. She'd driven by there looking for Eve just a couple of hours ago. Secluded for sure. "So he found out where she lived," Vera suggested. "Caught her there where no one was likely to see him." She hated the idea of where this was going.

"His only mistake was in not realizing I was there too," Eve explained. "It was a Saturday, and I'd come home with Suri that Friday and spent the night. My car wasn't there, so he had no idea she had company. He intended to rape her again, Vee. He was already tearing off her clothes and shoving her around when I intervened."

Vera closed her eyes. Shook her head. "What did you do?"

"I hit him in the head with a cast-iron skillet."

Damn. "It would have taken one hell of a lick to end his life."

Eve stared at the ground a moment. "I may have hit him a couple more times when he staggered away from her and at me." She stared at her hands. "I hit him until he stopped moving."

Vera reached out and took her hands. "I probably would have done the same thing." Maybe not the repeated-blows part, but the sister side of her got it.

Eve's gaze collided with hers. "I'm sorry, Vee. I should have told you, but I hoped they wouldn't find that part of the cave."

"How did you know about that part? Did you go back there after . . . Sheree? You must have seen the other piles of rocks."

Eve nodded. "I went back a few times. And, yes, I knew about the others."

Vera scrubbed at the tension throbbing in her temples. "Why in the world would you go back?" She had known this was coming, and still it threw her. "Why didn't you tell me about the others?"

"First off, you know how I feel about the dead. They had no one to visit them. So I did. I knew the others were there from the beginning, but I couldn't tell you."

Vera stood. Paced back and forth next to the water, wished she could jump in and swim away. But she wouldn't get far . . . that was the problem in her life. However she tried, she could never get away clean.

She stalled, glared at her sister. "Just tell me Daddy didn't kill those women." She looked away. "I know in my heart"—she stared at her sister once more—"that Mama couldn't have done it." Vera wilted back onto her rock.

"I honestly don't know who killed them, but it was Mama who hid them there."

No. Anger flashed. "I don't believe you." Just as suddenly Vera's insides went ice cold. No. No. No. Her mother would never have hurt another human. This was wrong. A lie. Eve had to have misunderstood whatever she saw or heard. Or made it up, damn it.

"It's true," Eve said, her voice small but firm.

"Mama would not have killed anyone," Vera argued, angry again.

"I wouldn't have killed anyone either," Eve argued. "But it happened."

"Frankly," Vera snapped, "I can see you killing someone before Mama."

Eve made a pained face. "Really? Thanks."

Vera ordered the intensifying emotions to calm. She had to think . . . rationally. "Just tell me what you saw or heard that makes you believe Mama had something to do with those remains." Not possible. No way.

"I only saw them hiding the first body."

"Them?" Vera thought of the things their father had said this morning when he thought she was Evelyn. Strangely enough, his words were beginning to make sense. And it made Vera sick.

"Two of her friends helped put the bodies there." Eve's expression shifted to one of deep concentration. "Or maybe she helped them. I can't be sure. And I only saw them doing the first one. I wasn't home when the second one happened." She bit her lips together for a moment.

"I didn't tell you, because Mama told me I could never tell anyone. That it had to be our secret. Hers and mine."

Vera could imagine how that would have made Eve feel special. She had always needed just a little bit more. Maybe because of being so much younger than Vera. Still, what she was saying . . . she had to be wrong. "Let's put the absolute impossibility of what you're saying aside for a moment—"

"I'm sorry," Eve said. "I know this is hard, but it's true."

"I can't . . ." Vera shook her head, crossed her arms over her chest. "I can't accept what you're suggesting."

"See," Eve fired back, "this is exactly why I couldn't tell you even after Bent found them. I knew you wouldn't believe me." The stark pain in her eyes warned she was being honest . . . at least on some level. "And I'm not suggesting. This *is* the truth, Vee."

"All right." Vera took a breath, gathered her spiraling thoughts as best she could. "How did you learn about any of this?"

"I followed them to the cave that first time."

"So you know who the friends were?" Vera felt confident of their identities—which oddly made her immensely happy, in spite of all the rest. She couldn't wait to wield this information over that pompous ass, Florence Higdon. Her hopes faded. Unless Higdon had only been helping their mother with what *she* had done. Shit! Shit! Shit!

"Florence Higdon and Beatrice Fraley."

Beatrice was like their mother: she would never purposely hurt anyone. Florence had to be the one who murdered those women. A bitter taste rose in Vera's throat. This wasn't as simple as that. Very little ever was. She, of all people, understood that sometimes a person did things they wouldn't generally do.

"Were they aware you knew?" Vera couldn't see that scenario . . . otherwise one or both would surely have spilled the story by now. Then again, the idea could explain the scenario the two had shared with Walt when Sheree disappeared. Make the sisters look guilty in the event Eve ever dared tell anyone. It would be Eve's words against those of pillars of the community.

"No. Mama said they couldn't know. No one could."

"The bottom line is you can't be certain who killed those women?" Vera's gut twisted into a few thousand more knots.

"I can't," Eve admitted. "But I know Mama felt bad for the women. We went there sometimes and left flowers and prayed for them. The last time we went, just before she died, Mama put cross necklaces on their graves."

Vera cleared her head and struggled to get the rest of the details straight. "How did Sheree get one of those?"

"I put it there. Like Mama, I felt bad for her."

Vera squared her shoulders and forced all the emotions aside. "Okay. Let's go back to the beginning and make sure I have the details right. When was the first woman put in the cave, and how did you see it?"

Eve cleared her throat. "It was the day you went to Lake Winnie with your friend—the year before Mama died." She waited a moment for Vera to find that place in her memory, then she continued. "Florence and Beatrice came over, and Mama said there was something they had to do. I was to stay in the house. But I watched from the window. They had something in Daddy's wheelbarrow. When they pushed it toward the barn, I sneaked out and followed them. I thought maybe it was a new mystery night set up. You remember those?"

Vera nodded. How could she forget? Those were some of her fondest memories.

"Anyway," Eve went on, "they went all the way to the cave. While they were getting her inside, Mama heard me in the bushes. I gasped or something. Later she took me to the cave and showed me, because she knew I would look anyway."

Vera's heart sank lower with every word. When her sister at last stopped talking, Vera took a breath, only then realizing she'd been holding it.

"Mama never told you who killed them? You didn't see how the body arrived at our house?"

Eve shook her head. "No, and I never asked. I'm not sure I fully understood the bigger picture at the time."

Of course she hadn't—she was what? Nine years old? Vera steadied herself and took stock of their options. "We have to find the answer to that question before we take this to Bent."

"There's more."

Vera's gaze locked with her sister's. Her heart squeezed and then started thumping wildly again. "What?"

"You said you wanted the whole truth."

Vera nodded; her throat closed.

"When Sheree died," Eve said quietly, "it wasn't just Luna's crying that woke me up. It was Sheree and Daddy arguing."

And there it was. Vera's absolute last hope evaporated. "He killed her in a jealous rage?" Jesus, had he killed Rimmey, too, as the FBI suggested? How could she not have picked up on any of this?

"No. Listen. I heard Luna screaming, just like I told you, so I climbed out of bed and went to see what was happening," Eve went on. "I heard him say, 'What were you thinking?' And Sheree said, 'I never wanted that damned baby.' Daddy warned that if she ever laid another hand on Luna, he would go to the police. He told her to leave." Eve rolled her eyes. "The idiot said she wasn't leaving without a little incentive."

Vera gritted her teeth. That sounded exactly like something the bitch would have said. How in the hell had their daddy ever gotten himself tied up with that woman? Vera instantly felt contrite. Without Sheree there would have been no Luna.

"Luna kept screaming, and Sheree was telling him to shut her up. It was awful." Eve shuddered visibly. "Sheree must have reached for Luna, because he said she better never touch her again, and then she went batshit crazy. I got to the bathroom door just in time to see her charge

Daddy. Luna was in his arms. He shoved Sheree back, and that's when she fell and hit her head on the toilet."

The imagery made Vera feel even sicker, but she had to hear the rest of this ever-worsening nightmare.

"I asked what was going on, and Sheree scrambled up and charged at me. Daddy grabbed her by the arm and pulled her off me and shoved her away. She flew backward, hit her head on the sink on the way down. I think she hit a lot harder that time, because she didn't get up."

When Eve didn't speak again for a minute, Vera prompted, "What happened then?"

Eve took a breath. "Daddy handed the baby to me. She was soaking wet with her clothes and diaper on. He said Sheree was trying to drown her. She had called him at work and said she couldn't take her crying anymore. That's why he came home. He had a flat tire on his truck, so he had to borrow a car. Vee, he showed up in the nick of time, or Luna would be dead. I don't think I could have stopped Sheree, even if I'd woken up in time and heard her in there. I'd never seen her act that crazy. She must have been on something."

Vera cringed at the idea of how the whole thing could have played out. "What did you and Daddy do after it was clear Sheree was dead?"

"He cried. He kept saying who would take care of his girls if he went to prison. I told him to leave, and I'd pretend I did it and that you would help me figure it out. It took me a minute, but I finally convinced him." Eve's expression turned confused. "The funny thing is, it was like he didn't remember it happening. Later . . . I mean." She rubbed at her forehead, as if the memory puzzled her. "Like after he reported her missing, I waited until you were in the other room with Luna and told him not to worry, that we had taken care of everything. He acted like he had no clue what I meant."

"Sometimes people block that sort of trauma." Vera reviewed the facts. Obviously what happened with Sheree was sad and unfortunate, but it wasn't murder. Their father had been protecting Luna and then Eve. Manslaughter . . . maybe. The rub lay with their mother and the other two female victims. This was the part that pained Vera the most. "According to the PI, Teresa Russ, one of the women Mama helped bury was having an affair with someone here. Someone wealthy and important."

Eve suddenly realized what she meant. "No way was it Daddy. He adored Mama. No way. I know he screwed up with Sheree, but that was different. He wasn't himself. Mama was dying, and he was out of his mind."

"You're right," Vera admitted. Not that there was ever any excuse. "That leaves either Charles Higdon or Walt Fraley—considering their wives were the others involved in the cover-up. Which would mean Mama was only helping a friend hide what she or he had done."

The scenario went along with the things her father had said. The longer Vera thought about it, the more momentum the idea gained. Maybe only because she wanted so badly for it to be anyone but her father, preferably Higdon.

"I know Mama felt sorry for both those women," Eve noted. "She said that no one deserved to die that way." A frown tugged at her face. "You think she would have felt that way if one or both were involved with Daddy?"

"Probably not," Vera said, working hard to think logically, "but the sympathy you thought she felt may have been regret for what he did and how it prompted her to do what she did." Her chest constricted, and a deep breath just wouldn't come. Then she remembered another aspect of that time period. "The second set of remains would have been placed in the cave around the time Mama got sick."

"That's right," Eve confirmed. "I didn't even think about the cave until way later."

"Right," Vera said, her thoughts zeroing in on the one detail that might prove a saving grace. "I can't pinpoint a particular memory of anything happening between Mama and her friends, but I also can't remember either one coming around after her diagnosis. No visits or calls to see how she was doing. No casseroles. I considered this before, but now that I know the rest, it might mean more than I first thought."

"Oh my God," Eve said, her face lighting up. "You're right. Those two never came to see her after she got sick. Not once. Wait . . ." She put her hand to her mouth before going on. "Mama was mad after the second woman was put in the cave. Really mad. I'm pretty sure that's when her friends stopped coming around. Mama said something like once was a mistake, but purposely doing it again was unforgiveable."

Anticipation zinging, Vera tried to think if she'd seen Beatrice or Florence at the funeral. She couldn't remember. She'd been far too devastated. Surely they had come. Their absence would have been noticed by the whole community, not to mention their husbands. It would have been scandalous not to show up.

A strategy fell immediately into place. "We have to figure this out before we tell a soul," Vera warned. "If Mama didn't kill those two, and we know she couldn't have, then Florence or Beatrice did. Or maybe one of their husbands."

Eve didn't appear so excited about the idea. "Are you sure we shouldn't just tell Bent? This sounds like we might be getting into a hornet's nest."

Vera resisted the impulse to tell her sister this was already a hell of a hornet's nest. Instead, she went with her gut on what the next step should be. Hoped it was the right one. First, she had to convince her sister. "There's not a lot the law can do to Daddy, no matter the outcome of any charges against him for what happened to Sheree. The same goes for Mama. The only damage would be to their memories." Vera pinned her sister with a look. "But you and Suri . . . and Gates—that's a different story. No matter that it's a fairly clear case of self-defense, your world would be turned upside down, as would Suri's. If none of the others he hurt testified, it would be a difficult case to prove."

Eve's face clouded with defeat. "I'm sorry, Vee. We handled it all wrong."

Debra Webb

Vera understood. These kinds of tragedies rarely occurred when people were thinking straight. "Let's see what our options are and then decide about going to Bent."

Eve visibly steadied herself. "How do we determine what our options are?"

A tiny smile tugged at Vera's lips. Oh, she knew exactly where to start that process.

She'd already tested the waters—the weakest link . . . where else?

37

Fraley Farm
Jenkins Road, Fayetteville, 8:00 p.m.

Vera checked the time again. Where the hell were the Fraleys?

"We've been here an hour and a half already. Is your plan to just sit here all night?" Eve shifted in the seat and stuck her head into the darkness outside the window, as if that would provide some sort of relief from the heat.

Not happening. No matter that it was past sunset. The humidity hung in the hot, thick air like molasses dripping from an open container. Her sister's whining did not help the situation.

"We're not leaving until one or both of the Fraleys come home," Vera reminded her, avoiding a specific time frame. "You agreed to see this through."

Eve hissed a beleaguered breath. "I get it. You're punishing me because I knew about the women in that secret part of the cave and you didn't."

Vera's jaw dropped. "That is the most asinine, childish statement I have ever heard." She shook her head. How had she forgotten what it was like spending hours cooped up alone with her sister?

It had been more than twenty years since they'd spent this much time together *alone*, with no background distractions like a television or a looming task that couldn't wait. Apparently, Vera decided, her sister had only one close friend—the same one she'd had since childhood. She worked where she'd always felt most comfortable, with the dead. Never deviated from the known and the trusted. Routine was her middle name. She was a textbook case of failure to move on to the next stage of emotional development.

Now Vera was just being mean. She pushed away the frustration. "I am not punishing you, Eve. You were a child, and learning what was in that cave was an accident. One I'm sure Mama would have preferred to protect you from. What we're doing right now is to protect Mama. You want to do that, don't you?"

"Don't be ridiculous. Of course I do." Eve dropped back into her seat. "And you're right. She didn't want me to see any of it, and I will do whatever is necessary to protect her memory."

Vera leaned against her own headrest. "It's exhausting."

Eve turned her head toward Vera now. "Keeping me and Mama out of trouble?"

A dry chuckle erupted from Vera's lips. "No." She turned her head as well, so her and her sister's faces were only a dozen or so inches apart. "I would do anything anytime to protect you and Mama. Daddy and Luna too. I meant keeping secrets is exhausting."

"No kidding." Eve breathed a laugh that held even less humor than Vera's had. "It's so much easier to just tell the truth."

"Except," Vera offered, "sometimes it's too painful to tell, or it creates a domino effect that ultimately will help no one."

"Especially Luna," Eve said, facing forward once more.

Especially Luna. Vera sighed. She didn't want to think about their secrets anymore.

Eve tugged out her cell phone and distracted herself.

Vera considered doing the same but preferred not to risk seeing her name attached to any lead stories.

"We have three potential *sugar daddies*," she said, thinking out loud in hopes of doing something constructive. "Dr. Higdon, Sheriff Fraley, and Daddy."

"My money's on Higdon," Eve said without looking up from her phone. "I never liked him. He was always so mean, even when he pretended to be nice."

"I thought you liked him," Vera countered, "since he works with the dead too."

Eve's face contorted into an expression of disgust that looked slightly blue in the light from her cell phone. "Not the same as what I do at all. Besides, he has always been like this sneaky old man who did things you couldn't see but that hurt just the same. All smiles and wearing those little bow ties."

A laugh popped out of Vera.

"What?" Eve shot a curious look at her.

"Every time I see him," Vera admitted, "I think of that old Porky Pig cartoon."

They both burst into laughter, the full-belly kind, until they had to stop to breathe.

"Oh my God," Eve said as she wiped away tears from laughing so hard, "me too."

Vera swiped at her eyes and cleared her throat. "Then I guess that makes his wife Petunia."

They dissolved into laughter once more. Vera laughed until it hurt. She understood that it was the exhaustion and the stress driving the moment, but she needed the relief and felt thankful for it, no matter the form.

"Oh shit." Eve stared at her phone.

Vera straightened up. "What?"

Eve turned the screen toward her. The image was of her and Eve sitting on the bench at their mother's grave. Vera grabbed the phone and tapped on the screen. There was another image, this one of their mother's coffin being exhumed. Fury lit in her belly. The accompanying story was about the exhumation . . . from the Memphis ABC affiliate and that damned Patricia Patton.

The ruthless reporter had gotten her story. Vera wasn't surprised, just pissed off.

Headlights bobbed in the darkness, jerking Vera's attention forward. She passed the phone back to Eve and collected herself. "Maybe this is the Fraleys."

Eve tossed the device onto the console. "I hope so. I'm starving."

As if the reminder had flipped some switch, Vera's stomach rumbled. "We'll stop at the Jack's pickup window before going home."

"You can have Jack's," Eve grumbled. "I'll take KFC."

Vera didn't argue. Who knew if either of them would still have an appetite when this was done. She refused to think about the images that went with that damned story of Patton's.

The truck Vera had seen parked in the drive the last time she visited Beatrice came to a stop now. As if the driver considered turning around and driving away, the vehicle sat for a moment, motor running, lights blaring into Vera's SUV, before shutting down and going dark.

"Beatrice is getting out," Eve said, peering toward the truck, which was parked on her side of the driveway, maybe ten feet away.

"Let's do this then." Vera opened her door and climbed out. Eve followed.

By the time Beatrice reached the front end of her truck, Vera and Eve were there. A second person—presumably Walt—was in the passenger seat. Vera could just make out the outline of a figure beyond the windshield.

"Hi, Beatrice," Vera said. "We've been waiting to see you."

"This is not a very good time," the former schoolteacher said, her voice too low, too quiet, as if she didn't want whoever was still in the truck to hear. "Walt had an appointment at the doctor's office in Nashville, and we visited our niece while we were there. We're both fairly exhausted, as you can imagine."

"I'm sorry," Vera said, feeling no sympathy whatsoever. "But this won't wait for another time."

Beatrice exhaled an audible breath. "I need to get Walt in the house."

Before Vera could offer, Eve said, "Let me help you." She followed the older woman to the passenger side of the vehicle.

Eve retrieved the folded wheelchair from the bed of the truck and readied it for its occupant. Beatrice helped her husband out of the vehicle.

"Evening, Vee," Walt said as he rolled past.

"Evening to you." She doubted he would be happy when he learned the reason for her showing up like this. Since Beatrice said nothing, it was clear she wasn't happy at all.

Her behavior was suspicious to say the least. Maybe only because Vera wanted her to know something about the murders. Wishful thinking could be powerful at times.

Eve rolled the wheelchair, Walt onboard, to the ramp that had been added at the end of the porch. Another, brighter light came on as they neared. Beatrice unlocked the door and stood back while Eve continued pushing the wheelchair until they were inside.

While Beatrice settled her husband in the living room, Vera and Eve waited in the front hall. Some folks still called the main rooms in these old houses *parlors*, but Vera's mother had used the term *living room*. Her mother hadn't really been like the other mothers. Maybe because she had grown up in the city. Even though Nashville was still in Tennessee, it was a different world from Fayetteville.

When Beatrice returned to the hall and looked from one to the other, it was clear as glass she didn't plan to make this easy.

She said nothing, just looked at them.

"Do we need to speak in private?" Vera asked.

The older woman turned and walked toward the kitchen.

Vera and Eve shared a look, then followed.

Beatrice sat down at the kitchen table. Vera and Eve joined her.

When they'd made this plan—or more accurately, when Vera had decided this visit was a necessity, she had concluded it would be best to proceed with caution. She and Eve did not need to reveal any aspect of what they knew about the disposal of the women's bodies or the fact that their mother had helped. The goal was to learn all possible without giving anything away or leading the story in any way.

"We've learned," Vera began, "the identity of the other remains in the cave." She left it at that for a moment to focus on the older woman's response, verbal and physical.

At the news Beatrice flinched ever so slightly, then she blinked. "Florence hasn't mentioned it."

"She likely doesn't know," Vera explained. "The lab in Nashville is handling the case. With the FBI involved, locals don't necessarily get all the details." This was basically conjecture on her part, since Bent hadn't said one way or the other, but it was the most logical assumption.

More blinking from their reluctant host. "Is it someone we know?"

"Latesha Johnson and Trina Sutton, both from the Huntsville area," Vera explained. "Latesha was having an affair with a so-called sugar daddy here in Fayetteville."

Another flinch. "Oh my. I don't recognize either of those names." Beatrice's tone sounded stiff . . . unnatural.

"Sheriff Fraley never mentioned those names?" Eve asked, her timing perfect. "There was an investigation when the second one, Trina Sutton, went missing."

Beatrice's face worked until she managed to speak. "I was so busy with my teaching and after-school programs, I rarely had any idea what Walt was investigating."

"Why don't you just ask me," the man himself said as he rolled into the kitchen. He looked from Vera to Eve and back. "My body might be betraying me, but my mind"—he tapped his temple—"works just fine."

"Do you need some water or something?" His wife shot to her feet. "I'm sure you're utterly exhausted."

He scoffed. "Why, I'm never too exhausted for these two."

Vera turned in her chair to face the man as he rolled closer to the table. "Do you remember an investigation into two missing women,

Latesha Johnson and Trina Sutton, from twenty-five years ago? They were from Huntsville but came to Fayetteville and were never seen again. I remember you said there were no unsolved missing persons cases under your watch."

Walt considered her question for a time before responding. "I do. The one—Sutton, as I recall—had gone missing after supposedly coming to Fayetteville to look for a friend." His face furrowed in thought as he searched his memories. "There was never any investigation conducted by the Fayetteville Police Department or my office on the Johnson case. I only recognize the name because it was a part of the Sutton case—which FPD participated in. It was never my case, so what I told you is true."

But he had known about the case, and he hadn't told her. *Slippery slope, Walt,* she mused.

"Was FPD able to determine if Sutton was ever in Fayetteville around the time in question?" Vera asked.

He shook his head. "They found nothing to suggest she was ever here or involved with anyone here. Now"—he gave Vera a look—"does that mean she wasn't? As you well know, it only means they didn't find a witness who had seen her or owned up to seeing her."

Vera wasn't surprised. This was the way those types of cases usually went.

"We're just trying to figure out," Eve chimed in, "how the two ended up buried in our cave. Do you remember any other details about the investigation?"

That she looked at Beatrice when she said this made Vera cringe.

"Now that is a hell of a good question," Walt confirmed, drawing Eve's attention to him. "I said that exact same thing about how they wound up buried in your cave when Bent called me while I was in Nashville today. I think we could clear this all up if we just knew how that happened."

Good to know that Bent wasn't dragging his feet. As for Walt, Vera couldn't quite tell if he was being facetious or helpful. She asked, "Do you have thoughts on the answer to that question?"

He chuckled. "You know I do. As I said, they never found a single thing on either woman. As for why those two were in that cave, I guess you'd have to ask your daddy about that."

Vera felt the punch of his words like a blow. She threw a jab back at him. "Do *you* believe our father was having an affair?"

"I am not suggesting any such thing, nor do I believe any such thing," he insisted. "Did he help out a friend by allowing him to use the cave? Maybe so. Vernon has always been a good-hearted neighbor."

Beatrice had remained silent and utterly still since her husband started to talk, but her face had grown paler with each statement he made.

"You were his friend," Vera offered. "Perhaps you were having an affair with one or both of the women, and it was you he helped."

"Vera Mae Boyett!" Beatrice shot to her feet, her chair scraping across the floor. "Why in the world would you insult my husband this way?"

Walt laughed, but his wife was not even smiling. Vera met her fierce glare. "A friend of my family put those bodies in that cave. I'm just trying to figure out who it was."

Beatrice shook her head. "I will not listen to a moment more of this." She rounded the table to go.

"But, what about Dr. Higdon?" Vera demanded, causing her to stall. "He was friends with my father, and like you, his wife was friends with my mother." Vera frowned. "Wait. Maybe I'm wrong, since neither she nor you came to visit Mama during her most difficult time. You seemed to fall off the planet when she needed you most."

Beatrice hesitated for two seconds, then she stormed out of the room.

Walt sighed. "This situation has us all upset." He rested his attention on Vera. "She's just trying to protect me. Bea adored your mama."

"I'm sure you're right," Vera agreed.

Except the only thing she was certain about was the idea that Beatrice Fraley knew something that was eating at her . . . eating her alive.

All Vera had to do was keep pouring on the pressure until the woman couldn't hold it in any longer.

38

Vera stood on the porch. She hadn't knocked yet. The house was dark. Bent could be in bed already.

She closed her eyes and drew in a deep breath.

She shouldn't have come. But after visiting the Fraleys, Eve had decided to go to Suri's. Luna was still staying with Jerome, and suddenly Vera hadn't wanted to be alone with her thoughts anymore.

What the hell was she doing *here*?

The porch light came on. She blinked at the brightness.

The door opened, and Bent was there, a wide smile on his face. "I was in the office, but I heard you turn into my driveway."

Besides being startled, now she was confused. How could he hear her half a mile away?

At her look of confusion, he went on, "I have an alarm and cameras that let me know when someone turns into my drive. Sheriffs aren't loved by everyone."

She understood. Made sense he probably had a camera on the porch and watched her indecision about knocking.

"It's late." Not that late but . . . it was the only thing she could think to say. Funny, she'd had this list of items she wanted to talk with him about, and suddenly her mind was blank, or maybe she was just too damned afraid to start spilling and end up saying far too much.

He reached for her arm and tugged her across the threshold. "Coffee? Beer? Something stronger maybe?"

"Stronger, I think." She watched while he closed the door and then walked over to the kitchen area.

Part of her wanted to collapse on his sofa, but she couldn't be that still with all the scenarios spinning in her head. Instead she started to pace. Beatrice Fraley knew the whole story. Damn it. Was the former sheriff covering for her? His theory about how the bodies got into the cave was reasonable but only pointed to her father's involvement, not her mother's—which, she supposed, would by association implicate his wife.

The idea that Walt knew what his wife and Florence Higdon had done and still protected them disappointed Vera, no matter that, in his position, she would likely do the same. She'd been protecting Eve for decades . . . except apparently it wasn't Eve who had needed protecting where Sheree was concerned. It was their father. Eve's confession had rocked Vera to the core.

Why, oh why had her sister not told her this in the first place? *Irrelevant. Move on.*

"Here you go."

She jumped. She'd been so deep in thought she hadn't realized Bent had appeared next to her. She struggled to recover and accept the tumbler, filled with something amber that promised relief. She sipped it, then indulged in a deeper swallow. The burn that rushed down her throat warned it wouldn't be long before that edge she tittered on would vanish, or at the very least soften.

"What's going on, Vee?" His hand was on her arm again, guiding her to the sofa.

She eased down onto the cool leather, and he settled next to her. His closeness had her going for another generous swallow.

"Eve and I stopped by to see Walt and his wife." She took a breath, hoped it would shore up her wobbly composure. "I wanted to know why he'd told me there were no unsolved missing persons cases on his watch—which as we know isn't true. He claimed it wasn't his case, it was FPD's."

The urge to tell him the rest was so abrupt and so strong, she barely held back. Would unburdening herself make her feel better in the end? She wasn't sure anymore. Couldn't trust herself to make the right choice.

Bent mulled over her words for a time before responding. Vera downed the last of her drink. Wished there was more but recognized the danger in going there.

"I can see his point," Bent said. "No one wants an unsolved case on their books. He told me the same thing when I called. But I'm not so sure that's his only motive."

Eve had been right. Bent really was a good sheriff. She studied his face, the lines and angles she had never been able to evict from her memory. Why wasn't he married by now? He was clearly a great catch. The sheriff . . . handsome as hell. Her gaze traced his beard-shadowed jaw, roved over his full lips. The remembered feel of those lips—

"Vee, you need to stop looking at me that way, or I'm going to get the wrong idea."

She blinked, told herself to shift her attention from the movement of his lips to his eyes. That piercing blue color zoomed into vivid focus . . . the move didn't help.

"I should go." She stood, swayed a little. Damn, maybe she should have taken a little more time with that drink.

He stood, set his glass on the coffee table, then did the same with hers. "I know this thing is getting more complicated every day."

For a moment she had no clue what he was talking about, then the image of the cave tumbled into her rambling thoughts. "*Complicated* is one way to put it."

The cell phone stuffed into her back pocket vibrated. She snatched at it, needing two attempts to drag it free.

Eve.

What now? Vera was so weary of the damned drama.

"Is everything all right?" she said instead of hello, when she wanted to demand what the hell had happened now.

"You need to come home," Eve said, her voice too quiet.

"What is it?" Fear blasted away the effects of the alcohol.

"I had to come back by the house for my phone charger and found Luna here. She is really upset. Someone was in the house again."

"On my way." Vera shoved the phone back into her pocket. She steadied herself and met Bent's expectant gaze. "I have to go."

When she swayed, he took hold of her arms and steadied her. "Hold up a minute. What's going on?"

"Someone broke into the house again." Damn, she should have considered that he would need to go too.

His expression hardened. "I'm driving."

Boyett Farm
Good Hollow Road, Fayetteville, 11:50 p.m.

Bent had searched the house and yard and found nothing except a broken pane of glass in the back door—the entry point.

Luna had calmed down after Vera's arrival. A fight with Jerome had prompted the mutual decision that a cooling off period was necessary, so she'd come home for the night and bumped into an intruder. Like the one Vera encountered: tall, muscled, outfitted in a black ski mask and gloves.

They—all three sisters—sat on the sofa, Luna wrapped in Vera's arms as if she were two years old again. Eve as usual looked stiff and uncomfortable at the closeness. She wasn't much of a hugger. Hadn't been since their mother died. Vera thought about that for a moment. Eve really had changed after that painful day. Vera reached her free arm out and draped it around her and pulled her closer, whether she appreciated it or not.

"This is weird," Eve muttered.

Vera smiled, her lips pressed against Eve's hair. "Little bit." She eased away, removed her arm.

Eve grinned at her. "Thanks for the thought though."

"It's always the thought that counts." Vera dropped her head against the sofa. This was so much like when they were kids. She glanced down at Luna. Except she had been a baby rather than a grown woman on the verge of marriage.

Luna was the baby of the family, yet she was the only one to get this close to marriage. Spoke volumes about just how screwed up Vera and Eve were.

Thanks, Dad.

Then again, for Eve apparently it had started with their mother.

And here Vera had been confident their childhood in the *before* period had been pretty perfect.

Bent entered the room, and they rose from the sofa in anticipation of whatever he had to say. For Vera her attention first swept from hair to boots and back before landing on his face. He really was far too handsome for his—or Vera's—own good, with her teetering in such a precarious emotional place right now.

So very cliché, Vee.

"What happened with the security system installation?" This question he directed at Eve, who had volunteered to take care of that detail.

"They can't come until next week," she said with equal measures impatience and frustration. She glanced at Vera.

She was supposed to have told Bent but forgot. Oh well. A lot of crazy shit had happened. "Sorry." Vera raised her hand. "I was supposed to tell you that."

He gave a nod. "I'll take care of the back-door repair in the morning. For now, I have it secured in a temporary manner."

Vera had heard a power drill. She suspected he'd picked through her father's tools until he found what he needed to secure the door closed.

"We appreciate that," Vera said.

After Bent's thorough look around, she and her sisters had explored the house and determined that nothing appeared to be missing. Evidently whatever the intruder had been looking for he didn't find, or what he found was something they hadn't yet missed. Vera was glad he hadn't ransacked their parents' bedroom again. She'd only just gotten it put back together.

"You ladies should get some sleep," Bent suggested. "I'll be on your couch tonight."

"I'm going back to Suri's." Eve was heading out of the room as she spoke. "Night, y'all."

Good nights were called after her. Vera knew better than to try to stop her. She wondered if Eve would tell Suri that Vera knew about the rapist.

Didn't matter. She could not think about that again tonight.

Luna folded her arms over her chest. "Thank you, Bent." She looked to Vera, smiled sadly. "Night."

There had been no time to discuss whatever had happened between her and Jerome. Hopefully nothing major.

Vera returned her smile. "Night." She watched her go, wishing she could make her feel better about her fiancé, but that was way beyond her control.

With her sisters gone, Vera figured it would be in her best interest to go as well. "I'll get you a pillow and a blanket."

Bent analyzed her for a long moment, then he nodded. "That works."

As Vera walked away, she wondered if he'd hoped she would invite him upstairs.

Oh yes, this whole situation just kept getting more complicated.

And maybe a little more dangerous than she wanted to admit.

What was the intruder looking for? There had to be something here, or he wouldn't have come back. Assuming it was the same guy. But what could it be? Vera had searched the house thoroughly.

She had a feeling the answer to that question was the match point in this game.

39

Saturday, July 27

Boyett Farm
Good Hollow Road, Fayetteville, 6:35 a.m.

"Another cup?" Bent stood at the counter next to the coffee maker.

Vera shook her head. "No thanks."

He had been up and making coffee by half past five. The smell of the fresh brew had drawn her down the stairs when she had thought she might stay in her room until Luna was up.

Waking up with Bent in the house was a first.

And no matter that his clothes had that slept-in look and his hair was just a little tousled, he looked far too good. Wore forty-something really well.

"Serious personal question," she said, before her brain could over-ride her mouth. She should have been discussing last night's intruder and what it meant, but here she was about to toss out a personal question that suggested things she didn't want to imply. She was just curious, that's all. At least that's what she told herself.

The way he paused to wait for the question made her want to crawl under the table and hide. Then he refilled his mug and joined her at the table once more. "Shoot."

No going back now. "Why aren't you married or in a serious relationship?"

"Probably the same reason you aren't." He inclined his head and studied her the way he had last night when she'd offered him a pillow and blanket. "Life in the military—for me—wasn't really conducive to a permanent relationship. Lots of folks handle it just fine, but it wasn't the sort of situation I wanted. When I came back here, Walt immediately recruited me to go after the position of sheriff. There was a lot of work to be done to straighten things out. On top of that I was busy renovating my place. No time, I guess, is ultimately the answer."

"Wow." Vera gave him a pointed look. "That's a lot of excuses for ignoring your personal life."

He chuckled. "Like you have any room to talk. Why aren't you married or in a serious relationship?"

Right there was the reason a smart person never asked questions like the one she'd foolishly thrown out.

Not at the top of your game today, Vee.

"Truth?" She might as well start there.

"The truth is always the better choice," he agreed.

"I was so burned by our relationship, I didn't want another one for a really long time." She held up a hand when he would have spoken— judging by his expression, an apology. "I'm not saying that because I want you to feel guilty or to apologize. We were kids. I suppose between Mama's death and you leaving, I just needed some time before wading in again."

He gave her a nod. "Fair enough."

"Eventually, I dated. I was almost engaged once, but when he popped the question, I said no. He was a very nice man, and we had fun together, but I just didn't get that forever vibe, you know?" She laughed. "Thankfully we are still friends."

The part she kept to herself was that she'd wondered once or twice if she'd made a mistake . . . if she'd missed her one chance at the things every woman was supposed to want. No, she'd decided. This was not her mother's generation. This was now, and people wanted different things. There was no need to follow a certain protocol.

Bent smiled that one-sided expression that always made her smile back no matter the circumstances. "I guess our time will come."

"Maybe." She laughed. "I won't hold my breath."

"Me either." He drank his coffee.

Vera toyed with the idea of changing her mind about that second cup, but she was already fidgety enough. Better not to push the limits of her caffeine rush.

"Fraley called me at the crack of dawn this morning."

The news surprised her. "Does he do that often? Check in on how you're handling things?"

"More so lately." Bent pushed his cup away as if he'd had enough as well. "He wanted to talk about the other remains found in the second cavern of the cave—in particular, the female victims."

"Really." Vera wondered if the man had passed along any new scenarios or complained about her and Eve's visit.

"He firmly believes your dad helped out a friend who'd gotten in too deep."

Vera had hoped for something different. "Yes, he mentioned something like that last night." She turned her cup between her fingers to give herself something to focus on as she worked up the courage to say what she really thought. "My thinking is if that's the case, then the friend was probably the former sheriff himself."

Surprise flared in Bent's eyes. "They were—are friends. Could be, I guess."

That he didn't argue the point was unexpected. "There are a number of others," Vera pointed out. "George Monroe, Daddy's longtime boss. They were friends." His name had popped into her head as she lay in bed last night, trying to pretend Bent wasn't down here on the sofa. "Charles Higdon." She ticked off a few other names of big shots in town with whom her father had been friends. "Where should we start our questioning?"

"Seems to me"—Bent leaned forward, braced his forearms on the table—"you already did."

She shrugged. "I suppose I did."

"Is there a particular reason you started with Walt? I mean he's a well-loved figure in the county. Everybody knows him."

She'd expected him to cut the man a little extra slack. Back in the day, Bent had told her how Sheriff Fraley had intervened on numerous occasions when Bent's daddy was on a rampage. A kid didn't forget that sort of thing.

What she couldn't say was that it was Walt's wife who'd been last night's target.

"We both know that doesn't exempt him from crossing the line," she countered. "Mistakes happen to the best of us." The tragedy in Memphis was a perfect example.

"No one is exempt," Bent agreed.

"Not even my mama," she said, tossing it out there so casually, she hoped he didn't see the motive behind it. "Or Beatrice and Florence or the wives of any of the other men I mentioned."

"Your mama would never have hurt anyone," he argued. "We can rule her out."

He really had adored her mother. "But not the other women."

His smile was back. "So that's it, huh? You think one of the wives did this because the husband was cheating with one or both of those women left in that cave. And maybe Evelyn helped a friend in need."

A shiver raced across her skin. "Maybe. Whoever it was has sent this same mystery intruder into the house not once but twice. The audacity of the move tells me this is someone who knows us well. The persistence suggests whatever she *or he* thinks is here must be incriminating." Vera considered the idea a moment. "She's looking for something my mama or daddy may have left. Maybe something that points to the scorned wife turned killer."

"Or the husband trying to hide his secrets," Bent proposed.

"Or that," she agreed.

"Then we need to figure out what that something is."

"We can start right now." Vera stood.

Bent did the same. But then he reached for his cell, checked the screen. "Bent," he said in greeting.

Vera took their cups to the sink while he spoke with the caller. Luna was still upstairs. She likely hadn't gotten much sleep last night, plus she had big shopping plans later. Any search of the upstairs would have to wait until Luna was gone. No need to upset her further.

Bent ended his call. "I have to go. There was a break-in over at the Claiborne place. Turns out their two teenage boys have a major drug operation going on in the barn. But we should go through the house together later today."

Just because it was a Saturday didn't mean the sheriff had a day off. Vera was well aware. "It's a date. But in the meantime, I'd like to interview some of my parents' other friends. I need to find answers, Bent."

"That will be our next step after the search. We will not stop until we find those answers," he promised.

Vera followed him to the door. "I appreciate you playing bodyguard last night."

"Any time." He settled his hat into place. "FYI, I've got someone assigned to watch the house until that security system is installed."

"Thanks. I, for one, will feel better." Luna would be at Jerome's—assuming they made up, and they would. Eve went to Suri's as often as she stayed home. So Vera would likely be alone.

Eve's relationship with Suri and the business with the Gates guy was just one more secret she could never tell this man—no matter that the cop in her wanted to do so more every passing hour. In truth, it was only a matter of time before Bent or the FBI found the same connection to Suri that Vera had found. Until then, she had enough to deal with without going down that road just yet.

"Keep me posted on what you're up to," he said before leaving.

"I will." Vera watched him walk to his truck. She actually intended to start interviewing the other potential suspects this morning. But Bent didn't need to know that until she had something to share. He didn't want her doing it alone. Not to mention, anything she learned would be considered hearsay. But she had to do it. She had to know. Had to find answers before this thing went any further south.

When he'd driven away, she grabbed her bag and keys. She glanced toward the upstairs landing. Still no sign of Luna. Maybe she needed some time alone. Vera ensured the door was locked and headed out.

She'd already pressed Beatrice for answers, and she had no doubt told Florence. The more time they had to work out their stories or cover any other tracks, the less likely Vera was to find the truth. She could not wait for Bent.

And she knew right where she wanted to start.

Higdon Residence
Mulberry Avenue, Fayetteville, 8:00 a.m.

Judge Preston Higdon didn't live out in the county as Vera and Bent did. He lived in the biggest historic house on Mulberry. He'd obviously taken great care to bring the massive home back to its former grandeur.

The open carriage-style doors of the detached garage showed off a high-end automobile with vanity plates. Vera knew from her research that the man had two daughters, both at Ivy League universities. His wife was a doctor. And, as Mrs. Higdon had boasted, his name was on the list of nominees for a Tennessee State Supreme Court post.

Dear Preston had done well for himself. Vera should give him the benefit of the doubt. He could be a very nice man. Just because he was a real shit back in school, that didn't mean he'd grown into a bigger one.

The door opened after a second ring of the ancient doorbell with its strange *bong*. Preston himself stood at the door. No butler or housekeeper doing it for him. No little wife dutifully manning the needs of the household. Possibly a good sign. No matter that it was Saturday and quite early, he wore neatly pressed navy trousers and a crisp light-blue shirt with the collar open. He looked ready for a day on the courthouse steps, speaking to the citizens whom he helped protect, or for a stroll around the square for first Saturday activities. He was clean shaven, his hair styled just so, and maybe even had a touch of makeup on his chiseled face.

His expression shifted to surprise. "Vera? Vera Boyett."

"Good to see you, Preston."

He looked her up and down, and a grin spread across his face. "Well, my word, how are you?"

"I'm good. Really good. I'm hearing all sorts of amazing things about you. Up for the state supreme court. That's just incredible."

He rolled his eyes. "My mother. God love her. She's told everyone in the county." He opened the door wider. "Please, come in. Would you like coffee? It's just me this morning. My wife, Charlene, is away at a medical conference."

Vera beamed a smile. "Coffee would be lovely."

"Well, come on then." He waved an arm, ushering her inside.

If she'd thought he had glammed up the exterior of this big old house, no adequate words came immediately to mind at what he had done inside. *Stunning* perhaps covered it. What she could see of the parlors on either side of the gorgeous entry hall had been beautifully restored, modernized only the slightest bit. The staircase was breathtaking. The woodwork and the plaster walls simply beautiful.

This was very Preston.

On the side table in the enormous hall was a photograph of the family. His daughters, thankfully, looked more like their mother. Next to that photograph was another: his parents. Vera bit the inside of her jaw to keep Porky and Petunia out of her head. The third photo was another older couple. Perhaps his in-laws.

"My daughters, Charlotte and Cassidy." He gestured to the first photo Vera had noticed.

"Beautiful young ladies," she said, meeting his gaze once more.

"Come on." He led the way to the kitchen—a chef's dream of course—where he immediately prepared coffee in a machine that looked like a small prototype of the base one might use to build a robot.

"Sit." His hand on her back, he leaned in close and gestured to the extravagantly long island with its Italian marble top. "I'll bring the coffee when it's finished."

Vera stilled—as still as stone—as he strutted across the room. A smile slid over her face. Oh, this was too good. She watched as he hurried to start the coffee. Eventually she slid onto one of the stools and reveled in this new discovery.

The machine sputtered and billowed steam, but it wasn't the pleasing smell just starting to waft from it that had captured her attention. It was his *aftershave*.

It couldn't be this easy . . . oh, but it certainly seemed so.

"I hope you don't mind me mentioning it, but what's happening at your farm"—he joined her at the island and passed her a cup filled with the fresh brew—"is pretty incredible. My God, to have four sets of human remains hidden there for all these years. You must be reeling."

Vera somehow maintained a calm facade as she sipped her coffee. "You're right, it really is incredible. I don't know how we lived there all that time and never had a clue."

He shook his head. "It's a shame about your father's illness. I suppose he's unable to shed any light on the situation."

She understood. He wanted to take the opportunity for a little fishing as well.

"Sadly not. I'm helping Bent interview people who were friends of my parents in an effort to learn anything I can about the time frame."

His forehead furrowed in thought. "It was what? Twenty-odd years ago?"

"Twenty-five or -six, yes, for the first ones."

He reached for his cup. Vera watched, noted how fit and muscular he was. Clearly he worked out regularly. The memory of the intruder's solid, muscled body roared into her head.

"I was preparing to head out to college," he said as he cradled his coffee. "It just seems so . . . unbelievable. Like a horror movie."

"You were accepted to Harvard," she said, ignoring his other comments. "I remember it being on the billboard in front of the high school."

He smiled, pretended to be embarrassed. "I was lucky."

Vera made a scoffing sound. "Please, we both know how it works. You were a spectacular student, obviously."

He bowed his head in feigned humility. "Thank you."

Vera savored her coffee for a moment before venturing into the deep weeds. It took every ounce of self-control she possessed to sit still and converse with him. "Our parents were good friends."

He nodded. "They were. I remember. I was usually busy with my own friends, so I didn't see you and Eve much, but I do remember several occasions when your whole family came to some big festivity my parents would host at the house." He rolled his eyes. "My mother was a regular party animal."

If he meant a show-off, he was right.

"Do you remember any tension between my parents during that time frame—twenty-five or -six years ago?"

"No." He shook his head. "Nothing comes to mind." He made a face that suggested he was confused. "Why do you ask?"

"If my father was having an affair," she proposed, "I thought perhaps there might have been tension between him and my mother or between him and their friends. I was so young, I doubt I would have noticed."

"Ah." He nodded as if he got it now. Then he made that concentrating face again. "I do seem to recall my parents being worried about your parents for some reason or another. I doubt it would have come to mind though if you hadn't asked. Interesting how the memory works. Sometimes it only takes a simple mention of a particular day to trigger all sorts of memories. Have you tried looking through family photo albums? Snapshots from the past can be so good at bringing back things we've forgotten."

"I have." Vera sipped her coffee. "They provided some help."

"I'm sure you have dozens of"—he smiled—"shall we say, *vintage* photo albums. Do you have them stored away from sunlight? It's particularly bad for the photographs."

Vera hadn't given a single thought to photograph storage. "We have so many albums. Mother loved taking photos. As far as I know, they're all lined up on bookshelves in her library. I guess I'll have to look into changing that."

He gave her a nod. "You'll be glad you did."

"Honestly, I feel like I'm running in circles. I have to tell you"—she looked him directly in the eyes—"it's a very difficult time for me and my sisters."

"I'm sure it is." He made a sad face.

Unable to help herself, she leaned closer and inhaled deeply. "What is that aftershave or cologne you're wearing?"

"Clive Christian number one. My wife buys it every year for my birthday." A startled look claimed his face, as if he'd just gotten the punch line of an insulting joke.

Vera hummed a contemplative note. "I'm sure I've smelled it somewhere before." She inhaled deeply again. "Hmm." She drew back. "Well, thank you for the coffee, but I really have to go."

She hopped off the stool and headed for the door.

He hurried to keep up with her hasty exit. "I'm sure I can arrange a meeting with my parents," he offered. "If you'd like to interview them."

Vera didn't pause until she reached the front door. "Well thank you, but that's not necessary. I'll just have Bent arrange it. Nice seeing you again."

She walked out, knowing that Judge Preston Higdon would be calling his mother the instant the door closed.

"Gotcha," she muttered.

Whatever else he had done, he'd damned well been in her house, possibly twice, caused her to take a tumble down the stairs, and scared the hell out of Luna.

Unless, of course, there was some other pretentious ass in this little town who wore $2,000 aftershave.

40

Vera had made calls and stopped at the homes of several of her father's friends. Keller Cole, a longtime work friend of her daddy's, had passed away last year. His wife remembered nothing relevant to the time in question. With no luck there, she tracked down Dennis Haynes. Haynes was the coworker who had, according to the FBI, lent his car to her daddy to go home the day Sheree . . .

Anyway, the man's wife informed Vera that her husband wasn't taking visitors. He had a terrible, highly contagious virus and was sequestered to the bedroom. She would have him call when he was well enough to chat.

Vera didn't believe her for a minute, but there was nothing to do but let it go until another time.

George Monroe was next on her list. She walked up onto his porch and rang the bell. Monroe had been the managing partner of Monroe & Floyd Distributors. Besides Higdon, he was her last hope as far as her daddy's closest friends went. But how personal did her daddy get with the man who was his boss? Maybe not so much.

Her best bets were Haynes and Higdon.

The trouble was, if Haynes was avoiding her, and Higdon would certainly be, then Monroe was it for now—assuming he was home and available.

The door opened, and an older, very petite woman peered up at Vera. Her gray hair was fastened into a neat bun, and the pink lipstick she wore matched her dress. "Whatever you're selling, I'm certain we're not interested."

It wasn't until she spoke that Vera remembered the lady. Back in the day—in the *before*—Mrs. Joslyn Monroe was known for her homemade tea cakes. Vera and Eve had loved when gatherings were hosted by the Monroes just for those tea cakes.

"Mrs. Monroe, you probably don't remember me. I'm Vera Boyett, Vernon and Evelyn's daughter."

Her mouth formed an *O* before her lips spread into a wide smile. "My goodness, you're so grown up, I didn't recognize you. Come in!"

Before the door was closed behind Vera, the woman was already shouting for her husband. "George! You won't believe who's here."

George, ninety if he was a day, shuffled into the entry hall. "My goodness. Look at you." He grinned. "It's like Vernon said, you're the spitting image of your mother."

Vera's chest constricted. "Thank you. It's nice to see you, Mr. Monroe."

"Good gracious, call me George."

"Call me Lyn," his wife tossed in. "Now come on in here."

Once they'd ushered her to the living room, Mrs. Monroe—Lyn— insisted on serving iced tea. George told Vera all about how he and her father had lunch once a week all these years until just recently. But now Vernon, more often than not, didn't recognize him. Then he moved on to a more pleasant topic, explaining how his sons had taken over the company and business was booming. He had four grandchildren—he showed her photos of every single one—and half a dozen great-grandchildren. He and Lyn were living the good life enjoying all those grands.

Vera suddenly wondered if her daddy had ever resented the fact that neither she nor Eve had given him a grandchild.

She brushed aside the unexpected thought. "I'm sure you've heard about the trouble at the farm. We're just stunned at all that's been found."

"It's quite the shock," he agreed. "We were all convinced that Sheree had taken off on Vernon. No surprise really. She had a certain reputation."

"She did." Vera pursed her lips and gave a somber nod. "It's just inconceivable that she's been dead all this time. We can't even imagine who would have wanted to kill her."

Lyn lifted her glass of tea but hesitated before taking a drink. "I can tell you," she said with a knowing look at Vera. "It was a wife, mark my word. That girl was just daring someone to come after her."

"Now, now, Lyn. No need to speak ill of the dead," her husband warned.

Lyn made a *tsk*ing sound. "Live by the sword, die by the sword."

Vera resisted the urge to smile. "It was a sad and difficult time."

"It was," Lyn agreed, then smiled. "What a lovely young lady that Luna has become."

"She has. Daddy raised her right."

"He did, indeed." George assessed Vera a moment. "I'm sure the rumors about your father having been the one who did away with Sheree have been heartbreaking. But I can tell you, I find that impossible to believe. The man adored her."

Lyn shot him a look. He held up his hands, as if to ward it off. "It's true, he did. Not like he loved your mother, of course. But he was smitten well enough."

"Evelyn was the one he loved most," Lyn added. "I'm convinced Sheree took advantage of his loneliness and grief."

"I will give you that," George confirmed.

"Do you recall any particular tension going on between my parents in the two or three years before my mother died?" Vera asked.

The two looked at each other, then shook their heads. "No," George insisted. "Your parents were the happiest couple we knew."

Lyn laughed. "We were all jealous of how close they were. If there was ever any trouble, the two resolved it quickly and never once let on."

Vera bit her bottom lip, hesitating before throwing the next one at them. Then she went for it. "What about any of the other friends? Any tension with them? I mean"—Vera looked to Lyn—"as you said, there were plenty of wives who were upset by Sheree."

George frowned, as if he were concentrating on the question. "I can't recall any particular issues." He laughed then. "That was the time frame when you and I were on the wrong side with each other."

Lyn nodded, her face somber. "We almost got divorced twenty-six years ago, right after our youngest son graduated college. I had this strange idea that I married too young and hadn't experienced life the way I should have."

"Thankfully," George put in, "she realized she was wrong."

Lyn made a little gasp. "Now that I think about it, I believe Florence and Charles were having a little trouble back then too."

George made a maybe-maybe-not gesture to back up the expression that insinuated the same. "It was always difficult to tell when Florence and Charles were fighting about themselves or that pom—" He cleared his throat. "Their son. Preston was a bit spoiled by his mother, and Charles tended to get ill about it sometimes."

Vera laughed. "It can be that way at times. Particularly with only children."

Lyn scoffed. "Admit it." She said this to Vera. "Preston was a little shit."

"Oh my," George said. "Perhaps we shouldn't go there, Lyn. After all, his father will likely be the one to pronounce us deceased when we die."

Vera struggled to keep the grin off her face. "A very good point, George."

George's expression turned serious then. "Vera, if your father or your family needs anything during this awful, awful mess, please come to us. We are glad to help."

Vera didn't hesitate. "I could use a little assistance getting Dennis Haynes to talk to me."

"Consider it done," George said. "The man owes me. I overlooked many a Monday morning when he crawled in late after a weekend of too much drink."

"Thank you, that would be much appreciated."

Lyn insisted that Vera stay for lunch, and as much as she wanted to rush out and find the next name on her list, she decided it was the least she could do after the couple had been so forthcoming.

Then she was going to find Pete Brooks if it took her the rest of the day. Although he certainly wasn't on the friends-of-her-parents list, he was considered Garth Rimmey's closest friend.

Whatever he remembered about that time frame, Vera wanted to hear it.

Kidd Road, Fayetteville, 3:30 p.m.

Vera had talked to a dozen people and driven to more locations. But she hadn't found Pete Brooks.

Anywhere.

Bob Phillips, the man who operated the gas station on Pulaski Highway just outside the city limits, had said the last he'd heard, Brooks lived in the Harms area on Ables Road.

Vera had headed there next. She hadn't heard from Bent or her sisters—which hopefully meant there had been no more drama at the house or the cave. Until some other action occurred to change her course, she intended to use every minute available in search of answers.

If she were lucky, George Monroe would come through and have Dennis Haynes call her. Unless, of course, the FBI had warned him not to talk to anyone involved with the case.

She rounded the next curve and found herself staring down a black SUV in her lane.

Her foot went instantly to the brake.

The SUV rocketed forward—still coming directly at her—in *her* lane.

Her heart rushed into her throat. She cut the steering wheel hard to the right. Rammed the accelerator. Her head hit the glass in her door as her vehicle bounced so hard she lost control of the steering wheel . . . her head hit the window again.

The shoulder belt tightened, jerking her against the seat until she couldn't breathe.

And then everything stopped . . . except the airbag.

41

Bent opened the passenger-side door of his truck and waited for Vera to climb in. Until that moment, he'd scarcely been able to breathe.

She said not one word until he was behind the wheel and driving out of the hospital parking lot. No surprise.

"Are you satisfied now?" She shot him a glare as she struggled to rip off the wristband the nurse had put in place despite her argument that she was fine and didn't need to see a doctor.

Bent took a necessary moment before he answered.

Twenty-three years. He had not seen or spoken to this woman in nearly twenty-three years, or thereabouts. He'd thought of her hundreds—maybe thousands—of times. Dreamed about her. Wondered about her.

Then she waltzed into town, and suddenly he was right back there, twenty-odd years ago, thinking he couldn't breathe deeply enough without her.

But he had, and he could.

He just hadn't wanted to . . . didn't want to now.

He was a fool. No question. She might not be going back to Memphis, but when this was over, she would land somewhere.

Anywhere but here. How many times had he heard her say as much back then about the future?

"You hit your head twice," he reminded her as he navigated onto Thornton Taylor Parkway. "The airbag deployed. You could have had a concussion or a skull fracture or even fractured ribs from the airbag. There was no way to be sure without the x-rays and the CT scan."

"And an EKG. And blood work. And every damned thing else you and that overly zealous doctor—who I'm guessing is a friend of yours—could think of! All for the four stitches in my hairline." She ended her rant. Took a breath. "Butterfly strips would have done the trick." She exhaled a big breath and braced her arms across her chest.

She was not happy. Vera Mae Boyett had never liked being bossed around or feeling as if she were not in charge. Evidently that hadn't changed. Or maybe she just got prickly when in a vulnerable position.

"I wanted to make sure you were okay." His fingers tightened on the steering wheel at the memory of finding her.

She had called Bent and claimed she needed a ride without mentioning the reason. Assuming she'd run out of gas or had a mechanical issue, he drove to her location. When he arrived, she was standing on the side of the road, not far from her *wrecked* vehicle, which was straddling the ditch in an odd position. As he drew closer, he saw the blood dripping down her forehead, and that was when he lost it. He would never get that image out of his head. Never. His gut clenched even now.

"Just take me home," she muttered.

Between x-rays and blood draws, he'd had one of his deputies take her statement about the vehicle that ran her off the road. He'd been in no frame of mind to do so. Though she hadn't gotten the license plate number, her description was damned good for someone facing an oncoming seven- or eight-thousand-pound vehicle with little time to react to the threat.

If he found out who did this . . . there would be serious hell to pay, and that was after he'd beaten the ever-loving daylights out of the driver.

The silence the rest of the way to her farm was deafening. Bent thought of several things he should ask her, but he wasn't ready to have his head bitten off again. While they'd waited for results from all the tests, she'd told him about her morning. The people she had interviewed and those she hadn't been able to locate.

He'd wanted to be pissed that she hadn't waited for him to do all those interviews with her, but he'd figured it was best to keep that to himself since he'd strong-armed her into an ER visit. It was always smart to tread carefully with Vee when she was this angry. A smile tugged at his lips, but he suppressed it. Nice to know she wasn't perfect all the time, even if she seemed damned perfect most of the time. He glanced at her. Damned beautiful too.

She caught him looking and glowered. "What? I told you everything."

His smile couldn't be stopped then. "I didn't say otherwise."

He made the right turn into her driveway, rolled forward until he reached the parking area. Other than the county cruiser, no other vehicles were there. Luna was likely closing at the library tonight or already out with Jerome, and Eve worked all kinds of hours at the funeral home. Bent climbed out, rounded the hood, but Vera was already out before he reached her door. She had never liked needing anyone else, especially when she was angry.

He nodded to the deputy keeping watch and followed Vera to the porch. He held out his hand for the key, and she gave it to him with a big exhale, as if doing so had been a tremendous burden. He had a feeling that being back in her hometown and having all this insanity from the past crop up was unsettling her. Damned sure was unsettling him. He unlocked the door and stepped inside. She followed.

"I should have a look around." He surveyed the hall and as far as he could see into the living room.

She slammed the door shut. "Please. If the intruder is back and he didn't hear your truck when you arrived or me slam the door just now and hasn't climbed out a window, he's pretty damned pathetic as an intruder. And your deputy would be a damned sad surveillant."

He shrugged, figured laughing would just piss her off all the more. "All right then. You need to lie down or something?"

Big mistake. Her expression shifted to some pissed-off zone he doubted he wanted to experience. Too late now.

"Are you serious? Four sets of human remains were taken from a cave on this property. Someone—Preston Higdon, I am confident—has broken into this house twice, no less, and another someone—maybe a friend of his—ran me off the road. No, I do not want to lie down. I want to know what he was looking for and why I'm a target."

All right then.

Bent took off his hat and placed it on the table next to the door. "Where would you like to start? Should I go to his house and kick his ass? Beat the truth out of him?"

She looked away, but his suggestions had done the trick. Her posture visibly relaxed. She plopped her shoulder bag and the keys next to his hat. "We should search the house. Maybe I missed something." She shook her head. "We can start upstairs, I suppose. We'll work our way down."

"Good plan," he agreed.

Room by room they took the upstairs apart and found exactly nothing relevant. Nothing an intruder could possibly want. Nothing that related to the case. Bent had to admit that he got a kick out of searching Vera's room. It was exactly the same as when she was in high school. He'd only been in her room once back then—one of the times he had visited her mama. Everything about it was pure Vee. The determination and the energy. She was something.

Downstairs they repeated the same steps. Every drawer, every shelf, every nook and cranny were searched. Vera was damned good at not missing potential hiding places. No surprise. She was a highly trained analyst who had helped create a cutting-edge team. She hadn't gotten so far without expertise in many areas.

She stopped in the middle of the living room and turned to him, looking exhausted and frustrated and just a little bit vulnerable. "I believe we've covered everything." Vera collapsed on the couch.

The bandage on her forehead made his chest feel too tight. When he found out who did this . . . He shook off the thought. "I should see what I can whip up for dinner," he suggested. "Then I'll get out of your hair and let you get some rest."

"Are you going to talk to Preston?" she asked, sounding incensed before he even answered the question.

"I will, yes." He set his hands on his hips and readied for battle. "But you get that he's a judge. I wouldn't want to walk in accusing him of a crime without any evidence."

"The aftershave," she argued. "It was the one the intruder was wearing, and how many men around here do you think wear two-thousand-dollar aftershave?"

"I get that." He nodded for emphasis. "But maybe it was a knockoff brand."

She made a face at the suggestion. "Does he or someone he knows drive a big black SUV? I find it a very big coincidence that this vehicle ran me off the road only a couple of hours after I spoke to him. Especially considering that during our conversation I mentioned the aftershave. I told you that, and it was not a knockoff."

She really was tired. She was repeating herself. Very un-Vera-like. And she had to know that black SUVs were a dime a dozen. God and everybody owned one.

The sound of the front door opening had them both moving into the hall.

Luna, then Eve, walked in.

Saved by the bell. Bent hoped he was off the hook about the judge until he could do some digging. As much as he wanted to charge into the man's house, he had to keep his cool and be smart about this. Vera was not thinking straight. She was emotionally involved and angry.

"Oh my goodness," Luna cried, staring at Vera. "Are you all right?" She threw down her bag and rushed to her sister. "One of Jerome's friends works at the hospital and called him."

Eve was a little slower, but she did basically the same thing. She flinched when she looked at the bandage. "You okay?"

Vera nodded, then winced at the movement. "I'm fine. Just pissed. That's all."

"I can vouch for that," Bent warned, holding up a hand.

The sisters laughed; Vera rolled her eyes, but she was smiling just a little.

"I ordered food from the Local," Luna said. "It'll be here any minute."

Maybe this was his cue to go. He had some research to do.

Maybe some ass to kick.

42

Sunday, July 28

Boyett Farm
Good Hollow Road, Fayetteville, 7:00 a.m.

Vera's head ached.

She closed her eyes and tried to force the pain away. No such luck.

Beyond the pain, her mind kept replaying the way Bent had watched her in the hospital. His hovering had made her almost as angry as the driver who'd run her off the road. She refused to acknowledge the other feelings his intent attention had roused. A quick call this morning to check on her before she'd been ready to get up, much less to hear his voice, hadn't helped.

"Not going there," she muttered.

She got up, grimaced. She needed to dig through her closet for something else to wear. She'd had a long, hot bath last night in hopes of heading off some of the aches and pains today would bring. Hadn't worked as well as she had hoped. Passing the dresser on the way to the closet, she got a look in the mirror and gasped. The bruise on her forehead was more visible now. The skin around the stitches was red and angry. Dark circles had formed beneath her puffy eyes. Damn.

She turned away from the mirror. Too early for that.

With effort and lots of groaning, she dressed and made her way downstairs.

"Morning," Vera said as she joined Eve in the kitchen. The smell of freshly brewed coffee had lured her here.

Seated at the table, Eve cradled her mug in both hands. "Morning. How're you feeling?"

"Not great, but I'm aware it could be worse," Vera admitted as she poured a cup of badly needed coffee. "My head hurts, and I'm sore from the seat belt and airbag, but otherwise I'm okay."

Eve considered her for a moment. "Do you really think it was the judge?"

Vera had told her about the visit to Preston's home and the calls and visits to the others.

"Of course I can't be positive," Vera admitted as she slid onto a stool. "But the aftershave is difficult to get past."

Eve made a face. "He always thought he had to have the best of everything. His mama spoiled him rotten."

"She did." Vera hated passing judgment on a man she hadn't seen in more than two decades, but it was difficult not to. "Let's look at this from the perspective of what we know."

"We know," Eve picked up from there, "that Florence and Beatrice were aware of the two women in the cave. For sure they helped with putting the first one there, and I'd be willing to bet any and everything that they did with the second one as well."

"With all that's happening now," Vera offered, "Florence may have asked Preston for help in protecting her secret. This is assuming she has no idea you saw them that first time."

"Only Mama knew," Eve insisted. "She never told anyone. I never told anyone."

Vera had to call her on that one. "What about when you and Suri put Gates in there. She didn't ask about the others?"

Eve stared into her coffee mug. "I told her I couldn't talk about them." She lifted her gaze to Vera's then. "I swear. That's exactly what I said, and she didn't ask questions. Suri isn't like that. She takes me at my word, as I do her."

Vera focused on her coffee for a few minutes. It wasn't that she didn't believe her sister or that what she was suggesting wasn't possible. It was simply unlikely that Suri would never tell. That said, she was willing to let it go for now.

"I couldn't sleep last night." Eve lifted her gaze to Vera's. "I kept thinking what could have happened to you, and it makes me sick."

"Hey." Vera set her mug aside and took her sister's hand. "I'm okay. Really."

"But if I hadn't told you the secret I shared with Mama, this might not have happened. I feel like it's my fault."

Vera took Eve's mug from her other hand and set it on the table, then she put her arms around her sister and hugged her. "This is not your fault. Nothing you did or said had anything to do with yesterday. I'm glad you told me."

Surprisingly, Eve hugged her back, but then quickly drew away. "I know we don't see each other often enough, and we don't even call enough, but I couldn't do this life thing without you. Just knowing you're wherever you are makes me okay."

"Come on now." Vera smiled. "We're okay. Don't worry about me. I'm not as easy to put down as you think."

Eve let go a big breath. "Just be careful. Keep Bent close."

"That might not be smart," Vera confessed.

A big grin spread across Eve's face. "I knew it. You are still hooked on him."

"Stop," Vera argued. "We can be friends, I think. That's all this is, but I need to be careful with him."

"Got it." Eve gulped down more coffee. "Gotta go. Mr. Hamilton is waiting for me."

Vera frowned. "Coach Hamilton from high school?"

Eve nodded. "Heart attack while mowing the lawn. His wife warned him that mowing the lawn in the heat at eighty wasn't smart, but he didn't listen."

"He was eighty?" Damn. The notion made Vera feel old.

"Time flies," Eve said. "See you later." She waggled her fingers and disappeared.

Somewhere between the kitchen and the front door, Vera heard her sisters talking. Luna must have come downstairs. It was rare that she slept this late. Maybe the trouble yesterday had kept her awake last night as well.

Luna rushed into the kitchen, already dressed for church—cute little yellow dress with matching sandals and purse. She looked like a doll ready to be boxed up and shipped off to a waiting little girl.

"I'm late for breakfast with Jerome and his family." She gave Vera a hug. "Are you sure you're okay?"

"I'm good." Vera smiled, ignored the pain in her forehead. "Don't worry about me, and drive safely."

Luna backed away, her lips pouting. "I will. You just stay home and rest today. Love you!" She started to turn away, then hesitated. "Oh, I borrowed one of your mother's photo albums. I know you were looking at them the other day. I saw a stack on the table in the library. I didn't want you to think one was lost. I had left it at Jerome's. I've been putting together some album collages for taking with me when I move in with him." She smiled. "Anyway, last night I finally remembered to bring it back. It's on the table in the library."

That was just like her little sister. Album collages. Vera had never heard of them. "Thanks. Have a good day."

Luna waved, and then she was gone.

Vera finished her coffee and listened to the silence in the house. The big old grandfather clock in the hall started to chime and then made eight deep *dong*s for the hour.

She should get going. Maybe stop by Bent's and see what his plans were for the day. All she needed were her bag and her shoes.

351

The bag she vividly remembered leaving on the side table in the hall. Shoes too, she hoped. She groaned and scooted off the stool. In the hall she checked out a front window and confirmed the deputy on duty this morning was there. No matter that she refused to be afraid, she was no fool. Trouble could sneak up on the most highly trained individual.

She picked up her shoes, sat down on the bench, and tugged them on.

A knock on the front door made Vera jump. She'd spoken to Bent, so it wouldn't be him. Eve would have called if she needed to talk further. Maybe Luna had forgotten something. But wouldn't she have just unlocked the door? Wouldn't be a reporter since a deputy was stationed in front of the house.

She could keep up the guessing game or just go to the door and find out who it was. With effort she got up, stretched her sides. Her ribs were sore. Her neck felt a little stiff as well. Forehead was still tender.

She peeked out the window and saw a deputy standing on her porch. A glance at the cruiser in the drive told her it was the one on duty.

Vera opened the door. "Is everything all right, Deputy?"

He gave her a nod. "Yes, ma'am, but there's a man here to see you."

Vera's gaze arrowed to the old—vintage, some would say—rusty, faded-red Mustang parked beyond the cruiser. No one she recognized. Dennis Haynes? She sure hoped so.

"His name is Pete Brooks. He's a local. Bit of a deadbeat." The deputy glanced in the man's direction. "I can tell him to get lost if you'd like."

The old friend of Garth Rimmey. Talk about surprises. "No. Thank you. Actually, I'd like to speak with him."

"Whatever you say, ma'am." The deputy stepped off the porch and waved at the man in the Mustang, then hitched his thumb toward the house.

Vera watched as an older man, sixtyish, climbed out and started in her direction. He was tall. Slim. His hair was gray. Despite the heat, he wore biker boots with his jeans. A T-shirt and a leather vest. What looked like dog tags hung around his neck.

His gaze was steady on her as he climbed the steps and crossed the porch. He stopped directly in front of her. With him this close, she could see that he was nearer to seventy than sixty.

"I hear you been looking for me."

"Come in." Vera stepped inside, and he followed. She closed the door behind him, then gestured to the living room. "Would you like coffee?"

He chuckled. "Only if there's whiskey in it."

"Have a seat, and I'll see what I can do."

She walked to the kitchen and rounded up the half-empty bottle of Jack Daniel's she'd indulged in the other night. She poured a good portion into two mugs, then topped them off with coffee. This meeting might very well call for something a little stronger.

With the bottle tucked under one arm and the mugs in hand, she joined her visitor. Mr. Brooks was studying the framed photographs on the mantel.

"You look just like your mama." He turned to her, accepted a mug.

"And proud of it," she agreed. Vera placed the bottle on the coffee table and settled on the sofa.

Brooks sat in the chair that had been her daddy's favorite. "What can I do for you, Ms. Boyett?" He took a long draw from his spiked coffee.

"Do you know anything about what Garth Rimmey was doing the day Sheree—my stepmother—disappeared?" Vera sipped her own warm brew, flinched at the burn.

He studied her a moment. "You sure you want to know?"

Vera took another sip. This one went down a bit more smoothly. Life was full of firsts, and this was certainly her first time having whiskey before breakfast. "I asked, didn't I?"

He gave her a nod. "Rimmey and I were buddies. We had a little business on the side—selling weed and a few other things. Anyway, that day we were at his place just chilling. Business wasn't usually very good on weekday mornings, so we were relaxing."

Another swallow of Jack and coffee slid down Vera's throat as she waited for him to go on.

"Your daddy showed up about ten-ish. I can't tell you the exact time, but it was midmorning."

Vera held her breath. "Why?"

He frowned, took another drink. "Why what?"

"Why did my daddy come to Rimmey's house?"

"He wanted to have a few words with him. Knowing when something was coming that I wanted no part of, I stepped outside for a smoke. I heard them arguing. Your daddy was telling him that he knew what he'd been doing with his wife. Rimmey said something stupid like 'What you gonna do about it?'" Brooks snorted. "To make a long story short, your daddy beat the shit out of him. Then he left."

"When you say *beat the shit out of him*—"

"I mean, he blacked both his eyes, busted his lip. Rimmey thought his jaw was broken, but it wasn't. That kind of stuff."

Vera nodded. "And you're sure it was my daddy."

Brooks laughed. "Oh yeah. Me and Rimmey had driven by this place lots of times looking for Sheree, and we'd watched the two of them, your daddy and her, once or twice when they were in town together. Believe me, I was well aware who Vernon Boyett was. Knew you too." He looked her up and down. "You were a little spitfire. Had yourself a crush on Gray Benton."

Vera ignored the remark. "What was my daddy driving that day?"

He frowned. "What?"

"Was he driving a truck?" Her father had bought his truck brand new twenty-five years ago. Her mama had helped him pick it out. He had always loved that truck.

Brooks thought for a minute. "No. It wasn't a truck. It was a car. A sedan."

"You don't remember the model or the color?"

He shook his head. "Nothing that stood out. It was generic, you know. An old piece of shit."

"Do you recall about what time my daddy left?"

He made a face. "Not the exact time, no. But what he came to do didn't take long. Twenty, maybe thirty minutes."

"Just one more thing," Vera said. "Were you with Rimmey the rest of that day?"

"If you're asking if he killed her, the answer is no. He drank himself into oblivion after your daddy beat his ass. When I left that afternoon, he was passed out cold."

"You're sure he didn't leave the house after you did."

"Positive, because I stole his hidden stash while he was out cold and had myself a party at a friend's house. Rimmey was pissed the next morning." He laughed. "Seriously pissed. If he'd woke up later in the afternoon or even that night and found it missing, he would've been pissed *that* day, and I would have known it."

Vera understood that he could be lying, probably was. "Who do you think killed him a few days later?" She held her breath. This was important. What happened to Sheree in that bathroom was an accident . . . Garth Rimmey's death was not. She didn't want her father charged with his murder. The best way to prevent that was to find out who did it or to find a solid alibi.

"Some believe it was your daddy." Brooks leaned forward. "But between me and you and the Jack sitting here, it wasn't. You see, Rimmey decided to get back at me for stealing his stash. He told my baby mama that I'd been fucking around on her. She got so pissed off she called the cops and told them I'd beat her up, so I got arrested."

Vera so hated men like this one. "Did you? Beat her up?"

He shook his head. "I didn't touch her, but I did fuck Rimmey up. As soon as I made bail, I went to his house. He was out cold again, stupid bastard. I gave him what he deserved. I was a little over-the-line pissed off, so I sort of went overboard. Now mind you, he was breathing when I left him." He shrugged. "Evidently he lost that ability at some point later that night."

"You killed him." Vera tensed. Killers didn't generally tell people—particularly ex-cops—about their murders.

"I didn't say that." He finished off his drink. "I said he was breathing when I left him. You wouldn't want to go around telling folks I did something I didn't."

Vera held up her hands. "It's usually better if you do the telling yourself. That's how plea deals are made."

"Well, if you do decide to spread rumors about me, I'd just have to swear that it was your daddy. That I witnessed the whole thing. I don't figure you want me doing that." Brooks stood, indicating the conversation was over.

Nice close. He was counting on her need to protect her father as insurance.

"It appears folks around here like their secrets," she suggested, rising to her feet to look him more directly in the eyes. "Otherwise, I wouldn't have ended up in a ditch last evening."

"I heard about that," he said with a nod. "Some guys—women too—think they own the road. You should watch yourself, because there are folks who will do anything to keep their secrets."

With that warning, he walked out of the living room and exited the house.

Vera was too absorbed in his final statements to react for a moment. The man had literally confessed to murder in her living room. But it was the other part that made her linger.

There are folks who will do anything to keep their secrets.

Her phone rang, the shrill sound making her jump and echoing through the big old empty house.

Where had she left it?

Kitchen.

By the time she reached it, it had sounded off for the third time. Bent's name flashed on the screen. She hit Accept in the nick of time. "Hey."

"It's me."

Like she didn't know. He surely knew she'd added him to her contact list, but that was the way he'd always identified himself—way before she'd had a cell phone.

"You holding up okay?"

"Sure." She touched her aching forehead. "How's your day going?" It was Sunday. Maybe he was at home taking care of things like those horses.

"Busy. I'm at the office going through reports and all the other routine stuff I've ignored all week. I have a meeting with Gallagher and Trotter in five minutes, but I wanted to call you first. I have some good news to pass along."

Vera dared to hope that he'd spoken to Preston Higdon and the judge had confessed to breaking into her house and running her off the road in an effort to protect his mother.

Don't hold your breath.

"I got an email from the lab in Nashville. A guy there did me a favor and expedited the review of your mama's remains. They found no evidence of past abuse or strangulation. No fractures of any sort."

Relief rushed through Vera, no matter that she had known this would be the case. "Thanks. I hope Higdon is satisfied. He did nothing but waste the county's money and make a fool of himself."

"He's not returning my calls this morning, so I'm guessing he's heard and feeling embarrassed. Oh wait. It's Sunday. He's probably at church."

"Thanks for letting me know." Vera wished she could see Higdon's face when he heard the news.

"There's something else."

Bent's tone set her on edge. Ugh. She did not want any more bad news. "Don't make me wait, Bent. Just tell me."

"The judge doesn't have a black SUV, but his administrative assistant has one. A black older-model Suburban."

"It had to be him!" A fresh wave of outrage swept through Vera. No matter that she was aware black was one of the most common colors of SUVs on the road, she couldn't help seeing this as confirmation.

"I need you to listen to me, Vee. I'm going to interview the assistant tomorrow. I've already set it up. Then I'll talk to the judge. Do not—and I mean do not—call him or go see him. I need to do this by the book. Got it?"

Vera knew all about the book, damn it. She wanted to race over to his house right now and confront him. But Bent was right. This had to be strictly by the book.

"I will not contact him in any manner." She grinned. "You know what this means," she said, hoping he saw the bigger picture. "Preston doesn't want me digging into what happened to those two women. He has to be protecting his father."

His mother as well, but Vera couldn't say that part without explaining how she knew the woman was involved in any capacity.

"I think you are definitely onto something," Bent agreed. "All you have to do now is be patient and let me do my job."

"I can do that," she promised, though her record to date was not so good.

"I feel like," he said slowly, "I should come over and babysit you."

"No," she argued. "I'm fine. Really. Just bored. I intend to go through all those photo albums again to make sure I didn't miss anything. Do not worry about me." With all that had happened, she wanted to revel in those good times from the past. To soak up the memories.

"I need you to stay home, Vee. Just take a break."

"Fine. Fine. I'll be here taking a break." Geez.

"I'm coming over at noon—right after my meeting," he warned. "Bringing lunch. Mexican or Chinese."

"Chinese."

"I'll see you then."

"Don't forget the chopsticks." Vera ended the call and slid the phone back into her hip pocket.

She went to the library and surveyed the shelves of albums. No one had been better at documenting the family history than Evelyn Boyett. Her mother had taken loads of photos at a time when it wasn't nearly as convenient as it was now.

The album Luna had borrowed lay on the table. Vera sat down and opened it. The first photos were from her thirteenth birthday. She smiled. This was *before* . . . before the cancer. Before all the pain and tragedy.

She slowly flipped through the pages. The memories tugging at her heartstrings. Their family really had been so happy.

A big Fourth of July bash showed the Fraleys, the Higdons, and the Boyetts together at the Higdon home. Considering the number of people mingling in the backyard, there must have been at least a hundred people in attendance. As Preston said, his mother had been a party animal in her day. Probably still was.

As Vera studied the photos, she noticed a lot of kids around her and the judge's age were at the party. Seniors mostly. Vera was sure he had liked showing off. They had a pool and a massive pavilion for just this sort of gathering. This would have been the last big family bash before he went off to Harvard. Some of the kids Vera recognized, but they were all older than her by a couple of years.

She started to turn to the next page but hesitated. She leaned forward and peered at one photo in particular . . . there was a girl standing at the edge of the shot. Long blonde hair. Long tanned legs.

Vera's heart stumbled.

Latesha Johnson.

She turned the page, studied the other dozen or so from that day, but a single photo was the only one that included Latesha. Vera turned back to that photo.

This was evidence the Higdons had known the first victim to end up in that cave.

Apparently the sugar daddy in question was dear old Dr. Higdon. Vera snapped a pic of the photo, then another, zooming in close on the face.

She sent Bent the photos in a text message and suggested he compare them to the photo Russ had given her. No sooner than the text was delivered, her cell vibrated, almost making her drop it in surprise. How had he responded that quickly? She took a breath and opened the text.

We need to talk.

Not Bent. She didn't recognize the number.
Who is this? She typed the words and hit Send.

Preston. Need to talk to you. Can you come to my house?

Vera had promised Bent she wouldn't talk to him . . . another text arrived.

It's important.

She thought of the woman in the photo . . . of the friend who'd come looking for her. And then she considered the damned SUV that had almost gotten her killed.

She had to go. A quick reply that she was on her way zoomed off, sealing her decision.

With a grimace, she stood. That little voice she always ignored warned that she should call Bent or at least let him know what she was doing. But he was in that meeting by now. And the pissed-off daughter of two of the people the Higdon family had hurt wanted to do this herself.

She would call Bent after the meeting.

Vera had made it to the door when she realized she had no vehicle. Hers had been towed away from the ditch on Kidd Road.

She did an about-face and walked to the kitchen. Her daddy's truck keys hung on the rack next to the back door.

Maybe that old truck would start after sitting in the shed for two years. If not, she would just have to figure out another ride.

One way or the other, she was going.

43

Vera parked near the judge's garage next to another vehicle. Not the black SUV that had run her off the road, but a sedan. Newer high-end vehicle. Maybe one belonging to his wife.

Or an attorney.

Vera scoffed. She could see him having an attorney present for this meeting. Bastard. Then why not just do this with the sheriff present as well. She got it. He thought he could intimidate her without Bent around and avoid the official route altogether.

Better men had tried.

She climbed out of her daddy's truck and closed the door. To her surprise the old Chevy had started right up. Eve or Luna must have driven it from time to time. The stick shift pattern had come back to her before she'd gotten out of the driveway. Just like riding a bicycle. Because the truck had been stored in the shed out back, she'd been able to cut down by the barn and leave without the deputy assigned to watch the house knowing.

Bent would be pissed, but this was something she had to do.

Deep breath. She headed toward the walkway. A row of ornamental grass marched along both sides of the cobblestone leading the way to the broad porch. Neatly manicured shrubs flanked the foundation.

Not much that bloomed, just varying sizes of evergreen plants. Less maintenance, she supposed.

She climbed the steps. Glanced around, then back toward Mulberry Avenue. No traffic. No pedestrians. Most folks were in church at this hour on a Sunday morning. Her instincts stirred, had the hair on the back of her neck rising. She passed an eye over the enormous front yard once more . . . then the driveway across the street. A small, white Victorian-style house was evidently being renovated. A dumpster sat in the driveway. Sawhorses stood on the porch. A board with a permit posted on it had been nailed to a post. Her attention settled lastly on the one out-of-place element—an old Mustang parked by the dumpster. Same faded, rusty red as the one that had visited her this morning.

Was Brooks watching her?

She scanned the block, left to right and back, without spotting a soul. If Brooks was close by, he was hiding. Maybe watching from the narrow front window on the second floor of that reno.

Vera dismissed the worry for now and headed to the judge's front door. As she lifted her hand to ring the bell, she hesitated. The front door was ajar.

Okay, now this was one of those moments when she wished she had her service weapon, but she'd left it in her lockbox in Memphis, along with her official credentials, when she'd rushed home.

The idea that this could be some sort of setup crossed her mind. Uneasiness started another walk up her spine. She glanced across the street once more. Surveyed the expansive yard.

All clear.

She took a breath and turned back to the door. Preston had sent a text to her phone. He had to know that if something happened to her, phone records would be subpoenaed and his text messages would be found.

He was a prestigious judge after all.

Stop stalling. Go in, or call Bent.

Maybe he'd left the door open to avoid having to get up and answer.

Yeah, right. She had a bad feeling about this. What the hell? No turning back now. She pulled her phone from her back pocket and held it tight. Then she braced for trouble, pushed the door open wider, and stepped inside. "Preston?"

The house was quiet. Way too quiet for comfort.

She took another step. Then another. "Preston? I'm here."

The whisper of a rubber sole against hardwood sounded a split second before a sudden impact from behind flung her forward . . . pain shattered her skull.

The phone flew out of her hand.

The cool hardwood floor slapped her in the face.

Then everything went black.

Vera tried to open her eyes.

Agony exploded in her brain.

Had she been in another accident? The memory of the big black SUV barreling down on her made her flinch.

Her eyes fluttered open.

Not in her SUV.

She looked around as best she could without moving her aching head. Dark. She tried to reach out but couldn't move her hands. Tied behind her.

Her head throbbed worse than after the accident . . . her eyes squeezed shut against the pain. There was something in her mouth . . . like a ball of cotton or cloth.

A gag.

Shit.

Vera pushed away the panic that attempted to rise and focused harder on the situation. Moving. She was moving. She was in a near-fetal position with her hands behind her back. She attempted to stretch one leg out, barely moved a few inches before she hit something. Small space. Cramped.

A big bounce rocked her forward, then back. Pain sheared through her skull. Light gleamed in the darkness.

Car. She was in a trunk. The brake lights had lit up for a moment. But they were moving again now. The car must have slowed after the bump and then turned.

She listened for any sound . . . a voice, a radio. But there was nothing but the growl of the engine.

The forward movement slowed.

She smelled smoke . . . no, cigarettes, and something else . . . stale beer maybe.

The car stopped, and she rocked again. More of that pain pierced her, and the urge to vomit rushed into her throat. She struggled to swallow it back.

A car door slammed with a whine. Then another softer thud close by but not from this car.

Two cars with doors closing . . . two *people*.

Her heart started to pound. She rubbed her bound hands over her hips. Her phone wasn't in her back pocket.

Damn. They'd taken it.

"What do we do now?"

The voice made her jump. Female. Vera listened intently. Her head was really messed up, but the woman sounded as if she were right outside the trunk. Too muffled for her to determine if this was someone familiar or a stranger.

"We get her inside."

Another voice . . . louder. *Florence* . . . Florence Higdon.

Vera made a face. Maybe she was mistaken . . . why would—

The trunk lid opened.

Light scorched Vera's eyes. She squeezed them shut.

"She's awake."

The other voice . . . softer.

Beatrice.

Vera forced her eyes open. Ignored the glare of light.

Beatrice stared down at her . . . her face pale . . . worried.

What the hell was happening here? Vera's pulse sped up, and her mind grew more alert.

"We have to get her inside," Florence barked. "Help me."

The two reached into the trunk and grabbed Vera and started to pull her upward.

Her skull exploded with more of that fiery torture. She winced at the agony. Wrestled with the urge to fight them.

She needed out of this trunk. *Relax. Let them get you out.*

Vera's feet hit the ground. Her knees buckled. Vomit rushed into her throat, and she gagged. Couldn't stop it.

The hot burn of the bile rushed into her nose. She couldn't breathe. Tried to cough. Doubled over in pain.

"Oh God, she's choking." *Beatrice.* "We have to help her."

Fingers clawed at her lips. Vera forced her mouth open wider.

Air. She needed air. Her heart pounded harder and harder. Her lungs seized.

"There's no time," Florence shouted. "We have to get her inside."

Need. To. Breathe.

Somehow Beatrice's fingers caught the cloth and yanked it out of Vera's mouth.

Vomit spewed from her throat. She gasped for air, then she spit and tried to blow the bile from her nose.

More air. She fought for another breath.

Florence yanked at her. "Walk," she ordered.

Beatrice took hold of Vera again and helped Florence half walk, half drag her forward.

Vera tried to take in the surroundings. Dilapidated mobile home. Grown up yard. Junked car sitting to one side.

She knew this place. Looked just like the description of the dump where Pete Brooks lived.

She turned her head further to the right.

SUV. Black.

Another burst of adrenaline had her straightening, her gaze sharpening.

Maybe not the one that ran her off the road but one like it. Seemed a bit of a coincidence if this was where Brooks lived.

Vera didn't believe in coincidences.

Fury tightened her jaw.

She tried to twist around. Spotted the rusty Mustang—trunk lid up—and another, newer sedan, before Florence yanked her back around. She recognized the second vehicle. She'd parked next to it at the judge's house.

It was a setup. Son of a—

"Step up," Florence demanded.

Vera concentrated on climbing the four steps that led onto the rickety deck. Three steps later they were at the front door.

The pain and anger twisted inside Vera. The sun was beating down on her head. She needed to throw up again. But first she had to get out of this insane situation.

Beatrice turned loose of Vera's arm and opened the door. Florence pushed her inside. She stumbled forward and landed on her knees. The crash landing had pain bursting in her skull.

When the world stopped spinning and the pain lessened enough, Vera's gaze settled on what was right in front of her.

Pete Brooks.

He lay flat on his back on the matted blue-and-green shag carpet. Eyes closed. The way his arms were tucked under him, his hands appeared to be secured behind his back. No visible injuries. Was he dead?

Holy shit.

"What did you do?" Vera dared to move her head so that she could glare at Beatrice. "Did you kill him?"

"Get her up," Florence ordered.

Beatrice grasped Vera's right arm once more and helped her to her feet.

Brooks stirred.

Vera stared at him. His chest rose, then fell. He wasn't dead. Relief flooded her chest. Then she considered what she knew about him and decided maybe she should be worried instead of relieved.

"He's waking up," Florence said. "We don't have much time. We have to do this now."

"Do what?" Not that it wasn't perfectly clear what they had planned, but Vera intended to make these two crazy old ladies say it out loud. She resisted the urge to shake her head. This was like something out of a bizarre comedy, with diabolical seniors playing thugs. Or in this case, killers.

But this was no movie . . . these women had killed before. If there had been any doubt in Vera's mind about that, it was gone now.

Florence removed the backpack she wore and reached inside. When she drew her hand out, she held a revolver. That was when Vera noticed the woman was wearing gloves. Vera wasn't surprised. Apparently Florence had learned a few tricks since the last time she committed murder.

"We have to do it now," she said to Beatrice. "Otherwise, we'll run out of time."

Beatrice nodded her understanding.

Florence aimed the gun—looked like a .38—at Vera. "Move her into position."

Vera steeled herself even as her heart pounded in time with the throb in her skull. Beatrice took hold of her again and ushered her toward Brooks.

"Wait. Wait. Wait." Vera stalled, digging her heels into that nasty vintage shag carpet. "What exactly are you doing here?"

"I'm sorry, Vee," Beatrice said. "You shouldn't have come back. You should have left it alone."

Vera took a breath. Ordered her heart to slow as she twisted toward her captors. "Where's Preston?" she demanded. "And Dr. Higdon? Do they know what you're doing?" While she had her back turned away from the two, she tugged at the rope holding her wrists together. "Answer me!" she shouted.

Beatrice jumped. Florence only glared at her.

If the spinning in her head would slow down and Vera could work her hands loose, she might just be able to stop this fiasco.

"Charles is at church," Florence said, lifting her chin arrogantly. "He's covering for Bea and me. She's at home with Walt since he isn't feeling well, and I have a stomach bug."

Vera's chest ached with disappointment. "Is he part of this too?" she demanded of Beatrice. "Does he even know what you're doing?"

Beatrice's lips trembled, and she looked away.

Hope pushed past the disappointment. Beatrice was still the weak link.

The man on the floor grunted. Vera stared down at him. He flinched. But his eyes remained closed.

"What'd you do? Drug him?" A librarian and a schoolteacher. Jesus Christ.

"Shut up!" Florence grabbed her. She glared at her partner in crime. "Help me get her into position."

Beatrice obliged, and the two of them forced Vera over to where Brooks lay.

"Put one foot on either side of him," Florence ordered. "Your back facing his head."

"No way." Vera wasn't cooperating.

Florence pushed her. She almost fell over Brooks, forcing her to throw out her right leg to stop the fall. She ended up standing astraddle of him just as they wanted. Fury erupted in Vera's veins. She was going to kick Florence Higdon's ass—no matter that she was an old lady—just as soon as she got her hands loose.

"Hold her still," Florence snapped.

Beatrice held onto Vera while Florence walked around behind her. She jammed the gun into Vera's hands and attempted to force her fingers around the grip.

"Oh hell no," Vera growled, fighting the woman's efforts.

She wanted Vera's prints on the weapon that killed Brooks—after his visit this morning. Convenient. Had he not realized he was being set up?

Vera needed to buy time.

"Just tell me why." Vera kept tugging her hands from Florence while she stared at Beatrice. "Is it because one or both of you killed Latesha and Trina and hid them in our cave?"

"I told you she would figure it out," Florence growled, her frustration mounting.

Beatrice looked away.

"It's because of that damned photograph, isn't it?" Florence demanded, forgetting her hands for a moment and getting in Vera's face. "You found it, didn't you? That nosy PI from Huntsville probably showed you a picture of those whores, and you put the two together."

"And I know the two of you killed them," Vera accused, "and dragged my mama into this."

"Evelyn," Beatrice said with a shake of her head, "had nothing to do with this. She just helped us hide the first body because we were her friends."

"Until we weren't," Florence snarled. "She wouldn't help us that last time. Wouldn't even speak to us anymore. But she got hers, didn't she?"

Vera barely restrained the urge to charge the woman. Instead, she twisted her hands harder in an effort to loosen the rope. She could feel the nylon stretching. Any second now her hands would be free. Then, she would take care of this, by God. Even if she died trying.

She turned to Beatrice again. Spotted the flash of sympathy in the former schoolteacher's eyes. "You have a chance to make this right."

Beatrice looked away again. Her trademark move.

"No more wasting time," Florence snapped. "We are on a deadline here. We have to finish this before church is over and this dumbass on the floor wakes up."

Vera racked her brain for something more to say or do. "All you've done is set your son up to take the fall," she warned Florence. "He was the one who lured me to his house with those text messages. I've already told Bent he was the intruder who broke into our house—his damned aftershave gave him away."

Florence cackled. "Do you really think I'm that stupid? That's why Brooks has Preston's phone and Preston is at home tied up in his wine cellar. Oh, and the aftershave, it's in the bathroom just down the hall. Brooks has a reputation for petty theft."

Vera shifted gears, looked to Beatrice again. "What's going to happen to Walt when you go to prison? Or is he going to prison too?"

Beatrice refused to look at her.

Vera shook her head. Ignored the scream in her skull. "For the first time in my life, I'm glad my mother is dead so she doesn't have to know what the women she trusted are doing to her daughter."

"Just shut up!" Florence reached for Vera's hands once more.

Vera wrenched her wrists harder. Florence grabbed at her right hand. The rope fell slack.

Vera twisted and plowed her shoulder into Florence. The woman toppled onto the floor. Vera hit the shag carpet face first.

The gun discharged.

Vera rolled and sprang up onto all fours and then to her feet. She swayed a little.

Brooks was rocking side to side and spewing curses.

Florence screamed and rushed toward Vera, the gun clasped in both hands.

"No." Beatrice stepped in front of Vera.

Florence jerked to a stop. "Get out of my way, or I'll shoot you too!"

"I can't let you do this," Beatrice argued. "This is not her fault."

Florence shoved her lifelong friend out of the way. "It's too late to back out now."

Vera slugged the woman before she could level her aim once more. She fell backward over Brooks and hit the floor flat on her back. The weapon flew from her hand.

Brooks rolled and flopped to get the woman off him, then struggled to his knees. He swayed drunkenly. "What the . . . hell?"

Vera scrambled for the gun. Grabbed it and pushed herself to her feet, adopted a firing stance. "Call 911, Beatrice," she ordered, "before I really do have to shoot someone."

Beatrice did as she was told.

"You," Vera said to Brooks. "Sit down, and don't move."

"They fucking drugged me," he roared. "I did what they said by coming to your house this morning, and then instead of paying me, they drugged me." His face contorted with rage mostly directed at Florence, who was rocking and moaning on the floor. "I'm going to kill that bitch."

"I'd like to myself." Vera exhaled a weary breath. "But we can't. She's going to rot in prison."

Vera steadied herself and hoped like hell help got here fast. The adrenaline was fading fast, and she wasn't at all sure how much longer she could remain standing.

Lincoln Medical Center
Fayetteville, 4:50 p.m.

Vera was fighting mad by the time Bent walked into her hospital room.

Eve and Luna had been trying to calm her since they arrived. The two had stayed with her through all the tests and scans. This time she had a serious concussion, and the doctor had already warned that she would not be leaving the hospital today.

The only upside was that the meds had toned down the pain. Even her fist where she'd slugged Florence wasn't hurting anymore. Vera was fairly confident the lethargy was the primary reason she hadn't stormed out of this room already.

"We'll . . . ah," Eve said, looking from Vera to Bent, "give you guys a few minutes." She jerked her head for Luna to follow her.

"Can we bring you something when we come back?" Luna asked, worry lining her face.

"No." Vera forced a smile. "I'm fine."

When the door closed behind the two, she glared at Bent. The man was smart. He'd stayed at the foot of her bed—out of reach.

"I am so angry with you," Vera said, her speech a little thick. Damn it.

He nodded. "I know. But I'm here now, and I'll tell you everything."

She had wanted to be there to observe the questioning while those two crazy women were interviewed. She had wanted to hear what Brooks had to say. Not to mention how badly she'd wanted to be there when Charles Higdon got his. Damn it!

But Bent had sent her to the hospital strapped to a damned gurney.

"You tricked me," she said, even angrier now than she was four hours ago. "You told me if I'd just let the paramedics have a look at me, you'd ensure I was with you for everything."

He stared at the floor.

"Instead, they strapped me on that gurney and brought me here."

He finally met her gaze. "If it makes you feel better, when you're well enough, you can kick my ass the way you did Mrs. Higdon's."

She might have laughed if she hadn't been so pissed off. "Just tell me what happened, and don't leave anything out."

Bent had already been at her house looking for her when the 911 call came in. He'd gotten out of his meeting a few minutes early and seen the text message with the photo.

"What about Preston?" she said, not waiting for him to begin. "Whatever he said, he was part of this too."

Bent nodded. "He was tied up in the wine cellar, just like you said. And he, of course, insists he had no clue what was going on other than Brooks attacked him. When we pressed the issue, he lawyered up."

Vera felt her face going red with another blast of outrage.

"Don't worry," Bent assured her. "Brooks told us everything—including Preston's part. Beatrice confirmed his story."

Vera closed her eyes a second to make the room stop spinning. "You're giving me the abridged version. How about filling in some of the finer details."

Bent dared to move around to the side of the bed. "According to Beatrice, Preston was the intruder—just like you said. Although his bottle of expensive aftershave was stashed in Brooks's bathroom."

"Florence bragged about having thought of that." Vera wondered how no one had seen the crazy in that woman.

"The black SUV parked at the Brooks's place belongs to Preston's assistant. We brought her in, and she confessed immediately to having run you off the road. Preston talked her into it."

Vera decided she couldn't stand waiting for the crescendo. "Florence killed Latesha and Trina, didn't she?"

"Yes. She's trying to get some sort of deal—as is her husband. But Beatrice has already rolled on both of them."

The tremendous rush of relief combined with the meds had Vera relaxing maybe a little too much. "Charles was the sugar daddy. I knew it." Well, at least she'd wanted it to be him.

"It started out that way," Bent said, "but Preston and Latesha got involved. Beatrice said Florence never cared what Charles did as long as no one in town found out. But she was terrified Preston would screw up his life—get kicked out of Harvard . . . ruin his reputation."

"Beatrice didn't kill anyone, right?" Vera hadn't believed her capable of murder. But how had such an intelligent woman allowed such an evil one to drag her into this mess?

"No, but she feels responsible. Apparently she and Preston had a thing during his high school years. When he got involved with Latesha, Beatrice got jealous. She's the one who told Florence. Got her all fired up about how Preston would be ruined if the girl got pregnant or folks found out." Bent shook his head. "Because of that, she feels responsible for what happened. In the end, it didn't matter, because Preston was no longer interested in an older woman. It was all for nothing. And two young women lost their lives."

"That's why she went along," Vera realized. "She needed to make sure no one ever found out about her affair." The reality went to show that even good people would do almost anything to protect their secrets. Just like Brooks said.

"She didn't want anyone, especially Walt, to find out." Bent shook his head.

Vera felt bad for Walt. But she felt utterly sick at what those two had dragged her mother into. "They used my mother to help them hide the bodies."

Bent's expression told her how sick the idea made him as well. "That's something else Beatrice regrets. She said your mother wouldn't talk to them anymore after what they did. She kept their secret, but she wouldn't have anything to do with them."

Vera realized then that her mother had shared this with her father, which explained the seemingly incriminating things he had said the other day.

Vera forced the painful thoughts away. "Did Brooks tell you that, when he visited me this morning, he basically confessed to killing Rimmey?"

"In a roundabout way," Bent confirmed. "He said they fought but that the guy was alive when he left him."

Vera rolled her eyes. The move sparked a pain in her head. "I guess a jury will have to decide that one."

"Maybe not," Bent countered. "Like the Higdons, he wants a deal. He says he knows who killed Sheree and he'll give up the name for the right options."

Vera's heart almost stumbled. "Did he give any clue who that person was?"

"He says it was Rimmey and that he can prove it—as I said, if the right deal is offered."

Vera rode out the wave of shock. "You believe him?"

Bent shrugged. "It makes sense."

Not exactly an answer, but Vera would take it.

"Looks like you solved a major part of your case, Sheriff." God, she was tired.

"Yeah." He grinned. "Your favorite reporter is begging for an exclusive."

Vera's gaze narrowed on him. "Do it and I will never speak to you again."

He held up his hands. "Don't worry. I already told her no."

"Good." Vera put her hand on his, where it rested on the bed rail. "Thank you."

He chuckled. "For what? You did all the work. I should be thanking you."

"Thank you for being here." Vera blinked to hold back the emotion rising in her eyes. Along with the exhaustion, her emotions were getting the better of her. "This would have been hard—maybe impossible—without you."

He reached out, traced her cheek, with its rug burn from that nasty shag carpet. "I'm here to stay, Vee. I'm not going anywhere."

Vera smiled. "I'm glad."

She wanted to say more, but the door opened, and her sisters arrived with balloons and flowers. Luna was all smiles and wanting to celebrate, while Eve looked uncomfortable. So different, her sisters. But she loved them both so much.

Vera watched as they prodded Bent for the lowdown on all that happened. She closed her eyes and let the exhaustion tugging at her have its way.

It was all good now . . . nothing else to worry about.

Mostly.

44

Tuesday, August 13

Boyett Farm
Good Hollow Road, Fayetteville, 5:30 p.m.

Vera scanned the documents on the table before her one last time. "Your offer is an intriguing one," she confirmed to the man on the other end of the conference call.

"As I said," Special Agent in Charge Ernie Cusack's voice floated from the speaker of her cell phone, "we're fully aware of the issues that happened in Memphis. We're aware, and we understand. We feel the events that occurred there have no bearing on your ability. The post in Tullahoma is available, and we would very much like to have you fill it."

"I appreciate your confidence, Agent Cusack, and I will consider the offer."

"We look forward to hearing from you, Ms. Boyett."

Vera ended the call and blew out a breath. "Wow." She stretched her neck and back. Just a couple of weeks ago, she had been unemployed, and now she had two offers on the table. One from the TBI and now one from the FBI.

Life was strange sometimes. She touched her forehead. The stitches were gone, and the headaches were pretty much history. She'd gotten an "all good" from the doctor at her checkup yesterday. Technically she could go to work anytime.

Things were settling down. On Saturday Luna finally got the memorial service she wanted for her mother. Eve and Suri had decided to make their more-than-friendship relationship official, and Eve was moving in with her.

Luna's wedding was next month, so she would be moving out soon as well.

Vera was not looking forward to rambling around in this big old house alone. She glanced around her mother's kitchen. Maybe she would get used to the quiet.

The security system had been installed, so no worries about intruders without warning.

She still hadn't fully processed the idea that Florence Higdon was a murderer. Or that Beatrice Fraley had betrayed Vera's family so thoughtlessly. The behavior of Charles and Preston Higdon was no surprise at all. Selfish men. Still, the whole thing felt surreal.

The memory of Sheree lying on that bathroom floor with Eve soaking wet and Luna screaming at the top of her lungs echoed in Vera's head. Followed immediately by images of Vera and Eve dragging her lifeless body down the stairs.

Desperate people did desperate things.

In the end, it all came down to certain realities. Both Charles and Preston Higdon had resigned their positions. Both had also agreed to plea deals that included testifying against Florence. Father and son would do a little time in a cushy minimum-security prison for their participation in the kidnapping of Vera and Brooks. Florence, on the other hand, was facing hard time. Her trial was still months away.

Beatrice was not charged with any crime related to the murders of Latesha and Trina, since she agreed to testify against the Higdons. For her part in the kidnapping, her further testimony had garnered her probation with house arrest. This allowed her to continue taking care of her husband. In Vera's opinion, it was fair. Beatrice made a mistake—a costly one—but she was also a victim. Both Preston and Florence had used her for years. The Brooks plea deal was still in negotiations. Vera couldn't help worrying a little about what he might have to say in the end.

A knock on the front door drew her from the troubling musings. She slid off the stool and wandered toward the sound. She checked out the window next to the door. *Bent.* A smile spread across her face.

She opened the door. "You're early."

He hitched a thumb toward his truck. "I could leave and come back later."

"Stop." She grabbed him by the arm and pulled him inside. She surveyed the yard and drive before closing the door. It was nice to be able to look outside and not see police cruisers or reporters. The Boyett family had pretty much fallen out of the headlines the past few days.

"You're not going to believe what happened this afternoon," he said as she ushered him to the kitchen.

"I could say the same thing." He would be stunned when she told him about the final offer from the Bureau's Knoxville office for the position in Tullahoma.

"You go first," he suggested as they entered the kitchen. "Mine's a little complicated, and you might want to brace yourself."

She wilted. "Oh God, that doesn't sound good." She scooted onto the stool she'd abandoned and made a worried face.

"Oddly enough it's good." He straddled a stool and lowered onto it. "So shoot with your news."

"All right." She cleared her throat for emphasis. "The FBI made a second offer for a higher grade." She grinned. "I guess they really want me."

"That's great." He smiled, but he didn't sound all that excited.

"Your turn," she nudged, not wanting to go into how she intended to respond, which would be his next question. Or why he didn't appear pleased for her.

"Pete Brooks got his plea deal," Bent announced.

No matter that she had every reason to believe his statements wouldn't affect her family, she still held her breath.

"He had Sheree's wedding ring. He said Rimmey had it on him when Brooks last . . . encountered him."

Vera felt gobsmacked. She'd had no reason to notice or check for Sheree's wedding ring . . . that day. She and Eve had been too focused on getting her out of the house. How had Rimmey gotten her wedding ring? Vera knew for a fact he hadn't killed her.

"Something wrong?"

Vera snapped out of the haze of disbelief. "No. No. I'm just surprised."

"He said Rimmey was all torn up about it and kept muttering how he didn't mean to do it."

"Wow. You win. My news wasn't nearly as shocking as yours." This was too bizarre.

"Yeah." Bent shook his head. "It was a strange day."

"Sounds like," Vera said as calmly as possible. As much as she wanted to believe the business with Sheree was settled and somehow behind them, she was too much of a realist to go anywhere near there. "So you've solved all the murders related to the cave except for Gates."

"We," he countered, "solved them. In fact, the talk in the community I'm hearing is that you're a true hometown hero. I expect the mayor to give you a key to the city."

"I won't hold my breath." She eased off the stool. "On that note, I think we should go out and celebrate."

"Sounds good to me. Just don't be surprised if someone asks for your autograph."

She laughed. "Yeah right."

His face lined with a frown. "But what about the offer from the FBI?" He searched her face, worry claiming his expression once more. "Are you taking it? Or maybe you prefer the one from the TBI."

The TBI position meant moving to the Nashville area.

She hesitated but then decided not to keep him in suspense any longer. "No and no. I've decided to become an independent consultant. I want more choice in the cases I take and the work I do." She shrugged. "Who knows? It could be very lucrative. I can work from right here at home. Or maybe get an office on the square." She laughed. "I guess that's the point. I can do what I want the way I want while being here for my sisters."

His relief was palpable. He really had been worried she would be leaving.

"I'm glad." He reached out, took her hand, gave it a squeeze before letting go. "Really glad," he repeated, "that you're staying."

She relished the feeling his words prompted. "Me too."

"In fact," he suggested, "with all the instrumental help you provided on this investigation, I believe you should submit a bill to the county. Might as well get you in the system. I'm sure we'll require your services often in the future. Not to mention, I know the sheriffs in most of the surrounding counties. I can put in a good word for you."

She smiled, hooked her arm in his. "Maybe I'll do that."

On the way to the door Vera grabbed her bag. Outside, she paused to survey the yard and all the beauty her mother had cultivated. This was home. This farm . . . her family . . .

She glanced at Bent. These were the things that really mattered.

And she would do everything in her power to protect all of it.

As they walked toward his truck, Bent said, "I was thinking about the Gates murder." He opened the passenger-side door and waited for her to climb in. "The story will come out eventually. Just like those remains found in the cave, secrets rarely stay hidden forever."

Vera smiled but let it go at that. Truth was, Bent was half-right.

Secrets only stayed hidden if you buried them deep enough.

ACKNOWLEDGMENTS

Fayetteville is a lovely little town in Tennessee on the border near Alabama. It's only a few miles from the Huntsville area, where I lived for more than two decades. As much as I love Huntsville, Alabama, moving to Fayetteville was a dream come true. We now have a small farm with a big old red barn, where we are surrounded by chickens, cows, sheep, and goats. We love it.

Living here has made the research for this book very easy. But with fiction it's often necessary to edit things, even real-life settings. I never want any real-life person or place to be negatively impacted by one of my stories, since I do write about murder and people who do bad things. With that in mind, I've created a fictional farm and house on a real-life road for Vera's family. Though some town shops and city or county offices in my story are similar to real-life ones, all are fictional, as are all characters in the book. Oh, and Dead Man's Curve is purely fictional as well, although the curve that inspired me is one that I still dread every time we take that road.

I hope you enjoy this story, and if you live in Fayetteville or nearby, know that I adore living here! This is a special place with the greatest neighbors!

ABOUT THE AUTHOR

Photo © 2019 Jenni M Photography LLC

Debra Webb is a *USA Today* bestselling author of more than 170 novels. She is the recipient of the prestigious Romantic Times Career Achievement Award for Romantic Suspense as well as numerous Reviewers' Choice Awards. In 2012, Webb was honored as the first recipient of the esteemed L. A. Banks Warrior Woman Award for her courage, strength, and grace in the face of adversity. Webb was also awarded the distinguished Centennial Award for having published her hundredth novel. She has more than four million books in print in many languages and countries. Webb's love of storytelling goes back to her childhood, when her mother bought her an old typewriter at a tag sale. Born in Alabama, Webb grew up on a farm. She spent every available hour exploring the world around her and creating her stories. Visit her at https://debrawebb.com.